THE STARLIGHT
HOTEL-CASINO

GUERNICA WORLD EDITIONS 58

WILLIAM A. DOUGLASS

THE STARLIGHT HOTEL-CASINO

TORONTO—CHICAGO—BUFFALO—LANCASTER (U.K.)
2023

Guernica Editions Founder: Antonio D'Alfonso

Michael Mirolla, general editor
Scott Walker, editor
Cover and interior design: Errol F. Richardson

Guernica Editions Inc.
287 Templemead Drive, Hamilton (ON), Canada L8W 2W4
2250 Military Road, Tonawanda, N.Y. 14150-6000 U.S.A.
www.guernicaeditions.com

Distributors:
Independent Publishers Group (IPG)
600 North Pulaski Road, Chicago IL 60624
University of Toronto Press Distribution (UTP)
5201 Dufferin Street, Toronto (ON), Canada M3H 5T8
Gazelle Book Services, White Cross Mills
High Town, Lancaster LA1 4XS U.K.

First edition.

Legal Deposit—First Quarter
Library of Congress Catalog Card Number: 2022943589
Library and Archives Canada Cataloguing in Publication
Title: The Starlight Hotel-Casino / William A. Douglass.
Names: Douglass, William A., author.
Series: Guernica world editions ; 58.
Description: Series statement: Guernica world editions ; 58
Identifiers: Canadiana (print) 2022039878X | Canadiana (ebook) 20220398828 |
ISBN 9781771837897 (softcover) | ISBN 9781771837903 (EPUB)
Classification: LCC PS3604.O975 S73 2023 | DDC 813/.6—dc23

To my beloved brother John,
lifelong companion and fellow Starlighter

Gambling promises the poor what property performs for the rich: that is why the bishops dare not denounce it fundamentally.
—George Bernard Shaw

I

God, Manny was nervous as he waited to be admitted to the in-progress meeting behind the closed doors. Manny Cohen had always thought of himself as a good adman, at least until he volunteered for the assignment in this burg. With Vegas's hands around its throat and Indian arrows pointed at its heart, Reno gaming was toast—only the shmucks in the inner sanctum failed to realize it. They were prepared to spend a hundred million dollars (borrowed money, of course) on a new casino.

They needed a theme. Manny contemplated the word "Bethlehem" on the cover of his proposal. The subtitle "Fear, Loathing, and Learning in Reno" conflated and paraphrased the Robert Venturi and Hunter S. Thompson titles—the two Las Vegas books in his briefcase.

Two weeks in southern Nevada had given Manny creative constipation more than inspiration. Pyramids and pirate ships, New York City and Venice imploded into caricatures of themselves, the French Riviera, riverboats without mosquitoes, the endless circuses and prize fights, the tallest phallic symbol west of the Mississippi with its Big Dick ride. Manny glanced out the window at the twin domes over the Silver Legacy and the National Bowling Stadium and mused, *At least this place has the biggest balls. Bowling for Chrissakes.*

1

And races, too—balloon, airplane, car, bicycle, camel, the rodeo, and chili and rib cookoffs (all "national championships" to be sure). What did Reno want to be when it grew up?

This could be it.

"If I blow this job, my next assignment could be Newark," he sighed.

He almost missed his boring former stint with the potato chip manufacturer in South Bend. Manny leafed through the report, which suddenly seemed flawed and silly. The Bethlehem Casino, replete with animated wise men, live sheep and cattle, and a birth of Christ show three times daily. Christmas 365 days a year—a consumer's delight! Think of the gift shop possibilities. Then there was phase two—simulated crucifixions and beheadings of baptizers, resurrections, assumptions, and ascensions. Manny wondered nervously if there was a Christian ayatollah lurking out there somewhere who might take vengeful umbrage over a guy just trying to make a buck. He knew that his visions were always of a grandiose ilk. Would it all be one huge turnoff to his clients?

"Naw," he thought. *Nevada's ready. Fuckin' America's ready.*

The programmed talking head behind the name plate proclaiming "Priscilla, Executive Secretary" blew off another caller. The word-player in him reimagined her name as "Godzilla."

Manny stared at the stone-faced, stern-voiced guardian whose purpose in life was to protect Fitzsimmons from the world. All ten of Manny's calls from Vegas to his boss had earned him an earful of Muzak, probably while she trimmed her nails before informing him that Fitzsimmons was not available. The buzzer interrupted his thoughts.

"The board will see you now, Mr. Cohen."

"Jesus, it's showtime!" Manny harrumphed. "Oh, and Mary and Joseph, too."

A confused Priscilla stared at the back passing through the door of the inner sanctum.

"Hey, Mr. Clinton, here are your books. I really enjoyed them," Manny lied. He had found the architect Venturi's work *Learning from Las Vegas* to be a slog. Hunter S. Thompson's novel *Fear and Loathing in Las Vegas* was more a criticism of America seen through the psychedelic distortion of Las Vegas hyperreality, certainly a more enjoyable read, but its relevance to his assignment escaped him. Never mind, he had struggled through both of them in the spirit that when your boss assigns you homework, you do it. There might be a quiz.

***

Yet again Jeremy Clinton had run into himself coming around the corner. He sat alone in the darkened boardroom trying to come down off the emotional plane of the heated exchange. He didn't regard himself to be a liar.

I just embellish a little, he thought.

There was the ninety-seven-yard touchdown run that gave his high school football team a state championship that, in his retelling over the years, became his own heroism rather than Cliff's. His cheeks burned anew as he recalled the time that he made an eagle on the par-four seventh hole at Reno's Lazy Creek Country Club while playing a solo round. At the bar afterwards, he claimed it was a hole-in-one on the par-three sixth instead. How was he to know that that damn reporter from the *Gazette-Journal* would make it an item in the paper? Since then he was the guy who'd sunk the shot that everyone wanted to talk about. Purgatory comes in many guises.

After that absurd presentation of the Bethlehem Hotel-Casino project, the board had turned its attention to "foreign gaming," meaning anywhere outside Nevada. Jeremy was a two per-cent owner and general manager of the Starlight Hotel-Casino, and he'd just had a confrontation with James Fitzsimmons—founder, chairman of the board, and majority stockholder in the enterprise. He was also the scion of one of the state's pioneer gaming families. Arkansas was considering legalization and the Starlight had a secret option on a prime casino site in Little Rock. But opposition was growing in the polls and it was rumored that the governor was about to come out against gaming.

"Jerry, I just don't understand why you can't call your cousin and ask him to influence the gov," Old Man Fitzsimmons had opined.

"It's not that simple, Sir. You don't just tell the president of the United States that you need that kind of favor. He's got many more important things on his plate. He's busy running the country, not to mention running for re-election."

"Even I could beat Dole. Hey, what are relatives for if you can't get something out of them once in a while? You're his cousin, aren't you? Are you going to make the call?"

"Of course. I'll make it, but don't expect much."

"Oh, yeah? Maybe we've got the wrong GM around here!"

Jerry brooded in the twilight of the waning evening, his face turned alternately crimson and blue by the blinking neon pulses of the Starlight's street sign. "Why in hell did I ever say ten years ago that I was related to that damn Arkansas governor?" At the time, it had seemed like such a little fib—a minor claim to fame by a guy otherwise saddled with the humdrum of a pit boss's life. What now?

"Shit."

***

James Fitzsimmons Kennedy summoned his son—James Fitzsimmons Kennedy, Jr., father of James Fitzsimmons Kennedy III—to his executive office. They all went by the first of their two surnames. In family parlance, the patriarch was James, his son—Jimmy, and the grandson—JFK.

"You know, Jimmy, people think that we're bulletproof. How can you lose with a casino? It's the proverbial license to steal. You build a box, hang some neon lights over the front door, the gaudier the better, put in several rows of slots and table games, and presto, your biggest headache is counting the money. Well, some people believe in Santa Claus, the Easter Bunny, and the Tooth Fairy. This just may be one of the toughest businesses there is. Everybody can see a good thing and wants in on it. Reno lost out to Las Vegas half-a-century ago. Nevada lost its monopoly when New Jersey legalized in the 1980s, not to mention the sneaky Indians in the 1990s. Gaming is spreading around the world—Macau, Australia.

"With all that competition, you give away the store—free drinks, cheap food, and beds—just to get players through the door. Hell, we've got so many loss leaders, you'd think we were in the losses business!

4

Look out that window, Son. Neon everywhere; so many boxes and all with row after row of the same product. To get to ours, the customer on Virginia Street has to walk two extra blocks down a pretty seedy stretch. We've got guys on the Great White Way handing out coupons for free shrimp cocktails to entice the biggest cheapskates our way. We're testing how far an elephant will go for a peanut. Even when we get those bottom feeders, you have to ask what we've accomplished. Anyone who will come two blocks for a puny shrimp cocktail will probably scarf it down and rush back to Virginia Street to check out the other freebie coupons on offer."

"I know it's not a great program, Dad, but we're desperate. What else can we do? We can't pick this place up by its bootstraps and move it two blocks."

"Jimmy, see that little white light next to the Flamingo's sign?"

"Yeah."

"Well, that's Bob's Goldilocks jewelry store—the best business in this town. It's been here for two decades and has an established clientele. Half the guys in our business shop there. It's a great growth industry."

"I don't get it, Dad."

"Think about it, Jimmy. First you need a little engagement ring. Then every Christmas Eve, when you're stumped, you go there to buy your little lady something that has to be a bit better than last year's afterthought. There comes the day when you try to dazzle the new girlfriend with a rock, followed by the colossal stone offering when the wife finds out. If Bob ever goes public, I'll buy the stock!"

***

Susan Johnson, *nee* Marinelli, and her husband, Red, had been high-school sweethearts in Youngstown, Ohio. He was the star halfback on the football team and she the head cheerleader. Most of the entries in her yearbook referenced the ideal couple and their inevitable marriage. Unbeknownst to the commentators, the prediction was already a reality. Sue and Red were man and wife. Neither the school administration nor her parents knew. Red's not-too-happy widowed mother had decided to hold her silence so the kids could graduate.

The winter of their senior year was filled with joyous anticipation of a football scholarship that never materialized. Their dream of going off to college together metamorphosed into the reality of two dull jobs in one dull town. Red was given preference in the steel mill where his father had worked for forty years before collapsing as he inserted coins into a coffee machine. Sue was a waitress on the night shift at Hoagie's Diner right across from the plant's illuminated front gate. The two nineteen-year-olds rarely saw one another except on weekends or when Red stopped by for a snack after work, a visit frustrated by the legitimate demands of other customers on Sue's attention. Sue got home at midnight and packed her sleeping husband's next day's lunch before retiring. She rarely stirred when Red arose at six to make his own breakfast before repeating the daily routine. It was a wonder that she got pregnant.

In her eighth month, Sue quit her job, exacerbating the already precarious state of their finances. The birth of their daughter underscored the fact that they'd assumed the baby would be a son; they hadn't even thought of a girl's name. Red's ecstatic mother held her granddaughter for the first time and proclaimed, "She's … she's the Queen of Sheba!"

The day after Sue returned home from the hospital with Sheba, Red walked through the front door at noon to announce, "The mill's in deep shit and might even close. They just let us new guys go."

"God, Red, what are we gonna do now?"

"We gotta go someplace; this town has had it."

Sue suggested Pueblo, Colorado. The mill had a branch operation there and her uncle Giuseppe had moved his family to Pueblo three years earlier. At least they would have someone to show them the ropes. Red shook his head. "Naw, I don't think so. That's another mill town. I got no stomach for this industry. Some of the guys was sayin' Nevada's the place. Sammy thinks it's the fastest growin' state in the country. He seems to know."

So, three weeks later, the little caravan left Youngstown—Red at the wheel of the U-Haul van and Sue driving their '75 Chevy behind. They pointed west on Interstate 80, headed for Reno, Red's concession to Sue's fear of raising Sheba in Las Vegas. Even though she'd never been beyond the Mississippi, for Sue the trip was more agony than adventure, something to be endured rather than enjoyed. Sheba, alternating between the cab of the U-Haul and the floor of the Chevy, was equally unhappy in both. Her colicky caterwauling provided the theme music for the westward odyssey.

Reno was a shock, particularly stark and arid Sun Valley, where they rented a decrepit single-wide trailer, depositing the last of their savings for it. But Sammy was right about the economy. Their first day Red found work as a construction laborer and Sue became a cocktail waitress on the casino floor of the Starlight.

"It'll just be for a while. You'll see, Sue; by the time Sheba's in school, we'll have our own place in Sparks."

It was not to be. For the next twelve years Red worked construction. In Youngstown he took union scale for granted, but in this right-to-work state, he earned half of what he'd made as a teenager. There were the periodic layoffs and he was usually without health insurance. He developed double hernias and had to have an operation. The bills piled up, as did Red's frustration. Twelve years in Nevada and, factoring in the normal rise in the cost of living, Red was essentially working for the same pay as his first day. They moved to Sparks alright, but as renters rather than owners.

Then there were the temptations. Red had begun staying out nights drinking and gambling with some of the single guys on his crew. Sue tried not to nag, but one sweltering August night she was waiting in the living room at midnight when her tipsy husband fumbled his way through the front door.

"Where have you been?"

"None of your damn business."

"Of course, it's my damn business; it's called marriage."

Red clenched his fists. "You want to know? OK. I just got back from Mustang. Yeah, the Mustang Ranch. You know why? Because at Mustang, they wash your pecker before, they wash it after, and in between, they don't say 'God, Red, what are we gonna do now?'"

His fist smashed into her left cheek, sending her careening across the sofa.

The next morning Sue pressed an ice pack against her face and said nothing while Red pleaded, promised, and apologized. She tried to regroup, if only for Sheba's sake, but the cheerleader in her was dead.

It was a week before she could return to her job at the Starlight, her bruise coated with a thick cap of makeup. That evening she picked up Sheba at Carol Bentley's house. Carol worked swing and the two impoverished cocktail waitresses shared childcare duties. Red didn't come home that night or the next one either. It was unlike him, even when on a bender. The third day, Sue went to the police to file a missing persons report.

"We need more than that to go on, lady," the police officer told her. "Do you have any evidence of foul play? Real evidence? People disappear all the time, only really they just leave."

After a near-sleepless and nightmarish month, Sue received a postcard from Fresno with a cryptic message:

> *Sorry, Sue. Words fail me. I couldn't take it anymore. At least here I found a job, even if it's only washing dishes. I'll try to send a little money someday, but it won't be for a while. I feel horrible about Sheba. I think of calling to tell her that I love her, but I just can't. Words fail me. I don't know what you have said so far, but at least tell her that her dad's not dead.*
>
> *Red*

***

Jim Fitzsimmons met Dorothy Evans in Seattle at a sorority dance when they were students at the University of Washington. Both were majoring in their parents' wishes—she in chemistry and he in business. Both were middling scholars. Dorothy was high class—or at least upper-middle—raised on an island in Puget Sound when not attending boarding school. She and her sister, Deidre, were the daughters of a Pacific Northwest timber magnate with important business ties and a second home in Vancouver. Their parents were Anglophiles, a love that they tried to instill in their daughters. But the usual sibling rivalry ruled that out.

If "Dottie" was the acolyte, the younger "Deedee" had to be the rebel. Such is the law of nature, the only question being the degree of their mutual antagonism and uncivility. Predictably, Deidre studied

French, praised the African and Asian Francophonie, and defended Quebec's right to secede from Canada. She would later meet her husband in Paris, settle there, and raise her two daughters—Monique and Angelique—as French citizens. She wasn't the family's black sheep; she was banned altogether from the flock.

Dorothy adored, and even emulated, with some vocabulary at least, the speech of her English governess. She loved *My Fair Lady* and fantasized over being the Canadian Eliza Doolittle converted into an English Lady, not to mention teaching the King of Siam a thing or two. She'd seen the Lerner and Loewe play five times and the film ten. She regarded English imperialism as divinely inspired and approved of Canada's membership in the British Commonwealth. Her favorite story regarded the party she attended in Vancouver for the British Governor General. Her first trip abroad was to England, as were the third, fourth, and fifth.

While the two sisters were respective vessels of Anglophilia and Francophilia, both lacked much substantive content. Dorothy had never read Austen or Dickens, and Deidre was oblivious to Flaubert and Proust. Dottie would have approved of Burke's denunciation of the French Revolution, had she heard of him, and Deedee would have seconded Voltaire's disdain of Shakespeare, had she known of Voltaire. Dottie collected English antiques and worshipped Wedgewood; Deedee was a clothes horse and adored Dior. Both were wannabe Valley girls, at least of the southern Canadian rather than southern Californian variety—replete with mini-skirts, tank tops, and prone to start every sentence with: "Like ..."

Nevada Jim, thoroughly smug in his *new-world* American naivety, thought that such *old-world* intrigues could be ignored. He failed to perceive that, for Dorothy, Nevada was a wilderness to be conquered and colonized. Reno was its potential Bombay. For Jim, Dorothy was a trophy bride, maybe an unconscious attempt to impress his parents, if only with the foppery of her high-fashion habilment. If so, that particular experiment had failed miserably. James Fitzsimmons could not stand his daughter-in-law.

After moving to Reno, Dorothy's pet project was to cultivate James so there could be no doubt about the identity of his crown prince. She fretted over Jim's brother, Sean, never mind that the elder Fitzsimmons sibling had defected to the East Coast after declaring his disdain for the casino business. What prevented him from returning to Reno one day to reconcile with his father and claim a share in the family's fortune? Even worse, Sean's son, William, was two years older than JFK, held a B.A. in economics from Swarthmore, and was studying for his M.B.A. at Wharton. What if he decided to journey westward to direct the Starlight's recovery? Even Jim had mentioned hiring his talented nephew, much to Dot's chagrin. Who knew what that little opportunist might do one day? This private Medean side to Dorothy's personality contrasted with her prim, even prissy, manner.

Dorothy had converted to Catholicism and, like most converts, become obsessive. Virtually all her conversation with James (initiated mainly by her, to be sure) had to do with religion. He was largely indifferent to that topic. In his childhood home, Easter had been more about uprising than resurrection.

Dorothy was masterful at crafting confused messages and bollixed symbology. She mistook her own Anglophilia, bordering on reverence, for James's sympathy for his Celtic ancestry—both being British and all that, right? James had little actual knowledge regarding his Irish heritage. Parnell might as well have been in Cooperstown as the pitcher with the greatest number of strikeouts of Babe Ruth. But if he wasn't entirely sure *why*, James knew that he *hated* the English.

His teeth ached every time he heard the names of Dorothy's daughters, given to them ostensibly to please their grandfather. There was Heather (who he quickly labelled "Heathrow") and Ivy (his little "Intra"—as in intravenous or IV). For Dorothy, the only difference between the English and Irish was their respective accents when speaking their common tongue. Albeit less of a student of history than James even, she could recognize that a brogue was Irish. She was, of course, clueless about the nature and status of Gaelic. She couldn't spell Ulster, let alone locate it on a map.

For Dorothy, an English accent represented proper affectation and claim to elite social status. For James, it was the clarion of the oppression of his esteemed working class, not to mention its beleaguered island.

There was no small irony in the fact that James was the capitalist boss and his son Jim the employee within the Fitzsimmons empire.

James loathed Dorothy's family gatherings, their meals replete with napkin rings and place cards—as if the relatives didn't know one another—and served with Sheffield cutlery on the Wedgwood plate he feared chipping. She always insisted upon seating Heather and Ivy across from him, ensuring that his conversation would be vapid at best when conducted across the hardwood and generational chasms. Lacking competition, Dorothy was able to garner every family holiday festivity. Thanksgiving, more than Easter, became an annual Calvary, since she always invited the bishop and seated him next to James. The Fitzsimmons patriarch, a liberal and agnostic at heart, would grunt feigned agreement with the prelate's monologue of stodgy, when not outlandish, conservative pronouncements. He would have far preferred to be at the other end of the table with his parish priest and friend, Father Carmody.

James endured his haughty daughter-in-law only to please his wife, Bess. When she died, it was over. He never again darkened Dorothy's (and his son's) door.

***

Jerry Clinton's gaze flitted over the casino floor and sized up the two alluring new blackjack dealers in the pit. The generic Asian was tiny, her burnished skin glistening as if oiled, the strand of the coif hanging down her back like a starched-straight ribbon. The other was pink, blond, and nubile, seemingly too young to play blackjack, let alone deal it. Her cascading curls brushed the precocious protrusions struggling to escape the regimentation of her cowgirl blouse reinforcing the Starlight's "western" theme. Jerry smiled at his own musings. Were this academia, his thoughts would be deemed lecherous and acting on them moral turpitude possibly leading to ignominious dismissal. In this world, they were not only accepted but expected.

Jerry had once been a graduate student of philosophy at Berkeley; thirty years later, the clock was still ticking on this intended brief interlude from his studies. Somewhere along the way, his life had shifted from the contemplative to the ejaculatory. If once his triumphs were measured by turning the last page in a book by Plato and Aristotle, Hesse or Kierkegaard, now it was the check on the scorecard after having bedded the latest Ms. Forgettable—Apollo displaced by Dionysius. He filed away in his mind these two embryonic possibilities for future affairs—or at least one-night stands.

***

The days since Red's disappearance had turned into months as Sue struggled just to feed Sheba. She was saddened by her inability to buy school clothes for her daughter's first day of class. Sue held and rocked her that evening as Sheba cried while recounting the teasing from her new classmates over her ill-fitting dress. Never the hoyden, the miserable child always repressed her feelings when in public.

And then there was the rent. Tomasso Gardella let it slide for a couple of months, skeptical of her excuse that Red was out of state on business and they would catch up soon. By October, her finances were hopeless. So, Sue had gone to her landlord to give him her thirty-day notice. But then he proposed an arrangement that would halve her thousand-dollar monthly rental. Tomasso thought briefly of forgiving the entire amount, but he'd reached the limits of his capacity for charity—imposed by both an *old-world* upbringing and his immigrant's frugality.

Sue's parents had come from Agnone to Youngstown and spoke Italian (or at least their dialect of it) at home. She only remembered vocabulary words and a few set phrases. Her father actually discouraged her use of them in the belief that English was more important to her future. So her Italian was weaker than Tomasso's English, but not by much. They had even once attempted to communicate in "Italian," but the exercise dissolved in laughter and mutual amazement over the chasm separating her Abruzzese argot and his Sicilian dialect. He was formal to a fault, and it was the only time she remembered seeing him merry.

Tomasso was now seventy and had been in the United States for half a century. After working for thirty-five years for the Union Pacific Railroad, he'd retired with the idea of opening an Italian restaurant.

Adela was a great cook; everyone who tasted his wife's dishes said so. Her many Sicilian recipes, learned in childhood, were the main part of her cultural baggage when she left Trapani for America.

But then he found himself awash in perplexing detail—non-plussed by all of the required permits and frightened by the accountability. Until then, the only government acronym he truly recognized was IRS, but now he was confronted by mysteries like SDI—the State Disability Insurance program. He had only vague notions about withholding taxes, Social Security, minimum-wage laws, business and liquor licenses. It would mean trusting an accountant and maybe an attorney, too—something that he'd never done in his life. So, his savings went into the purchase of three Sparks rental homes instead of opening an eatery.

Sue brushed her teeth for the second time this Monday morning, her regular weekly day off. She then wrote a check for $500, put it in an envelope, and placed it on top of her dresser. She showered and toweled off before slipping between the sheets. It was almost eleven, and she knew Tomasso would be punctual. It was the first Monday of the month, their regular appointed time, and she mulled over a future scheduling challenge. It was June, and Sheba's school year was about over, so they would have to improvise for the next three months.

Sue heard the landlord's key turn in the downstairs lock and then sensed the gentle shuffle of the slight man's shoes on the stairs.

"Good'a day to'a you, Miss'a Marinelli."

Tomasso insisted on using her Italian maiden name. He crossed the room to the dresser and placed a lilac bloom in Sue's most recent ceramic creation. It was his custom to bring her a single seasonal flower from his garden on each visit, beginning the previous October's first Monday with a marigold. There had been the purchased Christmas orchid and the substitute chocolate bar in January, prior to the February crocus.

He always wore a suit and slipped its jacket over the back of the sole wooden chair in the sparsely furnished room. He then carefully folded his pants and dress shirt and placed them on the seat, along with his underwear and socks. The toes of two precisely aligned black shoes peeked out from under the clothing tower. Tomasso and Adela had stopped cohabiting some ten years earlier, but as he had put it during the negotiation, "I'ya be old, Miss'a Marinelli, but I'ya not dead."

As usual, Sue forced her mind to wander during the action. It was entirely his act, since after receiving him, her body remained motionless. He struggled silently to maintain the concentration without which he was incapable of sustaining his erection. It was over in five minutes, and he was across the room, reversing in precise steps his earlier disrobing. He put the envelope in his inside breast pocket and turned to leave. "Good'a bye, Miss'a Marinelli. *Grazie.*"

***

Jerry sipped his tonic water as he waited for Priscilla's signal to enter James Fitzsimmons's office.

The old days are sure gone, he thought.

The time was past when the sybaritic GM could cull a cocktail waitress from the herd and bed her in one of the unoccupied rooms upstairs. It had practically been a perk. Different supervisors had different approaches. Jerry's was to attract the attention of his mark by ordering a scotch from her to be delivered upstairs while placing the room key and a $100 bill on her tray.

He wasn't without certain scruples. He always waited until a few minutes before her shift ended so the Starlight wouldn't be short a cog on the floor. After all, he was its general manager.

The ploy usually worked, and when it didn't, the denouement was usually gracious. The girls were used to being hit on. Those few who didn't want to be were masters (or rather mistresses) at deflecting advances without imperiling their employment. Escape from your immediate supervisor was always the riskiest, but not impossible. Jerry, as the Starlight's poohbah, could only recall once when the game spun out of control. That what's-her-name, tall blond from Kansas, had dumped a whole tray of drinks in his lap and walked out the door. She never looked or came back—not even for her paycheck.

Jerry recalled his blondes-phase—his string of non-casino mistresses. His rule of thumb then had been "single, blond, no kids, fancy car." He couldn't remember any last names, but there had been Jenny Mercedes, Stacy Jaguar, Catherine Audi, and Sally Porsche.

Over the years, Jerry had become so accustomed to his manorial privilege that his four marriages now seemed more like ill-fated affairs—

brief interludes in which he'd been unfaithful to his stable. But even feudal worlds change. The defining moment had come, as he answered the summons from Fitzsimmons.

The old man was uncharacteristically nervous as he cleared his throat. "Dammit, Jerry, we have to be more careful. I used to have my fun, too, but it's not such a simple matter anymore. Those union bastards are sniffing around here trying to organize our people, and we can't give them any ammunition. Our attorneys say this sexual harassment stuff is for real and getting worse. Those horny Japs got hammered in Illinois."

Jerry remained speechless; he just couldn't think of anything to say. So Fitzsimmons plodded on, filling the air to dissipate the awkward silence. Jerry knew that the lecture was over when his boss made a crude stab at humor. "It might come down to issuing chastity belts to the women and steel jocks to the men. We could start with you. We'd save a lot of money on the tiny size of the cup! Har, har."

While he hadn't received a direct order, the tea leaves were easy enough to read. Jerry knew that if the sexual harassment thing worsened, he already had plenty of ticking time bombs.

He certainly should not be fusing new ones, even if Sue Johnson was the latest blip on his radar.

Maybe, I'll just ask her out. A thought that had already become his decision.

***

Swede called the meeting to order and, since he couldn't issue one, lapsed into his new civilian strategy. A veteran of the Korean War and its peace negotiations, and now executive director of the Northern Nevada Casino Association (NNCA), he'd developed the capacity to drone on endlessly about any subject, gradually stultifying his audience into submission. A few of the victims struggled valiantly to follow the monologue and the minds of others wandered, while George Anderson, executive vice president of the Pumpernickle Hotel-Casino in South Reno, began to fantasize about throttling the speaker.

"Gentlemen, we either hang together or we hang separately." (Swede wasn't long on originality.) "I've asked our lobbyist, Bruce Barstow, to address us this morning about this year's legislative session. Bruce?"

The intense, balding attorney and political strategist par excellence commanded the audience's renewed attention. Several of the listeners produced ballpoint pens to possibly record particular kernels of wisdom on their notepads or the backs of their agendas. He felt a bit out of place with his sports jacket and tie. His audience was scarcely coxcombical, given that all but the two in Bermuda shorts wore some variation of Levis and a tee shirt.

"Rather than go into the details about our legislative strategy, I prefer to take up where Swede left off. We can't solve our problems in Carson City; we have to do so right here in this room. There are too many big egos in this business, which is a luxury you can't afford in these tough times. I don't expect you to help each other out—after all, you are competitors—but this goddamn room-rate war has got to stop. You can't talk to each other without violating the anti-trust laws; I can verbalize the issues for you and then you're each going to have to make your own decision.

"Guys, you know nobody wins when rooms are going for twenty dollars a night, except maybe a few parasitical customers. I mean the kind that hates the quarter machines because they won't take pennies. They'll eat your ninety-nine-cent breakfast, stand in line for half an hour to cash a coupon for a two-dollar roll of nickels, drink your free booze, and probably sleep with your wife if you'd let 'em. Is that what you want? A bunch of stiffs with a puny gaming budget, whose idea of heavy action is to get a little ahead and then come after you with your own money? You can beat 'em out of maybe a hundred, but if they get on a roll, the sky's the limit. You're going to make a living off that kind of action?

"Think about how those rates hammer the motels. Who's going to stay in a motel room when they can get a good hotel one for twenty bucks? When the motels are empty, so are the streets and you lose that walk-around business. So, what's it going to be?"

John Ferrarese, grandson of a Piedmontese Italian immigrant who cut wood in the Sierras for the steam locomotives and son of the shrewd attorney who'd parlayed the sale of the family farm to developers into what was arguably downtown Reno's finest property, took up the challenge. "I think Dad's a genius. He's got the Midas touch, and he believes in Reno. That's why we built the Golden Spur. We can still grow this market, only it's going to take a while. Vegas is the big challenge. Driving in from our own airport, you pass that big billboard put up by the Las Vegas Convention Authority. They're not just after our players in Seattle, Portland, and Vancouver, they're fighting us for them right here in Reno."

George Anderson interrupted. "John's absolutely right. Why don't we get the Reno Convention Authority to lease a sign at McCarran International Airport? We could put a big picture of Lake Tahoe on it—the mountains, the snow—and a caption that says 'Hot? Reno-Tahoe is Not!' See how them Vegas bastards like that."

At first, there was lively discussion of the concept, but then Swede began to recognize familiar signs. Mark Bengoechea, GM of the Flamingo Hilton, allowed as how the Reno Convention Authority was broke and its board divided over both mission and direction. So, Anderson suggested that each property in the association pay its share of the billboard. That triggered a debate over whether to contribute equally or if there should be proration according to a property's size, income, or number of slots. Swede knew the game was up once it was going to cost the members money. Some of them were in arrears on their NNCA dues, for God's sake!

Anderson tried to call his own question: "I'll put up my share any way that you guys choose to calculate it. We've got to do something. Are you in?"

Swede contemplated the room, trying to keep the bemused expression off his face.

Jim Hanson, CEO for another of the corporate players, was the first to speak. "I like the concept, but I'll have to see what my marketing director thinks." (Translation: "I have to run this higher up because corporate has me on a short leash.")

Carl Smith said, "There may be some problems with it, but it can probably be finetuned." (Translation: "These guys are nuts if they think I'm even going to propose such a confrontational move to headquarters. I'm not putting my career on the line over some billboard.")

James Fitzsimmons's epigone, Jim, opined, "We're for it, but I'll have to get back to you with a definite answer." (Translation: "I haven't a clue how Dad's going to feel about this.")

Then John Ferrarese spoke out. "We'll go along, but I don't see why we should include Tahoe."

Anderson exploded. "Why? Because the last time I looked, they were the ones with the mountain lake, Slick."

"I don't care. Why should we spend money on their image? The Tahoe casinos are our competitors, too, just as much as Vegas."

Swede thought, *Mission impossible! They've issued me a bunch of clones and kids. To think the public believes these clowns actually run this town. What a joke! They can't even get together to put up a damn billboard in some other place.*

John Douglass, CEO of the Comstock, commented, "When are we going to wrap this up, Swede? My tee-off time is in an hour."

Mark Bengoechea stood up to leave, and the meeting adjourned itself. "So, John, how do you manage to golf so much? I love the game and I'm lucky to get a round in a couple of times a month ... on Saturdays."

"You have a job, Mark; I have a position," Douglass joked.

***

Jerry felt like a canary let out of its cage as he braked in front of Sue's house and honked once. He was mildly startled at the apparition of the pert figure clad in Levis and a western shirt. Sue's hair was pulled back from her face into a ponytail. In hiking boots rather than high heels and only a touch of makeup, the approaching figure bore no resemblance to a cocktail waitress.

Sue had regretted the coming day and even thought of calling Jerry to cancel. There would be the perfunctory time at the beach, the meaningless foreplay, followed by the inevitable coupling in some yet-to-be-determined venue. Sue could have manufactured an excuse, but felt she could ill-afford to alienate her supreme boss. She was resigned to the inevitable.

She was ready when he arrived, her bathing suit and toiletry kit wrapped in a beach towel, the picnic basket by her side. She'd heard the faint beep of his horn and now sat next to Jerry in the cab of his Toyota Tundra. He gestured toward the back seat of the king cab, and as she placed her things there, Sue noticed the blanket and air mattress for their probable lovemaking.

"Good morning, Jerry. I'm a little surprised."

18

THE STARLIGHT HOTEL-CASINO

"Why?"

"Oh, I don't know. I guess I expected a fancier car."

Jerry chuckled and gave his explanation. "I have a Lexus, too. But I want to show you something different today. I said we'd go to Tahoe, but I hope you don't mind Plan B. I just need to be in my special place. I'll show you a secret there. I even brought you a sweater. We'll be close to ten thousand feet, and it can get pretty cool. It's where I go to get away from my problems, and boy do I have them these days. Everyone knows that the Starlight is in deep trouble. I'm not sure we're going to make it."

They rode in silence for a few minutes before she asked where they were headed.

"To the Sweetwaters, my private mountains. We probably won't see anyone all day, and the views are fantastic. My son and I used to ride ATVs together, and the best place we ever found was the Sweetwater range east of Topaz Lake." Jerry continued, "I haven't seen Tim for years. He's grown and has two kids of his own. He's an accountant, lives in Des Moines. I've never even met his wife."

"Did he grow up here?"

"Not really. When Joan divorced me, she moved back to her parents in Iowa. Tim was a baby, so of course, she got custody. I didn't really give a damn. I'm not much of a kid guy. Years later, Joan wrote me that Tim was fourteen and an impossible handful. He needed 'a male role model'—her words. She wasn't high on my qualifications, but she had no alternatives. She never remarried and didn't even date. I suppose after life with me she'd had enough of marriage. The letter was kind of a guilt trip; her only real hold on me was Tim's monthly child support check. Anyway, I was between marriages, had plenty of room, and was a little lonely. I was also a little curious. So, I thought, 'What the hell!'

"Tim moved in with me and attended Reno High. He wasn't a bad kid, really. Smoked some pot, cut a class or two, but came out the other end in one piece. He graduated from Iowa State with honors. I have great memories of our time together, even the day I thought he'd killed himself."

"God, Jerry, what happened?"

"It was where we're going today, actually. I was in the lead and we were keeping our distance because of the dust. Tim was maybe a quarter of a mile behind me. I waited at the truck for five minutes before I realized something was wrong. I backtracked and was shaking so hard that I could barely steer. Sure enough, there he was, lying in the road in a heap, his ATV upside down in a ditch with its motor still running. I shouted and thanked God when he moved his hand. I gave him a whiff of smelling salts and that woke him up. He was covered with blood; lots of cuts and bruises and gravel embedded all over his face. I drove straight to the emergency room in Carson. He wanted to sleep during the drive, but I made him talk to me. It was the longest ride of my life. It turned out that he was okay. He just needed a few stitches. His helmet was split down the middle, but it'd protected him from the worst of the blow. He only had a mild concussion.

"Soon after that, he graduated from Reno High and was accepted into Iowa State. Those two ATVs sat around in my garage for a couple of years until I sold them. I never could bring myself to look for a substitute companion. I guess I was also gun-shy after that last ride with Tim. You know, Sue, I actually miss him a lot."

Jerry felt liberated as he turned off busy Highway 395 just before Topaz and onto the two-lane highway that would take them through Smith Valley and onward to the east side of the Sweetwaters. He breathed deeply, feeling the Starlight's stale secondary smoke evacuating his lungs.

Once on the dirt road and beyond Sweetwater Ranch, they began a gradual ascent through the sage- and rabbit-brushed landscape until they reached their first juniper trees and piñon pines. Then they were in a grove of quaking aspens and Jerry pointed at a serrated scar on one of them. Its message was "Pedro Armaolea, 1928."

"He was a Basque sheepherder. He probably spent the whole summer alone with his dog and burro and a thousand ewes with their lambs. Maybe once a week, his camp-tender would bring him supplies and provide his only human contact for a few hours. Carving his name in the tree was a way of humanizing an otherwise alien environment. Maybe it was also a way of communicating with future herders—kind of recording that, before you, 'Kilroy was here.' They left other markings—a stick drawing of their house back in the Old Country or a naked woman. The oppressive months without female companionship could become obsessive."

"God, Jerry, it gives me the willies just to think about it. Poor guys."

"A few even killed themselves and some just went crazy. I think the other Basques called it becoming 'sage-brushed' or 'sheeped.' When Tim and I first started coming here, there was one Basque sheep outfit left in these mountains, on the south end towards Bridgeport. Now they're gone. All that remains of the era of the Basque sheepherder in the American West are a few carvings on tree trunks, and it won't be long before they fall to the ground and rot as well."

They forded a small stream, and Sue asked him to stop. She alighted to splash cold water on her face and erase the stupor of the hundred-mile ride. Suddenly, a grasshopper took flight with a whir of greenish-gray wings and a loud clacking that defied its minute size.

"*Porca Madonna!*" she exclaimed and then blushed instantly. "I'm so sorry, Jerry, I didn't mean to swear. I'm just a city girl, and I've been thinking about rattlesnakes since we left the pavement. It scared the pants off me."

He laughed. "What was that? Italian? You know Italian?"

"Sort of." Sue bent down to fill her cupped hands with water.

"Don't drink that. This is cattle and sheep country. It could give you liver flukes. Also, there are beaver dams up this canyon. You could catch giardia—beaver fever. Nasty stuff. If you're thirsty, I have a canteen in the back filled with Reno's chlorinated finest."

"What a shame. It's cold as ice and looks so pure. It's like so many other things in this world—not what it seems."

"How did you learn Italian?"

"I didn't learn it from a book. I was born in Youngstown, but Mama and Papa were from Agnone in the Isernia area of southern Italy. There were lots of immigrants in my neighborhood from there—the *Agnonesi*, as we were called. There were enough of us to have our own club separate from the Sons of Italy.

"Papa hated America, or what he knew of it, and talked all the time about returning to Europe. When I finished the fourth grade and my sister, Laura, was about to start school, my parents moved back to Agnone. They thought it would be better for her to start Italian school right from the get-go. They were right, too, because Laura hit the ground running. I hated it.

"I thought I spoke at least some, but the standard Italian they taught us in school was Greek to me. We had a pompous ass as our fifth-grade teacher, and I was terrified of him. He would pace the room spouting his lesson as if he were alone. Suddenly, he would nail one of us with a question. His favorite word was *quindi*, which I understood to mean 'fifth-graders.' For months, I thought he was barking out our rank like some little Mussolini. I mentioned it when I told my parents how much I hated school, and Mama just laughed. She said, 'Susana, *quindi* just'a mean well or so. Fifth, its'a *quinti*.' That didn't make me feel any better, only stupider. Also, I hated being called Susana, even if it was my given name. It made me feel ethnic."

"So, did anybody famous ever come from Agnone?"

"Have you heard of Eddie DeBartolo, owner of the San Francisco 49ers? He's from Youngstown and his ancestors were *Agnonesi*."

"Have I? I'll say!" For Jerry, Agnone had just displaced Rome as Italy's most important city.

They entered a glade ablaze with wildflowers—lupines, penstemons, saxifrages, and Indian paintbrush vied for the most outrageous color award.

"Can we stop here?" Sue asked. "It's so beautiful."

"I don't know. We'll have to ask his permission."

"Whose?"

"See those pines? Look at the base of the broken snag that was probably hit by lightning. He's watching us."

"I see the trees, but …"

"Look closely at the patch of thick brush. See anything wrong?"

Sue was about to voice her frustration when the deer took three or four steps, glanced back at them one last time, and then bounded off. "It has antlers, too. It must be a boy. How on earth did you see him before he moved?"

"A buck, not a boy, Sue. I'm a hunter. It comes from practice. Probably like the practice that it takes to learn a language."

The Tundra was now in four-wheel drive as it climbed the rugged switchbacks scarring the face of the ridge. The road clung precariously to one side of the canyon. Jerry grunted when Sue's fingernails dug into his right arm.

"Sorry, Jerry, I can't bear to look over the edge. What if we hit one of those rocks, and …"

"Don't worry. Trust me. I've driven this road many times. Believe me, it's harder to be the passenger than the driver. I know this buggy's limits. By the way, we just passed into California. We're now in the old Patterson Mining District of Mono County."

Sue tried to distract herself by continuing her Agnone ruminations: "Luckily for me, Papa never made the transition. He couldn't find anything to do with himself in Italy. The men in his family had been coppersmiths, and by the time he returned, that trade was finished. He began to miss his friends in the Agnonese Club. If he said anything good about America, it just irritated our relatives. At my cousin Margarita's wedding, Papa said something to his brother that started an argument. Enzo shouted, 'If you like Youngstown so much, why don't you just go back?' A week later, we were on the plane, and Papa said to me, 'Susan, I don' know me, my'a self. I'na stuck betwin tu'a countries. I no belong'a here an' I no belong'a there.' At least I knew who I was—he'd called me Susan."

"Are your parents still alive? What were they like?"

"Oh yeah, they're still alive and in Youngstown. They got little education in Italy and none in America. They both worked two jobs to give us the life they never had. But we barely saw them, so they were sort of strangers. I know I was a big disappointment. They assumed I would marry a nice Italian boy—preferably descended from *Agnonesi*. I'm sure that was part of the plan when we returned to Italy. It worked out in Laura's case. Her name is now Vecchiarelli, and she lives a few doors down the street from my folks. Louie's parents were born in Agnone and he runs an Italian restaurant. Laura and Louie have got two kids in Catholic school. I'm the loser.

"When Papa found out about my husband, Red Johnson, he told Mama and Laura that he never wanted to hear my name again. Laura calls me once in a while and I'm sure she tells Mama news about me. She would want to know about Sheba, but she would be devastated by my job. Mama couldn't imagine her daughter prancing around in a cocktail waitress uniform. I'm not sure I'll ever see my parents again, maybe I'll see one at the other's funeral. Laura would call me. I'd have to go back for that, no matter how hard. I wouldn't be able to live with myself if I didn't. Once an Italian …"

Sue realized that she might be boring Jerry with such detail about strange places and people. "Good grief, Jerry, how did I get into all of that? I guess it's this day and what we're doing together. Being on this mountain makes me think of Italy. Mountains are what I remember most, or at least most fondly. The Gran Sasso is a lot like the Sierra Nevadas, and when I look at Peavine, it reminds me of the bare Maiella. We went on a school excursion partway up it to a hermit's cave where some saint or pope once lived. That's the day that I learned how differently the world below seems from a mountain—so tiny and insignificant."

And then they were over the summit and into an alpine meadow flanked by a grove of tiny, weathered pines. Sue was startled at the sight of ruined buildings.

"This was Belfort, a silver camp founded in the 1880s," Jerry explained. "Tim and I researched its history for one of his term papers. Its best mine, the Kentuck, was just over that ridge. The miners here sank a three-hundred-foot shaft and took $450,000 out of it in 1880—big money in those days. In 1890, there were forty miners living here. See all those tailings? Those little piles of rubble are all that's left of many broken dreams. When they put down their tools at night, those dreamers believed they were six inches away from pay dirt. They could hardly wait to get up in the morning. Some of them died up here, and others just walked away. Those piles are little monuments to stubbornness ... and maybe madness, too."

"Kind of like our players, isn't it, Jerry? I mean, they all believe that today will be their lucky day. Even after they lose, they come back again. They believe that luck will make them a fortune with their next bet. I don't see where this is any different."

"You're right. Nevada has always been one gamble after another on a big dream. There's not much else here—harsh climate, little water, more rocks than dirt—hell, we've got way more in common with Afghanistan than with Iowa!"

Jerry parked the Tundra on a promontory, where it seemed possible to see a hundred miles in every direction. To the west, the crests of the high Sierras marched to the backside of Yosemite, now sheathed in blue mist. Due south was Nevada's highest mountain, Boundary Peak, its snowbecapped topknot soaring majestically to more than thirteen thousand feet. To the east, mountain range receded beyond mountain range, each becoming browner and more barren as its claim on Pacific moisture diminished. Topaz Lake lay at their feet, as if captured by a landscape artist as a painting's focal feature. Far below them, a golden eagle pirouetted while riding thermal uplifts—it almost seemed as if they could step onto its back and go for a ride. Jerry adjusted his sunglasses to counter the midday effulgence.

"Come on Sue. From here it's heel-and-toe."

They entered a broad valley well above tree line. The gray shale was interspersed with several massive snowbanks feeding a small creek framed by twin ribbons of green.

"In wet years, the snow doesn't melt all summer. It wouldn't take much of a drop in the Earth's temperature to trigger another Ice Age up here. This valley would become a glacial cirque again in no time."

They crossed a mud flat with a veritable tangle of animal tracks. Jerry began to decipher the many faint tracings on nature's palimpsest.

"See the large cloven-hooved ones? Range cattle. The smaller ones are deer. That really big track, the one bigger than my foot, is a black bear."

He dropped to his knees and asked for her hand. He used her index finger as a pointer to trace the faint outline of a weathered feline paw print.

"Mountain lion."

Jerry then led Sue to a sheltered glen dominated by an ancient, gnarled tree.

"It's a bristlecone pine, the oldest living thing on the planet, maybe five thousand years old. Think of it. This was a grown tree when Christ was alive. It's the only one that I know of in the Sweetwaters. The White Mountains to the south of Boundary Peak are famous for their groves, but they must be at least a hundred miles away. So, I ask myself how it got here. Did its seed travel in the intestines of some wayward bird? Maybe there were more, and the miners in Belfort cut them all down for fuel. This one could have been too far from their camp to bother with. There are lots of ways to end up alone in this world!"

"I've never seen anything like it. It's got a few live branches, but mostly it just seems dead … and chaotic. It has no symmetry. If God was nature's architect, what could He possibly have been thinking of?"

Jerry laughed. "I don't think it was God, Sue. Gaudí designed the bristlecone pine."

"Who?"

"Never mind, it doesn't matter."

She wanted a keepsake and found an attractive dead branch with patterned whorls serrated into its wood.

Back at the Tundra, Sue opened the picnic basket and spread their tablecloth on the ground. They began eating their salami-and-mortadella sandwiches, washed down with a bottle of pinot noir.

"I didn't realize Norwegian cuisine could be so tasty," Jerry joked.

"So, Jerry, which was it—Belfort or the bristlecone?"

"What do you mean?"

"Your secret place. You promised to show it to me."

"Neither. You're sitting on it."

"What?"

"I mean it. Crawl off this tablecloth, put your face down close to the ground, and tell me what you see." She did so.

"Oh my God, Jerry, they're amazing. What are they?"

"Alpines. They're so tiny, you don't even notice them unless you know where to look. Actually, I mean how."

"Do they have names?"

"Sure—ones you've never heard before, like Gray's cymopterus, Sierra podistera, dwarf daisy, strigrose cinquefoil, Gordon's ivesia, pussy paws."

"I can't believe the colors on the rocks—absolutely amazing."

"Lichen. It's just wonderful how brilliant their yellows, greens, and rusts can be."

"Hello. What do we have here?" Sue pointed to a strange grasshopper whose frantic leaps barely covered a few inches at a time.

Jerry caught it easily. "Touch it, but be careful. It's so soft, I'm almost afraid to handle it. It's unlike any grasshopper you've ever seen before. The grasshopper from Mars! Its whole life span must be a few weeks. There's snow here for nine months of the year."

It was getting on toward late afternoon, and they sat for a long while in silence, watching thunderheads form on the horizon. As dark clouds marched toward them, the wind picked up, and the temperature dropped. Sue and Jerry took shelter in the truck and contemplated the developing weather extravaganza through the windshield.

"Jerry, are you for real?" She meant it more as an expression of admiration for his impressive command of Sweetwater lore than a question.

"I don't know. It's been a long time since I've had any way of telling."

She was a little embarrassed by his reply and felt that maybe she'd stepped over some invisible line and deeply into his personal space.

"I feel like such a failure. It's not just the Starlight. I've done a lot of things in my life, but it reads more like a checklist than a book. I mean a book with a beginning, a middle, and a meaningful end—as in a purpose. I couldn't even begin to go into my failings as a son, father, and husband. That would be way too painful."

A dam burst within Jerry's chest, exploding into the guttural sob of a man who hadn't cried in forty years. Sue gently guided his head to her breasts and ran her fingers through his hair. For several minutes, he wept gently, soaking her shirt with his tears.

"It's okay," she said. "It's okay."

"Sue, I need you."

The storm had skirted them, surrendering the sky to a profusion of benign stratocumulus clouds scudding by overhead. The dying rays of the setting sun still managed to warm the chill some. They inflated the air mattress, spread their blanket, and crawled under it together. Sue undid the clasp that held her ponytail in place, allowing her beautiful black hair to fall around her shoulders. She unbuttoned her shirt, and Jerry's mouth sought out a firm nipple. Sue was aroused by the rhythmic pulsing of his lips, but then she began to realize that this wasn't foreplay. Jerry was nursing.

"My baby, my baby," she purred until he was asleep in her arms.

It was pitch dark as they drove off the mountain. They rode in silence, drained by the day's emotions. Jerry turned on the radio and hummed along with Elton Bishop's I *Fooled Around and Fell in Love*. He was superstitious about song lyrics; he regarded them as an omen.

He chuckled privately.

"What's the matter, Jerry?"

"Nothing. Nothing." His fingers patted her knee before settling on its cap.

When they arrived at Sue's house, he leaned over, kissed her almost fraternally, and said good night. "I'll call in the morning and see if Sheba would like to go out for a movie and pizza."

"Okay, Jerry."

Sue sat in her darkened living room, contemplating the glow of Reno's lights in the distance while sipping a straight shot of bourbon, then murmured aloud, "I think maybe I'm gonna need a divorce."

***

Jerry did his best thinking about anything and everything during the nocturnal ruminations that were one symptom of his chronic insomnia. Curing himself of the other, his alcoholism, had made things better, but hadn't fully conferred an uninterrupted good night's sleep. So, he always kept a lined yellow pad and ballpoint pen at the ready on his nightstand. He now fumbled to adjust the familiar reading lamp and noted from the low-lit face of the alarm clock that it was four.

Tonight's topic was familiar: women in general and his latest in particular. Names like Liz, Tess, Mary, and Alice had been scribbled on the pages of former pads, only to be scratched off by subsequent events. Everyone failed to pass his muster ... or he theirs. Was Sue different? He wrote her name in capital letters followed by a colon. Two lines below, after the numeral one and a period, he wrote the word "Looks" with a question mark. His answer: "Classic beauty." The reply to his next question "Intelligent?" was "Very." He concluded with "Personality?" followed with "The Best." He extinguished the lamp and crossed his arms under his head. Before returning to slumber-land, a Sue-besotted Jerry admonished the darkness with a plaintive: "Uh, oh. Here we go again."

***

"So, Mr. Fitzsimmons, you wanted two hundred million for your portfolio two years ago when gaming stocks were hot and now you're asking for fifty," Don McNeal mused. "It's clear you're looking for an exit strategy. You want to pocket maybe thirty million of the proceeds. I can tell you it won't fly. No one wants to buy a berth on a sinking ship. The Bethlehem project may be brilliant, but for most potential buyers, it's going to seem really screwball, if not desperate. For some, it might even be offensive. Nevada might shrug, but the rest of the country isn't Nevada."

Jim Fitzsimmons was unabashed. "Look, there's nothing sacred about that theme. We can change it. We can stick with the Starlight name; it has some recognition and an established clientele. That should be worth something. Fifty million is way less than it would cost if you wanted to rebuild this place from scratch; then there are the Indian Country initiatives. I see the present ownership selling out ninety percent of its stock for ten million, with the other forty going into a remodel of the Starlight and a ten-million-dollar reserve fund for Indian initiatives.

The new company would assume existing debt of about fifteen million."

"The operative word is 'wanted,' Mr. Fitzsimmons. Who'd want to build this place in today's market? Your location is mediocre at best. Then there's California gaming looming over your head. It's beginning to look like it's going to get Indian casinos—lots of them. Reno could be in deep doo-doo, not just the Starlight. Then there's my playing field, the stock market. Casino shares are way off, and no one knows if they're ever coming back. That party may be over. Our firm happens to believe that they will rebound—otherwise I wouldn't be here—but sometimes we're wrong—"

Jim interrupted the dark-suited talking head who seemed little older than JFK. "So, what's your assessment, Mr. McNeal? What's possible?"

"My recommendation is that we go for thirty-five. Pay off all the bank debt, put ten million in the property, and sell eighty-five percent of your ownership for five. The new entity can pony up, or borrow, funds as needed for any external initiatives. We get five million and five percent of the ownership for finding your buyer. So, you end up with five million, no debt, and ten percent of the new company. You'll have to front some expenses, probably half a million to conduct the audits of your books and your contracts. That should also cover the preparation and publication of a prospectus. Your present external auditor and legal counsel will have to go. We'll need the credibility of one of the big five accounting firms, maybe Arthur Andersen, and a nationally-recognized law firm. We're reasonably optimistic that we can get you an offer, but there are no guarantees. If we can't sell the deal, you pay us a one-million-dollar fee for our efforts."

"Is there any wiggle room? Can we fine-tune those numbers?"

"No, not if you want Singleton to take this on. That's our bottom-line assessment."

"Is that all?"

"Well, not exactly. We're concerned about management. Of course, the buyer may want to assume management with its own people. But we're probably looking at an out-of-state, or even foreign, entity, and it will likely want a management team in place. There will have to be a new board, probably with present ownership holding no more than one seat on it. We'll have to scrutinize staffing, and particularly payroll, for possible savings. A potential buyer won't have much confidence in the team that got you into your present predicament. I suspect that some of your key personnel will have to go. It shouldn't be viewed as personal; rather, it's just sound bus—"

The figure seated in the corner exploded to his feet. Jim had been so fixed upon McNeal that he'd failed to notice the magma rising in James's volcano.

"What the hell's the matter with you, Jimmy? Throw this snot-nosed kid out of here. He wants to steal this place, and you sit there acting like you'll hold his coat while he does it." Fixing McNeal with a reptilian glare, James enunciated slowly for emphasis, "Listen, punk, there's not going to be a sale. I built this place with my pennies, nickels, sweat, tears, and years. When everyone else was home being a husband and father, I was down here running this family. Seven days a week, including Easter and Christmas. I never had a single day off my first ten years. Now you sit here and tell us we can give up the Starlight for ten cents on the dollar, if we're lucky, and then take a hike. Thanks, but no thanks. Now get out of—"

McNeal rose slowly, clearly not intimidated by James's diatribe, and gave his laconic reply. "The ball's in your court. You obviously need to work out some things. Everyone has to be on the same page. I'm on the road until next Tuesday. I'm working on three other deals, but you can contact me through the office. You have my number. Either way, it's been nice meeting with you."

***

Things were moving so quickly. Two days ago, the trip to the Sweetwaters, Jerry's "date" with Sheba yesterday afternoon, and now their 7 a.m. rendezvous at the Lotus Blossom Coffee House before Sue logged in for the day shift. They were seated at the far table of the outside patio, perched over the rippling waters of the Truckee River. Neither were morning people, so they ate their croissants and sipped their cappuccinos in silence. Jerry stared blankly at three tatterdemalions sprawled on the grass of Wingfield Park, lazily passing around a bottle of White Wolf vodka. Gradually the caffeine stirred conversation.

"Look at those two ducks, Jerry." A hen and drake mallard swam lazily in the current. "They have to swim upstream to stay in the same place. Sometimes I feel like my life is like that—a lot of effort just to maintain the status quo."

"Sue, don't take this question the wrong way. You told me a little about Youngstown and the disappointment over Red's scholarship, so I assumed you never went to college. Yet sometimes your thoughts and words seem too profound for a high school graduate."

"I've had a few college courses. When we got to Reno, I thought I could do it all: serve drinks at the Starlight, care for Sheba, cook and clean, be a good wife and take evening courses at the community college. I loved making pottery and took a few ceramics courses. Maybe, craftsmanship is in my Marinelli genes. After all, I *am* related to a long line of coppersmiths and bell-makers." She laughed. "But my real goal was to teach English literature. Red thought I meant in middle school, but I even dreamed of becoming a university professor. For two years I took a course each semester, but I could feel things slipping away. It was hard to do the reading. Sometimes I could barely stay awake in class.

"Red tried to help in his own way. He'd watch Sheba on school nights, but his wheels were starting to come off, too. When I'd get home, Sheba would be in her playpen crying and Red sitting at the kitchen table, staring at several empty beer cans with a blank look on his face. I used to check her for bruises when I put her to bed. I never found any, so I don't think he actually hit her, but I was really frightened that he was going to lose it some evening.

"That last semester, my class was on social writers of the nineteenth century. Dickens and Hardy, Hugo and Zola. I began to see my own reflection in their works. The fit wasn't perfect, but it was too close for comfort. All around me, there was the evidence of Thoreau's thesis that the mass of men lead lives of quiet desperation. Sun Valley was a living laboratory for that. Our neighborhood had so much desperation—and violence. Anyway, I gave up on my girlish dream. I've put it behind me. It was whimsical and unrealistic. At the rate I was going, it would have taken a million years to get my B.A."

"I've got one from a good university—Berkeley. You'd never guess in what. I graduated with honors in philosophy, if you can imagine. A degree in philosophy is about as useless as it gets. It only opens the door to graduate school, certainly not life."

"I would have never guessed that."

"In May of my first year of graduate school I was in the People's Park demonstration and was so disgusted by the violence that I moved to Mendocino to join a commune. We were a bunch of drop-out hippies, half of us draft dodgers protesting Vietnam in the name of pacifism. We grew illegal pot and smoked as much as we sold. It made me feel in touch—in touch with nature through the dirt under my fingernails and in touch with my soul through the drugs. Pot and LSD were my pleasures and Timothy O'Leary my guru. Is mind-tripping with hallucinogens really an escape from oppression, or just its own form of dependency and incarceration? You know you are in trouble when you regard O'Leary as the prophet."

"Was there any one special, Jerry?"

"My main squeeze was Tanya. Her tangled locks, hairy and pungent armpits, and downy legs made her seem like a forest creature. We tried to be self-sufficient. We made candles to illuminate our nights. The makeshift shelves in our pantry groaned under the weight of dozens of scavenged mason jars filled with home preserves. Our front yard was a vegetable garden. That was both our source of food and rejection of the American middle-class obsession with grass— the lawn kind, I mean." He laughed. "I had this little pot plot about two miles away. I went there as little as possible and tried to use different approaches to avoid creating a tread-worn path that might lead either the authorities or the less scrupulous of my soulmates to my little trove."

"Were you happy?"

"Sort of, but there was this dilemma that I could never quite resolve. Maybe it was philosophy's revenge! Anyway, we all claimed to have a social conscience and were out to change the world—help the underprivileged, end the war, flaunt our moral superiority through the music and protests of the Summer of Love. There I was in a commune, smoking lots of pot and getting laid a lot. Yet I was also selling my forest product like any good capitalist. In a way, weren't we just self-appointed Robin Hoods who were as self-indulgent and elitist as any robber baron? So, life in the commune wasn't perfect, either."

"Why did you leave?"

"Every routine has the potential to become boring. You can only read so many issues of *Mother Earth News*. How much can you say about compost? I was never much for religion, and there I was living some neo-pagan form of it. I began to miss my stored books. Most were by old white males and therefore politically incorrect.

"There were also the guns. I hate them, or at least I fear guns since my Mendocino days. Funny thing for Jerry Hunter to say, no? Every grower had a firearm to protect his marijuana plot. We had a little hovel way back in the hills. I was sitting on this filthy bed with the latest member of the commune—a firearms virgin. I showed him how to load the magazine of my 30.06 and then ejected the bullets—four, five, six. I put that empty gun down on the blanket between us and we drank our beer and smoked joints.

"Well, he casually reached down and squeezed the trigger and all hell broke loose. In that tight space, it sounded like the end of the world. You could hardly see for the feathers flying everywhere. That bullet went right through the metal headboard and the wall. In the kitchen, it missed the cook's head by a few inches. That was my wakeup call. If it was a reprieve, it was also a message. Of course, I'm thankful to this day that nobody was hurt, but even more so for it blasting me out of there."

"From there to where?"

"A week later, I was on my way to Reno in my 1950 Studebaker Champion. I didn't really know what I was heading for, but I was absolutely certain about what I was running away from. Even if it was kind of my hegira, Reno seemed as good a place as any to get a short-term job to earn a little money before going back to Berkeley.

"I didn't know anyone here. I just rented a room by the week in the Congressional Hotel, a real flop house, and went to dealer's school. My biggest education was exposure to the human burnouts at the Congressional. Philosophy sure hadn't prepared me for that experience. I think I matured ten years that first summer, at least in a cynical sense.

I listened through the thin wall to a rape in the next room and was too scared to intervene. I've never quite been able to look at people the same since.

"Bottom line for me was that Reno was just meant to be an adventure, an interlude before going back to school. I planned to apply that winter for the following semester. I got a job dealing blackjack in the Starlight. I was twenty-three and a pretty handsome guy, so it was party time, if a string of one-night stands adds up to a party."

"So why did you stay here?"

"Well, Joan was a dealer on my shift. I can't remember why she came to Reno. I must have known at one time. She was really lonely and vulnerable. When she told me she was pregnant, I suggested Tijuana—you couldn't get an abortion around here in those days. I offered to go to Mexico with her. It was a real slippery slope. She'd say, 'Jerry, you want me to have the abortion so you can dump me.' I'd deny it. Then, one day, I tried to prove the point. 'Look, I'll marry you today and then we'll go to Tijuana. We're too young to have a kid.'

"We went to Virginia City that night and got married, but I should've known better. I mean, there never was a chance that she'd have that abortion—she was a practicing Catholic and now a pregnant wife."

"I assume she had the baby—Tim, right?"

"Yep. I used to resent it. For years, I felt I'd been set up. But I don't feel that anger anymore. She couldn't help herself, really, and she didn't get any bargain, either. I wasn't ready for marriage and I fooled around a lot. After eighteen months, she filed for a divorce and moved back to Iowa. By then, she hated this place and everything about it … particularly me. It couldn't have been easy for her to return to Des Moines to live with her Catholic parents as a divorced single mother.

"Joan's never remarried. You understand the Catholic thing better than I, Sue, but I think a strict Catholic only gets one shot at marriage. The last time I was in Catholic church it was with Joan—and to please her. For a year, I even enjoyed the sermons and the reading of the Epistle and Gospel. It was like consuming the Bible as a book on tape. But then, the second year's repeat of the cycle had a deadening effect on me. I resented the time away from the broadcast of the Sunday morning 49ers games. I couldn't buy into the concept of everlasting life in paradise either, because heaven came with hell. I couldn't afford to entertain that possibility since I was such a prime candidate for it."

"Don't be so sure, Jerry. We Catholics believe that there is always time to repent."

"Joan and I do have Tim in common. Those years that he lived with me were my happiest. After getting to know him, it's hard to even think about Tijuana. But, of course, that whole marriage business derailed my college plans. It's hard to work out a graduate student's budget when you've got a child support payment to make. So, I put off applying from one year to the next. I could feel myself falling behind. The knowledge from my Berkeley days was rusting."

The waitress interrupted to ask if they wanted more coffee. Jerry asked instead for the check, as their time was running short.

"By other people's standards, I've had my accomplishments. I've done so many things in my life. I've climbed tall mountains, been on a photo safari in Kenya, snorkeled the Great Barrier Reef. I've caught trout in Alaska, rafted the Biobío in Chile, and shot elk in Montana. I know my philosophers and my wines, too. Ann, my fourth wife, was very wealthy and cultured. I was her plaything and pupil. She showed me where to dine in Paris, how to listen to Wagner's *Meistersinger* in the Vienna Opera House and Verdi's *Aida* at La Scala. She showed me Gaudí's architecture in Barcelona. We did the Spoleto Festival in Italy and the Mozart one in Salzburg. We had reservations to attend the Wagnerian music festival in Bayreuth and the Oberammergau pageant. We had a condo in Maui and a timeshare in Aspen.

"I know it sounds great, but my two years with her were terrible, a real penal existence. For Ann, I was an insignificant human being attached to an important penis. Being a kept man, a paid performer, was its own velvet prison. Certainly, no place for a pantheist."

"A pan what, Jerry?"

"If I'm religious at all, it's because I believe that God, if there is a God, is manifest in nature—the rocks, the plants and animals, the clouds, the planets, and even in human history, in every one of the tales we tell about ourselves. Think of that deer we saw in the Sweetwaters as your cousin. If all life evolved from primal slime, then those aspens are our relatives, too. If the apes are our first cousins, then the deer is maybe our thirty-first and the aspen tree our sixty-fourth. But the point is the divine in the shared kinship, whatever the degree.

"If I have a belief system, then Einstein invented it and called his creation 'cosmic religion.' It has no rules, no sin, no grace, no priests, no divine father figure, no prime mover. It's divinity based in the sheer logical beauty of the universe and the magnificent complementarity of its components. It's the divine zoological sublimity in that deer's alertness, the botanical grace in the leaves of the quaking aspen shimmering in response to an imperceptible breeze, the symmetry in the geological layering of the rock faces, the astronomical azure of the sky, the anthropology of the sheepherder's carvings. Taken together, they are my cathedral. Cosmic religion, Sue. It may have been Einstein's folly and possibly I'm his only disciple—his fool. But I find it more helpful and hopeful than the spiritual wasteland of pure atheism."

Sue laughed. "I don't think Father Gabrielli would have approved of your religion. In our cathedral, there were paintings of Jesus and the twelve apostles, God the Father, the Blessed Virgin Mary, and even a dove for the Holy Ghost. At least your religion spares you the calloused knees. That's what I remember most about church in Youngstown. Stand, sit, and kneel—particularly kneel."

"Sue, the real meaning in life is in the doing. Think of those miners in Belmont, it's not the gold that makes them significant to us, it was their *efforts* to find it. For me, when we start our day, the divine isn't reflected in a morning prayer to some abstract deity; rather it's the getting up, the dressing, the going to work, the day's fatigue—the effort. It doesn't matter whether you own the joint or work for it; it's the sincerity of your effort, the honesty, that sorts out the saints from the sinners."

"And how do we keep track? Isn't there some reward? Maybe a raise?"

"If money is the way to keep score, Sue, then I'm a star. There aren't too many people in this town, or anywhere else, making a hundred and fifty thou a year. There's the power, too. At the Starlight when I give an order, it's carried out ... well usually. But you know, in the middle of the night, I have my ghosts. There's this little voice that says, 'Jeremy, you blew it. You could have entered the Promised Land, and you sold out to the pharaoh.' I should have gone back to school."

"Maybe it's not too late."

"Ha! For you, maybe; you're thirty-three. I'm going to be fifty in five months, the big Five-O. You can go from Socrates to the Starlight, but not from the Starlight to Socrates. Oh, I'm not saying that life is over for me yet. There are lots of ways of staying alive. I'm an impetuous guy. I know you probably find that hard to believe." He laughed at his own cant.

"So, what do you have in mind?"

Jerry raised his arms as if holding a shotgun pointed at the ducks, and then jerked them skyward from the recoil. "I don't know for sure, but I'm going to do something. Look at those ducks. They're still here, waiting for us to throw them some crumbs. They look like mallards, but they're phonies. They're impersonating wild ducks. It's July, and the real mallards are raising their young in a Canadian marsh. In January, real mallards are swimming on some lagoon in Mexico. Somewhere along the line that pair learned that Reno isn't too hot in the summer or too cold in the winter. Here, it's possible for a duck to settle into the rut of raising its family in Wingfield Park and begging its bread from people.

"It cuts out the work, the flying. So, after a while, even a wild duck can forget how to fly, Sue. I want to soar again before I die. I want to fly with the wild mallards and be oblivious to borders, state lines, time zones—all those arbitrary distinctions we humans create in the name of imposing civilization upon nature, but we really put on ourselves. My favorite philosopher is Rousseau, and in many ways, he was like your Thoreau. He said, 'Man is born free, and is everywhere in chains.' For him, the eternal question was, is there life *before* death?"

"Thoreau and Rousseau, Jerry, sounds like a lounge act at the Golden Spur! I've got to go now, or I'll be late, Mr. GM."

"Alright, Mrs. Mallard."

***

Jerry contemplated Sue as she served drinks to three blackjack players in the pit. Even at a distance, he could make out her smile and read her coquettish body language as she avoided a fanny pat from the sozzled. She was good at her job, almost too good. He had an urge to cover her exposed flesh with Levis and a western shirt.

Jerry entered the elevator and punched the button for the executive offices. Father and son were having a heated exchange and they scarcely noticed his arrival.

"Jimmy, you're willing to sacrifice everything for this business except your time and attention. All you care about is lifestyle. You think we've got a divine right to dividends around this place ... well, we don't. If we ride this pony hard and put it away wet, it's going to catch pneumonia. Then we'll have a dead horse to bury."

"Dad, look, I'm just saying that we've got to talk to the bank and see if we can renegotiate our ratios. They won't let us distribute anything out of here unless we're in conformity with certain conditions. We made money last year, and we're going to owe the taxes, like it or not. I can't make my quarterly payment to the IRS as it is. I just don't have the money. It's easy for you to say that business is down so we'll just skip a few dividends; with your money it doesn't make a difference."

"Those bankers aren't going to lighten up on us, Jimmy. Why should they? Casino loans aren't that great, particularly now. When it comes to our business, there's not a banker in this valley counting his fingers who can come up with ten. Think of the Riverside, the Mapes, the Gold Dust, the Onslow, King's Inn, Harold's Club, the Horseshoe. They're all closed, and some banker has scar tissue to show for each of them."

"You're always right, aren't you, Dad? I mean whatever you think, that's reality. You talk a lot better than you listen. You walk through this place and everybody loves you—the employees, the customers. You always have a greeting and a smile for anyone, at least anyone not related to you. Why are you so hard on your own family?"

James Fitzsimmons fixed his eyes upon his son like a mongoose measuring a cobra, confident yet cautious. "Jimmy, it's called 'tough love.' If I'm not hard on you who will be? Think of me as your crucible, I won't be here forever to watch out for you."

"You're more like my crucifix, Dad. You're right about the time frame. Don't you think we should start working on some pleasant memories? I'm sixty, for God's sake. If you haven't got me right yet, you never will. Look at Sean. He moved to Boston just to put a continent between him and tough love."

"I know. I miss him a lot. At times, I miss him more than your mother. To be honest, Jimmy, there were times when I resented you because you weren't Sean. He had the spunk and backbone to tell me off and leave. You stayed, and I didn't know what to do with you. I gave you a salary, some stock, an invented title, a board seat, and a hard time. I kid you about your fishing, but the fact is, I was happy when you went on one of your trips. It cut out some of my busy work trying to think up things for you to do—like representing the Starlight in some of those bullshit associations we belong to so you and the self-anointed hotshots in this town can sit around and talk endlessly about nothing while feeling important. At least it kept you out of operations."

Jerry had been hovering near the door, feeling supernumerary and embarrassed. It was time to interrupt. He cleared his throat and James Fitzsimmons motioned him to a chair.

"Good morning, Sir. Hi, Junior."

"Jimmy wants to hire the creep that made the Bethlehem pitch as our marketing director. I think it's nuts."

"Dad, we don't have a lot of choice. Our marketing sucks. We've lost three directors in two years, two to riverboats and one to the Indians. Those riverboat guys come to town, rent a room at the Holiday Inn, and hold their job fair. They've cherry-picked us to death. We've been running a blind ad for two months and have two nibbles to show for it. One's from a bellman at the Golden Spur who thinks he has such a great personal touch with people that he's qualified for the job! At least this guy, Cohen, has some credentials. He's got a degree in marketing from Cornell, and he's worked for ten years in ad agencies back East."

"Another college guy; that's just great, Jimmy. Let me tell you something—you can't learn anything about this business in college. It's not about computer whizzes with famous degrees and fancier talk, little smart-ass know-it-alls who couldn't deal a hand of blackjack if their life depended on it. All that academic theory is just crap. You learn the casino business on the floor, working with customers. The customer is everything; without the customer, we can turn out the lights and save on power. You learn this business by carrying the customer's bags, cleaning up after him in the men's room, serving his food and clearing away his dishes, pouring his drinks, selling him change, dealing his cards, and giving him a big smile and pat on the back when he wins. You've got to remember his name, his wife's too, and care about his kids. If you can figure out how to get someone here from Vancouver or Fresno, you better be ready to wipe his ass before you kiss it. The customer is the king, the queen, and the jack around here; we're just the joker in the deck. That was true last year and still will be a thousand years from now. They can't teach you any of that in Casino 101! Universities should stick to what they do best."

"What's that, Dad?"

"Football."

"The times have changed. Where would we be without those computers you were so against? Up Shit Creek. You can't run a place like this any longer by scribbling numbers on yellow pads. You always bad-mouth the corporate guys and their fancy management ideas and benefit programs. Well, if we're so smart, how come our occupancy was fifty-five percent last month? How come our last three marketing directors jumped ship? Harrah's, Hilton, Caesar's, Circus—those guys are all failures compared to us, right?"

James Fitzsimmons was opinionated and hidebound, but he was no fool. He knew that his son had pretty much nailed the Starlight's grim reality. "I don't know, Jimmy. That Cohen guy seemed pretty goofy to me. What do you think, Jerry?"

"I don't care, Sir."

There was a stunned silence that was finally interrupted by Jim's nervous cough.

"You don't care?" the old man exploded. "You're the general manager of this joint and you don't care who we hire as marketing director?"

"I think he means that it's okay with him to go with Cohen," Jim said. "Isn't that right, Jerry?"

Jerry remained silent and impassive, which James Fitzsimmons interpreted to mean subject closed. They would be interviewing Cohen. "So, Jerry, what did your cousin say about our little Arkansas problem?"

"He said to go fuck yourself, Sir."

The new silence made the former one cheery. The elder Fitzsimmons's face turned purple with as much blood as his ninety-year-old body could muster. He articulated his first words slowly: "Presidents—don't—talk—like—that, Jerry. Well, maybe except for Nixon."

"You don't know my cousin, Sir." Neither Fitzsimmons noticed the slight twinkle in Jerry's eyes.

"No? Well, I do know one Clinton, and as far as I'm concerned, his ass is grass. Put your keys on the table. Jimmy, tell Security to meet our ex-GM at his office so he can remove his personal things. I don't want one scrap of paper to leave this place with him. As for your two percent, Mr. Clinton, we'll give you sixty thousand a point, not a penny more. If you don't like it, you can take your chances of going down with this ship like the rest of us. What do you say?"

Jerry knew that his stock was probably worth twice the offer, even with business down. "I just don't care, Sir. Tell Arnold to prepare the transfer documents for Gaming Control and I'll sign."

Jim interjected, "Jerry, we don't have a controller. Arnold resigned this morning, right after the June numbers came out. We lost another three hundred thou in June. Arnold's a conservative guy; he's going to be the first one out of Dodge. It'll take a little time to prepare your documents. At least a month or two."

"No problem, Junior."

***

Jerry caught Sue about the waist and spun her around. "C'mon, we're out of here. We're getting married!"

"Jerry! You've got to be kidding. I can't do that. And ... and shouldn't you ask me? You may be the GM, but that's a tall order."

"Sue, I'm sorry. You're right. Look, I'm not the GM anymore and I'm thinking with my gut rather than my head. But, you know, I've learned that it's when I listen to my head and ignore my gut that I get into trouble. My gut warns me every time I'm about to tell one of my white lies. Right now, my head is full of reasons why a four-time loser shouldn't ever get married again. My head tells me to go upstairs, kiss ass, and beg for my job back. Sue, I'm asking you to marry me, *today*. I love you. Even better, I like you! I want to see Italy through your eyes. I've got a house, some savings, and a few investments. We'll be fine—you, Sheba, and me. Given the talent shortage in this industry, I'll have plenty of job prospects, even here in Reno. This town's been raided by all those new riverboats and Indian casinos. We'll be fine. What do you say?"

"Jerry, I can't marry you today. I'm still married to Red!"

Jerry removed his coat and put it over her shoulders. "Turn in your tray and put on your street clothes. Let's go somewhere and talk. It seems like between us, we've got plenty of loose ends. We just need to figure out how to tie them up together. I'm asking you for something you probably shouldn't give. I'm asking you for trust, Sue."

She scarcely paused before saying deliberately. "Alright, Blue Eyes. I'll be back in a few minutes."

***

"There's so much to talk about, Sue. Where should we begin?"

It was only 11 a.m., and this was their second stint of the day at the same outside table of the Lotus Blossom Coffee House.

"You and Sheba can move in with me tomorrow. I've got four bedrooms. My house is way bigger than yours."

"But what about Sheba's school? We're not in your district. What about my cats?" Jerry hadn't anticipated that the practical questions could be so pointed. He *hated* cats.

"There still may be time to get her into a new school for the fall. If not, we'll have to drive her." *Damn cats!* he thought, resigned to the inevitable. "Thank God I don't have a dog."

"Jerry, before you marry me you should know that I don't want more children."

"So, I've got a grown son. I'm out of that business. Remember I told you that I'm not much of a kid guy. I don't even know my two grandchildren in Iowa."

Sue fixed her gaze on the mallards again and Jerry realized that he'd gone too far.

"Don't worry about me and Sheba," he said. "Our little date together went pretty well. I'm not her pal or anything, but when I told her how my tall tales got me into trouble as a kid, she even laughed a few times and asked me a question or two. She's got a lot of pain, but she's a good girl. Besides, she's thirteen. We're not talking diapers here. In three years, she'll have her driver's license and we'll have to make an appointment to see her."

Sue gave him a forced smile. On the subject of children Jerry was neither profound nor persuasive, but she could see that, in his own way, he was trying hard. She took his two hands in hers and looked intently into his blue eyes. "This is turning into some kind of business negotiation. There's plenty of time to talk about moving my furniture, my car payments, our health insurance. Babe, I need you; I want you inside me. I want you to take me home and make love to me without Sheba in the next room. I want us to spend half an hour just undressing each other …"

Jerry's thumb and forefinger were pressed together as if holding a pen. He made little writing motions in the air to catch the attention of the waitress folding napkins at another table. He wanted the check now—right now!

***

Sue snuggled against his shoulder as they savored the afterglow of their delicious noontime lovemaking. "I feel funny, Jerry. It was so wonderful, but now I'm feeling a little guilty. It must be the hour; we're like schoolkids playing hooky."

"I know what you mean. I'm always so busy at the Starlight that it seems like I should jump up and give someone an order. It's going to take some getting used to, being unemployed. At least I won't be your kept man. And I've had a thought. Let's take a trip together. You should take the fall off—be a mother, see how you feel about making a real home for all of us. Sheba won't be a child for much longer; you could work on some good memories with her. You might even consider college again. I'm going to need a job—I'll go crazy without something to do. When I get one, there's no chance of our having some quality time together for a while. You can't start a new job and ask for time off the next day.

"There's plenty of time to combine our households when we get back. School doesn't start until the end of August; that gives us five or six weeks. Maybe we could arrange for Sheba to stay with someone. Think of it as our honeymoon, even if we can't get married yet."

"What do you have in mind?"

"Let's go to Italy, your Italy—Angone."

"It's Agnone, Jerry. Gee, I don't know. I don't even have a passport."

"I think we can get you one quickly if we go to San Francisco or even D.C. Let's do it; let's throw one more caution to the wind. In fact, Sue, let's go to Italy via Youngstown!"

She looked at him intently before replying, "Alright, Jerry, on the condition that we come back through Des Moines!"

***

Three days later Jerry stopped by the office of Charles Wilson on his way to the Reno airport to meet Sue and Sheba. The attorney had a wry smile on his face as he handed him the envelope containing Sue's divorce papers.

"It's not often that I get repeat business from a client, Jeremy."

"I appreciate the quick work on such short notice. Oh, by the way, shove it, Charles!" Jerry added, but without any real rancor.

***

Manny Cohen was his own worst enemy. In this Age of Correctness his speech was a paean to the impolitic. He never spoke of people in the abstract. Everyone was a Mick or Spic, Greaser or Nigger, Dago, Wop, Bohunk, Polack, Chink, Kike, Frog, or Kraut. Women were girls, dolls, sluts, or cunts; homosexuals were fags or dikes. Clients were schmucks and customers suckers. "Fuckin" was his favorite filler and adjective. Such talk had cost him two jobs, one wife, the affections of a daughter, a broken tooth, several black eyes, and countless insults and rebuffs. Still, Manny couldn't help himself. His speech was ingrained into his personality and the only alternative seemed to be silence—self-banishment from the human race. There was no redeeming Dale Carnegie on Manny's attenuated horizon.

Once again, he faced Priscilla across the anteroom to Fitzsimmons's inner sanctum, caught in the seemingly endless waiting game of nervous anticipation. If Manny was incapable of restraining his venomous verbal darts, he certainly knew their potential from bitter experience. Once people got to know him, they ceased to judge him by his banter. It was the transition from first formality to intimacy that was Manny's particular *Via Crucis* in life. In short, he didn't interview well.

After sitting opposite his inquisitor in the board room, Manny couldn't help cringing. He listened to Jim Fitzsimmons's opening gambit, but his real concern was with the slightly dour look on the chairman's face. "Mr. Cohen we've been reviewing your application and we may be interested in offering you the position."

"So, you guys liked my Bethlehem proposal? You want me to take point, is that it? You want me to develop the concept, fill in some of the blanks? When are ya gonna build it?"

Jim replied, "You don't understand, Mr. Cohen; we never had any intention of building anything. We were thinking of going public, and we needed some sizzle, as they say. The stock market doesn't look at today's numbers, it wants to know what you plan to do tomorrow. The investor public is bored by good operating results; it wants vision, it demands growth, preferably spectacular. We're interviewing you for our marketing director's job. Your responsibility would be to get bodies in the door and butts in the beds and keep them here for as long as possible. But then you must know how to do that, given your education and experience." For emphasis, Jim shuffled through the pages of Manny's CV.

"Well, I dunno. I thought I was gonna be a big shot in charge of developin' a hundred-million-dollar project. What's the pay for a marketin' director?"

Before Jim could answer, James Fitzsimmons blurted out, "Fifty thousand." Father and son had discussed sixty as their number before admitting Manny into the board room.

"Fifty thousand?! Geez, I was makin' fifty-two at the agency."

"Mr. Cohen, the job pays fifty thousand. Jimmy here likes your résumé; I prefer some of the others. We've got a lot of interviews today. Do you want the job or don't you?" Manny was far too intimidated to bargain. "Well, Mr. Fitzsimmons, it beats goin' back to Joisey. I'll take it. Will I get a fu ... uh, uh a title?"

"Yes, Manny, you'll get a fucking title and office of your own, only around here we don't like to use offensive words like *title*," James joked. "From now on, you're Manny, because we don't deal much in formality, either."

"Does that mean I should call you James, Sir?"

"I didn't say that!"

Jim laughed and said, "Maybe he could call you Sir James, Dad."

Manny stood up and turned to leave.

"Oh, one more thing," James said. "You have to learn how to say 'Nevada.'"

"Sir?"

"It's not Nuh-vaw-duh; Manny; it's Nuh-vaa-duh, like in sheep talk."

"Sheep, Sir?"

"Yes, sheep. Think sheep—b-a-a-a. You can't sell something if you can't even pronounce it right."

"Yes, Sir."

***

"Papa, it's me. Susan." Sue took her immobile father's hand in hers. "*Penso d'andare in Italia. Me ne vado ad Agnone.*"

She thought she felt a slight squeeze, but couldn't be sure. She stood up, kissed him lightly on the forehead, and went into a living room that was filled with her childhood memories.

"Mama, does he still recognize you?"

"I'na no sure, Susana. Before he had'a his stroke he was'a, how you say, Alza-heimer. Now he sit'a there all'a tine. He sleep'a in that'a chair. I put'a television. I'na no sure he can'a tell."

"Mama, Jerry and I are going to be married. We're taking a trip together. Sheba will be staying with Laura. I hope you get to know her. She needs her *nonna*; she needs all the relatives she can get."

Maria della Quadra nodded in assent, happy that the awkward visit was over. First Red and now this stranger who was practically old enough to be her daughter's father. "*Porca Madonna!*"

***

"Mom, I really need to speak to Red. You must know where he is."

Eleanor Johnson eyed her daughter-in-law suspiciously. "Sue, I don't know what happened between you. Red won't talk about it. He did say that it was your fault."

"Mom, all I want from Red is a signature on our divorce papers. I've met a guy, and Sheba needs a father. I don't want to say anything bad about Red. What happened, happened. He's your only son ..."

The two women were sitting together on the front porch of the Johnson house. Eleanor poured them each a fresh cup of tea. "Leave me the papers and I'll see if I can get them to Red. I don't even have an address for him, but he does call every month or so. I think he's living somewhere around Fresno. He says he's a successful building contractor. He's afraid you're going to track him down and make his life miserable with attorneys. Ever since he left Nevada, he's like a fugitive."

"Mom, tell him it's okay. I'm not mad at him. I don't want a thing from Red. I'm sorry to hear that he's so nervous about me. I had no idea. He can just sign the papers and get on with his life; I give you my word."

"Tell me about Sheba."

"She's going to be here for the next month, staying with my sister. I'll tell Laura to get in touch with you if you'd like. Sheba's smart; she's going to be a very interesting person. I'd love for you two to get together. She's old enough to travel by herself—she could come to Youngstown to visit her relatives."

"I'd like that. I get awfully lonely. Do you think Sheba could stay with me for a couple of days now?"

"Sure, Mom. I'll arrange it."

***

When the Alitalia 747 completed its ascent from Kennedy, Jerry put his seat back and adjusted his long legs as best he could within the torture chamber otherwise known as economy seating. "I'm confused by some things that happened back in Youngstown. Why didn't you tell your mother we were going to Italy?"

"If I'd told her that, we would've had to visit all my relatives. I did tell Papa, but I don't think he understood. I promised to show you the town, not introduce you to my kin. They wouldn't understand about Red, you, and me. The tongues would really wag. Until a few years ago, you couldn't get a legal divorce in Italy—the women voted against it in the referendum. Let's go as tourists and just let sleeping dogs lie. They don't know me, Babe; they haven't seen me for more than twenty years. I was a little girl when we went back to Youngstown."

"If that's what you want. Actually, after our Youngstown reception, it might be better. I mean, Laura and Louie seemed okay—he's got a great sense of humor—but the weather in the rest of the town was really chilly for the first of August!"

"I expected it. That's why I only wanted one day there on this trip. The next time, things will be different. Mama has to get used to the idea. She's not going to have Papa for company much longer. He's a project now, but at least it gives her something to do. She's going to need Laura and maybe even me. Let's see how she and Sheba get on. That'll be a big part of it."

"I have another question. How come you introduced your mother as Maria della Quadra? I thought your name was Marinelli."

"It is, Jerry. It's Papa's name. In Italy we take our last name from our father, but then we keep it until we die. Her father was Luigi della Quadra."

The flight attendants served them dinner, and Jerry noted the difference in quality compared to the inedible, rubbery sandwich they'd had for lunch on their domestic flight. The veal was tender and basted with a delicate sauce, the bread and salad were both fresh, the Italian red wine full-bodied.

"Actually, Jerry, it's appropriate that the women retain their last names. Agnone is a town run by women, by widows—both black and white."

"What do you mean?"

"All the middle-aged and older widows dress in black. When someone in the family dies, they're supposed to go into mourning for a year. If it's your husband, maybe you wear black for the rest of your life. The market in Agnone looks like a convention of crows."

"But what is a white widow?"

"Oh, the *vedova bianca*, that's the married woman whose husband is away somewhere as a migrant. There are men from Agnone working in factories in Germany and coal mines in Belgium. Some live in North Italy—Turin, Genoa, Milan. My cousin worked in Rome and came back to Agnone every other weekend. In the old days, the men went out to places like Youngstown, Bahia Blanca in Argentina, and Trail, British Columbia. Some stayed away for years, earning money to send back to their families; many brought out their wives and kids and settled abroad permanently. Others went back to Agnone to buy a farm or start a little business. A few were never heard from again. So, when we get there, you'll see men in the bars and on the street—many of them old emigrants back from Providence, Rhode Island or Sao Paulo, Brazil. In all the public places the men are center stage and the women stay around the edges. But don't be deceived by appearances. Agnone is a widows' town!" Sue paused, seemingly distracted, and then locked eyes with him before changing the subject. "So, Jerry, how did your marriage to Ann end?"

"With a whimper rather than a bang." He laughed. "I guess you have a right to know. I was an aging athlete who finally failed to make the team. One day, I came home from golf, and there were two suitcases sitting outside the front door. Everything that I owned at the time fit into those two suitcases! She'd left me a note with the business card of Charles Wilson, Attorney-at-Law, stapled to it. It said:

> *Ciao, Jerry. Nothing is forever. Off to Monaco. Contact Charles about the documents. I'm willing to settle for the house and $500,000. That's from me to you Hon! My advice is to take it. Not bad pay for a little night work. Don't bother to call, and, please, no Christmas cards.*
> *Love, Ann*
> *P.S. Genaro sends his best.*

"I tried my key, but it wouldn't open the door. I wasn't exactly stunned, but I was pissed. I'd never even heard of Genaro! I considered fighting her, but on second thought, I realized that it was the kick in the butt I'd been needing to get on with my life. And it was turning out to be a golden boot. My own place and half a mil, and we'd been married for about five hundred days. I had this crazy, even perverse, thought of Kennedy. I mean he was president for a thousand days and ended up with a bullet in his brain to show for it. Ann's offer definitely had its advantages.

"Charles handed me the new house key when I signed the settlement. I went back to work at the Starlight as assistant GM. When they made me the manager and offered to sell me two points, I used Ann's money. After taxes, I was able to pay cash for my interest. Not too bad, really. On the other hand, it does make you wonder about yourself when you start making your wives happier by agreeing to the divorce than to the marriage!"

"Dare I ask?"

"Ask what?"

"Your other two marriages, Jerry. You know about Red, and I know something about Joan and Ann. Your cast definitely has more characters than mine."

He shrugged. "Why not? It's a long flight. Carrie was my second wife. It was a total tits-and-ass thing. Pure sex. When I think about it, I still can't understand how I ever got myself into that mess. She was marvelous in bed, but then you had to talk to her. She had more brain matter between her toes than between her ears. I know that sounds cruel, but it was a case of total incompatibility—an affair that just spun out of control.

"The worst part was her dependency. She wouldn't make a single decision on her own. It was as if marriage suspended all her adult responsibilities. She quit her job and sat around the house watching soaps and quiz shows. I remember asking one night, 'Who are you going to vote for next Tuesday?' She said, 'Geez, I didn't know there was an election.'

"That was the final straw. I tried to bring up divorce as gently as possible, but she just didn't get the message. So, finally, I took her to one of those canned-music dance halls. I brought along my own tape—Dan Hicks and the Hot Licks. I also had the divorce papers. I slipped the disk jockey a hundred-dollar bill and asked him to play my song in five minutes. When I saw him getting ready, I handed Carrie the envelope and excused myself, supposedly to go to the restroom. When I got to the front door, the guy was saying 'the next number is from Jerry to Carrie.' As I opened the car door, I could still hear the muffled refrain of *How Can I Miss You When You Won't Go Away?*

"I never saw her again. A few days later I got a special delivery envelope with the signed papers. There was a one-word note: 'Asshole.' Actually, it pleased me. It was the first spunk she'd ever shown."

"Boy, Jerry, I'm kind of sorry I started this. I think I'll leave my seat belt buckled while you tell me about number three."

"Maris, or maybe Mavis?"

"Jerry! You can't even remember her name?"

"Hey, I can barely remember anything about our three months together. She was rebounding from some sort of personal disaster, and I had a big-league drinking problem." Jerry put his hand on Sue's. "Don't worry, that was five years ago. The AA program straightened me out. Ann made me go. Now I just drink a little wine. Anyway, Maris and I met in the bottom of some bottle and I don't think we drew a sober breath between us the whole time. When I look back, I'm not sure it counts as a marriage—certainly not a real one. Let's say I've been married three and a half times!

"Maybe we just live too long. I'm a half-centenarian, and I'm not sure how I got here. It feels just yesterday that I was a kid. When life was brutish, mean, and short, you took a bride at eighteen, probably picked out for you by your parents, had five kids, buried three of them, and died at thirty-five. If you didn't care for your wife or she for you, well, tough shit. The point wasn't some search for a soulmate; it was to procreate. Your nose was to the grindstone and you worked a little plot of dirt six day a week. Then, on the seventh, you listened to some priest tell you what a sinner you were. We now live to seventy or even eighty, and the life expectancy of marriage in America is about twenty years. Marriages have become like knees and hips—when they wear out, they need to be replaced."

Jerry and Sue watched an edited feature film that lasted until well past midnight. Most of the other passengers then prepared to struggle through a few hours of upright slumber, but Jerry couldn't sleep on planes and Sue was too wired with the anticipation of her return to Italy.

"Since we're playing Twenty Questions tonight," he said, "let me ask you one. Where did you ever come up with a name like Sheba?"

Sue laughed. "In Agnone it's the custom to name first-born children after grandparents. If your grandmother was Rosalba, then you might be Rosalba. But my parents were so upset about Red and me that I was afraid to make matters worse by naming my daughter Maria. I was hurt, and angry, too. Then Eleanor came to the hospital and held her granddaughter for the first time. Mom said over and over, 'She looks like the Queen of Sheba.' It was the only time Red and I had made anyone happy."

Jerry extinguished their reading-light and each lapsed into silence, lost in thought.

***

They picked up their rental car in the early dawn. While Sue slept soundly, it was all Jerry could manage to drive to their hotel through Rome's horrendous rush-hour traffic. His body screamed for relief after their red-eye flight. He lowered the window for some air, admitting a cloud of Roman pollution instead. Occasionally he slapped his face to fight off exhaustion. They slept through the day, awoke in the middle of the night, and then napped fitfully into the next morning.

"So, what's it to be? North or south?" Jerry asked, underscoring the peripatetic nature of their adventure.

Sue struggled to focus her jet-lagged mind on the vague question. They were seated across from the Coliseum after having toured the half-decrepit, half-impressive attraction. "I don't understand, Jerry."

"Agnone is south, isn't it? You said it was inland from Naples. Should we go there or would you rather try Florence, Venice, and Milan first? Shall we go to your Italy or mine—or rather, Ann's?"

Sue pondered her options for a moment. "Let's go north, Jerry. We only need a day or two in Agnone. August 15th is my day there. Well, sort of. It's called the Day of the Emigrant. Some of the *Agnonesi* and their descendants from all over the world come back to Agnone for the festival. Everyone gathers at San Onofrio, a little chapel in the mountains that's abandoned for the rest of the year. The priest says mass and then there's a big picnic—you bring your lunch and celebrate life and good companionship. It's like the festival in Capistrano to celebrate the return of the swallows, only, in Agnone, the swallows do the celebrating."

"It sounds fine to me, as long as we get out of Rome. After two days, I've about had it with the tourist traps in this town. I couldn't believe those nuns selling postcards and souvenirs on the roof of St. Peter's. I'm not a religious man, but it made me approve of Jesus driving the money changers from the temple."

They sipped their five-dollar Cokes and contemplated the fresh busload of gawkers preparing to enter the Coliseum, several munching upon takeaway McDonald's hamburgers and French fries.

Jerry grunted and gestured. "Take that place. The big top of the greatest Show on Earth during the *Pax Romana*, now a ruin to be visited by citizens of the *Pax Americana*. Or is it the American Pox? Things change, but only within fixed parameters. In ancient times, they fed the Christians to the lions. There were lots of lions and just a few Christians, so history tells us to feel sorry for the underdogs ... who were also the top dogs, because they were humans and the lions were beasts. Now there are lots of Christians and only a few lions. In fact, all over the planet, we humans have slaughtered the lions, and most other species as well. So, if they were to reenact that Roman spectacle for our benefit this evening, it would be hard for me to cheer for the Christians. Particularly if I think of the no-hopers that I lived with in the Congressional Hotel compared with the magnificence of the mountain lion that left the paw print on the Sweetwaters."

***

The Tuscan countryside and that open-air museum called Florence exuded their ageless charm even in the stifling late July heat and the annual mosquito infestation that prompted the wiser Florentines to abandon their city until September. It seemed to be operated by a skeleton staff, whose specific duty was to cater crossly to thousands of tourists until the first stirrings of autumn once again made Florence inhabitable. The city wasn't the cradle of western civilization for nothing.

One late afternoon, Jerry pointed the car onto the highway that ascended to the nearby town of Fiesole. They strolled through its ancient streets, and he guided Sue to a spot where the view of Florence and the entire Arno Valley was magnificent. They contemplated the sunset, and as the lights of the city came on one by one, she broke their silence. "You seem to know this place well."

"Come on." He took her hand and led her through a maze of twisted streets that were scarcely wider than pathways. They stopped before an iron gate with the inscription "Villa Belvedere."

"Ann and I lived here for a summer. She rented this little villa through some agency. You can't tell from the street, but there's a wonderful patio off the dining room. It has an unobstructed view of Florence, even better than the one we just enjoyed."

"I would imagine so. *Belvedere* means good view."

"That's what the agent told us. I wish I could show you this place. It really is charming, and I have some fine memories of our time here."

"It's okay. It would be awkward for the people living here now, and it really isn't necessary. I've got the idea."

They descended to the main piazza. As they were about to leave, the night was filled with strange yet beguiling music.

"Something's going on in the theater," Jerry said. "Want to check it out?"

At the entrance to the open-air amphitheater, they bought their tickets and then struggled to find their places in the dark. They settled onto the uncomfortable stone seating and turned their attention to the performers—the *Voces Andinas* presenting the airy folk melodies of their distant Peru. The audience erupted into wild applause at the first strains of the finale—*El Condor Pasa*—the only number that anyone had recognized.

Afterwards, as they descended through the darkness towards Florence, Jerry remarked, "The world has imploded. There's no uniqueness left anywhere. We were sitting there in a Roman amphitheater that happens to be built on an Etruscan site, listening to South American music along with an audience drawn from maybe forty different countries. It was an exercise in simultaneous time and space travel. Maybe virtual reality isn't such a bad idea. Like with those mallards in Wingfield Park—it cuts out the flying, not to mention the heat and mosquitoes. We could just sit at home and listen to Yanni at the Acropolis and the Taj Mahal. Bill Gates tied up the electronic rights to the world's great masterpieces so he can project them on his wall. Why come all the way to Florence to stand in line with us at the Uffizi and Pitti Palace?"

"Jerry, sometimes you do sound your age. It's progress; it's inevitable. Why fight it?"

"You've got me wrong, Sue. I'm as fascinated as I am frightened by it. I think of the potential, the future possibilities. Take the David, for example. Michelangelo's masterpiece is here on display, frozen in stone, just as Michelangelo left him to us centuries ago. It was originally installed in front of the Palace on the Piazza della Signoria, where it could only be viewed from the front. After nearly four centuries, it was weathering, so they moved it indoors to the Galleria dell'Accademia. There, they've thoughtfully made it possible for the visitor to circle the statue, see it from every angle, so we can marvel at the many Davids afforded by differing perspectives. But, in the final analysis, David is passive, and we viewers become the active agents of his transformation.

"Enter virtual reality and animatronics. Reconstitute David as a series of electronic codes, and suddenly the possibilities are endless. David, like Prometheus, is unbound. The slayer of Goliath is now free to take on King Kong in David II, the sequel. The sequel's sequel has David III, our intrepid hero, on the deck of the Enterprise, exploring outer space for ever more exotic adversaries. But there is a grave danger, because as we sit back in our seats to contemplate the new Davids, it is we who become passive. It's an entirely new way of experiencing culture, and I'm not sure that, as yet, we fully understand the consequences— maybe benign, maybe sinister."

"Jerry, I think I know what you're getting at; I'm just not sure that people will ever accept the canned program as a substitute for the live performance. There's something about being there. Can the reproduction ever be quite as good as the original?"

"In the case of my David scenario, the answer is probably 'not yet.' But won't it be possible one day to transmit and reproduce the David as a perfect hologram? What then? When I was in college, I read Hesse's *Steppenwolf*. It has a passage, actually a diatribe, that I've never forgotten. For no particular reason, other than the fact that it was obviously weighing heavily on his mind, Hesse suddenly denounces the phonograph as some kind of infernal machine. He condemns the scratchy parody of real music that seems to issue forth from every window in Prague to assault any true music lover's sensibilities. He compares the crassness of such street music with the ethereal atmosphere of the concert hall and predicts the phonograph's speedy demise once it was no longer a novelty.

"Yet one could argue that today, from the sheer standpoint of quality, it's possible to experience better music from a good CD recording played on a superior sound system than at a live concert. You cut out all the intangibles, not to mention the irritations. The acoustics of the hall and your location within it cease to matter. The nervous coughs, the tardy couple pushing past you to find their seats, the idiot behind you who insists on talking to his date—they all disappear as distractions from the unadulterated power and beauty of the performance. Arguably, it's becoming more difficult for the true connoisseur to attend a live concert. There's a better product on the market."

"Yes, but more people attend concerts today than ever before."

"You've got a point there, Sue. I guess it shows that the contest between people and machines is far from over. In fact, it's only just begun. Think of Garry Kasparov versus Deep Blue in the chess wars. So far, Kasparov is winning, but for how long? The smart money should be on Deep Blue."

***

Terry Martin, board member and corporate attorney, was the last to arrive.

"Late again, Terry?" James Fitzsimmons scolded. "You're going to miss your own funeral."

"Sorry," Terry mumbled, without need for elaboration, given his chronic tardiness.

James Fitzsimmons surveyed his five-man board. Terry, son Jimmy, long-time crony and former partner Daryll Evans from James's earlier years as part-owner of the Showboat Hotel-Casino, and Ted Seymour, a local television newscaster whom James had added to the group for a little bit of public image and, hopefully, a lot of (as yet unrealized) free publicity.

Founder James owned fifty-one percent of the Starlight. Jim Fitzsimmons held twenty, and Martin ten. Evans owned nine points and Seymour was sheer window-dressing. The remaining ten percent was held by investors, including Jeremy Clinton—limited partners without voice or vote.

Fitzsimmons seldom worked from an agenda and brooked no real criticism, let alone opposition. In this regard, he was faithful to his upbringing—James acted like an infallible, Petrine potentate. Indeed, it was the board's function to sit patiently through his monthly report, a monologue that alternated between harangue and *fait accompli*. If not particularly stimulating, it was an easy way to make a thousand-dollar director's fee for a couple of hours' "work."

James fingered the box of Kleenex and toothpick wrapped in paper he intended as props for his fiscal sermon. No wonder the Starlight was going broke when it put gratis Kleenex in every public restroom and hotel bathroom in the place. The hotel rooms alone meant a multiple of nine hundred boxes for an amenity that no one appreciated or would miss. He was sure that the maids threw out the whole box over one missing tissue and replaced it with a new one. Waste, waste, waste. And as for wrapping toothpicks in paper, that had to be a cost for nothing of value. The Starlight had toothpick dispensers that sat by the cash registers for years. He'd yet to hear the first customer complaint that the probes weren't wrapped in paper.

Today's meeting would be different—truly substantive rather than perfunctory. Jim distributed the brief text that he'd asked Priscilla to prepare, the Agenda:

1. Call—James Fitzsimmons
2. Discussion—General Manager—Jim Fitzsimmons

James held the sheet of paper as if it were a toad. He cleared his throat and began a bit defensively, "Um, right. As it says here, we're facing a call. Gentlemen, the Starlight is all but bankrupt. Our payables are nearly two million dollars and we've got vendors who haven't been paid for six months. Most of them have us on COD. We've got nothing in the kitty, and winter is only three months away." The chairman paused to invite comment, seemingly oblivious to the board's long-since neutered character.

Jim picked up the baton. "Dad and I met with the bankers yesterday. It wasn't fun. They're demanding a reorganization plan. They're willing to restructure our debt, but only if we put two million into the place immediately. Not only will there be no dividend this year; we have to pony up. The call doesn't affect our limited partners, so we have to raise the money around this table ... except from you, of course, Ted."

Daryll interjected, "I stood tall with James at the Showboat, and I sold out with him when we lost that proxy fight. Count me in. Let's see. I own ten percent of the place, so what's my call?" "With Ted out, a little over two-twenty," Jim remarked, and then continued, "I know this isn't easy. I'm selling my cabin at Tahoe and all of my stocks, and

I'm still light. I'll have to use my private line of credit at the bank to hold up my end. The bank's other concern is management. They want a new GM in here … now. We've got three apps for the position, but only one of them is worth considering. I've already had a preliminary conversation with Mary Beth—"

"You've what!?" James Fitzsimmons exploded over his son's crotchet. "Who authorized you? Who the hell is Mary Beth? You're talking to some broad about being GM? Our corporate culture would eat her alive."

Jim had anticipated the outburst, but he had to repress a smile at the language. It was the first time he'd heard his father use "corporate culture," or words even remotely similar. "Dad, I made the contact at the bankers' insistence. Mary Beth Adams has a great record. She's assistant GM at the Claridge in Atlantic City. She wants to come back to Nevada. She's fully aware of the challenges here, but she's willing to accept the professional risk. Ms. Adams actually sees it as a good career move. Last week, I talked to Larry Smith in Vegas, and he didn't even wait for me to finish before he said that I had to be kidding. Even living in Vegas, he knew about our mess, so the whole industry must. I make a motion that we hire Mary Beth, or at least interview her." There was stunned silence as the board contemplated its first ever formal motion. The disturbed faces augured ill, and Jim was about resigned to defeat, when Ted spoke up.

"I second the motion. Desperate measures for desperate times, gentlemen."

James Fitzsimmons commented icily, "Oh, you do, do you? What gives you the right to second anything around here, you fucking ingrate? Where's your skin in this game?"

Before Ted could respond, Terry held up his hand and remarked, "I support the motion. In fact, if you want me to meet my call, I insist that we hire Ms. Adams … that's if she interviews well, of course. I trust your judgment on this one, Jim."

James Fitzsimmons was on his feet. He wadded his agenda into a ball and threw it down on the table. The frail projectile ricocheted in Martin's direction and careened off his chest. "This board has my resignation as of right now. I'll be damned if I'll ride some mare to perdition!" The cantankerous patriarch slammed the door behind him as he stormed out of his own office.

Terry Martin broke the silence. "I move that Jim Fitzsimmons be our new chairman."

***

Venice was their last northern conquest. Sue and Jerry spent the better part of two days sampling innumerable varieties of *gelato* in the outdoor cafes of the Piazza San Marco to avoid close contact with the summer stench of the polluted canals. It was all beginning to feel more like an entomological field trip than the Grand Tour, as one exotic city after another fell briefly into their butterfly net—Modena, Verona, Pisa, Perugia. They headed south and, in Assisi, visited the cathedral and then climbed the mountain behind it to view the tiny cave that Saint Francis once called home. They were becoming connoisseurs of mountains and their dwellers, particularly the solitary ones.

Jerry eased their rented Fiat onto Rome's *Raccordo Anulare*, the ring road that skirts the Eternal City. They were immediately engulfed in the chaos of gridlocked vehicles and the cacophony of their protesting claxons. The periodic construction projects, devilishly spared to prevent anyone from getting out of second gear, contributed pillows of dust that invaded their eyes and nostrils while adding a thick gray patina to the dashboard and luggage on the back seat. Their tiny vehicle seemed all too frail in this land of behemoths, ruled by the three-trailered auto-trains.

"This is motorized mud wrestling!" Sue protested.

Whenever the traffic came to a full stop, prostitutes would appear, phantom-like, out of the sparse vegetation fringing the highway to proposition the truck drivers ... and everyone else, for that matter. Jerry was curious about the logistics and almost asked Sue where they went to consummate the tryst. To a filthy outdoor hovel hidden back in the weeds? To some sleazy roadside hotel dependent on turning over its room inventory several times a day? But then he laughed to himself, amused by the realization that the answer would scarcely have been part of the education of a fifth-grade girl.

"Sue, this reminds me of Fellini's *Roma*. There's this scene where they shot the chaos of the *Raccordo Anulare* at night. I don't know if it was staged, but it's one of the scariest film sequences I've ever seen."

Before she could reply, their promise of salvation appeared in the sign announcing the imminent turnoff onto A-1 to access E-45 towards Naples. Sue assumed the role of navigator as Jerry negotiated the Fiat into the appropriate lane. Liberated, they were now cruising along at 120 kilometers an hour towards the first toll gate, which promised them speedy access to South Italy—all the way to the toe of the boot should they so desire.

"Well, Sue, it's time for me to shut up."

"What do you mean?"

"I mean it's your turn to lead. We've seen my Italy—tourist Italy— now we go through the looking glass into the real Italy. After you, ma'am."

Sue laughed. "Don't set your hopes too high, Jerry. I might not measure up; Agnone might not measure up. The real anything has more to do with prose than poetry. One thing's for sure—there won't be any Peruvians performing during the Day of the Emigrant. Unless, of course, there happen to be some Agnone emigrants back from Lima. The townspeople who had never left would call them the *Peruani*, just like they call us Youngstowners the *Americani*. They also lump us together with themselves as *concittadini*—the "co-citizens." So, we're different from them, yet the same. A little bit of Youngstown lives on in Agnone, and a lot of Agnone is burned into hundreds of hearts and minds in Youngstown."

Well before Naples, Jerry's copilot indicated the appropriate turnoff. They ransomed their freedom at the last toll booth and followed the signs that announced "Cassino—Isernia." Just before the town of Cassino, they deviated onto a narrow highway that climbed yet another of their lives' mountains. The summit was capped by the modern incarnation of the centuries-old Benedictine monastery of Montecassino.

"We're more than a hundred kilometers from Agnone, Jerry, but in the Middle Ages the townspeople owed tithes to this monastery, and a lot of others as well. In those days, to work the land was to till the fields of the Lord, or at least those who claimed to have His worldly franchise."

Jerry was repulsed by the stark, monumental architecture of the compound rebuilt after its near-total destruction during World War II.

Even in late summer, the basilica chilled him and raised goose bumps on his arms. After ten minutes, they were ready to leave.

As Jerry turned on the ignition, an apparition appeared at the driver's side. In extremely poor Italian, it asked for a ride down the mountain to the train station in Cassino. There was no easy escape, so despite the man's slightly unkempt appearance, Jerry shrugged and rearranged their suitcases to accommodate him in the back seat. They were immediately overwhelmed by the pungent body odor of the modern pilgrim. While Sue translated for Jerry, the old traveler struggled to tell his story, impeded greatly by language difficulties. His sketchy tale tumbled out in a stream of simplistic Italian phrases laced liberally with strange foreign terms. "He's from Poland—one of the few survivors of the Polish unit that was part of the final assault against the German fortifications at Montecassino. He says he vowed to return here before he died to pray for his dead comrades."

As he described the assault, the old man became so agitated that his Italian gave way before a Polish onslaught. When reciting a litany of names of the fallen, tears poured down his cheeks, while Sue stroked his hand in sympathy. Finally, Jerry stopped at the train station and the pilgrim reclaimed the small cloth bundle that served as his suitcase. He proffered a wrinkled banknote in payment for the lift, and Jerry waved it off with an awkward gesture. His discomfort was compounded when he heard himself say "*Vaya con Dios*," not knowing the equivalent expression in Italian.

It was Friday, and they paused for lunch in Isernia. While Jerry washed down the last of his *tagliatelle* with sparkling mineral water, Sue scanned the provincial telephone directory for lodgings in Agnone.

"I better call ahead. Sunday is the Day of the Emigrant, and the town will be packed. It's not really a tourist attraction—most of the visitors will be returning emigrants who either still have a mothballed house or relatives to stay with. But I only remember two or three little hotels, and they could be full or even closed. It doesn't really matter anymore, because we could stay here and commute. I've heard there's now a freeway most of the way to Agnone." She dialed the number of the entry for the "Hotel Sammartino" and, after a brief conversation in Italian, told Jerry, "We're in luck, Babe. They were full for the weekend and so was everyone else, but they just had a last-minute cancellation. We're in."

Sue was amazed at the differences as they drove through Isernia's bustling suburbs and then began to smoothly ascend the stair-stepped foothills of the Appenines. "When I lived here, Isernia was half this size. At one time, Agnone was as big or bigger—maybe in the last century. But then Isernia blew by us. Actually, they created a new Province of Isernia not very long ago. Becoming a capital city sure helps. Before that, Campobasso was our capital. Agnone is pretty isolated up in the mountains, and the world just passed it by.

"But maybe that's changing. They built this freeway after we returned to Youngstown. It goes to Vasto on the Adriatic coast. All of us *Americani* knew about it. It was big news, and I can see why. It used to take two or three hours to drive from Agnone to Isernia or Vasto. The road was so curvy that I always got carsick and threw up. I can hardly believe this. Jerry, stop. I want to backtrack and take you to *my* Agnone on the old road." When they turned onto the two-lane road, Sue remarked, "Even this one's been upgraded, widened. Before, there were places where you had to pull over to let an oncoming vehicle pass."

Jerry contemplated the changing countryside, which became greener as they gained in elevation. The deciduous forest was broken by clearings outlined by crumbling stone fences and collapsing terraces. "It looks like there were more people here in the past than now."

"Emigration, Jerry. More than a century of emigration. There are many more *Agnonesi* living elsewhere than there are here."

The abandoned fields reminded Jerry of the tailings at Belfort—another example of mankind's fragility and folly expressed in rearranged stone. It seemed incredible that anyone ever managed to scratch out a living by farming these rocky, godforsaken plots. No wonder they had emigrated.

Eventually, he began to appreciate Sue's description of the parlous road. Not only was it becoming tortuous, in one place it narrowed to a single lane where a landslide had claimed the other. At the summit, the countryside flattened out into high mountain pastures dotted with cows and sheep, and he struggled to pronounce the tongue-twisting name of the town presumably at the end of an even narrower branch road that wandered off to the right.

"Pietrabbondante, Jerry. You have to broaden your b's. In Italian, you hold double letters a little longer. It can change the whole meaning if you don't. Sometimes it becomes a different word altogether."

"My God, what's that?" Jerry had caught his first glimpse of the enormous structure marching across the mountain valley that had suddenly appeared before them.

"It's the famous *ponte* or bridge. Twenty years ago, Agnone had maybe six thousand people, but it also had a senator and a deputy in the Italian Parliament. When we lived here, the big issue was the town's isolation, the need for better roads. People were saying 'what good is it to have a senator and a deputy from Agnone if they can't even get us a new highway?' So they did—beyond everyone's wildest dreams. There's Agnone way over there. See it high up on the other side of the valley?"

Jerry lifted his gaze slightly above where the massive structure fused with the distant hillside.

Sue continued, "Without that bridge, the engineers would have had to follow the old road, which winds all the way down to the river and then back up that steep hill to the town. The ponte cut out several kilometers of driving, so they built it. I don't know the full story, but either they never opened it to traffic or soon after they did, it came out that the contractor had cut so many corners, it wasn't safe. I think he fled the country or was put in jail. The *ponte* was useless, and it was the nail in the coffin of the highway project. God knows what it cost."

Jerry stared in disbelief at the supreme monument to human folly that so offended his environmentalist sensibilities. The soaring cement pillars, tied together by the concrete ribbon of a roadbed, reminded him of an ancient structure in modern guise. "Well, if it's defective it should be more degradable than a Roman aqueduct. Maybe it will only take one thousand years for that eyesore to disappear!"

For several minutes they descended the tortuous, battered road to the valley floor, then stopped at a small *trattoria* perched next to the piddling late-summer flow of the Verrino River. The leaves of ancient grapevines trained up and over an arbor provided delicious relief from the midday sun as they lingered over the regional specialty, *spaghetti a la chitarra*. Sue was already laughing in anticipation as he raised his first glass of the tart, full-bodied local red wine.

It puckered his mouth and made him grimace.

"Whew, that's somewhere between grape juice and vinegar!" he exclaimed.

"Yes, but it's *genuino*, as they say here and in every other South Italian town. When it comes to food and wine only *ours* is genuine; everyone else's is phony." From where they were sitting, they could crane their necks and contemplate the tallest pylons of the *ponte*. Its suspended roadway loomed closer to the clouds than the earth. "I believe it's a hundred and eighty meters high at this point. That's about six hundred feet. Papa used to say that it's the tallest highway bridge in Italy … maybe the world.

"Actually, it's just one more example of a bigger problem. The enigma of the South. This is the Mezzogiorno, which is totally different from your Italy, Jerry. Ever since the Second World War, the Mezzogiorno has been Italy's national development project. No one really knows how much has been spent here to bring the poor South up to the standard of the rich North or, for that matter, where the money went. During elections, the politicians announce new public projects and dispense pasta and banknotes from their party headquarters. They promise to fix everything from the roads to peoples' lives. After the ballots are counted, the deep slumber begins again … except, of course, for the occasional public boondoggle like the *ponte*."

"You don't seem very proud of your heritage."

"Yes and no. I appreciate some parts of it. When I meet so many rootless people in Reno, like Carol for instance, I realize that there were good things about growing up in a close family that was part of a tight little immigrant community. We watched out for each other. But, of course, there's a thin line between caring and prying. When I was a teenager, I was embarrassed by my parents' accents. I resented their control. I wanted to be an American kid—date boys, hang out. They wouldn't let me. They made me go to boring church dinners and Italian celebrations—christenings and weddings. I got tired of all the talk about Agnone. I'd only spent a few months in the place, and yet it was this big presence in my life. It was as if my behavior in Youngstown was being judged by a whole jury of faceless strangers in some mountain valley half a world away.

"That's how I got involved with Red. When the high school football hero paid attention to me, it was no contest. I would have followed him into hell. Now I appreciate the trade-offs. Nothing's really black and white; everything has its consequences."

Four boisterous young men commandeered the next table and clamored for service. The cook-proprietress, who doubled as the waitress, approached them to take their order. Jerry was sure that they were teasing the old woman, but she seemed jovial enough about it.

"They say they're off to Naples for the weekend," Sue told him. "Look at them, Jerry. They have to be about my age, but they seem like so many boys. I'll bet they're bachelors. In Agnone, it's the custom for men to marry late. In the old days even married men stayed home and the women married out. As long as his parents were alive, a married man was under their thumb. They ran his life, and his wife's and children's too. He might be fifty years old before he became his own man.

"Papa always said that was why he left. Uncle Enzo was the eldest in the family, and when Papa and Mama married, Enzo and Aunt Adela already had two children. Everyone lived together in the same house for three years before Mama said she couldn't take it anymore. *Nonna* ordered her around, and so did Adela. When we moved back to Agnone, Papa and Mama thought they could be independent. So, we got our own house, but it wasn't that simple. By then, Grandpa was a widower, and he still lived with Enzo and Adela. He couldn't understand why we didn't move in, too. He complained a lot about it. It was one more reason for going back to Youngstown."

"Shouldn't we get a move on? I'm nervous about losing our room reservation."

"You're right, Jerry. You know, as I sit here and look up at Agnone, I have real mixed feelings. I'm glad we didn't tell Mama we were coming. She would have called Enzo and Adela. I'm not sure what would've happened then, but it's better this way."

The road ascended a steep hill for several kilometers and then dropped gradually onto the relatively level promontory that overlooked the Verrino Valley. Its shape reminded Jerry of an arrowhead. They entered the wide base, driving through the non-descript "New Agnone" of tasteless three- or four-story apartments, petrol stations, regional government offices, and hospital. But as they penetrated the ever-more-constrictive urban space, they were transported back in time, the centuries accumulating before their eyes. The broad, asphalted promenade ceased to be two-lane, and was transformed into a narrow one-way traffic loop that stitched together the splendors of

"Old Agnone." Eighteenth-century churches became fifteenth-century convents; impressive nineteenth-century houses ceded to sixteenth-century mansions. They drove past the weathered statue of the Lion of Venice adorning the cornice of an impressive dwelling, maintaining its eternal vigilance over the *borgo*, or quarter, while providing sculptured testimony to the town's ancient ties with the Venetian empire. The chaotic maze of curvy cobbled streets in Old Agnone spoke of another world, a whole different human experience. Considered together, New Agnone seemed to be an upstart graft upon an ageless trunk.

Sue asked a passerby for directions to the Hotel Sammartino, which they found with ease. It was one of the structures that formed the outer wall that had afforded the town its military defenses during more unsettled times. Their room and the restaurant both overlooked the *agro*, or farmland, that spilled below the *cittadina* of Agnone proper, where it clung to its dominant perch.

It was late afternoon as they walked the streets of the town. Sue pointed out the panoply of license plates anticipating tomorrow's festivities—Rome, Turin, Milan, Genoa, Switzerland, France, Belgium, Germany, and points beyond. The vehicles themselves ranged from the most modest of Fiats to the occasional Mercedes, mechanical expression of South Italy's hidebound social hierarchy.

Each of the elegant bars and peasant cantinas was packed, its clientele spilling out onto the sidewalk, where temporary chairs and tables strained under the overflow. The daily *passeggiata*, or evening stroll, had begun and they joined the flow, which moved ceaselessly from one end of the tree-lined promenade to the other.

They passed a dry goods store that triggered school-girl nostalgia in Sue. "I used to play with Silvia, the owner's daughter. She was my best friend. Her father lived in Sydney for years, working hard and saving up to buy that place. All four of the brothers worked in Australia long enough to start their own businesses here. Silvia's uncle Giuseppe spoke English, but with an Aussie accent. It made me laugh. I wonder if they're still here."

Jerry soon learned how to nod and smile while offering the abbreviated greeting "*sera*" (sans "*buona*") whenever he happened to lock eyes with a passerby headed in the opposite direction. After their third trip over the same territory, he even began to recognize people he'd already acknowledged on two previous occasions. In his mind, they were moving from the category of total strangers to the more liminal one of acquaintances. He noticed the first faint stirrings of a sense of kindred spirit within himself—Agnone was beginning to grow on Jerry.

"C'mon, Babe, let's see some of the old part." Sue took his hand and navigated out of the ebb and flow of humanity. Now they were alone, walking along the traffic loop, mindful of the occasional speeder who periodically threatened them from behind with vehicular mayhem.

"Stop, Sue. I don't believe it! Look at that. I'll bet you don't know what it is." He laughed.

"You're right—it kind of looks like an Indian."

"Yes, Sue, but not just any Indian." They were contemplating the features of a bas-relief on the lintel over the main entrance to an impressive three-story house. "That's the image from the Indian Head penny. I'm sure of it. When I was a boy, there were still a few in circulation."

The door opened, and an elegant elderly man appeared carrying a cane, about to set out on his evening constitutional. Sue approached him and began a conversation, which persisted to the point that Jerry was becoming uncomfortable, not quite knowing what to do with himself.

"He says the house was built by his grandfather after he returned from the United States, about 1900. He was one of Agnone's most successful emigrants; he made a real fortune. He was so grateful to America that he wanted everyone to know he'd been there. Like those tree carvings by Basque sheepherders. We've been invited to see the inside if you'd like."

"Love to."

Sue and their host continued to chat as all three entered the marbled foyer. "He says that this was the first house in town to have central heating."

"I'm not surprised," Jerry responded.

They ascended a formal staircase that doubled back upon itself at a landing and then terminated in an ample salon on the second floor. A massive table flanked with eight baronial chairs formed a wooden island in the center of the otherwise empty room. The old man motioned them to be seated before leaving in search of refreshments. Jerry looked up at the ethereal mural painted on the ceiling, which seemed to depict human industry viewed approvingly from a celestial perspective, a small portrait tucked into each of its four corners. Jerry remarked, "That one's George Washington, and if I'm not wrong, his strange bedfellow over there is Karl Marx!"

"I recognize Garibaldi, Jerry, but I'm not sure about the fourth one." Their host reappeared and she put the question to him, then turned back to Jerry. "It's Mazzini. He was a philosopher or politician. I think I remember from school here that he was a hero of the unification of Italy, like Garibaldi."

Their host set down his silver tray with its plate of assorted stale cookies, bottle of sweet sambuca, and three glasses. He apologized for the paucity of his hospitality, noting that his servant had taken the day off to spend time with her brother, who was back from Belgium.

**

Jim, while liquidating every asset that he possibly could to meet the Starlight's call, surveyed the detritus of his investment portfolio scattered across his desktop. He picked up the certificate that verified he owned an improbable fifty thousand shares of a Mexican bank. His broker had informed him these particular shares were trading at a mere eight cents, or practically the fee for selling them. He examined the all-but-worthless paper listlessly and placed it in the pile of similarly valueless mining stocks.

He'd hoped to discover one or two overlooked convertible nuggets from which to squeeze out his overdue house mortgage payment, but to no avail. He picked up the deed for the undeveloped desert acreage he'd bought years before, when he'd harbored the implausible dream of escaping from his father's long shadow by transplanting his socialite wife and their toddler son to a central Nevada homestead.

The memory brought the first smile of the day (indeed, of the week) to his lips. For a moment, he imagined a slatternly Dot in gingham dress with sleeves rolled up to expose dirt-encrusted elbows, carrying water from the well back to their rough-framed ranch house. He appeared on the margins of his own fantasy, dust-covered, wiping streaks of sweat from his face with a red bandanna.

"Where's the baby?" he asked.

"Asleep in his crib."

"I'll feed the cows if you'll change the waterlines in the alfalfa field."

He now snorted in delight at the preposterous imagined honyocker scene. Jim stared at the legalese proclaiming his ownership of a total of ninety-seven of the most arid acres in North America, knowing he was more likely to lose the land through non-payment of his county taxes than through sale. Putting them on the market with any expectations was clearly a fool's errand.

Then there were the alternate fuel shares, the undivided interest in an all-but-failed California citrus farm, and the cattle ranch tax shelter guaranteed to lose money while generating a write-off larger than his investment. (Unfortunately, he no longer had the requisite income to make the program work.)

"Will any of these ships ever come home to port?" he asked, knowing he was surveying his own little pieces of the Spanish Armada. He then telephoned his personal banker. "So, Jeff, how much do I have in all three accounts? Uh huh … oh … ouch! I thought the money market one was higher. Oh, now I remember that check. Okay, so sell my CDs. I know, I know about the penalty. Sell them. Transfer everything into my checking account as I'm about to write one for $450,000."

Jim swept the tantalizing, if worthless, papers into a cardboard box. He extracted a chain from his pocket, holding it between thumb and forefinger while twirling its links through the air. He stared intently at the lazy pirouettes of the appended key to his personal escape and purest pleasure. His extremely rare Mercedes SL 73 was scarcely a year old, under warranty, and paid for. It had to be worth at least seventy thousand dollars.

He pushed the intercom button. "Priscilla, I want you to place an ad in the newspaper to read 'Nearly new 1996 Mercedes SL 73, low mileage. Only $75,000.' Oh, and bring me a copy of the used-car classifieds."

***

James Fitzsimmons Kennedy Jr. now decided to beard the lion in his den. Their dreaded first conversation after the palace coup was inevitable; it might as well be now. He sidled across the hall and tiptoed through his martinet patriarch's door. Jim prepared to field a stern or snide opening remark from his atrabilious genitor and was a little surprised by his miscalculation.

"Come in, come in, Son."

He sat down across from James, unsure of what to say or why. The old man was wrapped in a blanket and flanked by two electric heaters. Jim perused the office, for the first time really noticing the artifacts of his father's life. There were no decorations whatsoever; every wall was blank. The tacky wooden desk had been purchased by James thirty years earlier in a garage sale. Two of its six drawers were permanently jammed open by the progressive sagging of the relic. The inevitable half-emptied cardboard case of hootch sat nestled within easy reach of its owner's chair. Against one wall, there stood a tall metal filing cabinet filled to capacity with the stale documents of business deals long since concluded. On both sides, it was flanked with documents from more recent negotiations, stacked in little piles on the floor and tilted against the wall as avalanche-prevention. In one corner, there was a dust-encrusted set of vintage gold clubs, a reminder of James's golfing days. Jim retrieved the golf ball from the Giants' coffee cup on the desktop and read the inscription on the sphere: "Stolen from James Fitzsimmons." He smiled at this perfect manifestation of his father's black Irish humor.

Jim steeled himself against the blast. The temperature must have been in the eighties, yet he noticed that James was shivering.

"So, Jimmy, what brings you here?"

"I just thought you'd want to talk. You know, after what happened."

"Oh that. You mean the brown stuff hitting the fan?" James was a picture of insouciance. "I've decided it was about time. I'm ninety, for Chrissakes. My mind wanders. I can't get your mother out of it. You know, I don't even remember for sure when she died. Two, maybe three, years ago. Sometimes it seems like fifty, and others like yesterday. She died, Jimmy; she didn't pass away. I hate that euphemism. She's dead. I think about all the things I wish I'd said to her. I was such a lousy husband. I wasn't unfaithful, if that means sleeping with other women— well, not much—but I was never there for her, or you and Sean either.

"When we were first married, I was on the road most of the week, running my slot route. When I was home, I played golf and gin rummy with my friends. They were all mine, not hers. She cooked us great meals, and I ate them without giving her a compliment or even a comment. Not even one crummy, 'Thank you, dear.' She had to raise you and Sean without me. I wasn't much for getting down on the floor with you two to build things with Lincoln logs or erector sets. You didn't learn how to fish from me."

"You're right about all of that, Dad."

"For the last twenty years of Mom's life, I lived here at the Starlight and she was pretty much alone. And now it's too late to make amends, Jimmy. All I have left of her is a few memories and a lot of Catholic guilt. God rest her soul," James concluded with his only Irish saying.

Jim sat quietly, listening to his father's regretting. He wasn't surprised by any of it, only the confessional self-examination itself. "Dad, Sean and I never could figure out your arrangement with Mom. You were married, yet you lived in separate houses. You went home to her place on weekends and left Monday morning. You took trips and celebrated holidays together, usually at the house."

James chuckled. "Jimmy, marriage is one thing, living together is another. We cared a lot for each other, but that didn't make us compatible. Relationships age, wither, and die, just like the people who have them. I looked forward to seeing her Friday night, and she looked forward to saying goodbye to me on Monday morning. She cooked my Saturday and Sunday breakfasts, and I took her out for dinner both nights. We didn't talk much; we were out of things to say. During the day, I watched sports on TV and she mostly read. But there was a certain bonding in just being together under the same roof. We did enjoy traveling together, since there was the diversion. We didn't really have to discuss *us*; we could talk about the new experiences we'd shared that day. Holidays were a little like that—special time-outs in which to open gifts or drink to one another's health. Neither of us wanted a divorce. We didn't relish dividing our lives into two piles of stuff while having to explain the failure of our relationship to a nosey world."

"You remind me of the Sinatra song about doing things his way. But you did move back home when she got cancer."

"True. Still, while that might have seemed natural, even easy, being a caregiver was the toughest thing I've ever done. It wasn't just that she was terminal, which was hard enough; it was being around the wasting away. I wasn't wired to watch that, either emotionally or by temperament."

"I certainly understand the emotional part. Sean and I both got your inability to deal with emotion of any kind—particularly sadness and tears."

"I suppose you're right, Jimmy. I certainly don't understand crying. I'm not sure if I've ever cried, even as a child. In your grandparents' house, bawling was forbidden. It was weakness that deserved ridicule, certainly not sympathy. If I hurt myself, your grandmother would say, 'Nobody died, so get on with life.'"

"What did you mean when you said you didn't have the temperament to deal with Mom's death?"

"I meant that I couldn't stand the feeling of sheer helplessness. I'm used to being in control, a fixer, and she was terminal. I couldn't do a damn thing about it. It made me mad. It's far easier for me to accept my own diagnosis and face up to the consequences than it was to deal with hers. The whole year before she died, I don't think we had a single serious conversation. What do you talk about? The future? How could I tell her about my day? If I mentioned the enjoyable parts, it was like saying that my life was good when she was losing hers. If I mentioned something bad, it seemed like burdening her with another worry when she already had a full plate of her own. So, all we ever discussed was her condition at that moment. 'How's the pain today?' 'Can I get you something?'

"And you know, she never complained. The pain was always, 'not too bad.' I slept in the other bed in her room in case she needed something in the night, and I could hear her whimpering in her sleep and gasping for breath. In the morning, her face was etched with that horrible nocturnal struggle, but she'd force a smile and get on with living through one more day of being terminal. So, Jimmy, I suppose in the real world, marriage comes in many shapes and faces, not just the Hollywood variety or the one that Father Carmody pushes from the pulpit."

"And what was that about your 'diagnosis'?"

"Don't you know that living is dangerous, even fatal …? Actually, I'm glad you stopped by, Son. Believe it or not, I was writing you a letter." James tapped the yellow pad under his right hand.

"About what?"

"Well, it's sort of instructional."

"Putting down your thoughts about what's wrong with management—my management? I know you've never had much faith in me, Dad. You never gave me any real responsibility around here until the board took it away from you. I'm sure that must have hurt. I'm sorry—"

"No, no Jimmy, I wasn't writing about the Starlight. I—"

Emboldened by having brought up the taboo subject of their relationship, Jim interrupted. "Did religion come between us? I mean, when I quit going to church and we had all those arguments about it. Was that when you wrote me off? Have all these long years been my penance?"

"Jimmy, I've been thinking a lot lately, and you're right to feel as you do. No, it wasn't religion, it was me. I accept all of the blame. It was my ego, if that's what an inability to delegate anything means. No one could measure up to my standards, so I did everything myself. I was more indifferent to you than angry—just like I was to everyone else, including Mom. Hell, Jimmy, as far as religion goes, I'm not even sure I believe in God, let alone presume to lecture others about Him."

"I don't get it. You were certainly angry when I refused to go to mass. When I left the church, you thought I was wrong to do so. Wasn't that a way of telling me what I should believe? And now you say that you're a doubter. So far as I know, you still go to church every Sunday."

"I do when someone comes for me. But think of it as inertia, like having coffee and reading the newspaper in bed every morning before starting my day. And then there's my dear friend Father Carmody. What would he think if I failed to appear at his eleven o'clock service? He'd probably call 911."

"But what about faith, Dad? Do you believe all the dogma?"

"I'm not sure. For me, the trick is not to question it. If I really thought about whether it's a sin to eat meat on Friday or if Father Carmody performs the miracle of transubstantiation every Sunday, let alone the mysteries of the Holy Trinity, well, I'm just not sure where that would lead me. I prefer to take it all on faith, like you have to suspend disbelief at a magic show. Every time I go to Vegas, I never miss Siegfried and Roy. I just love them. But you can't sit there and question whether they can really make white tigers disappear and then move them around through thin air to reappear somewhere else. The last thing you want to do is ruin the illusion.

"Actually, Jimmy, it's harder for me to go to church nowadays. All those reformers have ruined *my* mass. I liked the Latin mumbo jumbo; it added to the illusion. I'll never get used to some teenage girl reading the Epistle and her boyfriend playing a folksong on his guitar from the altar. When you start to involve the congregation like that, the audience, you destroy the show. Everyone then knows that no one can make white tigers disappear, let alone produce miracles like the transubstantiation. It was far better to just sit there and be told by Father Carmody that God created us as sentient beings in order to adore Him. Hell, I don't even know what 'sentient' means. I thought of looking it up and didn't, because that knowledge might have threatened the illusion—the theater."

"Dad, I was scared of God as a little kid. The nuns warned us constantly about His wrath. One day, we would stand before Him, accountable for all of our sins, particularly those of the flesh. I'm not sure what I feared worse, God's final judgement or being blown to bits by a Soviet nuclear device. You know, I stopped going to church because of you and Mom. Because she was a divorced Protestant when you married her, it meant you were excommunicated automatically. It made her some kind of whore, and Sean and me bastards. I figured that out in the seminary, and by the time I finished Manogue, I was very irate about it. I was having a lot of trouble with the egotistical Catholic God that created us in His own image so we could worship Him. In his spare time, He had nothing better to do than count how many times boys whacked off so He could condemn us to hell for eternity. I still have a problem with Dot's blind faith. If Father Carmody told her that God wanted us to take off our clothes and stand naked outside all night in a blizzard while holding hands, she'd start unbuttoning her blouse."

"Har, har. That's a good one."

"I feel kind of sorry for you, Dad. You've spent countless hours of your life on something that you're so unsure about, when by your own admission, you are sure about everyone and everything else."

"Don't feel sorry for me. If you want to pity someone, think of Father Carmody. We have dinner together, maybe twice a month, and

THE STARLIGHT HOTEL-CASINO

we never talk about the Church. The new Church is too painful for him. I'm sure he can hardly wait to retire. As for me, well, I can say that although I have my doubts about God, I'm a firm believer in religion. I believe that anyone who accepts and acts on Christ's real message is likely to be a better person in this life than the unbeliever. I don't mean the doctrine twisted and manipulated by all the Christian churches to suit their own purposes, but the simple and true message of Jesus Christ himself. He who follows the Savior is given a moral roadmap. As for the afterlife—heaven, hell, and all that—I am less sure. I'm a Catholic alright, but an earthly one. From creation to cremation, Jimmy."

"Have you ever thought of looking into other Christian churches? There may be one closer to your way of thinking."

"Hell, no. That would be treason!"

"To the Catholic Church, the Pope, or Father Carmody?"

"To all of them, but particularly to my mother. I was her only child, and she used to say, 'My only accomplishment in life was to raise a good Catholic boy, and that's enough.' You know, Jimmy, it's possible to be unfaithful to someone even after their death. I'm not certain she convinced me to believe in Jesus Christ, but I certainly believe in Saint Patrick. He was an original, first-rate, not like the subsequent corrupt popes canonizing one another. Patrick got into Cooperstown before they moved in the fences and juiced up the ball.

"When I was a kid, our parish priest was straight from the old sod. His brogue was so thick, it was almost easier to understand his Latin. Once a year, Father Flannery gave a sermon on how it was a mortal sin to believe in the little people—fairies and elves. Well, I'm sure fa-a-ther was the only person in the whole church who believed in them. They weren't really a very big problem in Reno!"

They lapsed into a mutual silence produced by the lack of an obvious segue. Then James asked, "Do you ever pray, Son?"

"No, but sometimes I kind of talk to God. Like, if I'm going into a tough squash match, or maybe I'm trying to cast to a spooky fish and it has to be perfect, I kind of ask for a little help. And you know, it's not superstition or habit. You and the nuns hammered God into me so deeply that I guess I believe in Him, if not the Church. I must admit, however, that when I ask for His help, I feel a little like an ingrate—like calling up an old friend you haven't contacted for twenty years to ask for a favor.

"It would never occur to me to ask God for help in a business deal. Maybe I should have crossed myself like some Latin ballplayer coming up to bat before talking to our bankers. They might not have started the foreclosure proceedings," Jim joked. "I'm not sure that even God can stop that now!

"For me, Dad, it's tough to square the injustices in this world with an omniscient and all-powerful being who supposedly loves us and created us all the same. Look at our family's blessings as opposed to those of the Starlight's hourly employees. I also have trouble with the micromanagement notion—the idea the nuns pushed that God somehow knows about *me*, my every thought and action. Even when I was in first grade, I had my doubts about that. Of course, their stock answer was that my question was His mystery. But it just boggles the mind to think that God keeps track of six billion or so human beings. He must be the original hard drive and about the size of Guatemala!"

"You should read the Book of Job, Son."

"I didn't think we Catholics were supposed to read the Bible. I'm not sure that Father Carmody would approve. It would kind of cut him out of the loop. Reading the Bible for yourself was pretty basic to the Protestant Reformation, no?"

"Jimmy, I go to church as insurance, just in case. Life's a casino, and the house odds are stacked against each and every one of us. In the end, the Big House in the Sky cleans all of us out! I give my time, and some money too, to the local diocese, just in case Father Carmody is right and there is a God. If he's wrong, what do I have to lose? So, sure, I go to church—we Nevada gamblers always hedge our bets."

"Thanks for being so honest with me, Dad. I really never knew. I always thought of you as the truest of believers. I resented the fact that you seemed to accept a bunch of superstition and myth without a peep."

"I'm glad we've had this chance to talk, Jimmy. I think a lot these days about my parents and the things they told me as a kid. Our dilemma as a species may be death and how to face it. Yet we also trivialize it. Forty thousand Americans die every year on the highways, and nearly that many from guns. Yet we resist speed limits and any attempt to regulate firearms. The media talk about six million dead Jews in the Holocaust, the thousands of AIDS victims, and lately, 500,000 deaths in the Rwandan genocide. These are guestimates that simply boggle the mind. You can't really internalize and personalize that much horror and inhumanity. How much bad news can a person process?

"It's also unfair to the five-hundred-thousand-and-first victim of the genocide. His death—and life—disappear into that enormous maelstrom. For me, the human mortality rate is one death per person. Maybe it's actually *one* death per person—your own. But I've decided that our biggest tragedy is the deaths of our mentors, and the fact that we never really listen to their advice until they're gone. By then, it's too late to discuss it with them."

James tore the first sheet off his yellow pad, crumpled it, and threw it into the waste basket. "I won't be needing this now. I can just tell you the news."

"What news?"

"Yesterday, Dr. Cantlon gave me the results of my tests. My ulcer's been acting up a lot lately. Well it's no longer acid indigestion, Jimmy, and it's inoperable. Hopefully, it'll be fast."

Jim's voice quivered as he groped for an appropriate response. "Why don't we do something together? Would you be up for a father-and-son trip? I remember to this day when you'd take me on your slot route as a kid. I'd help you count the coins in some crappy bar, maybe in Gabbs Valley. There were the bumps, ruts, and dust of the endless dirt roads. I was about five or six, and all you talked about was business. Your plans and negotiations. What you were thinking and where the other side was coming from. What you believed it would take to seal the deal. You sort of mentored me, so it's no wonder that I thought I would one day be your heir apparent."

James smiled coyly. "What fond memories, Jimmy. But there's no going back, so I prefer to stay right here. I pray that it hits me while I'm in this chair going over yesterday's numbers. They're my religion now." He groped for a suggestion that might appeal to his son. "Maybe we could smoke a little pot, Jimmy."

"I don't smoke pot, Dad. Why don't we just kneel down and pray together? I'd like that."

***

The restaurant in the Hotel Sammartino was crowded to capacity. The parties at two tables were conversing in English; at another, the conversation slipped back and forth between Italian and Brazilian Portuguese, while in the corner, Venezuelan Spanish was the medium of admonition employed by an irritated father on his two bickering teenage daughters.

"This view is magnificent," Jerry remarked. "I love all those scattered farmhouses and their patchwork fields and meadows. It looks like some gigantic quilt."

"I've been thinking about that Indian Head penny, Jerry. I wonder about its message. Was it an invitation to fortune—'This is American money, emigrant, your pot of gold'? Or maybe a warning—'Be thrifty, emigrant, save every penny.'"

"Maybe he was just fascinated with Indians and happened to have that penny with him to show the sculptor."

"There are so many possibilities, Babe. I would have liked to talk with the man himself rather than his grandson. I'll bet he had some great stories to tell."

***

Jim Fitzsimmons was the first to arrive for the directors' meeting. His nervous anticipation irritated him. "After all, I'm the boss," he noted—a feeble ploy to pump up his courage. He was at best an uncomfortable public speaker, and the thought of running the meeting was mildly terrifying. The anxiety was magnified by the importance of the occasion. To his mind, it held watershed significance for the Starlight's future.

He struggled with his prepared opening gambit. It was crucial to walk the narrow line between informing his directors of the serious challenges and pushing them over the edge into a full-blown crisis mentality. If he failed to communicate and inspire, he might easily create further despair, gridlock, or even desertion.

Seth Harris, the casino veteran who'd risen through the ranks from change boy to games director, was the first to arrive. When his attempts to draw the preoccupied Fitzsimmons into casual conversation failed, they lapsed into awkward silence. Mercifully, Security Director Harry Andrews, Hotel Director Shelly Sherman, and Food and Beverage

Director François Broussard entered together, chatting noisily about the upcoming weekend's slot tournament. Manny Cohen arrived alone, as did Tim Saunders, the Starlight's youthful slot director. Tim conveyed the regrets of Andrew McDermott, director of engineering, whose wife was, at that very moment, being operated on for breast cancer at St. Mary's Hospital. The last to enter the conference room was Joshua Threadwell, director of human resources.

Jim motioned to Josh to close the door behind him. "I have some announcements to make before we begin. I know that either my father or Jerry Clinton usually runs your meetings. Well, today I'm here in my father's place as the new CEO. I also must inform you that Jerry is no longer with us. He resigned as general manager of the Starlight."

Jim's tone did not invite questions, nor did he plan to elaborate further on either absentee's fate. He feared that treating Jerry's departure as a termination would raise the specter that downsizing at the Starlight was now reaching into uppermost management. Jerry's fate meant that the Starlight was an ocean liner without a captain, and the recent defection of their gaming controller left the ship adrift in dangerous financial straits without a navigator. The Starlight could ill-afford new holes beneath its managerial waterline.

Jim hastened to reassure his directors by making his next announcement. "We have interviewed three candidates for general manager and hope to have one in place by next week."

Joshua asked the question that was on everyone's mind. "Will the new GM be bringing anyone with him?"

Stupidly, Jim had failed to anticipate the obvious concern that new leadership might mean a whole new team, or part of one. The tension around the table was palpable.

"No, no. I can assure you that the new general manager has an open mind and no plans to terminate any of you. You'll have every chance to prove yourselves. Though, of course, there could be consequences if you don't. Anyway, we've made our best offer and are waiting for an answer. She promised to give it by—" Jim stopped in mid-sentence, jerked up short by the body language of his audience. He felt traduced by his inadvertent pronoun use, since he hadn't planned to disclose the gender of Jerry's replacement quite yet. "Look, those are my only announcements, and it's still premature to elaborate on any of them. Please be patient."

His inaugural attempt to run a directors' meeting was scarcely off to an auspicious start.

"The real purpose of getting you together today is to work out a new business strategy for the Starlight. I scarcely need to tell you that we face big challenges. You've all been asked to cut back on staff, and I want you to know how much the owners appreciate your efforts. It's never easy to decide who to sacrifice so that the rest can survive. Hopefully, the downsizing is over.

"I know that each of you could make a good argument that your department is understaffed, that you can't be expected to do the same job with a skeleton staff. Well, I'm afraid that I must ask you for more than that. I'm asking you do to an even better job with existing personnel. We're up against fierce competition. Business as usual just isn't going to get it done."

The comments provoked a buzz around the table as several people spoke at once. Seth Harris's voice emerged above the din. "Jim, we've tried this before. I mean I've been here twenty years, and this is at least the fifth time I've heard that we've got to restructure to get better results out of our people. It's just not that easy. Where's the incentive? We don't pay 'em enough to be able to give lectures about efficiency, or loyalty either. So, what's different this time? Fewer sticks and bigger carrots? Are we gonna offer raises? Bonuses? I think we should give our hourlies a fifty-cent-an-hour raise."

Jim fingered his calculator. "So, let me show you what a touchy-feely raise of fifty cents an hour translates into. We've got roughly a thousand employees times forty hours weekly, or twenty bucks each, times fifty-two. That's a little over a million dollars a year. Last year we lost a million. Your plan takes the red ink to two million. That's when we close the doors and a thousand people lose their jobs."

Seth mused, "I'm not sure I get it. How can this place lose a million dollars and still be open?"

"Cash flow and kiting the payables. That loss includes about a million and a half in depreciation for tax purposes. So, we have a positive cash flow of half-a-mil to work with. That's razor thin for an operation this size. It's also temporary because you use up your depreciation and it goes down. We can't afford to reinvest in anything, so we pick up no new depreciation. We can't buy the new slots we need; we're just living off the seed corn. Also, the deferred replacement and maintenance means the property is running down and becoming less competitive. Why stay in a dump when the Golden Spur has about the same room rates, more games, and better food? With no cash, we can't hire decent entertainment, either. Our lounge acts are all has-beens, not-nows, and never-will-bes—not exactly headliners. So even our most loyal players are going somewhere else, and we're replacing them with cheapskate bus people.

"Kiting the payables for two or three months is also a band-aid on a deep, festering wound. Pretty soon, you can't be sure you have meat between the hamburger buns, let alone lettuce, tomatoes, and catsup to put on it. Actually, most of the vendors understand the game. They may work with you for a while, but they call up and bitch all the time. It's the old squeaky-wheel-gets-the-grease ploy. You dole out a few cents on the dollar owing to them. That's when you need a controller with a rhino's hide. In effect, your suppliers become your bankers, almost your minor partners ... at least until they snap. Some cut you off and others put you on COD. Our meat vendor just did that. How scary is that, when we're best known for our special $5.95 one-pound New York steak. We sell a thousand a day. It's what gets half our business in the door."

"What's the answer?" Seth asked.

"Maybe there isn't any. Last year, the stock market was gaga over casinos, but everyone knows Nevada is challenged. We've got too many. There are the Indians and all the new venues around the country, and more on the way. Nevada never had great location, just a monopoly. I think we've missed the boat."

"What went wrong? Nevada used to be such a great place," Seth said.

"'Used to be' is the operative phrase, all right. It's not just the Starlight; the whole industry has changed. In Vegas, if you don't have three thousand rooms, you're a glorified motel. The Golden Spur has that many to our puny nine hundred. That almost seemed like too many when we built them. We thought we were warehousing our future—a footprint to grow into. How wrong we were. The world blew right by us, and we can't afford to catch up. We don't have the money to expand. Hell, we don't even have the money to remodel. It would cost three million just to re-carpet this joint. The Golden Spur just spent ten mil on changing the décor in one of its restaurants. The whole industry is now on expensive steroids and we can't even afford a bottle of aspirin."

"Okay, then where are we headed?" Seth asked.

"I wish I knew. I don't see us hitting a brick wall at a hundred miles an hour. I think it will be more like sliding off the road in slow motion and ending up in a ditch without anyone even noticing that we're missing."

Seth refused to be dismissed entirely. "Well, our employees are never gonna believe vague promises. Three years ago, we told them to roll up their sleeves and increase business fifteen percent and a third of it would be distributed as bonuses. Then comes Christmas and the word from on high was no bonuses. Everyone was expected to take it on faith that we missed the target. No bonuses and no numbers either. Just take it on faith, Jim. We directors don't have a lot of credibility with the rank and file anymore. When we're that kind of messenger, why shouldn't they kill us? We need a better line than asking them to work their butts off now because, once things get better, management will take care of them. That dog won't hunt again."

Jim listened to Seth's analysis with surprising inner serenity. He'd never heard such thoughts verbalized before, but they were longstanding whisperings in the recesses of his mind. He chose not to controvert the obvious, electing for an oblique approach instead.

"You're right about vague promises and their false expectations. Even if the employees bought them now, we'd just be setting ourselves up for problems tomorrow. But you did overlook one thing, Seth. In the last two months, we've laid off a lot of that cynical rank and file. That's action that everyone can understand. We're not talking about rah-rah here, pretty words and slogans—Christmas promises. We're talking about simple job security in a not-so-secure world. The Starlight's not the Lone Ranger, you know. Every property in northern Nevada has downsized in the last six months, even the most successful ones. So, the message is, 'If you like your job, then do it. In fact, do it better.'"

Seth had nothing to add, though it was obvious from his expression that he remained unconvinced. It was less clear what any of the remaining directors thought—particularly since there was no scramble for the putative microphone.

Jim continued, "I'm not really asking today for your thoughts and suggestions on employee standards. In fact, I'm just giving you some advance notice so you can be mulling it over. It's an area that concerns our chosen GM candidate a lot. I know that if she takes the job, it'll be one of her front-burner issues and she'll appreciate any positive suggestions.

"The second thing that we need to discuss is cost-cutting. The way to avoid cutting staff is to find other means to save costs. We have to impress on everyone the importance of buying right. That means getting the best price and buying the right quantity. They're related … price and quantity. Last month, we purchased two thousand ashtrays because they were seven cents cheaper than if we bought one thousand. The trouble is that two thousand ashtrays represent a five-year supply for us, without even figuring in that fewer people are smoking all the time. So that's a prime example of a false bargain. We need to put our capital, our vitality, where it'll do us the most good, not lock it up in crystal stored in the warehouse. If I'm asking for better results from our rank and file, I have to insist that we become smarter managers ourselves. That's a big priority with Mary Beth, too."

Seth laughed. "Well, Jim, we almost have her name, can you tell us her rank and serial number?"

"In good time, Seth, in good time. For now, I'm trying to let you all in on a preview of where we intend to go. I know you've heard it before. I also know that past restructurings around here were an exercise in shooing pigeons off park benches. You scared them a little, so they took off, flew around awhile, and, once the coast was clear, landed right back down on the same park bench. What I'm telling you is that, this time, we're not talking pigeon-shooing. This time, we plan to hire a pigeon exterminator. I can't make you believe my words, but I can assure you that any skepticism now could well prove fatal. I would like for you all to survive the transition, but I can't offer any guarantees.

"I now turn this meeting over to Manny Cohen, our new marketing director. I'm sure you've all met Manny by now. I asked him to take the point for the third initiative in our new strategy—getting more business in the door. Manny?"

"Like Mr. Fitzsimmons said, if we're going to turn this place around, we've got to cut costs while getting the biggest bang for the buck. That's especially true of marketing. I've been here a month, so I've had a chance to go through our entire program. We've been spending seventy-five grand a month on the media—two billboards in the Bay Area at four thousand each, twenty thou for newspaper ads and radio spots in the Central Valley, twenty for Reno media, ten for the coupon program on Virginia Street.

"In my opinion, we've got to rethink the program. What good does image advertising do for a place like this? We got two billboards on some California freeway when the Golden Spur sponsors the 49ers' telecast! We offer a room special in the *San Francisco Chronicle* that's more expensive than some of the joints in Vegas. We're not Coke or Budweiser. If you can saturate the fuckin' world, then image advertising works like Chinese water torture. But, for a little operation, it's like tryin' to turn the ocean yellow by pissin' in it."

"So, what do we do?" Seth asked.

"I'm pulling us out of most of the print media. Adios *Sacramento Bee*. Sayonara billboards, too. The street-capture program is too expensive. Also, who does it dredge up? Ask yourself what kind of person walks two blocks out of the way for a dollar giveaway? Not Jackie Onassis. We've got to focus, and I plan to. We need targeted promotions, ones that have real value, realistic costs, and measurable results. If I can't fuckin' quantify it, I don't want it. I'm not interested in seeing 'Starlight Hotel Casino' on the top of some cab or the back of some bus driving down the street. I know what that costs, I don't know what it gets me.

"I need better demographics, customer profiles—actual names and addresses. Somethin' that lets me reach out to our best players, reward 'em, keep 'em comin' back. The worst thing we can do is lose a good customer. It costs a bundle to get a replacement, particularly in this market."

"Then," Seth asked, "what do you expect each of us to do?"

Manny replied, "I wouldn't presume to tell any of you how to run your department, but I know you think you can run mine. Why? Because we're all consumers, every one of us. So, we all got opinions about products and why we buy 'em. I'll make it easy for you—I'm asking for your help. It beats second guessin' me. I mean, like, François you got to be part of the thinking if we're going to push a fuckin' food special, or it won't be very special. We got a slot club, but in my opinion, it's not great. We should make it the best dollar value in town. Our slot hosts aren't that friendly. My first day here I asked one where the sign-up booth was, and he didn't fuckin' know. Not only didn't he know, I don't think he cared. I could see he just wanted to blow me off. I don't mean to criticize slots, Tim, but we got to do better than that. Good service is the best marketing tool—you can't beat it. So, bring your ideas. Let's see what we can come up with together."

At first there was silence, but then François said, "Ees okay, Manny. I want *une speciale—biftec* and lobster for only $9.95. Eet must be very popular."

Jim opined, "Fine, guys, but we're walking a fine food-cost line here. If the lobster is undersized and the steak hard to chew, it could be counterproductive. It might turn off more customers than it pleases." He then added, "We used to have a check cashing special. You cashed your paycheck and got a free spin on a prize wheel. Most of the prizes were small, but you could win up to five hundred dollars. I think we gave the customer two free drinks, too. It was really popular with the locals. We've still got that wheel in the warehouse. What do you think, Manny?"

"Let me check it out, Sir. I'll run the numbers. It could be a great promotion."

An hour later, Manny Cohen sat in his office, tapping a pencil on his desktop while sifting through his thoughts. Shelly Sherman had just left after exploring some possible hotel promotions. They'd agreed that amenities were the key to attracting scarce midweek business, rather than room rates *per se*. After all, last winter the Harrington actually gave its rooms away from Monday through Thursday to travel-agent wholesalers just to put some gamers in the place. It's tough to undercut gratis!

Shelly had some interesting wrinkles. What about a "Treat Your Special Person" promotion—two nights for $39.95 per person with a basket of fruit, split of champagne, box of chocolates, and a complimentary breakfast in bed? Her rough calculation was that the amenities had an actual cost of fifteen dollars. If you added the nine dollars a day to make up a room, it still left a small profit margin. It beat having a vacancy when the hotel's occupancy was likely to be under fifty percent, anyway. Some people would take full advantage of the lovebird offer without venturing into the spider's web otherwise known as the casino floor. But certainly not all. Besides, just having people around shilled the place, made it more exciting and inviting, even if they didn't actually gamble themselves. It also created traffic in the restaurant, which at least translated into tip activity for its beleaguered waitresses and busboys. Manny had told Shelly to perfect the numbers before their next meeting.

Still, there was something wrong; he felt a kind of hollowness that seemed to portend future problems. He'd acceded way too easily to Fitzsimmons's suggestion. He knew that half the casinos in town had a payroll-check-cashing promotion, many of which offered better value than his boss had proposed. At best, it would put the Starlight squarely in the middle of the pack. It had warts and smacked of selling potato chips. In short, it was far too prosaic for the visionary of the Bethlehem Casino.

Manny shuddered slightly and then shrugged, "What the hell, it's his fuckin' casino."

***

The Day of the Emigrant dawned bright and clear. Mass at San Onofrio was scheduled for eleven, by which time, it would no doubt be scorching. Jerry and Sue took a morning walk through the awakening streets of the town. Unlike during their previous day's random strolls, Sue seemed headed towards a particular place.

"There it is, Jerry, our ancestral home."

He looked at the sprawling, two-story structure, which reminded him more of a compound than a house. It seemed to encompass half the block.

"It has a workshop and a courtyard where the men in the family learned to be coppersmiths. Agnone was famous for its copper products. There were two foundries on the Verrino that stamped out the blanks, and maybe forty families here in town that hammered them into cooking pots and other utensils. Uncle Enzo and Aunt Adela have two photographs on their living room wall that were taken around the turn of the century. One is of my great-grandfather, his three married sons, and their teenage boys all working together in the courtyard. There must be twenty people in the picture, and the youngest apprentice is about ten.

"The other picture is of the family eating together at one long table. My great-grandparents are sitting at the head and my grandfather and each of his brothers is seated with his wife and family. Great-grandmother is dishing out the food. There are more than thirty people in all and under the same roof.

"There was a fourth brother, who was living in the town of Alfedena and running an outlet there for the family's copperware. I still have cousins in Alfedena. According to the story, each of the brothers in Agnone took turns going on the road from time to time with a little cart filled with copper pots. They would visit the markets in towns like Capracotta and Pescopennataro. So, the family did everything from making the product to transporting it to selling it, directly through its branch outlet in Alfedena. I guess it was sort of a primitive Mikasa—the original factory outlet store!"

As Sue finished her story, the front door opened, and an elderly couple appeared. Sue's Aunt Adela was carrying a chair and held her Uncle Enzo loosely by the arm. She arranged his seating to one side of the portal and guided him into it. The old man continued to protest long after she disappeared back into the shadowy doorway. Gradually, it became evident that he was babbling rather than conversing. He didn't seem to notice when Jerry and Sue approached him. Nor did he acknowledge her when she said, "*Zio Enzo, me conosciute?*"

Aunt Adela appeared again carrying a lap blanket, which she tucked carefully under Enzo's legs, despite the mild temperature of the August morning. Adela wore a black dress that covered her from head to toe, in perpetual mourning for the death of her parents. It made Sue feel more inappropriately exposed in her gaily colored blouse and slacks than she ever had in her scanty cocktail waitress garb. She greeted her aunt as if they were total strangers, secure in the knowledge she wouldn't be recognized after so many years. Adela nodded and then retreated into the maw of the ancient dwelling.

Sue then turned to Jerry and said, "Uncle is demented. He's been like this for two years now. I just can't believe it. Papa sits silent in Youngstown and Unc talks endlessly here in Agnone. Papa can't understand, and Enzo can't make sense. Two old men, brothers, hanging on to a tiny sliver of life at opposite ends of the world while their wives prepare for their burials. Babe, it's just too awful!"

Sue leaned over and kissed her uncle lightly on the cheek. "*Ciao, Zio.*"

The old man continued to rail at nothing in particular, lost within his own private universe.

***

Jim had informed Dot of the palace coup as they ate their supper. She nodded and grunted in the appropriate places, but was clearly unconvinced. To her mind, this was scarcely a definitive changing of the guard. James still breathed. He would surely react. Given his majority ownership, what prevented him from reasserting his control?

Jim rose and strolled through the house as if for the first time. It was all Dot. Bric-a-brac from their multiple visits to London and Paris—ostensibly cultural experiences but, in reality, shopping sprees—populated every flat surface. He recalled the fieldstone fireplace before the prising and replacement with marble. The frippery of form and color, fashioned by the many different woods, carpets, and wallpapers, was all hers. To a visitor, it projected thoughtful detail, understated opulence long since resolved, yet Jim had become accustomed to the impermanency of the perpetual rehearsal. He now contemplated the chatelaine's mansion's only permanent feature—the ormolu frieze surrounding the upper wall of the formal dining room and depicting sylvan scenes from Grecian antiquity, illuminated by gold-plated sconces.

Jim was never consulted about her constant changes. He might return from work to find his clothes missing from their closet and his toiletries removed from the master bathroom in anticipation of the next day's demolition for the latest remodel. He knew far better than to interfere with his finicky spouse. His real space was a small room tucked under the eaves that must have once been an attic before being converted by a former owner into a child's bedroom. Access was almost clandestine, via a narrow stairway that rose out of a former closet on the floor below. Jim had to duck during the ascent and was still susceptible to the occasional bruised forehead if distracted or a little tipsy. He sometimes fantasized that he could pull the staircase up after himself like the rope ladder of his childhood treehouse.

Jim's secret space was far too sequestered and insignificant to warrant Dot's attention and talents. Over the years, it had become his refuge. It was here that he could shelter his privacy and display his trophies. Photos of Jim-with-fish festooned the walls with memories of expeditions to Kamchatka, the Amazon, and Christmas Island. Five hard-earned trophies from squash-tournament victories were carefully aligned across the top of the chest of drawers that was just small enough to have negotiated the narrow stairwell. On the south wall was a poster of world champion Mark Talbott, squash racket poised for action, personally inscribed to Jim—his prize possession. A triangular table was wedged into one corner. It served as Jim's fly-tying bench, complete with desk lamp, vise, gooseneck magnifying glass, and tabletop cabinet with a myriad of drawers filled with various kinds of bling, thread, fur, and feathers. The only other furnishing was the single bed that he frequently used but seldom made, its crumpled sheets probably in need of laundering. A small plaque on the outer surface of the entry door proclaimed in black letters:

Jim's World

***

The chorale performance after mass was Jerry's favorite moment during the festivities. The children's choir, bedecked in traditional Alto Molisan costume, sang one lyrical emigrant's song after another. Sue translated the humorous lyrics of *Mother of Mine Give Me a Hundred Liras So I Can Go to America*. As a finale, the choir sang *Mama*, the emigrant's nostalgic lament for his mother in distant Italy, which brought tears to the eyes of more than one listener.

After the entertainment, the hundreds of spectators scattered over the hillside in search of shade for picnic lunches. Sue spread the borrowed blanket from their hotel under an olive tree, where they shared the valuable space with a family back from Milan for the week. Sue chatted with the wife while Jerry exchanged an occasional word or gesture with her husband. Their three children were indifferent to the awkward attempt at international relations and soon drifted away in search of playmates. When Jerry swallowed the last of his salami sandwich, rubbed his stomach, and said "*bene*" to his new friend, Sue interjected "You mean '*buono*,' Jerry," thereby sealing his aspirational Italic lips for the remainder of their trip.

After an hour, Jerry and Sue waved goodbye to their departing companions. The husband was required to be at work in Milan first thing the next morning, so they would be driving well into the night as it was. When the crowd thinned, Jerry noticed a faint footpath skirting the mountainside. "C'mon, Sue, let's explore."

They walked for a couple of kilometers, crossing several small gullies created by landslides and subsequent erosion. Some looked freshly made within the last few years. At times, they seemed to be in an abandoned garden overgrown with weeds and brambles, defined by crumbling stone walls. At others, the landscape was more forested, smudged with wildflowers and sprinkled with trees.

Suddenly, the trail terminated at the edge of a cluster of rustic houses. They startled a small pig, which let out a squeal as it fled into one of the dwellings. Several hens scratched the earth in front of a second, ranging back and forth with impunity over its dirt threshold. Of the eight households in the hamlet, these were the only two with television antennas, the ubiquitous modern sign of life. Four others were in such obvious disrepair as to raise doubt about their habitability.

Just then, the first of a string of goats appeared and began milling about. When all thirty of the flock were centerstage, they seemed to take their first simultaneous notice of the intruders, freezing in place and fixing them with stares. The goats then performed a caprine magic trick—producing a goatherd as if from thin air. Sue greeted him from a distance, triggering his right arm into the ageless gesture of *contadino* subordination—the instinctive uncovering of one's head in the presence of superiors.

Jerry and Sue approached the rigid figure, who now regarded them with both suspicion and curiosity. The peasant remained silent, deferring to Sue's right to ask the questions regardless of turf considerations. At first, he answered her queries in curt, monosyllabic fashion, but then he began to relax perceptibly, obviously convinced that the strangers were innocuous.

"*Favorite*," he said, indicating his house and seemingly inviting them to enter the frightened pig's refuge. Jerry walked towards it with mixed emotions, uncertain what they might find in what was little more than a hovel. At the entrance, the man gestured to them to wait while he made the arrangements. The muffled conversation from within included a female voice. He reemerged bearing a small table, and followed by his wife, who carried two chairs.

Sue and Jerry were motioned to take their seats while their hostess brought out a bottle of red wine, two large slices of goat's cheese, and a rock-hard piece of bread. Jerry shuddered a little at the glasses, which were encrusted with unidentifiable substances, but nevertheless managed to banish that from his mind once they were covered beneath the coal-dark liquid. The cheese had a dry and coarse appearance, and he avoided tasting his until Sue took the lead. As it turned out, he was amazed at its delicious flavor, enhanced by a rich, pungent odor. The snack was ceasing to be an ordeal, and Jerry relaxed with the realization that he could meet the responsibilities of a grateful guest.

It was then that he noticed that their hosts remained standing, almost at attention. Despite the summer heat, the man was wearing what seemed to be heavy corduroy pants, though his shirt was lightweight. His arms were crossed, and his cap dangled from his right hand, exposing his silver mane to the full sun. The wife was barefoot and draped, rather than dressed, in a black cotton dress that made her figure almost shapeless.

"They say that, when they were children, there used to be fifty people here, Jerry. Now there are only two families, or actually, remnants of two families. They live alone; their son is in Isernia, and their daughter is married to a *cantina* owner in the *cittadina*. Their only neighbors are another couple, who live in that house with the chickens. They're not here today; they went to town with their three sons, back from Germany for the festival."

Sue's translation for Jerry's benefit completed, the peasant pointed partway up the slope immediately behind the hamlet. For the first time, they noticed a more modern structure keeping its own company. Sue listened patiently and then translated. "He says that one of the men back from Germany today built it ten years ago. He and his wife had worked there for eight years, saving their money. He dreamed of returning here to build a modern house. He read books on the advantages of cement silos and stable floors, crop rotation, new fertilizers, and superior breeds of sheep and cattle. He was convinced that the government was serious about supporting agriculture here. With the subsidies and using modern techniques, he was going to succeed, and also show others how to.

"So, he spent all his savings on that house and moved his wife and two children into it. For three years, he struggled. He listened to the government's agronomists and endured his neighbors' scorn. He applied for the subsidies and instead drowned in the paperwork. First his children and then his wife began to complain about his folly. Life was so much easier in Stuttgart. They had friends there. Finally, the third year, there was a major drought. His crops failed and he had to sell his fancy livestock to cover his debts. The agronomists urged him to apply for drought relief; he moved back to Germany instead. That house has been vacant for seven years now. When he left, he told his father to use it any way he wished."

"So, what does his father do with it?" Jerry asked.

Sue posed the question.

"He uses it for a goat stable!"

***

The next morning, they checked out of their hotel and were about to depart when Sue said, "Let's take one last walk through the town. I have such mixed feelings about this place—I hate to come here; still, I hate to leave!"

Jerry noticed a sign over a curious looking structure which said Pontificia Fonderia Marinelli. "Are you related to them? What is that?"

"That's the famous bell-works, Babe. Papa said we're distant cousins, but too distant for any of us to understand how. The sign says that it's a papal bell-works—the Marinelli foundry has the papal seal of approval. It specializes in making bells for churches all over Italy and the world." They entered the front office of the foundry and were intrigued by a display of items for sale. There were tiny bells of various sizes and descriptions and other bronze knick-knacks, door knockers, etc. Jerry picked up a bronze tablet with a strange inscription.

"That's a reproduction of the *tavola osca* found here last century in some *contadino's* field. It's an ancient tablet in the Oscan language spoken here before Roman times. I think the original is in the British Museum. For the *Agnonesi*, the *tavola* is sort of a founding relic, the earliest real evidence of civilization here."

Sue picked up a handsome book with the title *Arte e fuoco. Campane di Agnone* by Gioconda Marinelli.

"It means *Art and Fire. Bells of Agnone.* It gives the history of the bell-works. Look at this chart. The family's earliest known bell was made by Nicodemo Marinelli in 1339 for the church of Frusinate! It says that until early this century, the bellmakers would travel to the site and found the bell right there, in order to avoid transportation costs. But they would do the artwork here first and make all the wooden molds for producing the bell's decorations."

They were given a tour of the bell-works, silent and abandoned for the moment, and a brief explanation of the founding process. The clerk or custodian in the front office, who doubled as tour guide, seemed to be the only person on the premises. They were also shown a museum room with displays of wooden molds used for previous castings—some centuries-old. The walls were festooned with photographs of famous bells, usually taken on their inaugural day. The blessing of a new bell and attendant festivities seemed to easily rival the hoopla of a ship's launching.

Jerry selected a small souvenir bell for purchase and a copy of the book as well. As he was paying for them, their attendant said something to him. Sue translated.

"He wants to know if you'd like to have it signed by the author."

"Sure, but it's your call, since I'm buying it for you."

She nodded, and the attendant disappeared briefly into an interior office, and reemerged accompanied by a vivacious middle-aged woman. She greeted them warmly and expressed her obviously sincere hope that they enjoyed their visit to her family's ancestral temple. Sue complimented her on the fine book, promising to give it a prominent place in both her home and heart.

"Gioconda is asking if there is any particular inscription that you'd prefer, Jerry."

"Let me write one out in English for her."

Gioconda copied out his words and signed the dedication. They thanked her and left. As the movement of the Fiat gradually effected closure to their Agnone sojourn, Sue idly opened the cover of her prized book. Gioconda and Jerry's common project proclaimed:

> *To my dear cousin Susan in anticipation of your next visit to Agnone.*
>
> *Gioconda Marinelli*
> *Agosto, 1996*

***

"I'm glad we did it, Sue. Agnone was wonderful. I felt like a detective, or maybe an anthropologist. You're quite a guide! It helped me get over some stereotypes I had about Italians, although I guess it gave me some new ones, too."

"I'm not sure I understand what you mean by that."

"Oh, you know, the hood thing. In Nevada, in fact in all of America, it seems like when you hear an Italian name, you think of the Mafia. Take the Ferrareses, for example. Last year, the Starlight blocked their plans to get the city to pay for a park near their hotel. Jim Fitzsimmons wrote a strong position paper against the idea and met with the CEOs of five other properties. They all signed it, and the city council got cold feet. The project was shelved, and two weeks later, the Fitzsimmons family received an anonymous death threat. It may have been coincidence, but you couldn't help—"

Jerry had struck a nerve without meaning to. Sue unfastened her seatbelt so she could turn towards him as he drove. There was an edge to her voice as she began. "It's not easy being Italian, Jerry. The damn Mafia image follows us everywhere. When people get comfortable with you, they say things like 'I've never really known an Italian before' or 'You're a really nice person,' when what they mean is, 'for an Italian.' Take the Ferrareses. They're a North Italian family, I think from Piedmont. The northerners have more in common with Norwegians than Sicilians. They don't have a history of organized crime. They hate the Mafia and us southerners too. They think we're uncivilized country bumpkins. That's why I didn't want to go to Milan—not even when you told me about La Scala and the beautiful cathedral. I'm not really welcome there."

"I'm sorry, Sue. I'm just like all the other insensitive people you've met. I guess I've fallen into the old some-of-my-best-friends-are-Italian trap." He laughed and added, "And my lover, fiancée, and future wife, too."

She released a long sigh, her anger deflating, and put her seat belt back on. "It's okay, Babe. Actually, even here in the South, it's not easy to sort out the Mafia business. It's hard to know who is and isn't a *mafioso*—or even what the Mafia is precisely. It seems as much a concept as a reality. Actually, strictly speaking, it's a Sicilian organization with tentacles into the peninsula. But in Calabria they have something similar, the *Ndrangheta*, and around Naples, there's the *Camorra*. In the mountains of the Abruzzo-Molise, there used to be brigands, bands of outlaws, just like in the American West, but that was different. Even so, it's hard to know for sure. Let me tell you a little story:

"Here in the Alto Molise, almost everyone has a vineyard and makes his own wine. But when we moved to Agnone, we needed to buy our winter's supply. We heard about a man in Castelverrino, a little village on the river, who had some extra wine to sell. So, Papa, Enzo, and I went there to meet him in the only tavern. There were two old men drinking at the bar. They said something in English, and Papa introduced himself. They were from Pietrabbondante, and one was named Luigi Capone. They had both moved back to Italy after living for years in Cicero, Illinois. When they left, Papa, Enzo, and the man selling the wine got into an argument. It seemed that Capone was a very common last name in Pietrabbondante. Was Al from there? Enzo thought it was possible; the guy from Castelverrino said no way.

"When I was in high school, I read a biography about Al Capone for a class paper. He wasn't from Sicily; the book listed Naples as his birthplace. But, you know, whenever an American asked Papa where he was from, the answer was Naples. It was the closest big city. It was just too much bother to explain places like like Isernia, the Alto Molise, and Agnone."

"Pietrabbondante would have been even tougher," Jerry laughed. "Alright, Sherlock, what's it to be—Naples or Sicily?"

"Let's try both, Jerry. We still have ten days. We'll need to buy a map and guidebook. We're heading into the third Italy—the one neither of us knows."

The filth and traffic in Naples convinced them to cancel plans to spend the night there. They had decided to wander, rather than travel, through the South, carried along by whim and fate instead of a plan. Near Cotrone in Calabria, they found a secluded beach at midday. The unrelenting heat from the fireball in the cloudless sky made the dark waters of the Mediterranean irresistible. It was then they realized that, in their hasty preparations in Reno, neither had packed a swimsuit.

"Let's go skinny-dipping, Jerry. We're alone."

Sue slipped out of her clothes, revealing her swarthy body, made browner by periodic, bikini-clad backyard sunbathing. Jerry's creamy torso seemed to turn pink instantly over surprise at the unaccustomed exposure. They dove into the cool waters and swam together about a hundred yards offshore. For several minutes, they floated on their backs in silence until voices reached them from across the water. Jerry rotated his feet under him to be able to gaze at the shore.

"Oh my God, Sue, what are we gonna do now?"

Two nuns waved at them while shepherding their bevy of schoolgirls. Some of the children were spreading a blanket on the sand while others unpacked bread, cheeses, and drinks from wicker baskets.

Jerry and Sue swam around a rocky point and took refuge in the mottled shade of some sparse bushes. For the next two hours, they hid there, trapped by circumstance, until the festive picnickers had departed. They retrieved their clothing and found a country inn, where Sue doused Jerry's burned body with vinegar to ease the pain.

"I always did like my meat well done," he attempted to joke, but his acute discomfort was evident.

The next day, Sue had to drive as they left Calabria, crossed the Straits of Messina on the ferry, and entered Sicily. In Taormina, they found a marvelous hotel built into a cliffside. From their corner room, they could see Mount Etna in the distance in one direction, while in the other, they contemplated a vertiginous drop to the sea. Jerry had blistered his chest, arms, shoulders, and back, so they decided to make Taormina their headquarters. He recuperated by reading quietly in the hotel garden and sipping countless cups of coffee in the numerous small cafes.

After their hectic pace, the enforced relaxation was welcome. Their last day, they drove to Palermo to experience the main site of Sicily's role as the crossroads of northern Europe and North Africa.

Sue read from the entry for the city in their Fodor's guidebook: "Phoenician colony, Carthaginian town, the capital of an Arab Emirate, the commercial hub of Europe and Asia under the Normans, intellectual center under Frederick II—Palermo wears all of these labels gracefully."

Their favorite place was the church of Monreale, with its mosaic murals, located in the hilly summer residence of the Norman monarchs. It was the last curtain call of their Italian play—the delicious icing on their honeymoon cake. All that remained was the next day's marathon journey back to Rome for the flight home. Their Italian odyssey was over.

***

Jim Fitzsimmons took one look at the *Gazette-Journal* and threw it on the floor. There was a front-page story about a lawsuit being filed against the Starlight by an irate customer claiming that a bartender he stiffed had used his dick as a swizzel stick to stir his second drink. Jim would need to confront François with this, but meanwhile, his bad mood was worsened by reading a two-page memo for the third time. Jim punched the button on his intercom hard!

"Priscilla, tell Cohen I want to see him immediately! If he's in a meeting, get him out of it. While you're at it, get Seth Harris here, too."

Five minutes later, the executive secretary opened the door to the Fitzsimmons lair for the agitated marketing director.

"Sit down, Manny. I want an explanation. Where did we get this advertising copy?" Jim waved the pages threateningly in Manny's general direction, then let them flutter like two wounded butterflies onto his desktop.

"I don't understand, Sir. I thought you wanted me to take off the gloves and sell this place. I stole some fuckin' ideas from the California lottery. They can afford top-notch ad types. Why reinvent—"

Jim interrupted with a wave of his hand. Before he could speak, the door opened again, and a somewhat winded games director settled into the other chair facing the boss's desk. Fitzsimmons slipped on his bifocals, retrieved a page of Cohen's text, and began to read: "Harry won the progressive jackpot at the Starlight last night. Next week, he's moving his family into a new house. What are you doing for yours?"

Jim slowly tore the sheet in two and handed the pieces to Manny, who made a lame stab at humor. "I used to have principles, Sir, but I got over them. They crucified the last miracle worker two thousand years ago."

"Manny, you're the only person I know who could run across a horse pasture and never miss a pucky."

"Mr. Fitzsimmons, I approved that ad campaign, too," Harris interjected.

"You did, huh? Fine. Well, let me give you a present, too." He fumbled through the papers on his desk, found Seth's supportive memo, and repeated his destructive ritual. Closing his eyes, he began stroking the lids with the thumb and forefinger of his right hand. For a full minute, livid and rigid, he wrestled with his anger.

Manny was simply intimidated by the reproof and squirmed in his seat.

Finally, Jim sighed deeply, his stooped shoulders proclaiming abject discouragement. He contemplated his casino manager's scarlet face and said, "Look, I'm sorry. I'm having a bad day. In fact, I'm having a bad year. I know I've put pressure on both of you to perform, but there *are* limits. We've got to maintain some scruples. That ad copy and, Seth, your other memo recommending that we scrap our player-limit policy step over the line—my line. They encourage problem gaming. Hell, they create it.

"Hopefully, we've come a long way since the old days, when if somebody gave you heavy action, you pumped him full of free booze and the GM became his personal buddy. It was the GM's job to do everything he could to make sure that player stayed put. I've seen guys pee their pants, puke, or pass out because they couldn't tear themselves away from the table … or we wouldn't let them. My father thought it was just part of this business; well, I consider that a velvet mugging. I won't tolerate it.

"Seth, there's a business reason for our player-limit policy. I'm not just being squeamish about it. If you tell someone to establish his limit when he first comes in, say ten thousand, and then hold him to it, you won't burn him out. When he starts to drink and play, he can let himself go without worrying about losing the farm. You've got the ten percent courtesy rule. If that ten grand player begs you to raise his limit, maybe gets belligerent about it, you're authorized to go to eleven—but no more. I don't want the authority to raise that guy any higher; I don't want Jesus Christ to have that authority. I've had some of our best players phone me at home on Saturday night to call me every name in the book for not giving them a chance to get even after they lost their limit—their own limit. Well, those guys call back sober on Tuesday morning to thank me. It's shortsighted to take out a good customer over one run of bad luck. You'll never see him again, so it's even a bad business ploy. You can clip a sheep's wool a lot of times; you can only skin it once. We're in the wool business, not the fleeces one."

The chastised directors retreated in silence, leaving their boss to himself.

Jim pressed the intercom button and told Priscilla, "Hold my calls. No interruptions until further notice." He suddenly felt bone tired. He slowly undid the knot of his tie and slid it out of his collar. The top button of his shirt came off in his hand as he tried to unfasten it. Jim removed his jacket and rolled it into a ball. He lay down on the floor behind his chair, his head on the improvised pillow. "This place needs a GM really bad," he said, then slipped into deep slumber.

***

Sue and Jerry were both contemplative as they settled into the return flight to America, the closing parenthesis of their vacation. What had transpired in Youngstown while they were away? What would transpire in Des Moines? And back in Reno? How would they transition their new household into a home? Sheba would be attending a different school, which meant a teenager's angst over the loss and gain of old and new classmates, and both Jerry and Sue were now unemployed.

Jerry tried to change such subjects by philosophizing about their trip. "Life is an illusion, Sue. I mean, you constantly run into yourself coming around some global corner. Staying home and turning on your television is the same as watching the one in your hotel room. All the

Hollywood world, the game show and sitcom knockoffs that stimulate our illusions ... and delusions as well. It plays with our desire to be frightened out of our boredom with everyday life. It makes us couch-potato voyeurs by challenging us with the seamiest sides of humanity— war, torture, crime—so we can feel smug and superior in our own little ruts. 'My life may be bad, but it isn't *that* bad!'"

Sue interrupted, "I think you're being too cynical."

"Am I? Why do you think the movie industry did so well during the Great Depression? Then there's travel—tourism. We just left Rome, city of the Caesars. Well, if you want to see their real palaces you'd better go to Vegas, Tahoe, or Atlantic City. Steve Wynn would say everything is a Mirage. I say it is more than a mirage, today the simulacra are the *really* real, the hyperreal, which is to say the superior reality." Jerry tapped the cover of his flight companion, Umberto Eco's *Travels in Hyperreality.*

"But Jerry, we were just where it all began. It wasn't *just* a copy. It was *genuino.* Why do you think people come from all over the world to see Rome?"

"Hype, Sue. The travel industry, cruise ships, airlines, alumnae associations, *National Geographic*, Hilton, Hyatt, and Marriott—just for openers. None of them are selling the destination so much as their own illusion of it. It's all about marketing; certainly not education. 'Come see the Coliseum. Take pictures.' Then, inflict them on your friends, along with your guide's spiel, supposedly to educate them but really to underscore 'I have seen the Coliseum; *you* have not.' And is that the genuine article where the lions ate Christians? Of course not. It's a caricature of its former self, constructed out of rocks that weren't even the originals lying in some pile of rubble. Those rocks were cannibalized long ago for other building projects in a city that's no more eternal than Vegas.

"Both constantly reinvent themselves. The original Coliseum meant something in peoples' lives ... and deaths. It wasn't some attraction illuminated at night to titillate tourists. So, like forty million other Americans last year, give me Caesar's Palace. Come to think of it, I prefer the Vegas Excalibur any day to riding around Merrie Old England in some tour bus filled with Mencken's 'booboisie' trying to imagine King Arthur's world. That was its own myth. To understand it, what's better—the seat on the bus or a ticket to a good production of *Camelot*?"

"I still see a difference between Europeans and Americans, Jerry. Europeans appreciate life more; they celebrate heritage."

"I wish that were so, but I'm skeptical. Don't you see all the ironies? Bilbao hires some Canadian living in LA to build a titanium museum franchised by New York's Guggenheim, while in LA, the Getty Foundation erects a medieval European palace out of Italian Travertine marble and, up the road, a new museum to house its world-class collection of Greek and Roman sculpture. France is about to open its Disney World, while Epcot erects a French pavilion in Orlando and Vegas creates anew Paris and Venice. Who is celebrating whose heritage and where?

"It's not just culture. Look at the world's botanical gardens. By definition, they're about displaying vegetation from elsewhere. We even have lions and emus running wild in Texas … well, sort of."

"Are you saying that we are all citizens of just one world, now? That there's no diversity?"

"Kind of. I mean, there's a whole lot of blurring going on. With this Internet stuff, maybe all reality is becoming virtual, and, in a few years, the only *real* place left will be cyberspace. But, you know, globalization has its own special hype. It's supposedly new and even futuristic. *Au contraire*. It's been around for centuries. Didn't you Italians send Marco Polo to Mongolia, and he came back with spaghetti and forks? Then another of your Italians sailed off to America and brought back tomatoes domesticated by Aztecs. Now western civilization was getting somewhere. So, in the nineteenth century, millions of Italians emigrated to new lands, opened restaurants, and today, you can find spaghetti in tomato *sugo* (billed as *traditional* authentic Italian cuisine) and eat it with a fork anywhere on the planet. It's not globalization that's new, Sue; it's the pace. If you're looking for a good investment, buy stock in US Pacemaker."

"Has anyone ever told you you're crazy, Jerry?"

"Of course. We all are. We just differ in our idiosyncrasy—each person's madness has its own special form. When enough of us get together and draw a perimeter around *our* idiosyncrasies we think we have defined normality. Woe be it to those who fall outside the circle, there are usually serious consequences … at least for them."

Sue's mental synapses had reached overload. She snuggled against Jerry's shoulder and placed two fingers to his lips. "Please don't say 'you Italians,' Jerry. I don't like it. I'm as American as you are. By the way, what are *you*?"

"Just an All-American mutt, Sue. I'm the map of Europe—a lot of English, some French and Serbian, a little Irish and a dash of German. Who knows, maybe some Jewish, too. That's without sorting through all the Ellis Island name changes. You know, when they clipped off the terminal vowels and extra consonants—anything that offended the American ear. It was part of the delousing."

***

Jim found himself standing in the anteroom of the executive offices staring at James Fitzsimmons's closed door. A sliver of light emanated from under it like some tiny beacon. Jim knocked lightly.

"Come in."

Jim felt a panicky urge to simply flee; it was as if he were sitting in the corner observing and listening to the father-son conversation. He heard his own voice say, "Dad, I don't know what to do next. My managers are leaving, and the bankers are at our throats. I'm not even sure we can make payroll this month. The vendors are all stretched as far as they'll go. Half of them have got us on COD already. It's August and we don't have a penny in the kitty for winter operating. I've had discussions with our bankruptcy attorney about filing for chapter-eleven. You remember Jeff Harmon? You have a right to know; it's your reputation, too—the Fitzsimmons name. You don't come to the board meetings anymore, so I'm not sure you're aware—"

"I know a lot more than you think. I've got my eyes and ears around this place. There are people here who tell me what's really going on, stuff that you and that woman will never hear—the real scoop. There's also Priscilla.

"So, Jimmy, what makes you think that there's anything left here to salvage? I look at the numbers every day, and they just make me sick. Freefall, that's all it is. I see where two more Indian joints opened up in Oregon and they're talking about legalizing Indian gaming in BC. The Washington and California tribes are in court, and they just might win. You're some kind of cockeyed optimist, Son, open up those eyes."

Jim struggled with his anger. He knew all too well about his father's network of lackeys—the old-timer, sycophantic employees who used James as a sounding board and rallying point to undermine the directives of the management team. Given the Starlight's more serious problems, Jim had long since decided to tolerate rather than challenge his father's rogue behavior, but he didn't have to condone it. *Steady, Jim. For God's sake, don't take that bait. That's not what this discussion is about.* "Dad, I need your advice. Hell, I need more than advice—I need your help."

"For what, Jimmy, to file for bankruptcy? Jeff can do that. What do you expect of me?"

"Expect? I don't expect anything. To expect would suggest that I have a right and you an obligation. That's not the way things are between us. I understand that. What I'm saying is that I want to work through this mess. If we have to do it under chapter eleven, so be it. I'd rather not. I'd rather fight the good fight, Dad, fight until there's not a breath left in the Starlight's body … or mine either."

"You're serious, aren't you? I see it in your eyes. In fact, I *like* what I see in your eyes."

"Look, Dad, I never asked to be CEO around here. I wasn't bucking for your job at that board meeting. It just turned out that way. I've been in the hot seat for maybe two weeks now. Well, it's no throne; in fact, it's more like an electric chair. Dad, I'm not sure that I know what I'm doing. It was a lot easier to be your critic than your successor. No one prepared me for this. I mean, where do you go to get owner training?"

James listened to his son patiently, even passing on the opportunity to comment whenever Jim's pause invited it.

"Dad, I always believed that one day, I would be in charge of the Starlight. In fact, I thought that was your plan, too. We've never really discussed it. Until recently, you've always acted like you think you're immortal. If it was never your intention for me to follow in your footsteps, you should have said so. I could have done something else with my life. I don't know if I'm an optimist. If so, then so be it. In fact, I'd rather be an optimist proven wrong than a pessimist proven right. If disaster comes, I'd rather take my medicine in one big gulp, and then get on with life, rather than sip it a little at a time while anticipating the worst. Someone has to come in here every morning, at least until we shut off the lights and lock the doors."

"Jimmy, I've never been able to read my sons. Sean's gone, I guess that's clear enough, but you … you just sort of hung around the edges. Maybe I should have brought you more into the business—the real decisions—but you know, Son, I was never quite sure of you. You'd come down here every working day when you weren't off on one of your fishing trips, but I never could figure out what you actually *did*. I put you through every department and nothing seemed to click."

"I know you did it because you couldn't decide what to do with me. I dealt cards, bussed tables, served wine, carried coin on the floor. You even had me mucking out the restrooms: bucket and mop, squeegee and toilet brush. Did I learn from all that? Something. A little bit of knowledge about a lot of things. Knowledge, but no real wisdom. I had no idea how it all fit together. It taught me about operations within a casino, but not how to run one."

"Actually, Jimmy, I was grooming you. I wanted you to have hands-on experience with every aspect of the business. I believed that then, one day, you would be—"

"You never told me that, Dad," Jim interjected. "When you transferred me to something new, it felt like I'd just failed at something old. I felt like my life was suspended or balked. It shows how little we communicated, really communicated."

"I admit that I never provided you with the way, but did you ever bring the will? Maybe we're both talking about original sin here. That should be Catholic enough for both of us! Dorothy would agree."

This latest stab at humor elicited Jim's first smile. "You know, Dad, you were partly to blame for my fishing and my squash. Around here, I was a nobody. I had no agency. In fly fishing and on the squash court, I'm in control. A good cast brought in a fish, a poor one spooked a lunker. A decent drop shot might win the critical point that meant victory; a crappy miss, and it was all over. Both gave me a sense of pride and personal worth." Jim nodded toward the dust-covered golf bag and clubs in the corner. "For most of your life, you played golf once a week and went on weeklong trips to play in Death Valley or Hawaii. You thought that was natural enough—well-earned time off. I'll bet you missed more days here than I did over the years. But somehow, I was goofing off, and you were just relaxing."

"Do you ever hear from Sean, Jimmy?"

"Not really. Just the Christmas card."

"I miss him, particularly the chance to have this conversation with him. He is my son, after all."

"What happened?"

"Happened?"

"Yeah. Something must have happened between you two. I've thought about it a lot, speculated."

"You know, that's the hell of it, Jimmy. I can't remember anything specific. I once knew a man who was sitting on his porch, as well as could be, when he felt a tickle in his nose. It must have been quite a sneeze since it left him a paraplegic in a wheelchair for the rest of his life. Sean's leaving was kind of like that. No warning, just a sneeze."

"You must have some kind of theory."

"Maybe it was the tough love and the seeming indifference. As I said, I was too busy to give either of you much attention. When his team played for Reno's Little League championship, I sent my slot manager in my place. I'm sure Sean got the message. So, he's twenty-five and Mom and I got a letter from Boston—not even a call, for Chrissakes. It wasn't much of a letter, either. Just, I'm in Boston and okay. I haven't seen him since. Well, Son, you are now in control here. Does any of that make you happy?"

"Am I happy? As opposed to what? Am I sad? Why? 'I'm not sure' is an unacceptable answer in our age of pills and counseling. No one has a right to unhappiness when it's now equated to clinical depression with quick fixes. 'On a scale of ten, Sir, rate your discomfort.' 'My lower back? My attitude? My soul?'"

James considered the comments patiently and nodded his agreement. "You're serious about this, aren't you, Jimmy? I mean, you're really getting into the trenches around here. So, what's the plan? You've got to have a plan. If not, you can just rename this place the *Titanic*."

"Why don't we work out a plan together? We need a GM and a marketing director. Maybe you and I could have a division of labor. You could oversee operations, like before. I'm not that good at the games side of the business anyway. You could teach me as we go along. Those are your strengths, and God knows the Starlight doesn't have the hang time for me to go through a learning curve. I'm not sure about Cohen. Whether we keep him or not, I want to put my efforts into marketing. We've got to improve the top line or die. We might win a few battles by tightening things up internally, but we lose the war if we don't get more customers. If I could count on you to stabilize operations, I could concentrate on marketing. We could make you CEO—"

"I don't think so, Son. I'm too old and sick of a dog to go on a new hunt. Fact is, I haven't really been in operations for years. I would just hire the best GM that I could afford and then tell *him* what to do."

"Well, I'm not sure what we do next, Dad."

James reached for his checkbook and scribbled out the Starlight's immediate fate.

"Five hundred thousand! Dad, another call won't work. I'm broke, and the board won't go along."

"Book it as a loan, Jimmy."

"I don't know what to say. Do we shake on it? We've never shaken hands before. I could hug you, but we've never done that, either."

"It's not necessary, Jimmy. Just get the job done."

***

Sue's anxiety subsided at the sight of Sheba in the Des Moines airport. The weakest link in their plan had been their coordinated scheduled arrivals in Iowa. Sheba had been chaperoned on her flights from Youngstown by the airline's personnel and Jerry's son, Tim, had agreed to meet her. But, after all, he was still a stranger to both mother and daughter. What if something went wrong?

Sue let out a little squeal and ran to embrace her Sheba, who flashed the nervous smile of an adolescent suddenly made the object of gushy attention. Nevertheless, she was obviously as relieved as her mother by the smooth connection.

"Sue, meet Tim," Jerry interrupted.

Tim extended a raised palm to his implausible future stepmother, who was only five years his senior. A handshake or hug seemed totally inappropriate, so they acknowledged each other with a tentative high-five. Seven-year-old Caroline and her little brother, Brett, had already bonded with their soon-to-be cousin. Given that she was twice their age, she was already their presumptive Aunt Sheba.

"We need a scorecard," opined Jerry, as he put his arm around Tim's shoulders while they walked towards the baggage claim area.

"I haven't even met Carla yet, Son. How's your wife?"

"She's fine, but awfully busy. She's a dental hygienist, and they're short on staff at her office. Sometimes I think she should quit and stay home with the kids while they're still young. I earn enough for us to live well. But for Carla, her job is about more than just money. It's about independence and self-esteem, so I don't really push it."

Jerry noticed that his son, dressed in a dark suit and tie, looked every bit the public accountant. While only twenty-eight, he was already balding and developing a bit of a paunchy waistline. He was certainly no longer the lean and muscular figure that Jerry had lifted from the desert floor for the stressful ride to the hospital.

"It's so good to see you again, Son. I don't know where the time goes. I guess it's been maybe ten years now. I just can't believe it. You know, I'm awfully sorry that I couldn't make your wedding. Actually, I was in the midst of a messy divorce at the time."

A slight look of pained resentment flashed momentarily across Tim's face and then evaporated into a smile. "It's okay, Dad. Ancient history."

"How's your mother?"

"Just fine. She wants to see you."

"Uh ... are you sure that's wise?"

"I'm sure. She's coming over to the house for dinner tonight. Dad, it was more than twenty years ago. She appreciates the time I spent with you and knows you didn't have to do it. Believe me, it's okay. She just wants to say hello."

Carla arrived home at four. By then, Sheba was reading a story to Caroline and Brett. The early return from work was Carla's way of acknowledging the importance of the visit. She was pleasant enough and seemed instantly at ease with the strangers in her house, skills that she'd cultivated in her profession. Carla said, "I'd like to call you Dad, Jerry." She then looked at Sue and added, "We're so close in age, I think I should call you Sue, if you don't mind."

"Sue's fine, Carla."

"So, you've been in Italy? I've always wanted to see Europe. Before

Caroline was born, Tim offered to take me, but I was just starting my career and it didn't feel right. Europe must be great."

Jerry volunteered, "Sue's from Italy ... well, sort of. Her parents were from there. She showed me an Italy that you can't get through any travel agent."

The doorbell rang, and Caroline ran to open it. "Grandma!"

Jerry watched the frail, silver-haired, figure enter the room. His first thought was that this must be Joan's mother, given the family resemblance.

"My Lord, how you've changed, Jerry," Joan said, laughing. "I hardly recognize you. What happened to my Berkeley boy? Too many frat parties?" The potentially sardonic remark was made in such a jovial fashion that it actually put Jerry at ease.

"Hello, Joan. How have you been? We're just passing through on our way home to Reno. This is quite some family we've got here. I wanted to meet Carla and the children. Oh, this is my fiancée, Sue, and that's her daughter, Sheba."

"Hullo," Sheba volunteered, glancing up momentarily before plunging back into her reading.

"I'm pleased to meet you, Joan," Sue said.

Joan nodded and smiled sympathetically at the next of Jerry's several clueless brides.

Carla excused herself for kitchen duty, and Tim took drink orders. Handing Sue and Joan their white wines and Jerry his tonic water, Tim said, "I prefer Chivas on the rocks myself, Dad. I thought that was your drink."

"At one time it was," Jerry replied without elaboration.

"I've got to set up the patio furniture and start the coals. I'll be outside if you need me," Tim announced.

"I think I'll see if Carla could use some help," Sue interjected in a thinly-veiled ploy to leave Joan and Jerry together. "Sheba, why don't you read to the children in Caroline's room?"

Suddenly, Jerry and Joan were alone.

"Geez, Joan, it looks like they insist we have some kind of private conversation. I haven't practiced my lines, have you?"

She laughed. "Me neither. But we can't disappoint them. We have to say something to each other ... or at least pretend. Maybe we could talk about your accident. You look like you've been skinned alive."

Jerry grabbed his left ear self-consciously and pulled at a piece of peeling skin. "I'm living proof that WASPs should never go swimming in Italy with Italians. Wrong genes! You ought to see my back. I'm some kind of snake shedding its skin."

"Just remember that it was you who called yourself a snake, not me."

"I've just met Carla and the grandkids, so there's obviously not much for me to say on that score. Of course, it's my fault for not having had much contact with Tim since he left Reno, but then, you know how I am. When it comes to husband and father, I'm scarcely Mr. Wonderful."

"I don't really know who you are. We were just babies having a baby, playing at being adults. I hope for your sake that you grew up. It's no fun being an overage adolescent. I know you've been married quite a few times; I sincerely hope this one works out for you."

"Thanks. You know, Joan, I've learned one thing the hard way—the grass is never really greener. Sometimes, I wonder why we ever got divorced. I've been married three times since, and none of those marriages were any better than what we had together. A little more mature perhaps, or maybe the better word is jaded, but I'm not even sure of that. It wouldn't have been so bad if you and I were sitting here today as a middle-aged couple, discussing Christmas plans with the grandkids."

Joan rubbed her finger across the gathering moisture in her eyes and said huskily, "So, why *did* we divorce, Jerry?"

The silence was becoming awkward by the time he broke it. "I think you loved me too much. You were so loyal and devoted, so accepting and unquestioning. I couldn't handle the emotion and *finality* of it all. I used to think that I couldn't handle the notion of *forever* then because of our youth, but I still can't. Whenever a woman's commitment to me becomes sincerely permanent, I panic and head for the exit. If that's immaturity, then I've never grown up. I also used to think that it must have been your religion—maybe it was the final nail in the forever coffin. You were so Catholic, and I was a pagan ..."

"Don't be silly, Jerry. You've never been a pagan. No one is. You can't grow up in this society without being a Christian of sorts. Christianity is in the air you breathe and the water you drink. It shapes our standards and laws. 'One nation under God' doesn't mean Allah. American morality isn't the good life according to Epictetus or Seneca either, Jerry. You walk around with a lot more Catholic guilt than you realize. Everyone does."

"You're right. This is bringing back some of our old debates. Maybe, rather than a pagan, I'm an anti-Christian, which makes me part of the fold in a way. My Platonism versus my hedonism was my own yin and yang."

"You used to claim you were an atheist. Do you still believe that?"

"Well, you've just convinced me that I am a monotheistic one. I guess I'm an ageing atheist, which means that I'm beginning to suffer from creeping agnosticism. It's becoming a rash on my soul—if I have one, of course!" Jerry laughed. "Joan, I've never told you how sorry I am about us. You deserved better. I feel like maybe I stole your life ... or at least a big part of it. I had no right."

"No one can steal another person's life, not unless they let them. Don't presume to have been that powerful or important. You didn't really know me well enough to steal anything of significance."

"I only meant to apologize, if belatedly. Please don't get me wrong. I don't want us to fight."

"Believe me, it's okay. Let me tell you something about myself. Before I came to Reno, I wanted to be a nun, but the thought of it scared me. I felt so unworthy. In fact, now I think I went to Nevada and got involved in the casino scene in order to sabotage my dream, to prove to myself that I really was just another unworthy sinner. Tim and our divorce actually turned out to be a good compromise. The shame of it all kept me from believing that I could actually profess religious vows, but my folks were a lot more understanding than I ever thought they'd be. Tim and I lived with them until he married.

"They're gone now, father died five years ago, and mother passed away last year. So now I live by myself in the family home. It's very nice and peaceful. It has a little chapel, my very own. I guess you could say that I'm a nun without a convent. And, of course, now I'm a saint, too. Ask any grandmother."

Jerry took her hands in his and pecked her on the cheek.

"So, why did we get divorced, Jerry?"

"My hunch is we just ran out of ways to hurt each other. How different our two lives have been! How very, very different!"

***

Jim stood in the Starlight buffet line behind a man accompanied by four kids. The offerings scarcely seemed scrumptious. "Having any luck?" Jim asked.

"Luck? Who plays? We come here to eat. They ain't got no mother; she's gone, who knows where. Cleared out and left me holdin' this bag." He gestured at his brood. "We eat in the clubs. The buffets are cheaper than cookin' at home, that's if I knew how. We used to come here for the $5.99 steak dinner. I'd order one and ask for two extra plates, but management wised up. They were nice 'nough about it, but we was asked to leave. In the buffet line, you pay by the plate. It's still a big bargain, and no hassles."

"So, you never gamble?"

"Are you kiddin' me? Of course not. I'm no sucker. I'm a maintenance man at the Cal Neva. I know what's goin' on. Their mom was a gambler, big time; look where that got us. Lies, fights ..."

Jim ate his salad, sprinkled with Lite Italian dressing, and contemplated the obese man at the next table diving into an overflowing plate that was a veritable sampler of the entire buffet. Half of a lit cigarette smoldered in his ashtray, and his fresh bottle of beer was flanked by two empties.

"You alone, too?" Fatso suddenly asked.

Jim was startled out of his reverie and felt a little embarrassed at having been caught staring. "Yes, yes I am," he mumbled.

"Join me if you'd like. You look like you hate eatin' by yourself. In fact, you look like you hate eatin' at all. Heh, heh."

Without quite understanding why, Jim moved his plate to the stranger's table. "Been here long?" was the best that he could muster as an innocuous icebreaker.

"Three days. I'm headin' home right after I finish this here dinner. San Jose."

"Had any luck?"

"The usual. I was up a thousand, but I gave it back. I always do. Heh heh."

"Come a lot?"

"About every two months. What are you, some kind of survey taker?"

"Sort of."

"Well, fire away. I like to answer surveys. Sometimes, I even tell the truth. Heh, heh."

"Are you sure?"

"Yeah."

"Alright. My first question is, do you know what you're doing to your health with all that food, tobacco, and alcohol?"

"Of course."

"Of course? Then why don't you stop?"

"Look, I like to eat; it makes me feel good. I like booze because it makes me feel good, too. Same with cigarettes and coffee, not to mention gambling and sex."

"But you're taking years off your life."

"Oh yeah? Well, you look like you're in pretty good shape. Eat right and work out a lot, I'll bet."

"Yes."

"Why?"

"I guess because it makes me feel good."

"I'm not so sure, Bud. You beat up your body in some gym and then starve it to feel good?"

"Well, not exactly. We're talking about two different things."

"Do you drink booze?"

"A little, very little."

"Screw?" Jim felt the instant warmth in his cheeks, flushed by growing discomfort.

"That's a complicated issue; a private matter, too."

"So, you do, but it makes you feel guilty, right? I think everythin' does, whether it's a piece of pie or a piece of ass! Me, I don't do guilt. You know why? Because we're all gonna die. Nobody gets off this planet alive, Buddy Boy, so you might as well enjoy. I'm goin' for dessert now. Can I bring you somethin'? Heh, heh."

***

Jerry contemplated his home from a different perspective as he ushered Sue and Sheba into their new abode. *Wow, this is stark by anyone's standards*, he thought. *Maybe even grim.*

The entire house was painted eggshell white and carpeted with tan shag. The living room had a sofa, flanked by a single easy chair and end table for his glasses and reading matter and illumined by the brushed-nickel, gooseneck floor lamp. All Scandinavian modern from Dania. Unquestionably a male universe, exacerbated by his minimalist tastes, even if for him, it was homey. Jerry disliked clutter of the frou-frou sort.

There was a single painting as the sole blemish on an otherwise blank expanse. Its three faces stared out of a background of swirls and confused colors. His first effort at portraiture was the product of a twice-weekly evening art class at Truckee Meadows Community College that had been part of Jerry's efforts to create a personal space that transcended both failure as a student of philosophy and success as a casino manager. *How perfectly hideous*, he mused as he studied the amateurish attempt to capture the subtleties in the visages of three of his former wives (Joan, Carrie, and Ann). The painting's privileged position on the house's most prominent wall was due entirely to its relationship with its owner. He resolved to destroy it before having to explain it to his new housemates.

This place obviously needs a lot of help … but not from me. Jerry resolved to invite Sue to Susanify the place. He suspected that her first move would be to hang the print of Georgia O'Keefe's *Sky Above Clouds* that she'd purchased for her living room while in Santa Fe on her sole vacation with Sheba. Jerry'd liked it at first sight.

He set down his suitcase in the front hall and went to the refrigerator for some ice. He mixed Sue's drink and poured himself a tonic water. Sheba had already disappeared into the room he'd assigned her, impatient to begin her poster-hanging.

"Home sweet home," he said, clinking his glass against Sue's.

She opened a window to allow the stuffiness of a dwelling vacated in Reno's summer to escape. "Maybe for you. It'll take us a little while to adjust. This is only my second time here, the first in daylight. Oh, I do love your backyard! I didn't know you had a green thumb."

Jerry laughed. "I don't. I have Javier Martinez from Zacatecas. He claims he's got a green card, but he can never find it. My next career better not be in the president's cabinet. I may not make it through the congressional hearing! We've got a lot to talk about, Sue, but let's wait until tomorrow morning. This is the last day of our honeymoon. Let's observe the ground rule until midnight."

Jerry was referring to their mutual agreement not to belabor the mundane details of their future while on the trip. Jerry sat on his chair and reached for the telephone to dial in his voice mail code.

"Fourteen messages. Not really very many if you consider how long we've been gone. When I was a GM, I'd get three times that many in a day. Usually fires to pee on."

He listened to the first eight and erased them without comment. Then a big grin spread across his face as he concentrated intently upon a lengthy spiel. Putting the receiver in his lap, Jerry exclaimed, "My, oh my! It's Jim Fitzsimmons. He says he wants to talk to me about a job—not GM, rather director of external relations. He thinks we could be a good team. He's even talked his old man into it. I would love to have been a fly on the wall during that conversation! It must have taken some sales job. Anyway, I want you to listen to the end of his message—it's a crackup." Jerry pushed the button that restarted the taped communication, waited until the right moment, and then passed her the receiver. "There's one more thing, Jerry. If we do this, I'm asking you for a favor—no, it's a condition. You have to stop calling me Junior. My name is James. I don't even mind Jim, but not Jimmy. If you want to discuss the job, I'd be willing to meet with you anywhere, even at your place."

Jerry pushed the button to start the tenth message and then handed Sue the phone again. "It's for you."

After a couple of minutes, her faced turned ashen.

"Bad news, Sue? What's wrong?"

She held up her hand to silence him while she concentrated on the mechanical communication and then replayed it to verify its date. "It's Red. He called two weeks ago. He says that he's signing the papers and sending them here. Have you checked the mail yet?"

"There's nothing for you. Maybe they went to your old address."

"No. I gave Eleanor this address and phone."

Jerry took Sue's hand and led her into his home office. She sat in the sole chair in front of his desk and he behind it; they faced one another across the divide that seemed designed to shield Jerry from any interloper. She was struck by the austerity—a row of bookshelves lining the entire wall from floor to ceiling behind his desk. Its surface was bare save for a single paperback with a prominent bookmark—Rousseau's *Social Contract* and two three-by-five cards.

Jerry was an inveterate collector. As a boy it had been stamps and coins; now it was women and words. Whenever he encountered a new word, he wrote it on a card to be looked up later in *The New Oxford Dictionary of English*. Before the trip, there had been two finds while surfing the Internet. The first was billed as the longest non-technical word in the English language, irresistible to Jerry. He now fiddled with that card and exclaimed "Wow!" He turned his back and fingered through the dictionary that defined floccinaucinihilipilification as "the action or habit of estimating something as worthless." This he scribbled on the card, and then, as was his custom, added his own take in parenthesis ("trashing"). *Oxford* provided him an entry for gallimaufry as well—"a confused medley or jumble of things" that he now inscribed on the second card, adding ("cluster fuck"). Sue watched him insert his new treasures alphabetically into a card file and then waved at his myriad of books.

"Have you actually read all of them?"

"Not all. The majority, I suppose. It was such a long time ago. I still carry them around with me—they're old friends. They keep me from being lonely."

"I've never seen so many books outside of a public library or bookstore. I'll bet I haven't read as many in my whole life as you have on one shelf. My library is mainly stacks of *National Geographic*."

"I refuse to subscribe to it as a matter of principle. There are piles of old issues, mostly unread, in millions of living rooms throughout the world. They supposedly project sophistication when, in reality, they are more about deforestation. No one's well-read, Sue. If you read every hour of every day of your life, you would barely scratch the surface of what's been written." He reached behind him and extracted a soldier out of the ranks of sentinels lining the shelf. "Stendhal's *The Charterhouse of Parma*—great literature and great political science. I could never sleep after reading a book like this; it gave me a high that sometimes lasted for days. It transported me to nineteenth-century Europe. But then there was the downer—I would compare myself to Stendhal, or whomever, and feel so inadequate. It made me very ambivalent about my studies. Still, I clung to the dream of one day producing a little piece of knowledge—an article, a poem, a short story, maybe even a book. Writing a book is the most egotistical of possible acts."

"Why egotistical?"

"Think about the arrogance of presuming that you have something to say to other people that's so important it deserves to be written down for those yet to be born. Nevertheless, I kept reading in the hope their brilliance would rub off on me and lead to writing. But that became its own dilemma. Once I walked through Stendhal's front door, I had to explore all his rooms. That opened up the labyrinth of French literature, which led to the European canon and eventually Russia. I spent two whole years reading nothing but Tolstoy and Dostoevsky. Then there was the other side of *Charterhouse*—it's political philosophy. That opens onto Hobbes, Locke, Montesquieu, De Tocqueville, and The Federalist Papers ... not to mention Plato."

Jerry waved broadly at his book collection. "I used to read obsessively to expand my awareness, and maybe even to find my soul in order to save it. I suppose I had to stop in order to preserve my sanity. I guess you might say I'm an addictive personality—booze, grass, tobacco, broads, cars, books. But I managed to give them all up. Several times, in fact!" Jerry glanced at his volume of Mark Twain's famous sayings and chuckled at their periphrastic private joke.

"When I was in AA there was this other addict, I can't remember the guy's name. One day after our meeting he invited me to his place for a cup of coffee. He had an unopened bottle of wine right in the middle of his kitchen table. I asked him what that was about, and he explained, 'Oh, that's my crutch. I can't resist liquor in the abstract; it's all I think about if my mind wanders. It's way easier for me to look at that bottle and resist opening it.'"

Sue was perplexed. "But why still surround yourself with the books? It seems creepy. It reminds me of the relics in Catholic churches. I could never get used to the idea of the priest performing the miracle of the Eucharist over a sliver of bone from a dead saint."

Jerry replaced *Charterhouse* in its slot and removed the fattest book in his collection. It was the complete works of Shakespeare. "I have never read a single Shakespeare poem or play. It is my intention to one day read this book from cover to cover. I'm saving it for my old age. It's my amulet against death, since no serious reader can die without having read *the* bard. It's my bottle of wine that I'll open when abstinence no longer matters."

"Why are you telling me all of this?"

"Sue, I want you to understand me, the real me, so you can be careful."

"I think I know you by now, Jerry."

"What you know is from airplane and pillow talk, mostly, snippets and sound bites. Mine are usually delivered with humorous sarcasm. I kid you about you and me about me, and the joking is my way of avoiding intimacy. It protects me against emotion; I don't do emotion well. In fact, I probably should have put what I'm about to say in a letter instead. I'm much better at writing than talking face to face. But here goes."

"Okay, Jerry."

"Sue, I'm a perfectionist and that has consequences. I guess it means that I can never live up to my own expectations of myself. No human is perfect. In my own mind, I was always half the person that other people made me out to be. I was pretty good at sports as a kid, but I never followed through. A three-hundred batting average and a forty percent shots-made percentage are regarded as good, but both mean that you fail about two-thirds of the time. That was unacceptable to me, so I always quit the team after proving to myself that I could make it. I learned to play the guitar, and my friends thought I was great. I hated hearing them say that. I noticed all the little flaws—the missed notes and broken tempos. So, I quit the guitar. It was the same with college. I always got A's, but *I* knew my ignorance—my limitations.

"Sue, I've had four marriages, all of them failures. Some of my friends think I'm a real Don Juan. Well, they don't see through my phony bravado. I know better because I'm the scared little boy inside the hotshot swordsman. I think I love you, Sue, but I'm not sure that I know what love is or if I've ever been in it. I've come to believe that you gals want to be loved and we guys want to get laid. I can never seem to get beyond the physical. Remember that book, *A Love Story?*"

"Yes. I liked it."

"Well, I didn't read the book, but I went to the movie. People all around me, grown men, were crying their eyes out and I was just embarrassed. Not by the audience, by the film. I went straight to a bar and drank several scotches by myself. They didn't help. I couldn't shake the misgiving that I was incapable of empathy, let alone love. If I had the only dry eye in the theater, it spoke volumes about Jeremy Clinton. I tried my hardest to cry, but just couldn't. It was like being constipated and trying to force your body to have a bowel movement. I'm emotionally constipated and trying to do something about it seems to just produce emotional hemorrhoids.

"I guess I'm warning you about me, Sue. I'd like to think I'm a little wiser now, and therefore not quite as self-judgmental. That came neither quickly nor easily. But the old Jerry resides deep within the real me, and we two are quite capable of hurting you. Beware of the Jabberwock and Minotaur. Protect yourself, Sue. Think hard before you make any irreversible changes in your life to accommodate me. We're glommed onto one another now, but I don't know if we will be next year, let alone five years from now."

"Jerry, I love you. I *do* know what love is and my eyes are open, wide open. I understand the risk, and I choose to take it. It's hard for me to imagine, but I suppose you could hurt me. I don't believe it would ever be deliberate. You know what? Even then, I wouldn't have regrets. I've never been happier than I am now. I want to be with you *forever.*"

Jerry grimaced slightly at her emphasis of the dreaded f- word. He then hid his discomfort by asking, "My ever or yours, Sue?"

"I'm not sure what you mean ..."

"I'm talking about our ages. I could just about be your father. I may be dead when you're my age. If not, I'll be a doddering old fart with both feet planted firmly on life's banana peel."

"Why do you have to say things like that? Whenever I try to really reach out to you, there's always some kind of wisecrack. Of course, I understand the difference in our ages and that I'll probably be alone again. But why can't we just enjoy the moment—the time we have together *now*? Let's take one day at a time. Let me be a joyful bride for a little while before I'm the grieving widow."

***

The following day, Jerry and Sue nursed their morning coffee. "Have you looked at that course catalogue we picked up before the trip, Sue? Classes begin in a couple of days."

"I'm not too sure about college. Red said he'd sign the papers and send them right away. They're not here yet, and I'm afraid to nag him. I don't know the guy anymore; he might get a funny idea about holding us up or something. Maybe I should get a job for a while. Carol tells me they need cocktail waitresses really bad at the Starlight. They'd take me back in a heartbeat, particularly now that they're not mad at you. I've got to run, Babe. It's Carol's day off and we're meeting at the YWCA to have a sauna. We've got to buy some school clothes for the girls, too."

Later, as she and Carol sat alone together in the semi-dark cubicle, Sue lazily ladled a wooden scoop full of water over the glowing rocks, creating a billow of steam. They braced themselves against its first searing lick across their naked bodies, then felt the perspiration rush to neutralize the sudden blast.

"So, are you coming back to the Starlight?" Carol asked. "How was your trip? I'll bet you could pick his dong out of a crowd of pricks. Did you ever get out of the hotel room?"

"Carol, I'm going to marry the guy!"

"Marry Jerry? What on earth for? He's a swordsman, not a husband. Testosterone dissolves male brain cells. He's poked every pussy at the Starlight, including mine. Well, maybe not Priscilla's. There's a limit to any guy's guts, and Jerry's no green beret! Fuck his brains out and work him on the side for a little spending money. He's a generous guy. He once gave me two hun—"

"Carol! Please! I don't want to hear about it. I'm going to marry him. Get used to it."

"Honey, I'm just tryin' to look out for you. Jerry's a seven-time loser."

"Four." Sue threw another scoop of water on the glowing rocks in the vain hope that it would change the subject.

Instead, she evoked Carol's brazened reply. "Alright, four marriages and maybe forty affairs and four thousand one-nighters. Jerry'd screw a rockpile if he thought there was a snake in it. If you want to sleep your way to the top, pick someone with real bucks and a guilty conscience. Take Jim Fitzsimmons, for instance. All you've got to do is take one look at that prissy wife of his and you know the guy's vulnerable. Adopt that orphan and you're either going to get a lot of hush money or a puppy dog that'll leave that bitch in a heartbeat to build you a pedestal. Either way, you win—that's what I call real pussy power!"

"You just don't understand, Carol. You know, you raise cynicism to a new level!"

"Look, Honey, I'm worried for you and Sheba. Seriously. You're ripping up both of your lives, and for what? Jerry? He's probably already asked you for a pre-nuptial agreement. If not, in six months, you're going to be sitting across the table from some junkyard-dog attorney whose telling you all the terrible things that'll happen if you don't stop hasslin' his client. Remember Mary? She bought into one of these hopeless marriages, and now she works the line at Mustang. She even had to send her little boy to live with his grandparents."

Sue tried to protest, but Carol pressed her assault. "Sheba's a real sensitive kid. What's going happen to her if she starts to trust Jerry and then the wheels come off? At her age, the next couple of years are really critical—particularly the boy-girl jazz. Think about it, Sue."

"I have, and I've made up my mind. In fact, it wasn't even that hard. Nobody knows Jerry the way I do."

"Honey, I sure hope you're right—for everyone's sake. Me, I prefer to look out for number one. If you expect nothin' from no one, you'll never be disappointed. I'm for a good time, but without emotions. I'm plum out of emotions. I learned to be a ravishing blonde rather than a raging bitch. No one hangs ornaments on a dried-up Christmas tree. Smile with your mouth and speak with your pussy. I'll bet I've fallen for every bullshit line that men can make up. I thought I'd seen every type of kinky male gig ... at least until I met Manny. The guy's a riot, a real weirdo."

"Who's Manny?"

"Manny Cohen. Our new marketing director from 'Joisey.' He's my latest rent-a-cock. The first time we're gettin' it on, the guy starts blowin' a kazoo. An honest to God kazoo! Then he's tellin' me this joke. I kid you not. I can't figure out what's goin' on. I mean, it's our first lay, and I don't know whether to moan or laugh—and it's gettin' harder to follow his story. He's like, 'Then the lawy—oh—the lawyer said—ahh.' He can barely get off the punch line. So, we're lyin' there restin' up, and Manny sez, 'So, how was it?' I sez, 'It was okay, Honey!' And he sez, 'Only okay?! Hell, Carol, that's my best joke!' I like the little putz. Manny and me, we speak the same language."

***

Jim found the bookcases in Jerry's home office and their contents to be incongruous. The somewhat incondite floor-to-ceiling rich cherry-wood shelving, constructed by Jerry, housed hundreds, if not thousands, of maybe $1.95 paperback editions—their pages with corners folded, margins annotated, paper yellowed, bindings cracked. He fingered several while pondering how different this was from "his" library in Dorothy's house—its one professionally-built mahogany wall displaying leather-backed volumes purchased by the yard and never opened. Once monthly, Dorothy always changed the single elegant volume on display on a hexagonal reading stand, a ploy to inform both the periodic guest and the cleaning lady that the Fitzsimmons household was no intellectual laggard. Whatever else it might be, Jerry's library was scarcely *décor*.

"My father is no longer the boss. I'm the new CEO. Jerry, we have to expand outside this market, and I want to delegate that to you. We don't have any money, but we do have something even harder to find; we have experience in gaming and some talented people. I have to stay on top of things here in Reno. That makes it all the more important that we hire a strong director of external relations. You're my first choice. I've always felt that we worked well together. You know the Starlight inside and out, our strengths and weaknesses. You can hit the ground running. We can't afford to waste time."

"Jim, I see you understand the need to delegate, but before you can delegate, you have to have a real team, which you don't."

"I thought you liked the department heads. You recruited most of them."

"They were second-raters, Jim, veterans of Reno's second-tier properties. Even in the best of times, the Starlight wasn't going to attract the best and brightest. You still don't get it, do you, Jim? I guess you haven't been close enough to the place on a daily basis. Maybe, there's a part of you that resists getting it. Think about how the Starlight's always been run—your old man called all the shots. There's not a department head he didn't humiliate, including me regularly.

"He's got his moles in every nook and cranny. He thinks they adore him, and in a way, they do, because they know his door is always open. He not only remembers the name of Molly the waitress, he asks about her two kids as well. Maybe he lent her a hundred and a handkerchief when she cried about not being able to afford a cub scout uniform for her little boy. Maybe he waved her off when she tried to pay him back. Six months go by, and Molly's supervisor terminates her for cause, so she's in the executive office in tears, telling James her version. Ten minutes later, the supervisor has been told to rehire her—end of the story. But not really, because, every time Molly pours your dad's cup of coffee, she tells him the latest rumor or the employees' bitch of the day. He takes it all as gospel—privileged insider information.

"So, Jim, there's no team; there's a bunch of department heads who expend their quality time and energy on covering their asses. Most understand that survival means learning to kiss up and kick down. Agree with anything the potentate says and shove his mandate down the employees' throats. You think the Starlight is braindead because of James's age, and it is, but it's also got a severe case of arteriosclerosis. You have to build a new team, your own team. I'm not sure you have much to work with in the old one. Each of them is too accustomed to looking out for Number One rather than taking risks for the Starlight."

"I know I need my own team, Jerry. You're my first recruit."

"How do you feel about your new responsibility?"

"Excited, but overwhelmed. You've been in the trenches and worked your way from dealer to GM. Can you give me some advice?"

Jerry closed his eyes as if trying to read the jottings of life's wisdom on the inside of the lids. "The main thing that I've learned is that to be a good manager, you first have to be a student of management. For me, the two greatest thinkers on the subject were Machiavelli and Sun Tzu."

"I've heard of the Italian, but who was Sun Who?"

"Sun Tzu wrote a very brief but insightful treatise on how to manage conflict. He didn't call it a skill; rather, the title of his little book is *The Art of War*." Jerry reached behind himself, took a slender volume from its shelf, and handed it to Jim.

"I'm not sure what you're getting at, Jerry. Could you give me an example?"

"Sure, take your dealings with your superior—maybe it's a person or, in your case, a board. It doesn't matter; it's the same. You want maximum support with a minimum of interference. But, if you think about that, there's an inherent contradiction. You want your supervisor's attention and involvement, tempered by minimal intervention. And your supervisor is similarly conflicted. There's the temptation to micromanage every detail, but carried to its logical conclusion, that would make you totally irrelevant and dispensable. It's also impractical, because there are only so many hours in the day. Your superiors, your board members, each have other obligations to attend to. You are not their only responsibility. So, they have to trust your representations and recommendations, but that always entails calculated risk. They want to succeed, but a part of their capacity to do so is now in your hands. They fear failure, and you've become the possible instrument of it.

"The key, or maybe it's the trick, to handling your relationship with your supervisor is to handle autonomy in a non-threatening way. The more you minimize the need for him to direct your operation, and the more you convince him of your commitment to furthering his agenda, the greater your autonomy and room to maneuver. But, of course, there is Machiavelli's caveat. He believed that the wise prince does not surround himself with sycophants. The wise leader should welcome constructive dissent. No one person has all the answers. The willingness to listen is the effective manager's antidote to egotistical myopia.

"When it comes to managing your inferiors, you can reverse everything I've just said. As supervisor, you need to cultivate competent team players and then delegate. The trickiest part for you is to understand the dynamic among them. They need to work together for the organization to work, yet they're competitors for your attention and approval. That evaluation translates into raises and promotions. So, no matter how much you try to convince your department heads that the hotel and food and beverage are apples and oranges as a way of assuring them they'll receive a fair individual evaluation, they still find it hard to believe they're not competing with each other for scarce merit pay."

"That's certainly food for thought, Jerry, but it still seems a little too abstract to me."

"Let me give you a concrete example. Your games manager's prime responsibility is to maximize play. The more rooms he has in reserve to comp high rollers, the easier his job. The hotel manager's prime responsibility is occupancy and room revenues, meaning paying guests. So the two managers' vested interests are at cross purposes. It's up to the wise supervisor to convince the hotel manager that it's okay to hold back twenty to thirty rooms for high rollers when the casino manager is holding a special event. But, take two weeks ago, for example—Hot August Nights. Every room for miles around was reserved, so we could charge our highest rates of the year. And those guests are not here to gamble. They came to ride around in their old cars and gawk at one another, buy a few parts, and listen to fifties music in the evenings. They're lousy casino custom. So that particular week the hotel manager should have rented every room at the highest possible rate, with the casino manager's initiatives pretty much put on hold."

"Hmmm. I think I'm getting your point. Will you come back to work at the Starlight?"

Jerry thought about playing coy by saying that he needed time to think it over and consult with Sue. But the fact of the matter was that she would go along with anything he decided. "I'll start tomorrow."

***

Sue entered Jerry's home office carrying two steaming coffee cups. "So, Mrs. Mallard, what brings you here? *Avanti.*"

"Jerry, I've been thinking. Maybe I will go up to the college tomorrow."

"That's great. What's in the bag?"

She showed him the three blouses and two pairs of slacks.

"How come they don't have tags? And that one pair of slacks seems a little bit … uh … a little bit used. The knees are threadbare."

"They're all used. Carol and I shop at the thrift-store."

Jerry was stunned. "The thrift-store? People actually shop at the thrift-store? You do!?!"

"Of course, Jerry, half of my clothes are from there. It's not so bad.

Actually, you'd be amazed at some of the nice things. I plan to shorten those legs and hem them above the knees—a like-new pair of shorts. How do you think we single mothers get by? Shopping at Macy's? You big-shot management people have so little idea of the real world!"

"Oh, we do, huh? And how about the rank and file? How much do you know? How good is your information? Isn't most of it just rumor? It's really easy to oversimplify complicated matters and then take cheap shots at management for making the tough calls."

"Right, Jerry. I suppose now you're going to defend the Starlight's wage scale, the industry's wage scale. You pay us close to minimum wage and expect us to make our living by hustling tips. If two of us get together to complain, it's a union plot and one of us is likely to get canned. It doesn't seem fair!" She sniffed, the edges of her mouth no longer at attention, albeit not quite at ease.

"You're right, Sue. There's nothing fair about competition. Mom and Pop are in trouble everywhere in this economy. What little hardware store can compete with Home Depot? How many of those neighborhood grocery stores that were everywhere when I was a kid are still around? It's questionable whether even a Barnes and Noble can survive against Amazon. Starlight versus the Golden Spur is just one more example of the same David and Goliath story. Except that David is now armed with a slingshot in the nuclear age!"

She sat on the arm of his chair and ran her fingers through his hair. "I shouldn't have turned my employee frustration into a personal attack on my lover. Looks like we've just had our first fight." She laughed.

"Not much of one. I don't think it requires an apology from either of us. Both points of view have some merit."

As she was leaving the room, she heard his voice: "By the way, I'm taking Sheba to Macy's this afternoon."

***

Priscilla seemed angry for no particular reason. She'd been short with Jerry and had just dismissed a caller without her usual feigned courtesy. She must have known about his outrageous comments that had led to his termination; sooner or later, Priscilla knew every inside scoop at the Starlight. Maybe she was wary that he was back to cause some kind of trouble.

The door to the outer office opened and a middle-aged woman entered briskly. "Priscilla, I want you to inform the department heads that I'm calling a general meeting in the conference room tomorrow afternoon at three sharp. No excuses. Tell Mr. Fitzsimmons that I've hired Samantha Edgars as our new controller. She's head and shoulders above that bean counter from Elko. The industry passed that guy by sometime during the Ice Age."

"Yes, Ms. Adams."

Mary Beth Adams was in and out like a desert dust devil. She hadn't even noticed Jerry.

"Who dat?" he asked.

"Our new GM," Priscilla huffed. "She's come to us from Atlantic City."

Priscilla's buzzer rang and she nodded while listening to her boss before informing Jerry, "Benedict Arnold will see you now," she said.

"Who?"

"Mr. Fitzsimmons."

Jerry entered the executive office and was slightly discombobulated to see Jim Fitzsimmons seated behind James Fitzsimmons's desk. It seemed almost sacrilegious for a mere mortal to sit on the celestial throne!

"Good morning, Jun ... uh Jim. Where's your father? I thought we were having a meeting."

Jerry was struck by the changed decor. Several potted plants gave the office a softer feel, and Jim sat beneath a family portrait of his wife and children, where formerly there hung a photo of Messieurs Fitzsimmons, Senior and Junior. Another wall was a virtual gallery of pictures of Jim with trophy fish. A pedestal to Jim's right displayed the silver cup that was his trophy for winning the 1985 San Francisco Olympic Club's annual squash championship.

"We are, Jerry, you and I."

"But—"

"I told you that I'm the new CEO. I'm hiring you as our director of external relations because Mary Beth is brand new and just learning the ropes. Jerry, America's on a gaming binge. Every politician who's afraid to tax his constituents sees gaming as a free lunch. Vote it in and tell the voters that it's harmless, only good clean adult recreation, but just in case, assure them that you can control it. Wrap it up in more regulations than lights on a Christmas tree, stick it on some boat, and make it sail out of sight before the games begin. Above all, assure the locals that it's a boost for tourism—another of the politicians' sacred cows. No one gets hurt, except for maybe a few degenerate out-of-towners. So, let's put on our masks, pull out our guns, and get ready to shake down those suckers.

"It works until the local family-owned restaurants start turning out their lights because the casinos give away their food. It works until the movie theaters and bowling alleys shut down. It works until the local racetrack closes and the state's tax receipts from the lottery nosedive. It works until everyone's got an old Aunt Sadie hooked on video poker machines. Binges and hangovers go hand in hand, Jerry, and this country's headed for a monumental headache."

"If you believe that, Jim, why do you bother? I mean, how can you justify expansion and still feel good about yourself?"

"That's a fair question without an obvious answer. Maybe it takes many sort-of-okay answers that add up, none of which would be convincing by itself. Take the activity, for instance. Do I think gaming's wonderful? No. I understand why some people call Las Vegas 'Lost Wages.' Every night when I leave here, a piece of me feels like a tavern owner stepping over the drunk passed out in his doorway. Can I defend the Starlight? Yes. I can defend it with the argument that it's human nature to gamble.

"Let me tell you about my earliest lesson about that. James was driving me to the seminary I planned to attend in Fresno, and we stopped in a diner. I was berating him about his business, pontificating on the evils of gambling. He listened politely and then said, 'Jimmy, watch those two guys at the end of the counter.' There was this gumball dispenser and one says to the other, 'I'll bet you twenty at five-to-one that the next ball is red.' And sure enough, it was red, so a hundred exchanged hands. James says to me, 'Remember that well, Son, people will always gamble, and they don't need to come to Nevada to do it. They've invented a thousand ways to bet since the beginning of time. No church or government has ever been able to stop them. It's human nature to take chances, particularly when it comes to the possibility of gettin' something for nothing, or a lot for a little.' So, whether we're talking about Paiutes betting with bones or the biggest casino in the world, otherwise known as Wall Street, people are going to bet. In fact, maybe we're the only honest business there is."

"What!"

"I mean that we're totally honest with our players. They all know about house odds and try to beat them. Most people think they're special, exceptions to the odds. Fearing the odds is for losers, schmucks. Ask God. Most of us sinners think we can get away with it and still repent just in time for redemption. Our naive players believe in luck, the stupid ones think they have sufficient gambling moxie to beat the house. But at least both have an outside *chance*.

"Compare that to the bullshit messages and games of, say, banks, insurance companies, and stockbrokers. In the stock market, the lemmings and the lambs rush to slaughter, blinded by their greed and convinced they're making shrewd choices based on study and expert advice. They think they're playing on a level field, when all they are is cannon fodder for the real insiders. I'd sooner put my money on the line in a back-alley dice game than pay some guy a commission to throw me to the Wall Street wolves.

"Everyone knows that in a casino, the odds favor the house, but not by too much. Competition sees to that. We've got maybe twenty-five joints in this town offering the same product. There are more than three hundred in the state. The player has protection, too. He knows that he won't be cheated. No operator in his right mind is going to risk his license to fleece a sucker or two. That would be more than greedy; it would be plain stupid. So, the player can count on a fair shake here. If you're going to gamble, it's smart to come to Nevada."

"Doesn't our product—gaming—bother you just a little bit? No one really needs it."

"Hell no, Jerry, not at all. Is our product any worse than that of the guys making cigarettes or soda pop? Buy a soft drink or a beer, and you get two cents' worth of liquid in a five-cent container, and after the twenty-five cents for advertising, you pay a buck or more. Five minutes later, you're burping up a bunch of dubious chemicals. Did you *need* that?"

"But why expand elsewhere?"

"A little bit of greed and a whole lot of fear. It's called survival. We've got nearly a thousand people working here, and most of them have families. That means there are thousands of people depending on the Starlight, and frankly, it's a falling star. We're in free fall. We haven't hit bottom; we're not even sure if there is a bottom—we might just flame out looking for it.

"While I feel responsible for *all* our employees and their families, I'm even more concerned about my own. It's just my lousy luck to have three kids in private schools—sixty-thou a semester. Dot doesn't have a clue. She just humors me when I try to talk finances. She's never earned a dime, let alone saved a nickel. But her reality check is coming big time. If something good doesn't happen soon, I'm going to have to put the house on the market—her house."

Jim gestured towards the family portrait on the wall behind him. "And then there's the kids. They don't want to believe money grows on trees because it'd be too much work to have to climb up to get it! Not one of them has a real plan—a goal. JFK has been in college for six years now. Don't ask me when he'll graduate. I doubt if even he knows. He's working on his third major at his fourth school—the San Francisco Academy of Art. He wants to be a sculptor. When you've only got one son, you think, well, just maybe … What the hell am I going to do with a sculptor?

"Last year, when things started heading south and we couldn't give out the usual dividend, Dad helped me out financially. I doubt I can count on that again. For the first time in my life I feel like a real man, like I'm standing on my own two feet. Well, I'm also standing alone and it's damn lonely, not to mention scary. I'm a little locomotive pulling a great big train. Everybody assumes that I can get us where we need to go … everybody except me."

Jim Fitzsimmons paused as if to invite comment, but Jerry couldn't think of anything to say, so the new CEO changed the subject. "As you can see, Jerry, there've been some big changes around here while you were away; I'm only one of them."

"So, tell me about the job, Jim. What am I supposed to do?"

"We've got a feeler from an Indian tribe in Washington. They're in gaming with bingo, but they need some professional advice because another tribe is about to give them some stiff competition. I need you to check it out and maybe negotiate a consulting agreement. We also have a chance to participate in a riverboat project in Louisiana. Someone has to follow up on that, too; we're inundated with queries."

Jim picked up some papers and began to sort them, one by one, into a little pile. "This one is for a half-interest in the Mongolian lottery if we'll put up the three million for the equipment. Here's another for management of a casino at Subic Bay in the Philippines—no capital required. This one's a sales pitch for a hole-in-the-wall property in Deadwood, South Dakota. A very crowded market; too much competition. Here's one for a management contract for the gaming on a cruise ship in the Caribbean. Ouch! Here's an option on a California card room—subject, of course, to a necessary change in the present law which keeps Nevada operators out of the state. Venezuela. Natal. Be a gamer and see the world!"

Jim had barely scratched the surface of the unruly stack of letters, faxes, and bound proposals. "You get the gist, Jerry. I can't deal with all of this. Hell, I can't get to any of it and keep my eye on this place. Somewhere in all of this horseshit, there might be a pony. I want you to try to find it.

"And that's not all. I need our director of external relations to represent us in the industry and civic associations, with the press, with the city council. Dad hated lobbying and public relations. He thought they were so insignificant that he assigned them to me. I happen to believe they're important, particularly now. There's a power struggle going on, Jerry; the whole future of the town—particularly the downtown—is riding on the outcome. We need to have eyes and ears in the public process. In fact, we need to have a tongue. If we don't, our destiny is going to be determined for us and we can just read about it in tomorrow's newspaper."

"Does the DER get to wear a blue suit and a red cape, Jim? You're asking for a lot. Would I have support staff?"

"Jerry, I'm asking you to take on the job without an answer to your question. Neither of us really knows what it entails. You can use Priscilla for now, and we can review the staff issue as things evolve. We let twenty employees go last month and thirty the month before. It would send the wrong signal to turn around and hire new staff so soon. What I can offer you is a hundred and eighty thou a year. After what happened, I can't expect you to come back for less money, or even the same salary. I know we'll work well together, Jerry. Maybe we can lick these problems. Here, let me help you."

Jim looked around for an ample container in which to place the pending proposals. Finding none, he took a framed photograph of himself holding a bonefish off the wall and used it as the backing on which to make an unruly pile.

"Not very elegant, but you don't have far to go. I've already told Priscilla to give you the first office on the left down the hall. Ask her for whatever else you might need."

Jerry paused in front of Priscilla's desk and tried to gather his thoughts. "I want you to order me two business cards. One should say 'Director of External Relations' and have our usual address and telephone numbers. The other should say 'Starlight Consulting Group.' I need a separate phone and fax line for that. Put voicemail on the phone line. I don't want calls delayed, misdirected, or lost through our regular PBX system. It seems like we've got a new trainee down there every week.

"I'll need a computer, too. I'm not real computer-literate or -dependent, so it can be a hand-me-down. I'll use it for email primarily. Check with marketing to see if we've got anyone who knows about setting up webpages. The Starlight Consulting Group needs its own webpage." He paused to ponder other requests, but then became aware of the weight of his awkward bundle. "We'll talk again tomorrow, after I've seen the layout." He turned to leave.

The door to Jim Fitzsimmons's former office opened and James appeared. "Oh hello, Jerry. Priscilla, what about my broker? Did he confirm that treasuries buy?"

Jerry was struck by the former chairman's appearance. He'd aged visibly during the past month; his face now sallowed. He even seemed to walk with a slight limp as he approached Jerry with his hand extended.

"It's good to see you again, Jerry. Oh, arms full, huh? Jimmy says you may be coming back to work for us. I noticed you were in his office. I guess you know about our little exercise in democracy. It never occurred to me that you count votes; I thought you weighed them. Har, har."

"I took the job, Sir. I look forward to working with everyone. I'll have some questions for you."

"Questions? Oh, questions. Sure, Jerry ... well maybe. Let's see how it goes. Jimmy tells me you're getting married again. You'll need a stone from Bob's. He gives out a thirty-day warranty. If she doesn't like your choice, he might exchange the ring for another of equal value, but he won't take it back. If you break up with her over the ring, he guarantees he'll find you another fiancée within thirty days. Har, har."

***

Now alone, Jim Fitzsimmons tapped a ballpoint pen on his desktop. "Thank God for that. One down and who knows how many more to go."

Having Jerry back in the fold was more than just a good hire, it represented a little piece of stability and a link, albeit tenuous, with former better times. Yet Jim also felt an instantaneous flash of seller's remorse over the preposterous salary. He knew that, in hiring Jerry, he was taking the first really desperate gamble of his life. Realistically, there was too little time to land a new venture, yet without some sort of coup with which to convince the bankers to extend their credit, the Starlight was finished. Jim sought slight consolation in the fact that the proffered salary was actually fifteen thousand a month rather than a hundred and eighty a year. Given the Starlight's present circumstances, a year was more of an eternity than a mere 365 rotations of the planet.

Jim did his own half-rotation in his swivel chair, and his gaze fell on the family portrait that manifested the Starlight's leadership transition. He scarcely recognized the seated central figure—the photo was only four years old, yet this apparition of his former self sported dark hair and an air of easy assurance. What a contrast to the prematurely gray new CEO with the drawn mouth and perpetual harried look in his eye. Unchanged, the stately woman standing next to him, with a hand on his shoulder, was the same person with whom he'd shared this morning's breakfast. Ivy and Heather, high school juniors in the portrait, were now young women—sophomores at St. Mary's of Notre Dame and Bryn Mawr College, respectively. Both were officers in their sororities and poured far more energy into their Hellenic obligations than their studies. Neither had settled upon a major yet. Indeed, their college careers seemed more about matrimonial than vocational aspiration.

James Fitzsimmons Kennedy III completed the contingent. The eldest of the Fitzsimmons offspring was, at the time of the photo, a junior at Loyola Marymount, majoring in business. But then there was the transformation, JFK's spiritual journey into artistic *Purgatorio*. He'd won some entity's "most promising artist of the year" award with a jumble of junk—a multimedia monstrosity of flattened tin cans speckled with superglued broken glass shards dangling by tiny gold chains from a car bumper of considerable vintage. JFK called the piece *Paradiso*, a name blazoned across the bumper with tampons and condoms. The overall impression was of a grotesque and enormous wind chime. After that dubious achievement, JFK transferred schools to the San Francisco Academy of Art. Jim suspected that his son was more indolent than inspired.

Just the typical American family—husband, wife, three children … and five therapists. He recalled Dot's reaction to the suggestion that they economize by using one psychologist for the twins. She'd opined, "Don't be ridiculous, Jim. Twins are in perpetual litigation; you can't expect them to use the same lawyer!"

An ironic smile flitted along Jim's lips and played with the corners of his mouth as he contemplated his son's staid appearance. The blue-suited costume and crewcut of the counterfeit business major were just too much, given subsequent developments. Jim's thoughts turned to the night about a year ago when, watching the late news while lying in bed next to his sleeping wife, he saw a report on a gay demonstration in San Francisco.

His casual attention had suddenly peaked when the image of a male couple exchanging a passionate kiss dissolved into two sassy young men mugging for the camera. JFK, stripped to the waist with his long hair bound into a ponytail, stuck out his tongue and then wiggled it obscenely, reminiscent of Joel Grey's performance in *Cabaret*. The scarlet letters tatooed on his chest proclaiming "Gay Power" seemed written in fresh-secreted blood. Jim hadn't discussed this revelation with Dorothy. He wasn't certain that his wife *knew*.

***

"It went well, Sue. I'm back in the Starlight saddle and with a big raise to boot. I'm out from under that President Clinton shadow. Neither Jim nor James brought it up; I'm sure they never will."

With bemusement, Jerry contemplated Sue's unflattering appearance—the tattered bathrobe, disheveled hair, and unpainted lips and face. Following his innumerable one-nighters, he usually experienced the shock of the morning after as closure—the beginning of the end. *This must be love*, he thought.

"I had a great yesterday, too. I started out for the community college but ended up at the university instead. At first, it was a little intimidating, but I kept telling myself there was nothing to lose. I met with a friendly old professor in the English Department and told him about my dream. He was great; I mean, he really encouraged me. So anyway, I'm enrolled in two courses this semester: Modern Drama and Western Literature—that's literature of the American West. We agreed that two courses would be enough for now—a chance to see if I can do the work. Jerry, I'm so excited, but a little scared. My first class is tomorrow."

"That's wonderful. I'd like to read some of your assignments. It would be fun to discuss them together. Maybe I could learn something through you. When I first came to Reno, I tried writing a little as a way of keeping up my philosophy. But even I could tell that my prose was screed and my poetry doggerel. As the director of external relations, I'm likely to be on the road a lot, or rather in the air. I should have time to read.

"I don't read much contemporary fiction. Although in Mendocino I did trade out Plato and Aristotle for Kerouac. There are so many writers today that keeping up is kind of like golf. You have to put in the time to be on top of it. I just chase the caboose. I read the obituary of some novelist and then buy his or her masterpiece. After I read it, I'm saddened. I might have liked to write the writer with questions or praise, but now it's too late. There's some letdown as well in the knowledge that it's over, since that particular writer will never speak to us again."

"Jerry, dear, would you mind if we got rid of some of the fish?"

Jerry blinked at this sudden change of subject. When he first acquired a spacious, largely empty, house, he'd experienced an atavistic stirring from his youth. As a boy, he'd been a serious tropical fish enthusiast … on a kid's budget. While it had been his dream to be the first to breed the Amazonian discus fish in captivity, their $75 cost, plus the need for a large (ergo expensive) aquarium, had squelched that ambition. He'd sated his passion with more mundane guppies, mollies, and swordtails. Dismantling the fifteen tanks lining the walls of his boyhood lair had been the hardest part about going off to college. And here he was with the financial wherewithal and seemingly endless space.

Jerry became a regular at Ofishal Aquarium on Vassar Street. First, it was a trio of tiny bowls for the three male bettas that came to inhabit his kitchen countertop. Next, there was the twenty-nine-gallon kit, perched strategically in the bay window that held his television. That way, he could take his meals while switching his gaze back and forth between Peter Jennings and a pair of dwarf gouramis, four sailfin mollies, several variegated platys, and a clown loach.

Jerry's burgeoning fish fever then erupted into an endemic illness that claimed the kitchen annex—a cubicle that would, for most people, serve as a walk-in pantry. He purchased three 130-gallon tanks, each with space-age support system of water-filtration and circulation devices. Temperature control and testing the chemical composition of his many tanks became as much a part of his day's-end routine as flossing his teeth and swallowing his expanding handful of pills.

One of the aquariums was devoted entirely to African cichlids from Lakes Tanganyika and Malawi. Their brilliant colors flashed furtively against the backdrop of yellowish white sand and porous brown rock as they darted between the latter's many crevices. They required acidic water, which had to be monitored carefully and brought to perfection with additives.

Another tank became Jerry's first excursion into the realm of salt-water fish husbandry. Since Reno was scarcely an oceanfront, this meant the weekly task of dissolving salt in the two five-gallon cans of water to be overnighted to dissipate the chlorine before being added to replace evaporation. Once monthly, the entire tank had to be cleaned and refurbished with new, treated saltwater. Jerry's zeal stopped just shy of that particular commitment, although he practically suffered a nosebleed whenever he had to write the several-hundred-dollar monthly maintenance check. It had cost two thousand dollars to have this service care for his whole collection during his recent Italian sojourn.

His third creation was the subdued world containing the verdant shapes of live plants. Its kaleidoscope of shade, mottled light, black mud, and sunken driftwood bespoke an Amazonian underwater wonderland. Schools of cardinal and rasbora tetras provided color and movement, while an active black angelfish asserted its dominance with false charges at the swifter passersby. Four large discus fish observed his antics regally from their preferred recesses.

A leather recliner and ottoman provided Jerry with his perch for observing his watery empire for an hour each evening. He didn't regard his fish as pets. Their only interaction with him was their rush to the surface when he removed the lids during feeding. You couldn't scratch their tummies or ears. They didn't sit in your lap or lick your face. Jerry liked dogs and planned to have one someday. But not yet. He felt that leaving a golden retriever, his favorite breed, at home alone for his entire workday, or worse, checking it into a kennel cage during his frequent trips, would be too cruel for words. A retriever might be a welcome companion during *his* golden years, but Jerry wasn't yet prepared to play his canine card.

Jerry ruminated over Sue's request to downsize his fish collection, struggling with his usual tendency to pamper her. There was a little suspicion in the recesses of Jerry's mind. Was she resentful of the distraction—the time they took away from her? Was she *jealous* of her finny rivals? "Let me think about it, Sue. Sheba likes animals and I did say no when she asked for a dog. Maybe the fish …"

Sue nodded her agreement, and then opted again to change the subject.

"Since I'm not going back to work, at least for a while, I have another project to discuss with you. I love the backyard, but I think it could use more character. When I got home today, I sat out there, just thinking about everything. Before I knew it, I could see a gazebo, deck, and fishpond over by that apple tree. In fact, I think the tree should come out—it's old and half dead. What do you think? I mean it's your yard and I don't want to be pushy."

Jerry laughed. "It's our yard, Sue. Actually, until now, it's been Javier's yard. He may be your tough sell. Tell you what, I'll give you a $25,000 budget, and you go for it."

"Jerry! I wasn't considering anything like that. I can't imagine spending so much money."

"You'll see. When you get into design and then push a pencil, it won't be nearly enough. But I still say go for it. I am not pandering or being beneficent. I want you to realize your dream; it's worth way more than the money to me."

"I like gardening myself. In Youngstown, I was the family's flower girl. I played in the dirt a lot. Frankly, your flower beds are dreadful. After the spring tulips and daffodils, they turn to seed. Dandelions. Can we garden together?"

"I'm a vegetable guy, Sue," Jerry replied, thereby displaying the practical side of his nature, or possibly the delusional self-sufficiency of his Mendocino days.

"We eat dandelions, you know. Were you growing them for the table?" she teased.

"We who?"

"We Italians."

"Well, fine, let's garden together next spring. We'll have a division of labor. You're in charge of flowers, and I'll do veggies. I'll till your beds if you'll weed mine. I hate weeding. I'm not planting dandelions … or eating them either."

Despite their mutual humor, bordering on the facetious, they were bonding. Both recognized the importance of discovering common interests if their relationship was to sprout, grow, and blossom.

Jerry observed, "Tim and I used to plant vegetables together. Maybe, Sheba and I …"

***

Jim scratched his head as he and Jerry surveyed the casino floor from an observation post. Understanding slot players was his particular aporia. Nothing appealed to him less than sitting endlessly in front of a lifeless, insensitive, hyped contraption exuding harsh light and a mechanical voice cajoling the player to pour money into its insatiable maw.

"What in the hell do they see in it, Jerry? They're like zombies or robots. They look so bored."

"Fun. It's their way of having fun, relaxing, maybe escaping."

"Look at that lady with the cigarette hanging out of her mouth and cocktail glass in her hand. She's on automatic. If she didn't have to push the buttons to make the machine work, she might as well be stuffed—a mannikin in a gaming-museum display. She's having fun?"

"Not everyone can play squash or go hiking. Twenty years ago, maybe she was a backpacker. Maybe she holds some kind of Olympic diving record. You scratch the mascara off, and you'll find a person underneath—a story. Gaming may not be for everyone, for you as an example Jim, but neither is hiking the Pacific Crest Trail. It's easier to criticize a seventy-year-old when you're fifty and haven't walked in their moccasins yet."

Jim hadn't anticipated such a pointed response to his casual remark. He felt slightly flushed by the recognition that Jerry's barbs had drawn blood. "You're right, of course. Jesus, I've always defended everyone's right to choose. Scratch my mascara, and you get some kind of half-assed libertarian. I even sent a donation to the libertarian candidate for governor in the last election. I was just venting; I wasn't really talking about that lady in particular. I know that she's more than a slot player. She's someone's mom, grandma, sister, wife. I guess I was really talking about myself—my inability to understand the main thing about this business. I don't get gambling's appeal, so I don't have a clue about what makes our customer base tick. I come to work every day as if I were a blind optometrist. I'm supposed to know how people see, and I can't read the eye chart myself."

"That's not the patient's fault."

"I know, I know."

"Maybe you're not permanently blind, Jim. Maybe you just need a cataract operation."

"What are you getting at?"

"I mean maybe your attitudes are cataracts, keeping you from seeing clearly. This business isn't rocket science. Like any other, it has its peculiarities and challenges that can only be addressed with a positive will and curiosity. You should read what some of the great minds have said about gambling—Giordano, Dostoevsky, Erving Goffman. Giordano says ..."

"Whoa, Jerry. Maybe the thing I admire most about you is your way with words. But you're all throttle and no brake. I haven't read very much, and I'm not sure that I get much out of the little I try. Sometimes, I have to reread Grisham two or three times. I don't mean a line or paragraph; I'm talking whole pages, and even chapters. But, you know, in some ways, I believe I'm more in touch with reality than you. I've never read your Rousseau, so here I am—what's the expression?—'blissfully ignorant.' My idea of 'research' is to channel surf between CNN and Fox News.

"Maybe there's more than just bliss in ignorance. The more you read the less you know, you told me that. I didn't learn much in college because my frat was more important than my studies. But I had my Berkeley, too. It was no four-year course. It was more like twenty-five sitting in an office down the hall from Dad's. I know what you're saying. I'm just not sure how to get there. Becoming genuinely interested in this business is about as tough for me as believing in God. I'd like to, but I can't just will it to be so. Faith doesn't work that way, nor does curiosity."

"Maybe you haven't ridden the right ass towards Damascus yet, Jim. Your life's trip isn't over. You'll probably be zapped by a few more lightning bolts along the way before you reach the cemetery."

"My trip to the cemetery?"

"Everyone's, Jim."

***

"So, Manny, you think this is a good promotion? Let me get this straight. If we pay an extra ten bucks a head the bus stops at the Starlight first, right?"

"You got it, boss."

Jim's skepticism was evident. "Walk me through your reasoning, Manny. Convince me that it's worthwhile."

"Well, it gives us first shot at the business. Some of those bus people don't care where they play. They blow their real wad at the first casino and then just cash in their coupons from the other joints before catchin' the bus back to Oakland. Maybe, they eat somebody's discounted lunch, first." Manny then added, "You think marketin' this place is tough? Let me tell you 'bout tough. Try to sell potato chips. They're overpriced for what you get, turn stale if you don't open the bag on time, and soggy if you don't eat them right away. They're salty, greasy, and just plain bad for you. I had to convince housewives to buy 'em to feed to their families. Selling a casino is a piece of cake!" He struggled to read Jim's expressionless face during the two-minute pause in their conversation.

"Alright, Manny, I'm going to approve this for now. But I intend to check it out."

"Sure, Boss, I'll run the numbers for you."

"Fine, Manny, but I meant that I intend to ride one of those buses."

"Are you fuckin' kiddin' me?"

***

Jerry took stock of his boxy, sterile surroundings. The pile of proposals he'd left doing its imitation of the Leaning Tower of Pisa had somehow managed to topple in the middle of the night, disjecting papers across the otherwise bare desktop and onto the floor beyond. A cord ran from the telephone jack on the back wall to the lower left-hand drawer of his desk, into which it disappeared mysteriously, like some transatlantic cable plunging into the ocean. Along the right wall, there was a bookcase devoid of material and a single-wide metal filing cabinet. A Playboy calendar displaying August's playmate was the only interruption on the white expanse of the left wall. Matched chairs, one behind the desk and one in front, and a wastepaper basket next to his feet were the only other items in the room.

If it weren't for the view, this would be totally Kafkaesque, he thought, encouraged by the living mural of Mount Rose provided by the array of windows over his shoulder. He loved its pine-green skirt and summit ermine-draped by the season's first snowfall.

Jerry came out from behind his desk, removed the calendar, and made his first contribution to the Starlight's paper recycling campaign. In its place, he hung a square of cardboard with a printed message that he'd taken from his briefcase. He stood back to contemplate the alignment of his favorite motto:

If you do not wish to be criticized, think, say, and do nothing

Jerry then dropped to his knees to retrieve the errant proposals. He paused superstitiously to examine the first that came to hand on the off chance that Fate had nudged his pile. It was a Request for Proposal from the Tuolumne tribe in California. They were looking for an operator for their future gaming facility. Jerry set it aside to be read in full, since he had to start somewhere.

For the next two hours, he attempted to domesticate his new challenges by arranging them into four separate stacks according to his own mental categories. The first contained Indian gaming proposals, while the second regarded riverboat projects, mainly in the Midwest. The third were international opportunities. The last pile was a grab bag of miscellaneous items—sales pitches for collaboration with existing gaming properties in a variety of venues and initiatives in possible emerging new ones, such as the Little Rock deal.

"Organization is progress!" he said aloud, but without conviction. He then examined the drawers of the filing cabinet. The top one was bursting with folders detailing the past eighteen months of efforts in Arkansas. The second and half of the third contained the sad history of the Starlight's descent into disaster with the Pé-Oné tribe.

"Whew! And Sue thinks she's got a lot of homework!" he muttered.

Back at his desk, he paroled the telephone from its dungeon drawer and was pleased to note that it was activated. He dialed a familiar number on the intercom and summoned Priscilla to his office. "I'll need a good atlas, a globe, and a wall map of the Indian nations of the United States. I also want phone directories for Phoenix, Portland, Seattle, Vancouver, New Orleans, St. Louis, Kansas City, Detroit, Chicago, Indianapolis, and Atlantic City. Oh, don't forget Little Rock. We have to subscribe to several magazines and newsletters—the *Adams Report, Casino Executive, Casino Journal, Indian Gaming, International Gaming and Wagering Business*, and *National Gaming Summary*. I'll also need a desk calendar and an organizer."

"An organizer, Sir?"

"Yes. One of those datebooks that you can use to keep track of your appointments," he elucidated.

"Most people are going to cell phones, Sir."

"An organizer, Priscilla. I'll leave it up to you to flesh out a list of office supplies. The usual pens, paper, and pads."

"Yes, Sir."

"One last thing. I'd like you to have whoever decorated Jim's office take a whack at this one, except for maybe the fish."

"That was Mrs. Fitzsimmons, Sir. I think it was her opportunity to get those photos out of their house."

"Oh, never mind. I'll take care of it myself."

Alone again, Jerry picked up the Tuolumne proposal and began to read. It seemed to have promise. The tribe had reservation land on an important state highway within easy drive of Fresno. They needed a contractor-manager and financing for a modest gaming facility.

Jerry liked the logistics of potentially managing a project within driving distance of Reno. He knew that the Starlight wouldn't, indeed couldn't, put up its own money, but it looked like a turn-key Phase One might only cost about three million dollars. They could lease the equipment, and it might just be possible to smoke-and-mirror the rest. Jerry knew that the banks, pension funds, and insurance companies had shown little interest in financing Indian gaming so far. The tribes had sovereign immunity from lawsuits, and most of their fixed assets were held in trust by the federal government and couldn't be used as collateral on loans. Such extraordinary rules didn't make for playing fields on which traditional bankers loved to cavort. But things were changing. The financial markets were again awash in cash and anxious to infuse at least some of it in moderate-risk, high-yield projects. While the signals from Indian gaming were certainly mixed, there were a number of successes, some spectacular. Connecticut's Foxwoods, Indian gaming's crowning glory, was literally the world's most successful casino.

Jerry debated whether he was ready for a real project. He didn't want the deal to wither while he got his sea legs, but he needed to buy some time. He called the number of the Tuolumne's contact person. Marv Gibson, the tribe's administrator, could scarcely contain his enthusiasm. Indeed, they would be delighted to meet with him the first week in October (nearly a month away). It was such a pleasure to get a call from a Nevada operator. They'd been really disappointed by the poor response to their RFP. Years of hassle with the governor and attorney general, several court cases that seemed to spawn yet others, and the decision by several tribes to defy state and federal authorities by putting in electronic gaming devices without first compacting with California had all cast a pall over Indian gaming in the Golden State. Jerry was favorably impressed by the ingenuous frankness of the man with whom he might be negotiating a business deal. If it made Marv vulnerable, it was also endearing.

Jerry copied down the rather complicated instructions for how to find tribal headquarters.

***

The telephone rang. "Mr. Clinton, this is Ms. Adams, your replacement. Mr. Fitzsimmons just told me that you're coming back as our director of external relations. We're having an important directors' meeting at three today. I'd like you to be there if you can make it."

"Of course."

"Mr. Clinton, I don't exactly know what happened. I mean, you know, between you and the owners. I'm sorry if—"

"It certainly had nothing to do with you, Ms. Adams. There's no reason that we can't work well together—" Jerry caught himself and amended, "Actually, that was presumptuous of me. I meant to say that there's no reason that I shouldn't be able to work for you."

"See you at three in the conference room, Mr. Clinton."

Jerry sat for a while, pondering the ponderous telephone exchange. He concluded that the most awkward part was the Mr. Clinton-Ms. Adams's formality. "I hope we get beyond that just as soon as possible," he said aloud.

Jerry decided to stop by Mary Beth's office on the way to the directors' meeting. It would be the first time for both of them in their new capacities. He wanted to meet her formally in private rather than under the gaze of Fitzsimmons and the other directors. There would be obvious curiosity regarding the rapport between the present and former general managers. For that meeting, at least, they would be on stage, like two puppies displayed in some pet shop window.

She was alone, busily making marginal notes on her agenda. "Oh, hello, Mr. Clinton. Do come in."

He thought he detected a faint hint of weariness in her voice and resignation in her demeanor. *But, of course*, he thought, *how could it be otherwise, given the problems around here?* For the first time, he realized that it hadn't been all that difficult to decide to provoke James Fitzsimmons into firing him. He wasn't a quitter—indeed, he'd come back—but he was no fool, either. It wasn't fun being in charge of the Starlight during the year of its spectacular nosedive. In fact, with the exception of his marriages, it was the only true failure he'd ever been associated with. Was it his? Could he have made a difference by doing things differently? Or was the Starlight perforce doomed by circumstances, just another buggy-whip factory in the new age of the automobile?

"Ms. Adams, I wanted to reiterate what I said on the phone this morning. I'm behind you one hundred percent. In fact, if you'd like, I'd be pleased to say a few words to that effect at the beginning of your meeting."

Mary Beth's face erupted in a broad smile. "That would be very nice, Mr. Clinton. Welcome back!"

Jim Fitzsimmons was late, and since Mary Beth was loath to start without him, it gave Jerry the perfect opportunity to make his little speech. When it was over, Seth said, "Rumor around here has it that you're engaged to Sue Johnson. If so, congratulations."

"Thanks. It's true, Seth, we're going to get married sometime this winter."

Jim Fitzsimmons entered the room and took his place at the end of the table opposite Mary Beth, providing the gathering with its second bookend of Starlight authority. He muttered an apology for his tardiness and then turned to Andrew McDermott. "How's Margaret, Andy? Home from the hospital yet? How're the kids doing?"

"Last week, Sir. She asked me to thank you for the flowers. We're fine, as long as we don't die from ptomaine poisoning. I'm the cook," he quipped in his thick Highland Scottish.

For an awkward moment, it was unclear who would moderate, Fitzsimmons or Adams. He quickly resolved any doubt by stating, "Before Ms. Adams begins her meeting, I want to say that she has the board's full support. This is not an experiment; the Starlight doesn't have the luxury of experimenting. I'll be attending your meetings for a while in my new capacity as CEO, but don't misread that as some kind of limitation on Ms. Adams's stewardship. She's not on trial; she has a mandate. I'm here to listen rather than to talk, because I need to become more familiar with operational issues myself—particularly in this time of transition to a new Starlight."

"Thank you, Mr. Fitzsimmons. I certainly appreciate that vote of confidence." She paused momentarily to focus her thoughts. "Before going into the specifics of our agenda, I think I should make a few comments about my management style and philosophy. I know there's a lot of informality around here—everyone's on a first-name basis. I see a lot of backslapping, but also quite a bit of backbiting. I've never seen such a beehive of rumors. In fact, I've had a little heart-to-heart with the queen bee. I want you all to come to me directly with your problems, suggestions, and requests for information, rather than consulting with Priscilla.

"In short, I believe in an open-door policy, but also in professionalism. I prefer 'Ms. Adams' to 'Mary Beth,' and I plan to address you the same way. I won't be attending your son's or daughter's graduation, either. Please don't interpret that as indifference or disinterest in your lives. It just has to do with my need to maintain the proper professional distance to retain my objectivity. I plan to be scrupulously fair with each of you. Whether I'm rewarding you with a raise, chastening you for a blooper, or terminating you for cause, the decision should be based on merit rather than sentiment. I owe you nothing less."

The door to the conference room opened, and a waiter entered with coffee service and ice water. Ms. Adams paused until the silent intruder had departed.

"If I were to state in a word the fundamental key to my management philosophy, it would be *teamwork*. From now on, we're all team members; we're fielding the Starlight team. For it to succeed, it's just as important that a busboy does his job as for me to do mine. 'Team member' sounds a little trite or cute; however, it's the cornerstone of modern management theory. The team won't happen just because I say so. It's going to take a lot of work on everyone's part. There'll be many fits and starts, most of them false. We'll have our successes, but lots of failures and disappointments too. The important thing is that the successes become cumulative and the mistakes get rectified. If we all work together on the team concept, I guarantee you that, a year from now, we'll have a restructured and stronger Starlight organization—one that's able to slay its dragons." She paused. "Are there any questions?"

Since no one volunteered, she decided to force the issue.

"Mr. Cohen, what's your opinion?"

Manny was unprepared for the attention. His face reddened, and he blurted out, "Geez, I don't know, Ms. Adams. I may be too old to try out for some fuckin' team. But I can try." He laughed nervously, looking around him for some sign of support. There was none.

"Mr. Cohen, I would ask you to be more respectful. Please understand that I'm not shocked by such language; I just find it highly unprofessional. You've just given us a prime example of what to avoid if we're going to raise the Starlight team's level of professionalism."

"What the fu ... uh, what has respect and professionalism got to do with it?" Manny protested. "I didn't mean to be disrespectful. It's just an expression, just words."

"Mr. Cohen, words are very powerful. Much more powerful than you obviously realize. Words are what separate us from the animals, but they can also make us into beasts. I must insist that you be more judicious in your choice of language."

Manny nodded assent as he lapsed more into a state of mild despair than anger. His predicament was all too familiar.

Mary Beth continued, "Item one on our agenda is how to improve cooperation between the pit, slots, hotel, and food and beverage during next weekend's tournament. I've talked to some of you individually already about turf issues. It's obvious to me that, in the old Starlight, each department was its own little kingdom defending its borders. I asked several of you to define and describe cooperation for me, and what I received was a lot of rhetoric and little substance. What passes for interdepartmental cooperation around here is actually more like standoffs and shaky treaties. I want each of you to put on your thinking cap and tell me how we can improve the situation. In a word, I'm looking for *genuine* teamwork."

Andrew McDermott was by nature a quiet man. He would frequently sit through a directors' meeting in silence. When he did speak, it was always in response to a direct question. So, all heads turned when Andrew interrupted the new general manager. "Ms. Adams, engineering interfaces with every other department in the place. Everyone needs maintenance at one time or another. Since we fix other peoples' problems, I would say that everything we *do* is teamwork. So, I, for one, am not sure how to interpret your comments. Are we the one department that is exempt from this criticism?"

"No, Mr. McDermott, you're not inviolate. I hadn't planned to go into specifics because I didn't want to put any one department on the spot. But you brought up engineering, so let's use it as an example, but with the clear understanding around this table that I will be reviewing each department's shortcomings with its director.

"It's certainly no secret to any of you that business is flat. Midweek, you could fire a cannon across the casino floor without hurting anyone. But last Wednesday was different. We had that large bus-tour group from Redding and the place was hopping, even though it was the day shift. So, that happens to be the day that engineering decides to shut down half of our main entrance to varnish the hardwood floor. It made the guests feel like they were caught in the middle of a construction project. It also took a bank of quarter machines offline for a day in which they might have actually seen some play."

"But Ms. Adams, I scheduled that work because Wednesday morning is always slow."

"Obviously the more accurate operative word is 'usually.' The point is you didn't check with any of the other directors before disrupting business on what turned out to be a busy day. The primary consideration was engineering's convenience, given its other commitments and scheduling problems. What I'm saying is that true teamwork means that each of you has to think of the bigger picture, not just in terms of your own department's druthers."

Shelly Sherman, the hotel director, protested, "Yes, Ms. Adams, but how do I justify sacrificing my department's staff time, and maybe even income, when it might not be noticed? Whenever I was asked to defend my department by Jerry … Mr. Clinton … the issues were always room rates, occupancy, more efficient scheduling of the maid service, and the quality of customer service at the front desk. My evaluation and the evaluations of my staff all turned on how well and efficiently we ran the hotel, particularly as reflected in what it contributed to the bottom line."

"You've made some excellent points, Ms. Sherman. Under the new Starlight team concept, there will be fundamental changes. In the future, whenever we hold a tournament or other special event, I plan to evaluate the results from a property-wide perspective and not by individual departments. When I do annual evaluations, I will apply the same standard. I'll be announcing a bonus program that will diminish departmental accountability. I said diminish, not eliminate, because I also plan to work with each of you to make your individual departments more efficient, but always as a cog in the larger Starlight machine.

"It's all about detail. I'm not talking about losing the game because we tripped over the basketball. Keeping track of the big picture—the basketball—is pretty easy. I'm thinking of the pratfalls and the dropped balls caused by overlooking the thousands of little ball bearings that life strews in our paths. Take a step without noticing the ball bearings and—wham!—you're flat on your back with a broken leg."

Mary Beth was apparently prone to mixing her metaphors.

Jerry nodded his approval, awash in the déjà vu of his recent soliloquy on effective management to Jim. He would definitely be able to work with Mary Beth Adams.

"What this all means," she said, "is that each of us has the same stake in the global outcome. When we're doing our retrospective analysis of last week's tournament or tourist bus in order to improve next week's, I don't want finger-pointing from one director at another department's performance. During any future Starlight event, the operative policy is that customer satisfaction is our paramount goal. Ms. Sherman, if you see a customer who needs change, make sure that someone attends to it. Don't look the other way because you're the hotel director and change isn't your responsibility. What I'm saying to all of you is that if you happen to see a piece of paper on the floor pick it up; don't make a special call to housekeeping or simply ignore it because you know that housekeeping will get around to it, maybe two hours later. Think of how many customers could have their impression of the Starlight influenced by that piece of litter in two hours' time. We all need to take pride in the property and feel personally responsible for every aspect of its performance. None of us are supernumeraries. The most important thing is that we each try to see the place through our customers' eyes. They don't care about our organizational chart and turf wars; they just want to feel comfortable. They come here to relax in a clean and friendly atmosphere—end of story."

It was also the end of the meeting.

***

Sue found Jerry in the family room watching a San Francisco 49ers game, seated beneath his beloved poster of Joe Montana placing his hands between his burly center's legs in anticipation of the snap that would initiate some new football miracle. Sue, as a former cheerleader, wasn't oblivious to the homoeroticism characteristic of most verbal and visual depictions of male contact sports.

The room was a virtual museum of Jerry's former devotion to bird-shooting. There was the gun case that protected his prized shotguns from intruders—not to mention himself, given that he'd long since misplaced the key. One wall was adorned with autumnal trophy photos: Jerry and two hunting buddies, each holding drake mallards one November morning at Stillwater Marsh; Jerry displaying a brace of pheasants amid the frosty stubble of a Smith Valley field; Jerry and Ann spreading the wings of a fallen goose by each holding a tip. The most prominent feature of the room was the collection of wooden duck decoys perched precariously on the amateurish shelving that he himself had made with his table saw.

In one corner, there languished two scarcely touched, good-as-new, first-generation exercise machines. There was even an old Schwinn bike lying on its side, souvenir of Jerry's youth.

Sue's slight smile spoke volumes about the many calculations informing her imagination. She could see a flight of wooden decoys heading south to Mexico, or to the garage, to be replaced by her handcrafted pottery. The displaced hunting mugshots would likely become accustomed to the walls in Jerry's new office—or suffer a far worse fate in some dumpster. This space had possibilities ...

Jerry pointed at Joe Montana and said, "It probably won't mean much to you, Sue, but I saw 'The Catch.' I really saw it, right up close and personal. It was January of eighty-two, and the Niners were playing the Dallas Cowboys for the National Football League championship and the right to go to the Super Bowl. Several of us decided to attend the game at the last minute, and of course, we had no tickets. We took a chance and drove to Candlestick. We bought scalped tickets in the parking lot, and they were awful seats behind the north end zone. Well, with less than a minute to play, Joe Montana threw a touchdown pass to Dwight Clark—right in our face. So, we had the best seats in the house for the greatest moment in 49er history.

"It was the beginning of a dynasty. Three years later, the 49ers played the Miami Dolphins in the Super Bowl held in the Stanford University Stadium. I had tickets for that one, a thousand bucks each. Only they were in the middle of the Dolphins' fan section. Three of us were wearing our Niners gear, and there was a lot of kidding and banter back and forth. The Dolphins were undefeated and had a superstar quarterback named Dan Marino. By game's end, Montana himself had run and passed for more yards than the whole Dolphin offense, and we won easily. The Dolphin fans around us were in the dumps and I turned to them and said, 'Don't be discouraged; there's always next year, and you have the second-best Italian quarterback in the NFL.' No one threw anything at me!"

"You seem to be a real sports fan, Jerry."

"It's how I spend my weekends. Actually, I'm a news junkie and I *hate* weekends. The pundits take them off, probably to watch damn sports," he quipped.

"Maybe the world takes the weekend off."

"What? Sue, do you think they observe Sunday in the Middle East or China?"

"Sort of. I mean, if we run the world and we take Sunday off, then the rest of the world has to as well. You called it globalization, didn't you?"

"You have a point. I miss my news on weekends, but I realize that professional wrestling is journalism's first cousin. Both are about theater more than reality. Both create the entertainment they present. Maybe I should see a therapist who can wean me off my CNN obsession. God knows, I have plenty of good books to read."

"So, what have you learned from all your books?"

"A little about life, I hope."

"And?"

"I guess I've learned that life is like a kaleidoscope. I don't know if kids have them anymore, but I'll bet you did. I had three or four as a child. Remember how you could hold it up to your eye, and there was a geometric pattern of shapes and colors that seemed perfect and permanent? Then you gave the cylinder a little twist and everything was in motion, a chaotic blur. And when you stopped, suddenly there was that perfect symmetry again, only the pattern was entirely different than the one before. To a kid, at least, the possibilities seemed infinite. If I came up with a really beautiful one, I'd try to save that pattern. That's how I learned that life's arrangements are fragile. If you were extremely careful, you might be able to put your kaleidoscope in a safe place and then, say a week later, lift it ever so gently to your eye and again glimpse that same infinity. But the slightest little jar, or maybe just holding it at the wrong angle, could dislodge one of the glass chips. The others then rearranged themselves as well, and that special saved *infinity* was gone forever. I still feel the sense of loss just talking about it. It was the only true mourning that I experienced as a child because it gave me my only real glimpse of death.

"I mean, Mother died when I was six, and all the adults in my life talked about her pleasant journey to visit Jesus—they made it sound like she was going on a long vacation, so long that I would eventually get used to her absence. Father died when I was a teenager, but they were divorced when I was a baby, so I'd only met him once or twice. He lived in Atlanta and had a whole other family there. I got this letter from his widow; I'll never forget how it began: 'Dear Jerome: We don't really know one another, but I thought you should know …' She meant well, but it was about as comforting as one coming from the Army informing you about your son's heroic death in combat. Only in my father's case, the victim was a total stranger to me."

***

Priscilla passed the call to Jim and he now listened to an echo from his past. "Joe Conroy, Jim. Do you remember me from the Bahamas?"

They'd met while fellow anglers at the Andros Island Bonefish Club years before. Conroy was a partner in a major Manhattan law firm.

"Sure, I do, Joe. That was some trip—a misadventure. Bad weather, poor guides, few fish."

"You've got that right," Conroy said. "Anyway, I represent Premier Oil and have its president, George Hoskins, right here in the office with me. They're all over the East, South, and Midwest. He says they're expanding in your direction. I told him about you and suggested this call. Would you speak with him? I'll stay on the line, too."

"Sure, Joe."

"Hello, Mr. Fitzsimmons. Let me tell you the deal. We have some land optioned off Interstate 80 in Sparks and plan to build our next travel center there. The Sparks City Council is hearing our request next week for the zoning change that we'll need. You come highly recommended by Joe. We've never been in gaming before and understand we could be in Nevada. We know nothing about it. What can you tell me about our prospects?"

Jim composed his thoughts and feelings. Should he refer the call to Jerry as his director of external relations? No. The Conroy tie was personal rather than professional, an anglers' bond. He owed it to Joe to be frank with his client. "A question, Mr. Hoskins. Do you plan to build rooms?"

"Certainly not for the present. We're in the travel center business. We hope to expand to every one of the lower forty-eight states. That will tie up our capital for the foreseeable future."

"Understood. But that means you'll be limited to a maximum of fifteen slot machines. Both Washoe and Clark Counties have a room requirement for an unrestricted gaming license. We hotel-casino operators at both ends of the state put that in to prevent slot-route operators from competing against us without first paying their dues, as it were. Some of them were sticking a hundred machines out on the highway into Reno and Vegas to pick off our customers. They were lean operations without our overhead—unfair competition. We took care of that. As for your zoning change, I doubt you'll get it."

"What?! Why?"

"There's a major travel center in Sparks that has been there for decades. I imagine it's given campaign money to every member of the city council. Also, the former chairman of the state Democratic Party is building a second travel center in Sparks. My hunch is that they'll both oppose your application; quietly, of course, but effectively."

"Thank you, Mr. Fitzsimmons. I appreciate your candor. However, our attorneys have met with Sparks officials and assure me that the zoning change is a formality. No red flags."

"Thanks, Jim," Joe Conroy interjected.

"No problem, Joe. Tight lines."

***

"It's Red! He's in town and he wants to meet me to talk," Sue told Jerry across the kitchen while covering the telephone receiver with her hand.

"Tell him to come over. I want to be here for your sake. I don't mean as part of the conversation. You can go out on the patio to talk … or I will—but I should be around, just in case." Sue nodded and communicated the invitation to Red. "He'll be here in fifteen minutes."

Jerry opened the front door and the two men contemplated each other with mixed feelings, curiosity mingled with animosity. For Jerry, Red's auburn hair and freckles were familiar from Sue's photographs, but he weighed easily forty pounds more than the figure in the visual record. There was also a hardness in his face that differed markedly from the youthful exuberance of the Lake Tahoe shots. Red was clearly nervous. He looked about him for a place to discard the extinguished cigarette butt in his hand.

"Give it to me. Sue's waiting for you. I'll show you out to the patio."

Red walked behind Jerry, taking in the opulence. He seemed totally out of his element and somewhat intimidated by the stylish house.

Sue awaited him on the patio. "Hello, Red, long time …" She struggled to start a conversation for which there was no easy beginning, also a bit taken aback by her husband's changed appearance.

"Wow, Sue, and you look just the same … maybe better."

She didn't know whether to thank him for the compliment or reciprocate with a lie.

"I'll sign the papers," he said, "but I wanted to see you and Sheba first. It looks like you're doing all right for yourself. Who's Gramps? Is that the guy you want to marry? A little old for you, isn't he?"

"That's him," she said matter-of-factly, her inflection measured to head off further conversation along that avenue.

"I want to see Sheba. I've got a right—"

"A right?" she exploded. "You've got a right? What about the wrong, Red, all the wrongs? You just walked out on her. No support was bad enough, but do you know what was worse? The Christmas with the little girl who missed her daddy. The sad birthday that ended in tears because he never called. I watched that sadness become pain, and then anger. You've got a right? *Madonna!*"

Red's face was crimson, but he repressed his desire to smack her, aware of Jerry's presence behind the sliding glass door. He said slowly and deliberately, "I want to see my daughter. I won't sign anything until I do."

"Red, I'm asking you to think harder about this than anything else you've ever decided before. When Sheba was twelve and about to become a teenager, she needed you desperately, and you left her; now that she's thirteen, she needs you to leave her alone. She's got plenty to do just adjusting to Jerry and me. She's at a very delicate age. I'm begging you to give her some space. Do it if you care for her at all. It may not have to be forever. She's going to need to work through her resentment. It's not healthy. I think someday she may come looking for you, if only to put matters to rest. You'll have your chance then, maybe when she's eighteen or twenty. But not *now*, Hon—" Sue caught herself before completing the rusty term of endearment.

Red averted his eyes, abruptly stood up, and disappeared through the sliding door without a word. "Don't bother, I'll let myself out," he said to Jerry who'd started to rise from the breakfast table.

Jerry heard the front door close and then observed Sue through the plate glass. She sat immobile, lost in thought, her face expressionless. Jerry left the house quietly out of respect for her need for privacy.

***

Jim ascended the stairs and sat in the only vacant seat in the first row, beside a plump matron who was sorting through her coupons from the different Reno properties. She waved them over her shoulder at the rest of her church group, Baptists no less, which made up the passenger load. "We're off, Sisters." Ten minutes later, the bus entered Interstate 80 eastbound and exited Oakland.

She divided her stash into free offers and two-for-ones, reading through each of the latter and discarding some. She then noticed Jim's smile, which invited conversation.

"Do you go to Reno, often, Ma'am?"

"'Bout once a month. Right after I gets my Sosh Shurity check."

"So, you spend it in Reno?"

"Lawdy, no." She laughed. "Ise spends dese in Reno." Referring to her coupons. "The Sosh Shurity check is for luck. If I goes to Reno widout it, I alays lose. Sounds like supastishun, don it?' But dat's true."

THE STARLIGHT HOTEL-CASINO

"Thanks, Ma'am."

"My name's Carrie, Suh."

Her reference to superstition caused Jim to ruminate about its role in gaming. In fact, wasn't 'luck' just another word for superstition? Is it science when the house changes dealers if a player gets on a roll? He remembered the Starlight's decision a few years earlier to terminate its Hawaiian promotion. The Hawaiians would wait until one of them got 'lucky' and then flock to place their bets alongside that player's. It seemed to work so well that the Starlight basically eighty-sixed the Hawaiian Islands. So much for house odds!

As the bus left Auburn and began climbing into the foothills, Jim surveyed the passengers. *Two-thirds full; not bad for mid-week in October*, he thought. He smiled to himself at the memory of Bruce Barstow's diatribe against bus people. No one in this crowd was about to sleep with his Dot. He then rose, steadied himself with a hand on his headrest and cleared his throat.

"Ladies let me introduce myself. My name is Lance James," he said, "and I'm in the marketing department of one of the casinos you'll visit. I've been assigned to conduct a survey, and we're prepared to reward you for participating. I'll give ten dollars to anyone willing to show me how much cash she has and then fill out a short questionnaire regarding her plans for this trip." Over the next hour, Jim passed up and down the aisle, asking his questions, receiving only one refusal, and handing out twenty-eight ten-dollar bills.

There were three non-starters. The only man in the group, Roy, was likely also the eldest and suffered from some form of dementia. To each of Jim's questions, he answered, "My name's Roy. Glad to meet ya." His caretaker explained that Roy was along for the ride so she could come. Jim made a mental note that the man would probably occupy the seat in front of a slot machine for the entire weekend without playing it once. Then there were the two white college girls who reversed American history by sitting in the back of the bus. They admitted to Jim that they used the casino buses for free transportation. One was from Reno, and both planned to visit sorority sisters at UNR.

On their arrival, Jim scanned the black faces of the animated ladies streaming out of the bus and through the Starlight's front entrance.

"Ellie, Ellie can you believe we're finely here?" Carrie said. She and and Ellie moved across the casino floor to a particular bank of slot machines. "There it be!" Carrie squealed, delighted that her favorite machine was available.

Meanwhile, Ellie surveyed the others like a champion cutting-horse rider assessing cows. Applying criteria known only to her, she plunked herself down decisively on the raised seat in front of a nickel slot. "Now you be good to Mama," she cajoled as the device flashed her its neon greeting. After her third play, they were bonded by the twenty "coin" payout, registered simply as a number in her credits account. The marriage was consummated a few minutes later when Ellie hit a jackpot and shouted the good news to Carrie. Ellie had definitely found her co-conspirator—a machine prepared to be disloyal to the house. She removed a marker pen from her purse and wrote a capital "E" on the faux leather seat so that, after lunch, her ample fanny would be certain not to stray mistakenly.

Six hours later, Jim returned to the floor and observed the two women each fixated before her chosen machine. Both were discomfited by the need for a restroom break—yet unwilling to risk it—fearful that mercurial Lady Luck might visit during their absence.

Next morning, the disconsolate casino owner sat at his desk. He'd just collated the results of his "scientific experiment." The cash stake of the entire busload of "customers" came to $406, or a little less than fifteen dollars each! Several had credit cards, but only two expected to spend more than $100 for the weekend. That, of course, assumed they lost. All reported having had a few winning trips in the past. All expected to spread their custom among the three sponsoring casinos; otherwise, how could they expect to maximize their coupons? Only six ranked the Starlight as their favorite.

As Jim descended in the elevator, on his way to the meeting he'd scheduled with Cohen to cancel the bus program, he was more annoyed than usual by the Lawrence Welk intrusion. "Has-been music for a has-been place," he muttered. Likely he should have included Mary Beth, but he was adamant and didn't wish to waste any more of anyone's time on further analysis.

His whole experiment with the bus people underscored the disastrous decline in the Starlight's prospects. It was as if he'd just contemplated the remaining remnants of a doomed endangered species. Long gone were the British Colombians who once rode a Starlight bus for a day and a half each way, the riders playing cards and singing songs, their favorite diversion marking a chalk arrow on a tire, then betting among themselves on whether it would be pointing up or down, left or right, at the next pit stop.

Jim saw that as a north-south version of the trek of last century's wagon trains settling the American West. Like that famous westward-ho movement, this modern one dealt with Indian ambushes. The first tribal casinos appeared in Washington State, then it was Oregon, followed by California and, eventually, British Columbia itself. The flow of business from western Canada to Reno went from torrent to trickle. There was no way that interminable bus-ride comradeship could trump convenience.

Jim recalled the evening in Vancouver when he realized that the Starlight's game was all but up. He was overnighting after his annual steelhead-fishing trip on the Dean River. Somehow, during the conversation with the waitress serving his dinner, it had come out that he was from Reno.

"Really? My husband and I love Reno. We used to go there all the time."

"Used to?"

"Well, yes. Now we go to Vegas. Not as often as before, of course. A slot is just a slot, and when we feel like gambling, why not just stay here or drive a couple of hours to Washington?"

When Jim mentioned his ownership of the Starlight, she became uneasy, almost as if she'd somehow been caught *in pari dilecto*. "Bill and I have been to the Starlight. I liked it a lot. But he prefers Vegas. He says there's so much more to do there. Besides, it's cheaper. Can you believe that airfare from Vancouver to Vegas is actually cheaper than to Reno? *The Sun's* full of Vegas discount offers. So, we haven't been to Reno in maybe ... five years."

It was all such an uneven contest. How was Reno to survive competition from tax-exempt tribes on the one hand and the industry's greatest visionaries like Steve Wynn on the other? The corporate behemoths with the deep pockets all preferred Vegas. Surely most of Reno's properties were doomed, and the few survivors would be locals' joints. And even then, they would be competing with slots in every pharmacy and grocery store.

***

"They're here, Jerry!"

It had been a week since Red's visit, and Sue had just opened the envelope containing the signed divorce papers. She read the note written in Red's familiar block letters: "It's not over, Sue. Not by a long shot."

***

It was a signal event of sorts, the first visit ever by James to Jim's office.

"Well, Jimmy, long time no see. I thought maybe you drowned on one of those stupid trips of yours. Are you still spending thousands of dollars to fly thousands of miles to fling feathers on a string so you can take some fish's picture and throw it back?" When James' crude attempt at an icebreaker failed to amuse his audience, he added his own belated sound effects, "Har, har." Then he asked, "So, Son, how goes the war?"

Jim was taken aback by James's alacrity. "Not great, but we're still standing and trying to return fire. It's not easy to be in the Nevada casino business, despite what the public might think."

"Jimmy, there is no such thing as *the* Nevada casino business, just like there's not one kind of player. I've pretty much lived through it all, seen all the changes. I can tell you that, while they both have slots, a joint in Winnemucca is about as different from Wynn's Mirage property on the Strip as Tonopah is from New York. I've seen this business go from the days before Bugsy Siegel, when the house and the players had to watch out for each other, to today, when everything is regulated and the biggest gamer in the state is the state."

"What do you mean watch out for each other, Dad?"

James chuckled as he visibly picked through the detritus of his memory. "Well, back in the thirties, most of the gamers came here from other places, and there wasn't a choir boy among them. To Reno, Jimmy, not to Vegas. They wanted a new start, maybe after ducking a bullet or jail time for running an illegal operation in another state—mainly California. They set the tone, Pappy Smith and Bill Harrah in particular. When Nevada legalized in the early thirties, the county sheriff pretty much regulated gaming in his jurisdiction—and a lot of those so-called regulators were paid to look the other way. The player might get dealt seconds or pull the handle of a rigged slot. If he won and tried to leave, he might be relieved of his winnings in the back alley as he headed for the parking lot. It was a two-way street, though—the cheaters came after the gamers. They might try to introduce their own shaved dice into the craps game, use marked blackjack cards, or shove wires up the slot to trigger a jackpot. Some arms got broken."

"Were you a part of all that, Dad?"

"Well, on the margins, you might say. More Tonopah than New York. I never hurt anyone. But I didn't always report all my winnings to the state, either. Anyway, everything changed right after the war. That's when the State of Nevada realized what it had—a monopoly on gaming in America. And, of course, the taxes went up. I doubt we paid one percent in the early years, and today, as you know, it's around six and three-quarters on the gross. Not the net, Jimmy, the gross. Do you know any other business in America that pays its taxes before deducting its legitimate business costs? We're losing money every month and the first check out the door is to the State of Nevada. I believe that, directly and indirectly, the casino industry pays half the state's budget. Then the counties and cities got in on the act with their licenses on devices. It took a while for the politicians to catch on to the potential of the closest thing to a free lunch that they'd ever see. It was perfect, because no one would object to taxing those profligate gamers. We're not talking family farms here."

"Sometimes I wish I was into farming instead of this, Dad."

"People think a gaming license is a license to steal. Everyone understands that any retail merchant keystones his merchandise. He doubles or even triples its price to pay his overhead and make a profit. No one objects to or regulates that. But our "house advantage" is resented by the public, and our overhead is unappreciated. We have enormous costs— particularly for labor and electricity. This is a very labor-intensive business—even with our cuts, we probably have close to a thousand employees. Do you think anyone appreciates what it costs to light this place up 24-7, 365 days a year? Every machine is turned on whether it's being played or not.

"Loss leaders are standard fare in the grocery business. They're regarded as sinister in ours—a way of enticing unwary sheep to the slaughter. Disney charges you several bucks for a few minutes on a thrill ride, keeps your money, and wins countless awards for good citizenship and providing wholesome family entertainment. If you bet that same money on a blackjack hand you might actually win it back, and more.

"Don't ever feel sorry for the player, Jimmy. If a guy gets on a roll and is up on us for fifty-thou, does he ever stop to think that we might be hurting? Do you believe that any of our clientele loses sleep over the plight of the Starlight? If we put up a display explaining all our current problems and concluding that we might go broke and close, what do you think the response would be to 'All Donations Gratefully Accepted'? Underwhelming, right?"

"I guess so."

"Then there's the State of Nevada. Once it was the biggest gamer of all, the state had to protect the integrity of the game. Today, you get investigated more for a Nevada gaming license than for a national security clearance in Washington. They turn your life inside out, and all on your nickel. If you did some business in England, well, two agents were sent there to snoop around, and you paid their bill. I was born here in Tonopah, for Chrissakes, and was licensed for my slot route for a decade before the first time I applied for a gaming license in Vegas. That little boondoggle took them nine months and cost me a hundred grand.

"When the tax was one percent of the gross, we did our own count and reported the result. Today, an owner isn't even allowed in the counting room. Do you know of any other business where the owner can't even count his own money? Now, if you expose a cheater, whether a wise guy or an insider, you have to bring in the state. They always want to prosecute, to set an example. You're never going to get that money back anyway, and it's going to cost you legal fees. You might prefer to just eighty-six the cheater and be done with it, but a casino cheater is stealing from the State of Nevada, and it's unforgiving. I remember the trial of one down-and-out guy who cheated us to feed his family. It amounted to a couple of thousand. I felt sorry for him and would have dropped the charges. No way. We still get a check for a few hundred a couple of times a year—principal and interest. He earns a little making license plates in prison, and I think they call it something like 'restitution.'"

"And what about the players?"

"What players?"

"You said there wasn't one kind."

"Oh, that. Well sure. We have the locals who come in to cash their paycheck in order to stuff their family on our cheap food. They might put five dollars in the slots or buy a couple of keno tickets. We have the high rollers who fly in, maybe in their own plane, for a stag event with raunchy entertainment and blow thousands over a weekend. We have golfers who come for our little tournaments or have us organize theirs—mainly Californians. We fill up with bowlers during the men's and women's national championships. We used to have players who rode the bus all the way from British Columbia. We used to have a lot of Indians until they built their own casinos. We do promotions to attract Blacks from Oakland and Hispanics from Stockton. All that diversity, and northern Nevada is a small fry compared to Vegas. We get a few million visitors each year, mostly from nearby, and they get tens of millions from everywhere. Casino owners around here say 'watch out, the Indians are coming.' Hell, Jimmy, there's nothing to come for. Vegas fixed our wagon twenty years ago. Today, its neighborhood casinos alone have a bigger gaming win than all of northern Nevada, even if you throw in the Lake.

"The lights are going to go out in this town one by one. Maybe we'll be among the first, and that wouldn't be so bad after all. We'd get it over with and avoid more pain. I don't know what you do with a closed casino. Maybe they should take the biggest one and turn it into a museum, a casino museum of the days before gambling became gaming. The days before it became recreation for bored little old ladies pushing the button on a slot for hours. In the old days, slot players pulled the handle hard. They pulled hard because it gave them the illusion of influencing the outcome. If they lost, their next pull was harder to change their luck. I've seen them break a machine. People threw the dice so hard that they might bounce off the table and have to be retired. They could be damaged or disappeared by someone slipping his own shaved ones into the game.

"Yessir, gambling was real serious business, then. The serious business of guys with a cigar in the corner of their mouth, a shot of bourbon in one hand, and a pair of dice in the sweaty palm of the other. Whether you were on a roll with a nice pile of winnings in front of you or down to your last dollar, I can tell you it wasn't recreation—it was damn serious business. I miss those days, Son. I really do. And they're not coming back.

"Anyway, as I was saying, there are the smart gamblers and the dumb ones. If you know what you're doing, the odds in craps are about even. A smart poker player never draws to an inside straight. A smart keno player and sports better doesn't bet on multiple number- and game-parlays. We used to have roulette wise guys. I mean there were players who tracked the outcomes on a wheel for days. They might figure out that there was a slight flaw in it that biased the outcomes over time. Or they might notice that a particular dealer was on autopilot and giving the same push to the ball every time. I've seen a demonstration where a guy was able to spin the ball on a wheel so precisely that it landed on the same one-third of the numbers more than half the time. That's a huge swing in the odds. Then there are the card-counters in blackjack. None of that wise-guy stuff is illegal, but it is intolerable. That's why the industry passed its 'privilege' legislation. In Nevada, to gamble is a privilege. You do so on private property, my property. If I want, I can eighty-six you, ask you to leave. I don't have to give a reason."

"It seems to me that the card-counters are the worst, Dad. There are all those books about how to do it."

"Jimmy, every blackjack player is a card-counter, a little or a lot. They all try to keep track of the aces and tens. Personally, I think those books help us. Most of the wannabes who buy one are lousy card-counters, but they give us more play trying. During their learning curve, they pay their tuition to us. Actually, any pit boss worth his salt can identify, and then monitor, a card-counter. If he's good at it and aggressive in his wagers, you eighty-six him—he could take you for big money. Bottom line is that the counters have to bet a little during the early deal from a deck, so they can count the key cards that have already appeared, before betting more once they think the odds are in their favor. Of course, there are the out and out cheaters who use concealed devices to keep track of the cards. You probably eighty-six them if you catch on. Some joints use shoes; put several decks together in a dispenser. That complicates the counter's math; he's no longer dealing with just fifty-two cards. It also depersonalizes the game some. Here at the Starlight, we try to overcome our poor location by advertising 'hand-held, single-deck' blackjack. The big joints don't have to do that."

Jim had heard this spiel from James umpteen times before and had been playing along with his questions. Rather than listen to the answers, he concentrated on his father's appearance—so fragile and … terminal! James was no longer capable of having new experiences that might generate fresh stories. His past was now his entire present, arrayed against a miniscule future. Jim realized that he was preparing for James's death—indeed, he was actually beginning the mourning.

***

As Jim walked from Virginia Street to the Starlight, he ignored the two drunks lying in the doorway of a decrepit mini-mart, which had sold them their gallon of red plonk in return for the proceeds from their day's panhandling, and tried to ignore the flashing lights in front of the catercorner sleazy motel renting rooms by the week to itinerant drug dealers as Reno's finest carried out the bust of a makeshift meth lab. Two-thirds of the businesses were closed, a few with windows boarded up to keep out street people in search of a night's shelter. Jim fixed his eyes on the Starlight's new flashing neon, Reno's most elaborate and expensive—a beacon designed to attract customers down the dark and dank tunnel separating his casino from the Great White Way. The signage had purposely been attached high on the building in order to encourage approaching pedestrians to raise their eyes above the squalor.

Too small, too boring, and two blocks off the main drag. We're an island that somehow floated away from the mainland, he thought. We're trying to be an island resort, but without the palms and white sand.

He tried to imagine the mind-set of a curious new customer as he entered the Starlight. As he walked by the banks of slot machines, the irony that they were his living yet bored him to death wasn't lost on Jim. To sit mindlessly for hours in front of a mechanical device struck him as tantamount to serving a limited jail sentence for a misdemeanor. He conjured up an analogy that made him chuckle. "I guess I'm a rancher who hates his cattle."

He tried to concentrate on the slot mix, while remembering Tim Saunders's dissertation on that changing world, particularly how the Starlight was lagging behind the competition. Like Detroit's automakers, the slot manufacturers brought out new products every year in order to make last year's models obsolete. The trend was to copy such cultural icons as television game shows and popular movies. Simultaneously, the traditional coin-fed machine was being eclipsed by electronics. Instead of spinning flywheels randomly halting reels to produce an outcome, slot play was now simulated on a video screen by a computer chip. Instead of being activated by coins, the player now introduced currency into a slit and was informed of her number of credits.

Activating play meant pushing a button. Payouts were check outs—pushing a button to get a paper receipt of one's credit balance to be redeemed at the cashier's cage. Gone were the sounds of cranked slot handles and metallic winnings falling into metal trays. In short, compared to before, the slot floor was eerily silent; its denizens, each in isolation, concentrated intently on a machine. No more of the jackpot bells and whistles that used to elicit the congratulations of fellow players. It was all one more incarnation of the solitudinous world of virtual reality.

Each machine cost a small fortune, close to fifteen thou and rising precipitously each year. There wasn't a single new machine on the entire floor. Tim was converting some of the inventory with kits from the manufacturers that themselves cost a couple of thousand dollars. But these fixes weren't available for the current year's games. Indeed, the latest wrinkle was called "participation," whereby the most popular games weren't even for sale. Rather, the manufacturer put them on your floor in return for a percentage of the win. So, you had a new partner, as it were.

Tim was in negotiations with IGT for some of its participation-only games as a way to have some cutting-edge product without having to purchase it. However, the initiative was stalled over the manufacturer's hesitancy to tie up scarce and valuable equipment in a notoriously failing enterprise. Jim tried to do the math in his head of what it would cost to replace all of the Starlight's nine hundred machines—maybe 13.5 million. It was more likely that the United States could retire its national debt first!

Later, as he sat across from Mary Beth Adams, Jim cradled a yellow pad on which to illustrate his thoughts. "We have to downsize the gaming. Right now. Monday, the payment for the next quarter's licenses is due. Given our lousy play, we should reduce the slot inventory by a third. We could weed out the oldest machines. That itself might give the impression that we've updated our mix. We can eliminate ten of the table games as well. That would help with payroll.

"How to redesign the floor is a head-scratcher. It's a boring rectangle, a big box. Do we wall off a third of it and move everything forward? Maybe so. But that has its own costs. My idea is a little different. Why don't we jumble the long straight rows of slots into little islands of five or six machines and arrange them in a labyrinth? We could lower the ceilings; engineering could do that, recycling the same materials. Maybe we should dim the lights, too. It might make things feel more intimate and less empty. It would give us the same feel as the Cal Neva. God knows *it's* successful."

***

Jerry contemplated the stranger staring back at him out of his vanity's mirror, looking at himself with the clinical eye of a physician. "Can that really be me?" he questioned aloud. The face retained the allure, which had facilitated his career as a womanizer, but there were now the noticeable wrinkles. The gold caps on his yellowing teeth weren't flattering, nor was the slight pouch of loose skin forming under his chin. He glanced down at his atrophying biceps and the bulge of flesh around his waist. There was the nagging twinge in his left knee where bone met bone, the intervening cartilage having succumbed long since to the rigors of pursuing high school football glory. There was the numbness in the ball of his left foot, a legacy of his drinking days.

The self-examination had been triggered by yesterday's experience at the Department of Motor Vehicles while renewing his driver's license. He'd filled out the form as always—eyes blue, hair brown, height 6'2", weight 180—but then the clerk's puzzlement made him realize that said description was belied by the salt that flecked his peppered mane, the slight stoop that had become permanent, and the portly frame that had long since broken the 200-pound barrier. He stepped out of line, threw out the form, and filled out another: hair gray, height 6', weight 210.

He groused as he assumed last place in the irritating line. The gaffe had cost him easily an hour of his life. "I've got to go to the gym," he noted to the fellow suffering stranger in front of him. Yet he knew that it wouldn't be the first time that this particular exasperation, become intention, had collided with his procrastination and shattered.

The next morning, Jerry eased his Lexus onto 1-80 and adjusted the volume on the radio so that the soft rock music was perfectly calibrated to his mood. The long rays of the early morning sun peeping over the desert hills to the east reflected off the highest peaks of the Sierra Nevadas, revealing rocky outcroppings and dense pine forests softened by the white chenille overlay of a modest early-season snowfall. The light show moved rapidly down massive slopes, searching out the recesses of canyons where it settled on the irregularly shaped gold bars of the autumn foliage of aspen groves. "Some Indian summer," he chuckled to himself, anticipating his midday meeting with the Tuolumnes.

While Jerry had allotted two hours for the trip to Sacramento, his clumsy efforts to find the unfamiliar address by consulting a map while navigating busy traffic made him late for his 9:30 appointment with Walt Maddox, the Starlight's Indian gaming attorney. Jerry was normally punctual to a fault, and his apology was excessive, prolonged in part by initial surprise. Jim Fitzsimmons had neglected to tell him that Walt was Sioux.

Jerry was having his first real glimpse into his own latent prejudices. In his mind, he was fully prepared for the early afternoon meeting with the tribe. He had a nearly memorized opening statement designed to allay any suspicions that the Starlight was more interested in making money than in the tribe's welfare. As he struggled through the preliminary pleasantries with Walt, he realized that his canned speech was simply hypocritical, not to mention ingratiating rather than gracious. He resolved to scrap it, but then felt totally disarmed for the upcoming contest.

He didn't even have a Starlight brochure to hand out. The afternoon before, he'd thought of asking for some, but by that time, Priscilla had already left for the day. No one on the swing shift had a clue as to where they were kept. *Kept, for Chrissakes,* he thought. *Aren't they for promotional purposes? They should be out where the public can get its hands on them.* Just one more crack in the Starlight's *modus operandi.* It was his own fault, however, that he was without business cards. He'd left his little leather card case next to his car keys the night before, and then forgotten it in the stupor of his early morning departure.

Jerry heard someone's voice inviting Maddox to stop calling him "Mr. Clinton," then realized it was his own attempt at some sort of bonding.

"Alright, Jerry. I prefer Walt myself. Now let's get down to business. First, let me tell you that I'm usually on the other side in these negotiations. The Starlight is my only non-Indian client."

"I didn't know that, Walt. In fact, I'm not sure I understand it. I mean, we're such a small player compared to the big boys. Take Harrah's, for example ..."

"Exactly! Harrah's made their presentation to the Tuolumne last week. What a dog-and-pony show. Three black Lincolns showed up at the reservation and eight executives got out dressed in dark suits and carrying briefcases. They had videos, graphs, and fancy brochures. After they left, there was just silence around the table. Half the tribal council never graduated from high school; slick white guys scare them. Thanks to a century of dealing with slick white guys, they're down to a few families, largely unemployed, and scratching a living out of a hundred acres of nothing. Now, for the first time in their lives they've got a real opportunity—it's called gaming."

"Yes, but why the Starlight?" Jerry asked.

"Last year, Jim Fitzsimmons sent out letters to all the California tribes. Since I represent several of them, I wrote back and said so. Frankly, I was a little fed up with the way things were heading. I'd just come back from a meeting in Vegas. The Mirage wanted to get into Indian Gaming and had invited reps from several tribes around the country. They gave us the deluxe tour and then sat us down for the pitch. Steve Wynn got up on the stage and started talking about his latest helicopter flight over Vegas with Disney's Michael Eisner, as if to say, 'come fly with us, blood brothers.' He handed out photos of

Michael and himself. Most of the people in the room would rather have had a Mirage cap, or, better yet, a jacket to take back home. If the Mirage has signed an Indian deal, I'm unaware of it.

"Then Jim Fitzsimmons came to see me, and we hit it off from the start—no bullshit, no big I. He knew that the Starlight was coming to the party late and without a costume. The more he talked, the more I liked him. Family is big with Indians—maybe the most important thing. I could see the fit between the tribes and a family-run casino. Even so, when Jim asked if I'd represent the Starlight, I had to think about it. Like I said, I'm used to being on the other side. But I checked the Starlight out and it came up clean, so I agreed to take you on. The Starlight needed me; it was well along in signing a flawed contract with the Pé-Oné tribe in Arizona."

Jerry was beginning to feel comfortable with this affable young man with the deep laugh and toothy smile, which flashed periodically like white lightning across his brown face. "So, when do we leave for Tuolumne?"

"I won't be coming, Jerry. I represent both of you and it would be inappropriate—a conflict of interest—for me to sit in on your negotiations. Later, if you both agree and will sign a waiver, I could draw up the documents. What I can tell you is that there are now several gaming companies interested in this deal. Think of it as a grape more than a plum, but a very sweet grape."

"I'm not sure I get—"

"What I mean is that there are California tribes with better locations for bigger projects. However, this is a good, solid, second-tier opportunity. The location is reasonable, not great. The Tuolumne should be able to give the casino at Table Mountain competition for the Fresno market. By the way, I'm also authorized by the tribe to tell prospects like you that they expect an up-front, non-refundable deposit from the successful bidder. They're going to use the money to remodel the houses on the reservation. They're expecting around $50,000 ..."

Jerry was disturbed by this unexpected news and almost said so before resolving to wait until after his meeting with the Tuolumne. "Can you tell me anything else that I should know, Walt? I guess what I'm asking is for advice on how to deal with Native Americans. This conversation has to be the only real one that I've ever had with one."

Walt studied Jerry for a moment and was apparently satisfied that the question was totally ingenuous. "First of all, forget that white liberal 'Native-American' crap. You're headed into Indian Country and you'll be dealing with Indians who are proud of it. Indian sovereignty antedates the United States, going back to an international treaty signed by the European colonial powers in the mid-eighteenth century. Under its terms, whenever one of them claimed a territory, it was also accepting responsibility for its people. In fact, the idea was that the colonizer was to prepare the so-called primitive peoples of the world for eventual self-rule, so the usurper was also the long-term guarantor of the sovereignty of the colonized. After the American Revolution, the new United States assumed and accepted this guardianship of its Indians. That's the foundation of the reservation system.

"God knows, our history is one long litany of abuse. It's only recently that we have won a few concessions, particularly regarding the land. But if Indian territory on this continent is shattered and fragmented into tiny little parodies of its former glory, the political concepts that underpin it are intact. In many ways, your negotiations today might just as well be with the Mexican government as with the Tuolumne Tribal Council. Every white who tries to do business in Indian Country goes through the sovereignty learning curve. That's why you've hired me!" Walt laughed.

Jerry almost held back his thought, but then risked it. "It didn't seem to do us much good with the Pé-Oné. I haven't had time to get through the file, but that deal cast a long shadow over the company. It seems to be a real mess—mine now, I suppose."

"When you're ready, Jerry, we'll talk about it. I was able to renegotiate that contract. Actually, I think you'll find that, all things considered, you came out pretty well on the deal. Jim told me that the monthly payment from the Pé-Oné is the Starlight's one bright spot these days. He says it's buying you your hang time."

***

The best that could be said about State Highway 49 was that it was paved. The two-lane ribbon of asphalt ran against the grain of the Sierra foothills stretching like fingers into the San Joaquin Valley. Jerry enjoyed the challenge as his Lexus smoothly negotiated the curves of one of the hillier knuckles. Such coupling with his metal paramour always filled him with a sense of power, but from a business viewpoint, the terrain certainly underscored Walt's point about second-tier locations. This was no ride for the hurried or those prone to car sickness. It reminded him of Sue's childhood ordeals on Agnone's by-ways.

It was fortunate that he'd followed Marv's instructions and set his odometer. Exactly 3.6 miles beyond Chinese Camp, a weathered, all-but-illegible, signboard identified a vague turnoff as the entrance to the Tuolumne Rancheria. Jerry drove slowly, picking his way between the many potholes and occasional rock that threatened to eviscerate his Lexus. His dainty lady seemed suddenly as helpless as a city girl attempting a wilderness hike in a tight skirt and high heels. The dull thud of stone against metal caused him to shudder. As his Lexus pitched forward, Jerry glanced in the mirror to see if she might be leaking one of her several vital fluids. He resolved not to examine the car's undercarriage until after the meeting, fearing that it might upset him. He certainly didn't need any bad news now; he was nervous enough.

The first house, or rather run-down shack, came into view. He couldn't tell if it was habitable and expected an Abruzzese goat herder to appear at any minute. The next had a gaping hole in its roof. Its sagging porch dipped precariously in the general direction of a vehicular graveyard that might have been a sculpture garden arranged by JFK and his classmates to mock late-twentieth-century neoliberalism. Jerry noticed the lifeless hulks of seven flivvers, some so deteriorated as to defy identification without the assistance of a forensic mechanic.

He negotiated the road, which descended a hillside, grimacing as a tree branch carved its initials in his passenger door. And then the road ended abruptly in the midst of a small clearing that contained the rancheria's only truly level land. He'd counted twenty dwellings, including several ancient, terminally immobile mobile homes.

Twenty times fifty thou—a cool million, he thought. *They sure need it, but I'm probably wasting their time and mine.*

A man emerged from the modest tribal headquarters building wearing a big welcoming grin on his mustachioed face. He was clearly non-Indian. Behind him, four teenagers slipped out of the same doorway, one bouncing a basketball. They feigned disinterest as they headed for the single backboard dirt court. Yet Jerry could sense their eyes on him. What he couldn't decide was whether they were hostile or just curious. He suddenly felt like an army scout in a Hollywood western, listening to drumbeats without knowing whether they presaged a powwow or an attack.

Marv thrust his hand through the open window and was greeting Jerry warmly before he could even extricate himself from his wounded chariot. "So glad you could make it, Mr. Clinton. We really appreciate your coming."

Jerry felt Marv's hand on his arm and followed him down a narrow corridor lined with tiny cubicles. He poked his head into each, introducing Jerry to its occupant and explaining her job responsibilities, usually while she giggled nervously. Mary Allen, grant writer; Sharon Allen, grant administrator; Betsy Allen, financial officer; Corinne Allen, social activities and health coordinator. Marv's own office, slightly larger than the rest and better furnished, was the only one bearing signage that identified his mission—Development Officer.

Mary then led Jerry down an improbable side hall that attached a hodge-podge mobile home annex to the main building. "Meet Julie Stern, Mr. Clinton. Julie has her B.A. in anthropology from Sac State and an M.B.A. from Stanford. Could you explain what you do to our visitor, Julie?"

Jerry fell instantly into the clutches of the intense young woman who kept referring to her war room. The walls were covered with topographic maps of the area, outlined and shaded in a variety of felt-pen colors and bristling with pins. "The red lines show the land that we can prove was Tuolumne during historic times. The green lines circumscribe the territory that we believe was ours in the prehistoric era. The blue is what we shared, according to early white settler accounts and our own oral traditions, with the Mokuolumne. The pins identify our sacred sites."

"Julie's our main resource person in claims cases and lawsuits," Marv interjected. He explained that the tribe was pressing its demands for more land, or at least compensation, in a variety of federal, state, and private arenas. Julie finished her presentation with a spiel about the impressive capacity of her computer and its links with others, unaware that her cyber talk was over Jerry's head.

They then went to the main building, where the entire seven-person council— four women and three men—awaited them, seated around a conference table. Jerry noted the standard male dress code—tee shirt and Levis—and congratulated himself for wearing neither coat nor tie. A jukebox spewing forth metal rock drowned out Marv's introductions, but Jerry did manage to return the welcoming nods of the tribal leaders. Two young men, no doubt their musical benefactors, were playing pool, seemingly oblivious to the impending meeting. The walls were covered with announcements, mainly warnings against drug and alcohol abuse. A young child wandered in and bought a soft drink from a vending machine, eliciting neither comment nor reprimand. Clearly, the meeting was not to be insulated entirely from casual interruption.

Jerry had assumed that Marv was the tribe's spokesman; however, at this stage at least, that wasn't the case. Rather, he slipped into the role of facilitator. Marv first introduced the council members—four people by the name of Allen, two Sterns, and a Wilson. He then told the council what he knew about the Starlight, mentioning that it came well-recommended by Walt Maddox.

Jerry was seated at one end of the table, facing Jenny Allen at the other. Everything about her was rounded—her squat torso, short arms, full face, and cropped hairdo. Before conceding the floor, Marv made a little speech about the relevance of gaming to the tribe's future and the importance of selecting the right company to help them get off to a good start. Jerry tried to read the reaction, but as far as he could tell, there was none. Every face remained expressionless, as if Marv was blithering in a foreign language.

Then it was Jenny's turn. "The Tuolumne Tribal Council welcomes you, Mr. Clinton. Tell us what you propose to do."

Jerry felt blood rush to his head. He had no real answer. He couldn't have. He hadn't seen their site, thought much about its logistics, or listened to their plans and expectations. About all he knew was that the ante in this particular poker game was around a million dollars and he could never sell that back in Reno—not even if this deal were Indian-gaming Valhalla. He was on a fishing expedition, and the first order of business was to cut bait. His mind rushed to catch up with his mouth, since, in desperation, he'd already cast platitudes instead of pearls before unimpressed shoppers. Not one of the stone faces had, as yet, revealed the slightest hint of a reaction. Jerry decided on an anodyne opening.

"Look, I have no proposal. I haven't the slightest idea what you're looking for. The fact is I came here to listen rather than talk. I don't have any pretty speeches or pictures either. What I can tell you is this. Should we make a deal, I give you my commitment that you will receive quality attention. The Starlight is just a few hours from here. That's critical when it comes to troubleshooting. The Starlight's a small operation, which means that you'd be getting my services and those of our department heads. Mr. Fitzsimmons has a personal interest in the Tuolumne casino. He told me to tell you that. So, if you do business with the Starlight, you're going to get the services of the same people you negotiated your deal with. I won't be turning you over to the company's Indian gaming director—I am our Indian gaming director."

Jerry's eyes flitted from one impassive face to another, vainly searching for any sign—he'd even settle for hostility at this point. "The last thing is that, if you're interested in the Starlight, I think that before we go any further, you should come to Reno and look us over. I don't know your schedules, but I would like you to be our guests for a couple of days—you pick the dates and Mr. Fitzsimmons and I will be there to meet with you. We'll give you a tour of the place and introduce you to our directors."

Marv came to the rescue. "I think that's a great idea. I could make the arrangements. I know most of you would prefer a weekend."

Jenny asked if Jerry and Marv would leave the room. Marv smoked his cigarette and Jerry drank his Pepsi in silence while they both paid vague attention to the in-progress two-on-two basketball game. Then they were seated again in their appointed places.

"Do you have anything to ask us, Mr. Clinton?"

"Just one thing, Mrs. Allen, what are you looking for? I mean, I assume that you want to make money for the tribe; that's not the point of my question. What I need to know is what kind of a facility do you have in mind and what are your expectations of your partner?" His one question was beginning to spawn offspring.

Jenny welcomed the opportunity to share with him her obviously oft-repeated vision. "Mr. Clinton, the Tuolumne are a very proud people. We believe that our gaming facility will be just part of a much bigger tourist complex. I believe that gaming is for now, but tourism is forever. We own a quarter of a mile of frontage on our side of the highway, and we've got an option on forty acres of land on the other. We expect our partner to lend us the money to buy it." (Jerry's mental calculator ratcheted up the likely cost of this deal.)

"Julie Stern will show you the plans. We're going to build an RV park, a waterslide, and an Indian cultural center—our own Tuolumne museum—on that land. We expect help from our partner for the museum." (Ratchet, ratchet.) "It will preserve our culture for our children and children's children. It will give them pride in their heritage and a desire to maintain it."

Up to this point, the exposition struck Jerry as reasonable, if increasingly expensive. But then his jaw began to tighten at the evolving surrealistic twist.

"People will come from everywhere to see our museum and enjoy our water park. It's not very far to the San Francisco airport, and there are more tourists every year, mainly from Asia. Asians like to gamble, and they're very interested in Indian people. There will be tour buses with Japanese tourists. We'll have to build a big parking lot for buses— we expect our partner to help pay for that."

Jerry was at a loss for words. He began slowly. "With all due respect, Mrs. Allen, I rather doubt that anyone is going to come all the way from Japan to visit the Tuolumne Rancheria, no matter what you build."

The council's reserve collapsed immediately into a buzz of agitated conversations around the table. It was clear that Jerry's simple business observation had far-reaching implications. He had challenged their voice of authority. Still, Jerry represented gaming expertise. With a few words, he'd unleashed a titanic contest of wills between the aged dream-spinner and the modern technocrat. It was then that he noticed that councilman Frank Wilson wasn't participating in the discussion. He continued to fix Jerry with a stare that was more a glare.

"They will come, Mr. Clinton. I have no doubt that they will come," Jenny said.

Heads began nodding in agreement as the council regained its former composure.

"I hope you are right, Mrs. Allen. But it would be dishonest of me not to share my misgivings with you. I know the San Francisco market. You're right about Asians; they're gamers. But the local Asians have got their own cardrooms in the Bay Area. Nevada spends millions of dollars in that market every year, and we don't get the play we used to. Vegas has tour offices and agents all over Asia. Why land in San Francisco and take a three-hour bus ride when you can fly straight to the big show, and maybe for less money? I'm just trying to be realistic."

"They will come, Mr. Clinton."

Marv rose and motioned to Jerry to follow him to his office. Jerry was certain that the game was over, and he'd failed to score. But then he heard Jenny Allen's parting comment. "Marv, work out the details with Mr. Clinton for our Reno trip."

Marv and Jerry discussed some potential dates and settled on the last week of October. They pored over the relief maps of the reservation and discussed the need to level a small ridge along the highway and the use of that material as fill in the low spots. On balance, it looked possible to come up with a four-acre building site, about enough land for a twenty-thousand-square-foot, phase-one building, complete with snack bar, bingo hall, gaming tables and room for about two hundred VLTs (video lottery terminals) or slots, the latter depending on the outcome of the current negotiations between the California tribes and the state. So far, Governor Wilson and Attorney General Lungren were sticking to a hard line, but there were rumors …

"Marv, I might as well be frank about something. We could probably loan the tribe money for the land acquisition, but forget about a million-dollar housing subsidy."

Marv was clearly confused until Jerry related that morning's conversation with Walt. "You've got it wrong, Jerry." He laughed. "We're talking about $50,000 to remodel *all* the houses—$2500 per family. We do our own work; we've got twenty unemployed guys with building skills. We just need to buy some materials."

Jerry nodded in relief, then added, "I guess we're on for the visit. But I've got mixed feelings about it. I mean there was a lot of concern when I criticized Jenny's dream about the Japanese tourists. Frankly, it's preposterous, and I couldn't in good conscience—"

"Is it preposterous, Jerry? Let me tell you a little story. Two years ago, there was a group of Japanese investors courting this project. Jenny and three of the council members went to Tokyo as guests of the developers. The deal was all but done when the Japanese showed them the mockup of their plans. They had this topographical map of the reservation—every hill and gully. Except that the existing structures were gone, and all of the best land was covered with condos. Instead of our roadside casino, there was a hotel tower, and our water park was a golf course.

"When Jenny told them to forget it, the Japanese were so mad, they cancelled the return-trip portion of the air tickets. It was a real hardship for us to bring them home at our expense. But don't try to convince Jenny, at least for now, that the Japanese won't come. She knows better."

Jerry mulled the day over as he drove back to Reno through a spectacular fall evening. "Welcome to Indian Country, Jerry. This is going to be a wild ride," he said aloud.

***

"How do you like it?" Jerry beamed as he contemplated her face in anticipation.

"Oh, Babe, it's ... it's ... overwhelming!"

Her response was scarcely what he'd expected. "Overwhelming? What does that mean, Sue?"

"It means overwhelming. I wasn't prepared for such a large stone. I've never even seen one that big. It must be real, but it looks like a prize out of a Cracker Jack box."

She noted the pained look on his face and hastened to add, "Oh Jerry, that was terrible of me. I didn't mean it the way it sounds. I'm just, well, overwhelmed. Red never gave me a *ring*."

He slipped the token of his love on her finger and watched as she stretched her arm to its fullest. She rotated her hand slowly to allow the diamond's multiple facets to catch elusive sunbeams. Jerry felt confident that Ben had scored again.

"It really is lovely, Jerry. Thank you so much."

She pecked him gently on the cheek and then cupped her hands around his face, kissing him on the mouth long and passionately while trying to ignore the nagging constraint of the cumbersome band on her unaccustomed finger.

That evening, Sue looked through the bedroom window, beyond Jerry's lightly snoring, sheet-shrouded body, at Reno's perpetual nocturnal neon light show. She felt overwhelmed by the day's many stimulations—the gift of the ring, the aromas and tastes of the French cuisine at the Petite Pier restaurant on Tahoe's North Shore, the drive back to town through the pine-flanked corridor of darkness in which they almost struck a deer, the late-evening lovemaking to the strains of Sinatra's mellowest melodies.

Something was definitely bothering her, and she struggled to bring it into focus. It must be the ring. She winced slightly as she twisted it off her finger and contemplated the refracted colors of the neon landscape trapped in its crystalline universe. It seemed ludicrous that such a tiny, insignificant object could command so much attention. It was worth more than an immigrant could hope to amass during a five-year stint in a Youngstown steel plant before returning to Agnone. Its value surpassed the impossible cost of the double-hernia operation that proved to be the beginning of the end of her marriage. It far exceeded the absent rent money that would have liberated her from Gardella's attentions and their permanent scar upon her memory.

It was then that she realized how disdainful she'd become of jewelry—probably because no one, not even Red, had ever given her any. Her inexpensive silver wedding band had been less an ornament than their way of notifying the customers at Hoagie's Diner that Sue was off limits. She didn't own a bracelet or broach. Her one matched set of imitation ruby necklace and earrings, the present of a long-since forgotten, would-be seducer, never saw the light of day. She kept them in a plastic baggie tucked away in the back of her underwear drawer, as if they were some kind of shameful secret.

Sue curled her fingers around the lifeless crystal and then stared intently at her clenched fist. She knew that she couldn't banish Jerry's ring to her reclusive baggie.

"This is gonna take getting used to," she murmured at the realization that she *hated* her ring.

***

Jim settled into the spare chair in Jerry's sparse Starlight quarters. "I like your view better than mine, I should pull rank and switch offices," he said. "You should get a plant or two, maybe paint these white walls some pastel color."

"I need a hobby like your fishing. Then the walls would take care of themselves," Jerry said, laughing.

Before proceeding with the business conversation, Jim asked about Sue and their trip to Italy, and Jerry extended Jim an invitation to his upcoming wedding. "Thanks, but I'll be fishing on Christmas Island in the South Pacific that day."

The small talk turned to Sheba. "She seems like a good kid, but a bit too quiet," Jerry said. "Sometimes, I catch her just staring at me. Sue says she has a lot of anger bottled up inside, more than the average teenager. I'm not sure how to handle her. My only parenting experience is with my son, and it wasn't that extensive."

"Girls are different, and no two are alike. Take my twins for instance; they look like two Barbie dolls out of the same package. They dress, talk, and walk the same. But, you know, Ivy's tough as nails and Heather's all silly putty inside. Ivy leads and Heather follows. Go figure."

Priscilla entered carrying a tray with coffee service for two.

"We should discuss the Tuolumne, Jim. They're coming here for a visit next weekend and I promised to have you there. Walt says the personal touch is really important. The fact that we're a family-owned place—a Fitzsimmons family place—plays well in Indian Country. They talk in terms of tribes, but they act as close-knit families."

Jim nodded in assent as he blew on the black liquid in its delicate china receptacle. "Walt's right. I've been there, and I'll be here next Saturday. Have you had a chance to review the Pé-Oné file?"

"Not really."

"Well, let me give you the thumbnail version—or at least the Starlight's side of the story. I'm sure you'd hear a different one from the Pé-Oné. We were approached by that Arizona tribe, which needed financing for its casino and management to run it. Under the terms of the Indian Gaming Regulatory Act of 1988, Indians everywhere have the right to conduct on their reservations any form of gaming that's already legal in their states. The states, in good faith, have to negotiate a compact with the tribes.

"In Arizona, some of the tribes jumped the gun and put in slot machines without a compact. Things got real tense for a while, and it looked like there might even be violence when the federal marshals went onto the reservations to confiscate that equipment. Only the feds had a right to do that; the state had no authority to enter onto Indian lands. Then the governor decided to head off a showdown by agreeing to compact for slot machines according to a demographic formula—so many tribal members translated into so many slots. The Pé-Oné qualified for six hundred machines, but their reservation was too remote. So, they wanted to buy property closer to Tucson on a state highway, and then have it taken into federal trust as reservation land. It was a really complicated deal that had to get congressional approval and a presidential signature. It took three years and a lot of lobbying.

"Anyway, by then we were involved. The Starlight had signed a five-year management contract with the tribe. We had to lend them the money to buy the land and find them financing for the casino. We were to get twenty percent of the profits. It looked like our share might be five million a year. But then it all bogged down over approvals. Under IGRA, our contract had to be approved by the National Indian Gaming Commission, and it had a big backlog—fifty or sixty pending deals. The delay was at least a year and getting worse.

"Meanwhile, we hired Walt, and he came up with a solution. Instead of managers, we could be consultants at a fixed fee. That contract would only require Bureau of Indian Affairs approval, a matter of a few weeks. That was the good news; the bad news was that we had to concede the final say so. We were only there to give advice—the tribe could take it or not."

"What was the story with Jeb? I know he's still working there."

"That's right. We had our GM down there as part of the consulting team. The casino is way out in the desert, and they couldn't attract their own person. It was getting closer and closer to the grand opening, so they made Jeb an offer he couldn't refuse and he went to work for the Pé-Oné. That's what gave you your chance to become GM here. As you know, a number of our departmental directors stayed on there for a while to get the new place up and running. Some never came back. Jeb hired them for the tribe, and things became pretty disorganized here. Really, by concentrating so much on the Pé-Oné project, the Starlight lost its bearings. We just weren't ready when the Golden Spur opened last year and suddenly there was too much product in the northern Nevada market. The Ferrareses talked about growing the market; in reality, they just cannibalized Reno's existing one."

"I sure remember those days."

"Anyway, I knew we were in big trouble in Arizona from the get-go. The day of the opening, the whole tribe was gathered in the showroom to hear the chairperson speak. Her first words were, 'Now we're going get even!' The crowd roared. We weren't open for two weeks before the problems began. Several members of the tribal council had been working on the gaming project for a couple of years. They'd visited several casinos and attended Indian Gaming conferences and they'd learned enough about gaming to have opinions, strong opinions—just enough knowledge to be dangerous. They started micro-managing the place and fighting among themselves. Sometimes they ignored our advice, particularly if it wasn't what they wanted to hear; other times, one tribal faction would use it against another.

"A few months later, they escorted our people off the property and tried to tear up our consulting agreement. Thank God for Walt. Thanks to him, we had about as much protection a non-Indian can have in Indian Country. We had waivers of their sovereign immunity—a right to sue. I thought we were headed to court for sure, but then the attorneys for both sides brokered a settlement and they bought out our contract.

"It was all pretty amicable in the end. Our five-million-a-year dream became a five-million buyout over five years, certainly better than a lawsuit. As it turned out, it was the pontoon under this damaged ship. Without that monthly payment, we probably would have closed the Starlight's doors last winter.

"So, Jerry, I'll be with you next Saturday with fingers crossed. I once had more arrows sticking out of me than General Custer, but I think I'm healed enough to consider doing another Indian deal—the right Indian deal."

***

Jerry surveyed the expectant faces around the table in the Starlight's conference room. The entire Tuolumne Tribal Council was present

... or was it? He fingered the letter from some California attorney, putting the Starlight on notice that he represented a group contesting the outcome of the last tribal election. He claimed that his side had won, but the vanquished had refused to relinquish physical control of tribal headquarters, even going so far as to post a twenty-four-hour guard on the premises.

In yesterday's hasty conference call, Walt had confirmed that the issue was indeed unresolved and would likely have to be adjudicated by the Bureau of Indian Affairs, which might even mandate a new election. Jerry and Jim were therefore unsure as to how to proceed. Chairperson Jenny Allen and her council had accepted the Starlight's invitation and had yet to even mention, let alone explain, the tribe's deep schism.

Then there was Frank Wilson. He was just as sullen as a guest as he'd been when one of the hosts of Jerry's initial visit to the reservation. Jerry found it difficult to take his eyes off him, sensing that Frank might actually exercise more influence over the outcome of the negotiations than Jenny. Indeed, two Wilsons—one a white California governor and the other a tribal member—each, in different ways, seemed to hold the Tuolumne's gaming future in the palm of his hand.

Jerry opened the meeting with the requisite formalities: "Welcome to the Starlight. It's good to see all of you again. I hope your dinner and rooms were satisfactory last night. Jim Fitzsimmons here, is part-owner and CEO of the Starlight."

Two of the councilmembers began to whisper to each other, looking confused, so Jerry hastened to add a clarification, "Mr. Fitzsimmons is the new boss around here. His father, James, just retired."

Jim took a last sip of water and cleared his throat to dispel his initial nervousness over public speaking. "I ... I would like to add my sentiments to Jerry's welcome. We plan to take you through each department, and have you meet its director. I think of the Starlight as one ... as one big family. If we all decide to make a deal, you'll be joining it. It's important that you know us well before you make that kind of decision."

Jim believed his own spiel ... sort of. He'd made it before, when personally negotiating the Pé-Oné contract. As he looked over the blur of unfamiliar brown faces, he struggled not to allow the hint of *déjà vu* to grow into a full-fledged warning signal. *These people are not the Pé-Oné*, he reminded himself. "Jerry will take you through the property … after you've finished your rolls and coffee, of course." He motioned to the continental breakfast buffet set-up. "I'll rejoin you once you've seen everything. I'll try to answer any questions you might have at that time."

As the tour progressed, Jerry had a growing sense of unease. Hotel Director Sherman's succinct description of the sales and registration procedures, the company's policy on guest services, and the procedures for adjusting rates according to available room inventory at any particular point in time elicited neither questions nor visible reactions from the audience. The Tuolumne were equally unresponsive to Food and Beverage Director Broussard's tour of the restaurant and bar facilities. The main point of his presentation, the importance of controlling food and labor costs when he was already providing a loss leader to the Starlight's product mix, seemed entirely lost on his audience. As they exited the main kitchen to proceed on to the slot department, Jerry overheard Wilson's comment, "You have to speak Spanish to work in there."

The gruff edge to Frank's voice brought into focus the mild standoff Jerry had just witnessed. The swarthy Mexican kitchen crew had feigned indifference while being scrutinized by the even swarthier visitors. Under other circumstances, they were competitors for the same manual jobs. There was no small irony in their present respective fates—the one group condemned to wash dishes, the other possibly destined to own them.

What was beginning to bother Jerry was his growing awareness of the complexity of a casino operation, a complexity that he'd long taken for granted. Trying to explain it to unsophisticated laymen was a far more daunting challenge than he'd imagined. He resolved in future to meet with the directors in advance of any dog-and-pony show to streamline their presentations. It seemed far more important to boil them down to a few salient, easily comprehensible points, rather than to be comprehensive. But there was the other side of the matter, too. Jerry thought that even if they might be boring the Tuolumne, they were certainly snowing them as well. The meta-message—"the casino business is very complicated, so you need our help"—wasn't all bad in the circumstances.

Slot Director Saunders's talk was equally arcane in many respects, but did elicit the first real questions.

One council member asked, "Are the machines fixed? How do I know when there's going to be a payout?"

"Good question. It doesn't work like that. We're dealing only in probabilities here. The machines are fixed to pay out a certain percentage, but the individual outcome is totally random. Theoretically, any machine can hit two jackpots in a row. Where the percentages enter in is over the long haul. After hundreds of thousands, or even millions, of plays, the house's hold, its win from a machine, should be very close to the programmed expectation."

"What's the percentage here at the Starlight, Mr. Saunders? What do you set your machines at?"

"Again, a good question. A lot of the public think that way. Actually, the reality is a little different. The percentage varies from one machine to the next. Some are looser than others. Part of the challenge for a slot director is how to mix them, how to lay out the product—the loose and the tight, not to mention the various types of games—so as to achieve maximum player appeal. There's more than one philosophy on how to do it. That's where the art, rather than the science, comes in—the slot director's gut feeling.

"We monitor everything carefully. We have a daily computer printout on every machine and track actual play and win against expected play and win. It can get pretty streaky over the short term, so you can't knee-jerk. But if, over several weeks, a particular machine is failing to get enough play or isn't holding well, then you may have a problem to examine."

"So, are the Starlight's machines loose or tight?" interrupted Chairperson Allen.

"We try to be a 'loose' house. We're pretty small by Nevada standards, and we don't have the attractions of, say, the Golden Spur's headliner live entertainment. So, we try to maintain the reputation of being a loose-slot house. We also have the town's most liberal rules on the table games. You can't expect people to walk a couple of blocks off the Great White Way if all they're going to find is more of the same.

"But I would emphasize that whether you're loose or tight refers to your overall slot mix. You might be 'loose' as a house and still have some pretty tight machines. The opposite is also true. Like when you see an advertisement that talks about a 'hundred-percent payback.' There may be only one machine in that entire establishment set at that percentage. Under Nevada law, you only have to deliver what you advertise. We can put a machine on the floor that pays absolutely nothing, as long as we say so. When you see the payouts listed on a machine, the state only demands that each of those combinations *can* come up—that's all. The state does random checking. They can come in any time and pull the chip from the machine and run a test on it. As long as it's possible to hit every advertised combination on that machine, you're okay. The state doesn't care how easy it is for, say, the jackpot combinations to come up. That's where the house's decision regarding loose versus tight enters in."

Another of the tour's stellar attractions from the visitors' point of view was the counting room. Jerry gave the spiel himself, as the Tuolumne gazed in rapt attention at their real future dream. Four employees scurried about a hopper feeding thousands of coins into it, which were then segregated and moved by conveyor belt to wrapping machines before being stacked on heavy-duty carts like so many Tootsie Rolls in some candy display.

"The coins never leave the Starlight, except for a few in customers' pockets. We just recycle them between the cashier's cage, the change persons, the machines, and this counting room. Sometimes, we have to buy additional change from the bank. We do the drop three times a week. That is, we take the coins out of the drop box in every machine. Security is always present. When uncounted cash is your inventory, well you're real vulnerable to employee theft.

"The first step, I mean our first control, is to weigh the coins. One hopper of ten thousand quarters pretty much weighs the same as another. Two hundred pounds of quarters equals approximately so much money. We then put the coins through metered wrappers and compare that actual count with the weight estimate. If there's a discrepancy, you look into it."

The council members took turns, two at a time, looking through the small window in the soft count room as Jerry pointed out the surveillance cameras monitoring the process.

"This is where we count the currency—that's what we take to the bank. The state requires that there be two money counters, and that they be filmed at all times. If one needs to use the restroom, the other has to step out as well. We're required to keep the videotapes of the count for ten days or so, and the state can come in at any time to check the procedures."

"Mr. Clinton, why is the state so involved in everything?"

"The short answer is that the state is the biggest winner from Nevada gaming, through its taxes. Directly and indirectly, we provide more than half of Nevada's budget. So, the state has the biggest vested interest in an honest count. I'm sure you've all heard the word 'skimming.' It used to be a big problem when the house just counted the money and reported the results. Procedures are much tighter now. In fact, Mr. Fitzsimmons, as an owner, is prohibited from being present in that room while the count is going on."

The back-of-the-house tour was to terminate in the ever-fascinating peek, or surveillance, room. It so happened that the Starlight's director of surveillance was Running Buffalo—a Blackfoot Indian. The gray-haired Asian woman monitoring the screens flashed a welcoming smile at the visitors, and then slipped back into her eternal scrutiny of the changing black-and-white images on the bank of twenty flickering screens.

"Look, there's the soft-count room," Jenny remarked to no one in particular.

Running Buffalo took command. "We monitor every machine with a large progressive jackpot. If it hits, we review the tape before paying it off, just to be sure everything is on the up and up, no tampering. See those other screens on the pit? Their cameras are set to cover a whole game. Chen, could you zoom in on a hand, please?"

The two hands in the image went from insignificant to monstrous. The three playing cards were seemingly highway billboards. "If we think something might be suspicious, we monitor the play carefully. As you can see, we're able to sweat a game without the dealer or player even knowing it. Possible collusion between a pit employee and a crony is a big concern—a real window of vulnerability."

"Sweat?" Jenny asked.

"It's a gaming expression for watching closely. Now, Chen, could you run the tape for our guests?"

All eyes were on the monitor, which showed a former dealer's theft from the Starlight. Running Buffalo explained what to watch for. Under his tutelage, most, though not all, were able to discern the sleight of hand move whereby the dealer ostensibly used the 'paddle' to shove a twenty-dollar bill through the slot of a blackjack game's cash box but, in fact, employed his little finger to press a corner of the banknote against the green-felt tabletop. He then deftly slipped his hand over the opening and used a sliding motion to retrieve the money from the recess, rolling it into a ball, which he palmed and then shoved under his shirt cuff.

"When we confronted him, he had two hundred and forty dollars up his sleeves … literally. He wasn't an employee any longer; he'd become a partner," Running Buffalo joked. "Sometimes they out themselves. My favorite was the guy who wore big cowboy boots and was good at dropping dollar tokens into them. He never missed. But one shift, he got too greedy, and when it was time to go on break, he could hardly walk. We just followed the clinking sound to the culprit!"

After the show, Running Buffalo handed out used decks and dice to his delighted audience. Jerry then took the Tuolumne to GM Adams's office, where she and Controller Samantha Edgars awaited the perfunctory courtesy call.

"As GM of the Starlight, I'd like to add my welcome to that of Mr. Clinton and Mr. Fitzsimmons. I know you are in good hands. In fact, Mr. Clinton used to have my job, so he can address your concerns as well as I can. However, if you have anything in particular that you would like to ask me, or Ms. Edgars …"

There being no questions, the group was headed back to the conference room when James Fitzsimmons appeared from around a corner. "Busy as usual, I see, Jerry. Who are our visitors?"

Jerry was a little uneasy as he introduced the Tuolumne. He hadn't factored an encounter with the Starlight's patriarch into the day's equation. His anxiety increased at the Fitzsimmons invitation: "Come into my office."

Priscilla scrambled to provide as many chairs as possible, giving up her own and cannibalizing three others from Jim's office. Even so, two of the visitors remained standing in the doorway, as did Clinton next to the seated host.

Jerry hastened to gain control of any possible agenda. "Mr. Fitzsimmons is one of the venerable pioneers of our industry. He was in the business in the forties, when Harold Smith was king of this hill and Bill Harrah was getting his start. Mr. Fitzsimmons knows as much about northern Nevada's gaming history as anyone alive."

"Jerry's right about that," James said. "You just can't imagine how much the business has changed in my lifetime. When I first started out with a bingo parlor on Virginia Street, why, Las Vegas was nothing. Bugsy Siegel hadn't even heard of the place. In those days, Reno ran this state—everything about it. Harold's Club was the biggest casino in the world. They had those 'Harold's Club or Bust' billboards all over this country, and a lot of other countries, too. It's owner, Pappy Smith, taught me the importance of low house odds. He always said, 'You have to send out winners to get players.' Bill Harrah taught us the need to have decent rooms, restaurants, and service—a sparkling image.

"It was the gambling business, then, not some squishy little thing called 'gaming.' We were real gamblers because we sat on both sides of the table. We understood the customers' perspective, because we, too, were players. Some guys, like Harold Smith and Bill Harrah, were so hardcore that they were always betting the farm, their farm, in competitors' joints. That sure wouldn't have passed muster as a business plan, but it was their plan and it was real. It was written with booze, broads, tobacco, and gaming chips. We're not in gambling anymore; we're in the percentages' business. We've become a bunch of boring bankers.

"In the old days, there was no air conditioning, and you couldn't stand to be in Las Vegas in the summertime. Until they invented air conditioning, Vegas wasn't even possible. We had maybe thirty thousand people in Reno and Las Vegas didn't have ten. The other day I read in the paper that Vegas has passed a million. We haven't stood still—they say there are a quarter of a million people in this valley now—but compared to Vegas …"

"Like I said, Mr. Fitzsimmons is a living authority on Old Nevada." Jerry interjected, hoping to quit while they were ahead. It didn't work.

"The gaming business is no good anymore. This town is dead, or at least dying. We used to know our customers, talk to them, drink with them. Now it's all college guys with computers. They use fancy words like 'demographics' and 'marketing strategy.' They worry about occupation, per capita income, geographic distribution. They still talk about fun and excitement, but they don't mean it. Hell, they don't have a clue—just words.

"The customer today is a number—a series of numbers. That's why I try to spend my time down on the floor. I circulate and try to talk to our old customers and long-time employees. I want the guests to feel welcome at the Starlight. I try to learn what's going on from the people who really know—our front-line employees. I almost never see any of our management on the floor. They're too busy having meetings or sitting in their offices writing reports."

James's reiterative exposition on gaming was new to the Tuolumne, if not to Jerry and Jim. But then James shot the dreaded arrow into the heart.

"You can't imagine how much this business has changed. And now they've got gaming everywhere. Take the damned Indians, for instance. They've got an unfair advantage. The feds let them have gaming and pay no taxes. We pay huge taxes. How can Reno compete against no tax? What did you say you were here for? Jerry?"

His worst fear realized, Jerry now struggled to say something intelligible. He knew that his face was as beet red as that of any magician whose trick had suddenly unraveled pitifully in mid-performance.

Jenny came to the rescue. "Mr. Fitzsimmons, it is an honor to meet with you. On behalf of the council, I want to thank you for giving us your time and knowledge."

As the Tuolumne filed out of the executive offices, heading for the conference room, Jerry took Marv aside and expressed his concern over the gloomy depiction and possible insult.

"It's all right, Jerry; Jenny meant what she said. The Tuolumne venerate their elders. No matter what an elder says, you listen and suspend judgement out of respect. Meeting Mr. Fitzsimmons was a big plus, a privilege. The meeting is what counted, not the speech."

Jim Fitzsimmons was already seated at the head of the table, awaiting their return. Jenny took her place at the opposite end, Marv at her side. Jerry sat next to Jim. The council members, save one, arranged themselves between the two negotiating forces. Frank Wilson lingered by the refreshments, refusing to take a seat.

Before either Jim or Jenny could open the meeting with a remark, Frank said, "I want everyone here to know that as long as I'm alive, there will never be a casino at Tuolumne. First the white man sent in the cavalry, then the anthropologists, and now the gamblers. Our language is gone—we have three elders who know a few words of Tuolumne—our culture is all but dead. Jenny wants to build a museum. I say we need more than that. A museum is a tombstone over the corpse of our culture.

"You call some of us traditionalists. You say we want to revive the past when what we should do is plan for a better future. Well, to me working for these guys as a blackjack dealer is a lousy future. To me, watching our people sell their souls to the white man, and on his terms, is to break faith with our elders and ancestors. What can possibly remain of the Tuolumne way of life after the casino is through with us? When we're all living in nice white-man houses and driving big white-man cars, who will we be? Tuolumne? I don't think so!"

The silence following Frank's monologue was deafening. All eyes were fixed on the door through which he'd just departed. The letter from the dissident faction's attorney, followed by James Fitzsimmons's speech, and capped by Frank Wilson's diatribe, had scarcely created a propitious climate for a serious negotiation. Jerry whispered a suggestion in Jim's ear.

Jim nodded and said, "It's been a pleasure to have you here. I have a thought—rather than discuss business, why don't we leave things as they are for today? Hopefully, you've had a chance to get to know the Starlight family. Jerry and I can drive down to the rancheria to meet with you there at your convenience."

Jenny responded, "That would be acceptable, Mr. Fitzsimmons. On behalf of the Tuolumne Tribal Council, the *only* tribal council, I thank you for your hospitality."

After she'd left, Marv and two council members took Jerry aside, and Marv said, "It's been great, but what about the girls? I told the guys that you'd get us some hookers. I thought casinos always did that. The dinners, rooms, and souvenirs were okay, but ..."

"Sorry, Marv, the Starlight's not in that business."

***

Jerry answered the front door and was momentarily stunned by the sight of Tim, Carla, and the children. "What are you doing here? I mean

… what a pleasant surprise! But why didn't you call?" He struggled to reconcile this unexpected development with the impending event—in an hour, he and Sue were to be married quietly in their own living room.

"Where is everyone, Dad? I thought this was going to be a wedding."

"You know about it?"

"Sure, Sue told Carla last week. They talk on the phone now, you know. We decided to surprise you. It's about time someone in this family attended someone else's wedding." Tim laughed, a little too close to the abyss.

Once over the initial shock, Jerry was enormously pleased. "Come in, come in."

Manny Cohen, Carol Bentley, and Tracy were the next to arrive, Manny festooned in a loud sports jacket and pair of slacks that probably glowed in the dark. It was the first time Jerry had ever seen Carol in a dress. *From the thrift shop, no doubt*, he thought, but then conceded that it actually became her. Manny and Carol were to be the witnesses.

The roar of a motorcycle engine announced the arrival of Bruce Thompson—Reverend Bruce Thompson, that is. The pastor of the Center for Religion and Life at the university had agreed to perform the ceremony. Reverend Thompson, dressed in a leather jacket and Levis and carrying his crash helmet, greeted the gathering.

"Let's get started," Jerry said.

"Dad, this is it? Nobody else? I've seen larger crowds at life insurance sales pitches!"

"Tim, when you've been around this track as many times as I have, it's a little ridiculous to hire a hall and send out invitations."

The reverend invited Sheba and Tracy, Caroline and Brett to sit on the floor at his feet. The living semi-circle of children had the effect of elevating the marriage couple onto their own little stage. He then conducted a brief ceremony that was both solemn and appealing in its simplicity. The bride and groom stood before the picture window that framed the distant Sierra Nevadas. The tallest peaks were wreathed in gray clouds, and wispy snow squalls flowed down the highest canyons, harbingers of an impending early December storm.

After exchanging the traditional vows and kiss, Sue read a poem that she'd composed for the occasion, her first ever. Then Manny activated the tape player that contained the two songs that Jerry had chosen. They all listened attentively to R. Kelly's *I Believe I Can Fly* and Bette Midler's *Wind Beneath My Wings*.

Reverend Thompson asked Jerry, Sue, Manny, and Carol to sign the wedding certificate, then wished the newlyweds all the best and was practically out the door before Jerry was able to convince him to accept a token payment for his services.

"See you at school, Sue," he said as he adjusted his chin strap and straddled his Harley. He and the bride were classmates in the same Western Literature class.

Jerry's attention immediately turned to the wedding dinner. They had a reservation for four at the Vecchia Varese Italian restaurant. He found both Manny and Carol shallow and coarse, but had deferred to Sue's wishes in the matter. As a veteran groom, Jerry had learned at least one lesson: weddings were a female affair. The wise groom did as he was told. They could scarcely leave Tim, Carla, and the children out of the dinner plan, but Jerry experienced mild panic at the thought of the volatile mix. He wasn't certain that Manny wouldn't use his favorite adjective, even in the presence of Caroline and Brett.

He needn't have worried. Cohen approached Jerry with a big grin and hand extended. "Congratulations! You're a lucky man! Say, Carol and I been talkin', and we think we should change our dinner date. You probably want tonight to be a family affair. Could we take a rain check?"

Jerry found himself alone with his new wife and stepdaughter, son and daughter-in-law, and two grandchildren. He was struck by the fact that he was the only representative of his own generation present. "I can't remember when I've been blessed with so much family. You know, kids, I left home at a real tender age and never looked back. Until today, I don't think I ever realized what a lone wolf I've been. It's kind of nice to have a pack."

Sue laughed and said, "So, I'm one of the kids? I guess that makes me a child bride. It sure does beat being an aging cocktail waitress!"

Jerry framed her face with his hands and kissed her long and lovingly, "Thank you so much for agreeing to fly with such an old reprobate."

"My pleasure I'm sure, Mr. Mallard."

A voice chimed in, "Dad, the whole day has just been beautiful."

Jerry turned in its direction. "One of the nicest parts was your surprise visit. Welcome to Nevada, Carla."

***

Will this never end? Jim bemoaned to himself as he insinuated his handkerchief beneath his shirt collar to absorb the flop-sweat generated by his fear of public speaking. He walked to the podium in the Starlight's ballroom and nodded at the sea of five hundred faces, each connected to an unhappy employee. Manny Cohen had been delegated by Mary Beth Adams to moderate as Jim steeled himself to deliver his two pages of prepared remarks. It was his annual duty to hand out the token honors for the Starlight's best this and that. It was a transparent management ploy to spread the glory as widely as possible, since the certificates of excellence, pins, and plaques were often a nick out everybody's annual pay raise. The audience knew that these cheap fripperies would be the entire substitute for money this year. The wooden applause for Jim's appearance was polite at best.

He wondered how many people in the room had applications under consideration at other casinos, thereby exacerbating the general rumor that the Starlight was on the ropes? He averted his eyes from those of the audience just in time to wince at Manny's japery, his lame attempt at levity as he handed a certificate to the septuagenarian in the maintenance department. "Just remember, Ed, honors are like hemorrhoids, sooner or later every asshole gets one!"

***

Two weeks after their initial conversation, Jim again heard Joe Conroy's familiar voice over the telephone.

"Hi, Jim. Mr. Hoskins is with me and wants to speak with you again."

There was a rustling sound, then Hoskins said, "Hello, Mr. Fitzsimmons. You won't believe what the Spark City Council did to us."

"Oh, I can imagine."

"Anyway, we've dropped our option on the Sparks dirt. We just bought three acres in Fernley. Our truckers can reach the Bay Area and return on a single tank of fuel, so that will work just as well as Sparks. We're also building a travel center in Las Vegas. My question to you is whether you'd be interested in being our gaming operator in Nevada? We'd prefer to lease you space in the new centers, rather than becoming your partner."

Jim processed the request. "I would need to run the matter by my board and directors. My first reaction is that Vegas would be out of the question. It's more than four hundred miles from Reno, and with no rooms, you'll be limited to fifteen games. It wouldn't be cost effective for us to set up an organization down there for that few. As for Fernley, which county are you in—Washoe or Lyon? The line runs right through there."

"I'm not sure. I can get back to you about that."

"If you're in Lyon, which has no room requirement, we may be interested. We might start with thirty or so games, and there could be an upside if we're successful. It's thirty miles from here; the Starlight could run the Fernley operation out of our slot department. We might pay you so much per slot machine or lease the premises. I can tell you that it couldn't be based on a percentage of the action. Nevada Gaming Control would treat that as participation—it'd make you our partner and you'd need a gaming license. They'd investigate you, and on your nickel, in every state where you operate. I imagine it'd be very expensive—maybe in the hundreds of thousands. Being a landlord also requires state approval, but the investigation is much easier and far cheaper."

"We'd prefer that. Time is of the essence. We're finalizing our construction plans and need to pull building permits in the next couple of weeks. We hope to open both Nevada sites within six months. We have a standard footprint for our travel centers—our own architect and preferred contractor. It really streamlines everything. But, of course, none of our other centers have gaming, so we would need to modify our standard design ... with your input, of course."

"I'll get back to you in two days, Mr. Hoskins. Thank you for thinking of the Starlight."

"Wonderful. If it's a go from your end, I'll fly out to finalize the details. Could we meet on Saturday? I know it's the weekend, but you wouldn't believe my work week. I have to visit three potential sites in California on Sunday."

"Of course."

***

The Fitzsimmons family was gathered for its Christmas dinner. Ivy and Heather were heading off together the next morning for a skiing holiday in Switzerland before renewing their studies. JFK was about to depart for Hawaii—ostensibly to "hang out" in his mother's parents' condo until spring semester classes started, but actually to commune with the goddess Maui Wowie for his next inspiration.

No one was prepared for a crushing speech by the family patriarch. Jim had startled the assemblage by first announcing that the following fall the children would have to attend the University of Nevada, Reno, if they expected his support. The resident tuition at the public institution was a fraction of their current expenses. He then informed Dot that they were putting the house on the market. Ivy blurted out, "D-a-a-a-d!!" Heather simply burst into tears and ran out of the room! JFK mingled disappointment with indifference as he mildly probed and debated the issue.

"So, we're broke, huh? Why didn't you say so sooner so we could plan for it? Just how broke is broke?" JFK's tone was more bemused than indocile.

"Son, you don't make plans to go broke. In fact, it involves a lot of denial. You keep hoping things will get better. In my business, you tell yourself that a strong weekend will make up for the weak weekdays. When it doesn't happen, you struggle to survive until the next big three-day holiday. When I walked through the Starlight today, there were three employees for every player—it looked like death eating a cracker. I don't know where it all stops. What I do know is that it's high time to take our heads out of the sand around here. It may even be too late to adjust our lives so we can get on with them without first having to walk away from a crash landing, but we'd better start trying."

JFK listened to his father with a slightly bemused expression, simultaneously panicked over losing his free ride and secretly relieved at the prospect of no longer being the remittance man in a Nevada casino family. Neither his mother's social pretension nor his father's dubious enterprise were easily reconciled with JFK's leftist politics and self-appointed artistic mission. The thought of being plunged into the netherworld of San Francisco's starving artists' scene through some fault or failing of his father had definite, indeed redemptive, appeal.

There was a piece of Jim that was actually enjoying the exercise. He suddenly realized just how alienated he was from his children— seeing them not as people but as products, products of their mother's upbringing. At every step of the way, he'd acceded to her desires, whether when purchasing their ostentatious house or giving preposterously affected names to their daughters.

"Jim, stop talking nonsense. You're upsetting the children. Sell the house? No one sells their house except to buy a better one. I couldn't bear to face my friends. Get real! James, go see if your sister is all right."

Jim and Dot Fitzsimmons sat in silence, glaring at one another across the excessive expanse of the table. The oaken surface was now the no man's land dividing two intractable forces that had battled to a draw. Raw hostility mocked the elaborate decorations and barely audible Christmas music emanating from well-concealed speakers. Jim hadn't a clue what might follow. Then Dot rose abruptly and left the room without another word. He sat for a while, half expecting her to return to put some exclamation point on the evening—her Parthian shot. She did not, so he ascended to Jim's World to catch a few hours of sleep before the next workday.

***

Jim entered Dot's capacious mansion the following evening and was drawn to the kitchen by the aroma of cooking. He noted that the dinette table where they took their meals when alone remained unset. He entered the dining room and found his wife revisiting the scene of last night's crime. She sat motionless, presiding over the wreckage of her shattered dreams. Her taut posture and drawn expression bespoke unpredictable danger, but also a pathos that elicited his first tender feelings toward her for some time. He approached his wife, and placed his hand upon her arm.

"I know this is all very hard for you, Dot. I tried to warn you. But we haven't been able to talk for years, not really. Maybe we never could."

It was then that she began to blurt out her obviously rehearsed lines. "I've made a decision. I want you gone from this house. I mean tonight. If you won't fight for our home, our children's home, then I will. I don't know what we've got left, but I intend to get every penny of it. I don't know who comes to the front door to evict women and children, but I'll fight them with every breath in my body. I will not accept this, Jim."

He lingered momentarily in silence, and then patted her arm twice before moving to the other side of the table to take a seat opposite his fuming and estranged wife. Jim waited vainly for several minutes, to give some unspecified outside force the opportunity to intervene, then rose slowly. "I'll be leaving in a few minutes, Dot."

"Oh, one more thing, Jim. Don't you ever, ever call me that again. I *hate* it. It makes me sound like one of those Silicon Valley businesses you're always talking about. I dislike Dottie, too. My name is Dorothy. You won't have any trouble remembering it—it'll be on the divorce papers."

He paused behind her, absently kissing the back of her head out of habit. "As you wish, Dorothy." He was relieved by her anger; he'd feared pleas and tears.

Jim ascended the stairs to Jim's World, where he spent the next hour packing. After putting two suitcases in his car, he walked through the foyer with his overnight bag. He noted that the kitchen was dark, and Dorothy was no longer seated in the dining room. She'd turned off the stereo, with its endless carols, and disappeared somewhere into the recesses of the mansion. The only signs of life were the twinkling lights outlining the crèche and those illumining the front door. As he left his home of twenty-five years, Jim absentmindedly fingered the baby Jesus figure, and then turned it face down in the straw of its manger.

***

Jim Fitzsimmons sat at his desk, hoping that a piece of flotsam might bob by that he could grab onto. He contemplated the card that Jeremy Clinton had given him that morning when he'd unburdened himself

... perhaps too incautiously. He now felt a little vulnerable should Jerry ever turn on him.

Charles Wilson, Attorney-at-Law.

Jim needed outside counsel, someone who had not known the family for years. His personal solicitor was Dorothy's second cousin and lived in Seattle. For Chrissakes, Jim wouldn't trust him with a minor personal injury suit, let alone his whole life. At least Dorothy had been quite clear about the playing field and her goals. Jim knew he required a *good* attorney.

He failed to find the thought of divorce disturbing. Given all of his other problems, it held no great prospect of either relief or release. The imminent unraveling of his marriage did underscore for Jim its fragility and frigidity. For more than a quarter of a century, he had preserved the appearances of marital bliss with the Seattle socialite.

Jim opened his desk drawer and took out his diary. For twenty years, it had served as a safety valve when he was burdened by the alternating boredom and stress of being James-Fitzsimmons-in-waiting. In his usual cryptic code, he wrote:

Dear Diary:
Last night it hit fan. Out of house by eight. Nowhere to go. Drove to Fallon, Schurz, Yerington. Clear night, hoarfrost on sagebrush. Got to Carson at one a.m.—still no plan. Woke up night clerk—checked into Bo Peep Motel. Didn't know still had such places. Reminded me of vacation trips when kid—rundown Central Valley, Spanish-style dumps. Palm trees out front— linoleum floors inside. Took three pills—woke up at ten. Couldn't shave—forgot razor. Got to office at noon. Mary Beth/Samantha waiting. More disastrous numbers. Food costs for the two-for-one lobster-steak dinner through roof. Payroll check cashing promotion hemorrhaging money. Locals taking advantage of both. A double whammy. Costs dollar ten to get dollar of business. Called in Cohen. Says food special his idea, but payroll program mine. Mary Beth said measuring promotions all talk if run simultaneously. Can't tell what's working. She fired him. Pretty extreme. Suspicious too. Mary Beth/Samantha can't stand Cohen style. Said nothing. Have to back my GM or remove her.

Jim replaced the leather-bound diary in its slipcover and contemplated his bleak prospects. It was 10:30 p.m. and he felt hunger pangs. He realized that he hadn't eaten since lunch the day before! He descended the back stairwell from the executive offices to The Westerner restaurant and took a seat at the counter. Since he never frequented the Starlight at night, no one recognized him. Despite his fast, the clubhouse sandwich seemed tasteless. It filled his biological need more than his whetted appetite. He read the day's newspaper while he ate, but found it impossible to concentrate on even the simplest of stories. By 11:30, he was wandering the casino floor, aimlessly experiencing its tempo. The irony of being the owner of this unfamiliar world wasn't lost on him. What was the Starlight like at 4 a.m.? That was a completely unexplored Night-Town for Jim Bloom, former meal ticket of Dorothy Fitzsimmons and her brood.

He found himself in one of the Starlight's several lounges and took a seat in a darkened corner. The cocktail waitress approached, and he realized that he'd have to order something to defend his territory. "Vodka and tonic, please. Make that Absolut." He was about to imbibe his first drink ever in his own place.

"Coming right up, Sir."

He'd expected a little less formality.

As she set his drink in front of him, she asked, "Will you be signing for this, Mr. Fitzsimmons?"

"Oh, so you know who I am?"

"Yes, Sir, I've been here for a lot of years."

He took a five-dollar bill from his pocket and told her to keep the change. He preferred not to leave a paper trail of his nighttime ramblings. What might Samantha think if the signed check came across her desk? He shuddered at the thought of Priscilla armed with rumored boozing by the boss during the wee hours.

"What's your name, Ms ...?

"Bentley, Sir. Carol Bentley."

"Have we ever met, Ms. Bentley?"

"Not really, Sir. Well, once you shook my hand at an employees' award banquet as you gave me my five-year service pin."

Jim watched while Carol attended to two other tables. Then she was back to ask if he wanted a refill.

"One more, and then it's decision time," he mumbled somewhat distractedly.

"Sir?"

"Another drink, Ms. Bentley."

When she returned, there was a moment of awkwardness. He'd already paid her more than three times the cost of his first drink. Now he sat immobile after she served the replacement.

Finally, she blurted out, "Sir, I'm going off shift. It's midnight."

"Well, thank you Ms. Bentley."

She was halfway across the floor before he realized his gaffe. "Ms. Bentley," he said in a raised voice that failed to get her attention. "Carol," he shouted, causing a few heads to turn, including hers.

"Yes, Sir?" she asked, coming to stand once again in front of him.

"Look, I've got no more money on me. Can you wait here while I go cash a check at the cage?"

"It's not necessary, Sir. I don't mind ..."

"Well, I do. Please, I insist."

"Sir, I'm not allowed to sit here in uniform. If you want, I'll go change and come back."

"Great, that'll work."

"Give me ten minutes."

It was only as she walked away that Jim noticed Carol's comely figure, clad skimpily in sequined folds of fiery red satin and accentuated by sheer black nylons.

Jim crossed the casino floor, finding it vaguely threatening. As he passed the pit, he winced at the aggressive screams of four intoxicated craps players trying to intimidate the dice. At the cage, he waited patiently before the bloodless automaton who seemed oblivious to his presence. After a considerable pause, the aged cashier raised her eyes from her book work and mouthed, "Yes?" She said it in a tone that simultaneously conveyed indifference and annoyance.

He felt anger rising within him. Jim now understood the conversation at a recent directors' meeting in which Mary Beth lamented the Checkpoint Charlie atmosphere of the cage, only to be told that several of the cashiers were among the Starlight's original employees and were way too old to learn new tricks. Given all of the other problems at the Starlight, she'd decided not to open up a new Pandora's box. Jim managed to cash his hundred-dollar check by providing the crone with the standard photo identification. She obviously failed to make any connection between her client and employer.

"How do you want it?"

"Four twenties, a ten, and two fives."

She counted out his bills, then turned away without another word.

No *thank you*, no *good luck, sir,* no *have a nice evening,* he thought. *No nothing.*

He made a mental note to ask Mary Beth to put discussion of the cage on their next agenda. *If the goddamn bank can train young kids to be friendly tellers, I sure don't see why we have to put up with that service,* he thought. *If we're down-sizing anyway, we may as well clean out that little nest of vipers!*

***

"What do you drink, Carol?"

"Mineral water, Sir. Never mix business and pleasure. I'm around booze too much to like it."

"Please call me Jim. 'Sir' makes me feel really old … especially tonight."

"What's so special about tonight, Jim?"

He laughed at the question. "Nothing. In fact, pretty much the opposite. I always think of 'special' as something good." He lapsed into silence, mired once again in trying to sort out the confusion of the last two days. "You know, Carol, tonight is so un-special that I have no idea where I'm going to sleep. I have three suitcases in my car and nowhere to put them down. Last night, I was Bo Peep's house guest in Carson. Tonight, who knows. But I better get on with it. It's late." A fleeting thought of Priscilla's waggish tongue immediately ruled out checking himself into one of the Starlight's many unoccupied rooms.

"You can stay at my place if you like."

"What?"

"I mean it."

When they parked in front of Carol's apartment, the lights were on. Jim thought he heard her mutter something under her breath. He removed his overnight bag from the trunk and followed her up the stairs.

"Cohen!" Jim exclaimed. "What the hell are you doing here?"

"I might ask you the same thing. Fuckin' A!"

"Manny, shut up!" Carol interjected. "And keep it down; you'll wake Tracy."

"I'll be going now," Jim Fitzsimmons sputtered, then felt Carol's restraining hand.

"No, you won't, Jim. Manny's just leaving, aren't you Manny?"

"I don't believe this. Carol, Honey, I really need to talk to you tonight. The cunt fired me today! Probably with his approval. Your fuckin' wheel cost me my job, boss. You should've stood up to her. It's not right."

"I said out!" Carol ordered, thereby adding one more brushstroke to the portrait of Manny's ignominious existence. She followed him outside, and Jim heard their muffled voices carry on for a couple of minutes. Then he and Carol were alone in her living room.

She extinguished the lights, and he felt her fingers kneading the muscles at the back of his neck. They were so tight and sore that he almost let out a little squeal of pain. She took his hand to lead him though the dark to her bedroom. It startled him when she flipped the light switch.

"I'll take a shower while you make yourself at home."

She closed the bathroom door behind her, and he contemplated the room. The queen-sized bed took up most of the space across from a wall adorned with a television screen, small to be sure. There was a dresser drawer, and a sliding door in another wall that suggested a closet.

Jim backtracked to the living room to retrieve his bag. He then gazed at the bulging contents of Carol's closet. The tiny space made her wardrobe seem impressive. Jim noticed the men's pajamas and bathrobe suspended from the last two hangers. The row of women's shoes also contained an interloping pair of men's slippers. He surmised that they were Cohen's. God, he hoped so, because he wasn't sure how many more Jacks, coiled to spring out of their boxes, he could stand.

Jim opened the drawers of the dresser, and found them all bulging with Carol's lingerie, costume jewelry, purses, and other accessories. No whiff of a male scent trail there. In fact, despite the naivety from his long years of total marital fidelity, Jim thought he'd figured out this drill.

Manny was her boyfriend, but not of the live-in variety. He stood holding his pajamas and too hastily assembled toiletry kit when Carol emerged from the bathroom wearing a see-through negligee. The blood rushed to his ears, not to mention the rest of his anatomy, and he was awash in the first real passion that he'd experienced in years.

"I need a shower myself, Carol. Have you got a razor?"

Next morning, he awoke in strange surroundings and circumstances. He was alone and disoriented. For a moment, he couldn't decide if he was remembering a true passionate night or merely one of his occasional wet dreams. The closing of the front door brought him back to reality.

Carol breezed into the room. "Awake, I see. I took Tracy to school and stopped at the bakery on the way home. Hope you like glazed doughnuts. I'll put on the coffee."

He dressed slowly, and then noticed the slightly ajar, empty drawer. Investigation behind the baffles revealed a void in exactly half of the rack and floor space. Manny's things were gone, and some of Carol's, too.

"I made space for you, Jim. You can bring up your suitcases now."

***

Jim Fitzsimmons lay awake, listening to the rain pelting horizontally against the windowpane. Carol was working graveyard, so he was alone. It was 3 a.m. of the first day of 1997, and the weather augured ill. Normally, a winter storm in Reno meant arctic cold and snow—at least a dusting in town and up to several feet in the nearby mountains. But this was a "pineapple connection"—part of a huge cloud mass stretching to Hawaii and beyond. Jim pointed the remote control at the gloom, and the Weather Channel sprang to life. For years, he'd been a devotee of any weather report, experiencing *schadenfreude*, along with his fellow watchers, while contemplating others' disasters. While anticipating the plight of tornado and hurricane victims, Jim always muttered his 'poor bastards' mantra, while shaking his head in mildly hypocritical dismay. And now …?

He listened to the foreboding forecast—a new, relatively warm front was racing across the Pacific and threatened to pummel the already sodden region. The snow level in the Sierra Nevadas was at nine thousand feet and rising. Given the deep snowpack in the mountains after a wet, record-breaking December, flood warnings had been issued from central California to northern Washington.

The grim news was underscored by the sound of rain across the window, lashed horizontally by the gusting wind. Jim arose and dressed slowly, aware that sleep was now out of the question. He drove to the Starlight through the intensifying storm along streets that shimmered and undulated as they shed the torrent. He carefully negotiated one intersection where a clogged storm drain raised the water above his hubcaps.

Andrew McDermott was already on-site, directing the sandbagging of the main entrance by a skeleton crew of the four of his engineering department's employees he'd managed to roust out of bed. "Looks grim, Sir. The river's already out of its banks in the warehouse district east of Sparks. It's only got a couple of feet to go here in Reno. We may be in for quite a spate. What's the forecast?"

Andrew's use of "spate" reminded Jim of his disappointing fishless week pursuing Atlantic salmon on Scotland's River Esk. "It could get a lot worse, Andrew. Another one's moving in—" Jim paused in midsentence as an agitated Hispanic employee interrupted.

"*Agua por todo, señores. Abajo.*" Porter Juan Gonzalez waved in the general direction of the stairwell leading to the accounting department in the basement. While Andrew and Jim descended, suddenly the power went off. They felt their way along the banister.

"Shit!" Jim exclaimed, having suddenly stepped into ankle-deep water halfway down to the basement level. Andrew's men arrived, their flickering flashlights lending a Halloween air to the stairwell. Just then, the emergency power came on as the Starlight's backup generator sprang to life.

The Dantesque scene was devastating. Andrew recollected vaguely that there was an underground municipal irrigation tunnel running alongside the Starlight's south foundation. For the twenty years of the property's existence, the waterway had been nothing more than an arcane, subterranean feature, hibernating out of sight along with the city's buried sewer line and the phone company's cables. Now, somehow, the artery containing the flow had suffered a coronary, bursting and breeching the wall it shared with the Starlight.

The five figures on the stairway to nowhere gaped in silence at the watery chaos. Chairs and desks rotated in a circle upon a sea of paper, ten feet above a seabed littered with computers, calculators, and typewriters. The maelstrom threatened to suck the Starlight down into a Neptunian grave.

When Jim Nemo and his crew resurfaced on the main floor, Shelly Sherman, her figure framed by the first faint gray of a soggy dawn, announced ominously, "They've closed the Comstock and Riverboat; they're both under water."

Jim nodded. "We're not far behind. We've got to move our guests to another hotel. There's no real danger, but for all practical purposes, we're closed. Try the Peppermill or some other outlying property. Get ahold of François and see if he can set up a free breakfast buffet for last night's guests. You'll have to work out alternatives for tonight's reservations."

"Right, Sir. We were going to be pretty full, but with the forecast, we had quite a few cancellations yesterday. I'm sure that's true of the whole town. We ought to be able to place everyone, even with such short notice. I'll get right on it."

For the first time, Jim stepped back in his mind to truly survey the situation. He was pleased that someone had clearly taken the initiative to inform the day shift people of the Starlight's plight. Several had arrived early, dressed for physical labor. He recognized several dealers and two hotel clerks decked out in Levis and wool shirts, some with leather gloves. "Shelly, can we get coffee and rolls together for everyone? Talk to François. Where the hell is Mary Beth?"

"I think in Europe, Sir."

"Europe? Well, never mind." An irritated Jim filed the information away, wondering what his GM was thinking of, taking her vacation over New Year's. Nor could he recollect having been informed, let alone consulted.

By early afternoon, the Truckee River was running down First Street, and, by nightfall, Second Street had become a side channel, converting the Starlight into an island. For the next twenty-four hours, the staff— those who were not cut off from the property by the flooding—fought valiantly and with some success to save the casino floor. Jim stayed the whole time, napping once in an upstairs hotel room.

The receding floodwaters left their own souvenir—tons of mud and debris. It would be four days before the Starlight was able to reopen its doors to the public. Jim had long since ceased to calculate the damages to the property and its trade. Rather, he'd become the leader of a magnificent team whose sole purpose was to play defense.

As he oversaw the removal of the last of the sandbags and contemplated the newly activated neon marquee, Jim was filled with pride. In a perverse sense, the floodwaters seemed to have washed away the Starlight's recent travails, bonding owner to busboy. There was a palpable collective sense of accomplishment pervading the Starlight team. Jim basked in the afterglow and made a mental note to tell Mary Beth to organize an employee-appreciation party as soon as possible. At the same time, he was aware of the nagging question forming like a new storm front on the margins of his mental horizon. *Well, poor bastard, what now?*

***

The recent irruption of robins in their backyard portended spring.

"Sheba, could I see you for a minute?" Jerry held open the door to his home office. "I want to talk to you about a miracle."

"A miracle?"

He led her to the library table, which was covered with little piles of good intentions. Jerry carefully rearranged several of the unattended-to projects in order to clear a space for his drawing. "I'm going to plant a vegetable garden. In this climate the delicious delight of a garden in summer is a true miracle! Even when it hasn't rained for two months, we can turn on the spigot, and last winter's Sierra snow flows out of the hose and down to the roots. We're living in the desert, and all around us, the world is shriveled and brown, but we have our precious oasis—our miracle."

He spread out the sheet of paper that outlined Javier's efforts. "You see, Sheba, we have three rectangles separated by two paths. Each bed is four feet across, which is just right so we can reach the middle comfortably from either side. Those black lines are the irrigation system, that Sierra lifeblood. So now we have to decide what to plant and where. What's your favorite vegetable?"

"Corn."

"Okay, so take this pencil and show me where we could put our corn."

She pointed to the front of the left bed.

"No, it won't work there because corn is very tall. If we put it in the front, it will shade anything we plant behind it."

Jerry placed his fingers around the back of Sheba's hand to move her pencil. He felt her recoil slightly, but then her arm relaxed and she allowed him to proceed. He moved her pointer so that the corn patch was now at the rear of the middle bed.

"See, if we put it here, then the back of one of the side beds will get the morning sun, and the back of the other will have sunlight in the afternoon. It's like working out a puzzle. Each of the pieces has to fit."

He blew gently in her right ear, and Sheba giggled at the tickling breeze. For the next hour, Jerry and Sheba pored over seed catalogues and fashioned their summer dream—onions, peas, two varieties of lettuce, radishes, tomatoes, zucchini, squash, beets, and carrots. Sheba had ve-toed broccoli—ugh! Still, Jerry had convinced her to include mysterious kohlrabi. They contemplated their work with mutual satisfaction. Jerry filled out their order on the form in a copious seed catalogue.

"Sheba, honey, there's one more thing. I know you don't know what to call me. I've never heard you say my name—not when talking to me or even about me. It's always 'you' or 'him.' Don't you think I should have a name? Would you like to call me something ... like 'Daddy'?"

He watched her stiffen visibly, her mouth drawn into a tight line as she shook her head. He chastised himself with the thought, *too far, too fast*. "It's okay, Sheba; it's okay. But we need something. I mean, one of these days you're going to want to get my attention, and it'll be tough. You'll have to say, 'hey you.' Tell you what, I have a suggestion. Why don't we settle on Jer? No one else calls me Jer."

Sheba nodded slowly.

***

"Don McNeal with Singleton Securities, Mr. Fitzsimmons. Remember me?"

"Of course, Don. How're things in the world of mega-dinks?" Jim shifted in his chair, his gut twisting with discomfort at the recollection of the Starlight's abortive attempts to go public earlier. He tried to conjure up the face of the voice on the telephone.

"I know we haven't spoken for a long time, but I wanted to try an idea out on you. That is, if the Starlight might be for sale?"

For sale!?! I hope to shout, Jim thought to himself. "We're not for sale, Don. I mean, we don't have a for sale sign hanging around our neck. But, you know, anything's for sale at the right price." He laughed weakly, his casual humor representing the opening ('we're disinterested') ploy of a possible negotiation.

"I've got Asian clients that are big in the gaming business in their part of the Pacific Rim. They've got a project in Uruguay, and they want to acquire a small, respected Nevada casino as their *pied-à-terre* in North American gaming. They plan to grow their presence here, including in Indian gaming. They're fascinated with Foxwoods. When no one else would lend those Indians the money, a group from Kuala Lumpur stepped in and made millions. That venture is famous throughout Asia. You've got experience with Indians. Didn't you make a deal with the Pé-Oné?"

"Sort of. What exactly are you proposing, Don?"

"My clients are out of Bangkok. They've got two casinos in southeast Asia, and they're working on something in mainland China. Gaming is just a small part of their portfolio. They're big in manufacturing—electronics—and they hold several franchises for marketing American products in the Orient. They're a three-billion-dollar company. Anyway, their advance people are here in L.A. with me now. We'd like to come up and meet with you on Wednesday. If that goes well, their owner will come to tour the Starlight and finalize the deal."

"Well, Mr. McNeal, the Starlight isn't interested in paying you a million dollars for your trouble if the deal falls through."

"It's highly unusual for us to proceed without the bigger game plan in place, but our Asian client really needs a foothold in North American gaming and wants to come to Nevada. He knows that our analysis justifies a purchase price of thirty-five million for eighty-five percent of your Reno property. He knows that it also involves possible Indian gaming initiatives. He's also interested in retaining the current management team. Of course, I haven't disclosed the identity of the Starlight as yet. Would you be willing to sign an agreement limited to this particular transaction? In the event that there's a deal, Singleton would get five million and five percent ownership of the new Starlight. The present ownership would get five million and retain ten percent and one seat on the board of directors. The buyer would do all his own due diligence without cost to you. Are you interested?"

"I'll run that by the board and my father. I suspect that they'll approve. I'll give you to my secretary. Priscilla will arrange rooms for you."

"That's not necessary."

"My pleasure. See you Wednesday."

Asian buyers, for Chrissakes, Jim thought. *Gaming Control would have a field day with that one. Licensing ought to cost them about a cool million and take at least a year. That's assuming they're clean—big assumption. Shit. In this business, 'exit strategy' is an oxymoron.*

Jim rose and went to the picture window of his executive office from which he could contemplate his more successful competitors lining Virginia Street two blocks away. A scant two blocks, yet in terms of location, location, location, an all but unbridgeable chasm. The conversation with Don invoked memories of Jim's earlier grand scheme. Acquire the two blocks of blighted real estate between the Starlight and Reno's main drag and use the proceeds from a $200 million IPO to build another nine hundred rooms, an events center, and a parking structure. Take Mohammed to the mountain! Valhalla! Sweet Promised Land!

At first, there had then been the cadre of facilitators—the smart, aggressive young men in their dark business suits who flew into Reno in teams, listened to the Starlight's story, and privately salivated over the prospect of the hefty commission.

What he'd failed to appreciate was that the dinks were short on patience and time. While it might be his obsession, they were only prepared to budget a small portion of their attention to the Reno deal— possibly one face-to-face meeting with the principals. The ambitious young men from the major brokerage firms had no interest in listening to Jim's concerns as he attempted to strategize with them over how to sell the concept to his crusty father and spineless board. By the time he'd learned that dinks weren't into handholding or procrastination, it was too late to make any kind of deal. Wall Street's psyche and the dinks' collective attention had soured on gaming and were refocused upon hi-tech.

For Jim, illusion became delusion and, ultimately, disillusion. The whole failed effort had cost him considerable credibility with the senior Fitzsimmons. Afterwards, whenever Jim proposed any kind of strategic move for the Starlight, James's comment was, "Is this another fool's gold deal, Jimmy?"

Jim Fitzsimmons shuddered out of his reverie.

"Asians!" he said aloud. For Jim, the planet was piscatorial. Canada meant steelhead, the Caribbean invoked bonefish, Russia was spelled Atlantic salmon. Chile and Alaska were rainbow trout, Australia barramundi. Brazil had nothing to do with the beaches of Rio's Copacabana; it was Amazonian peacock bass. Genghis Khan was a Mongolian historical accident; that country's real essence was defined by the mighty taimen. Paraguay? Jim knew Paraguay. He'd once fished for dorado in the Apa River, which separates Brazilians from Paraguayans. That geographical fact was the extent of Jim's understanding of their international relations. "Bangkok? What the hell kind of fish have they got in Bangkok? Never heard of the place!"

***

Manny shifted between drive and reverse to free his wheels from the sand trap, an antediluvian monster in the guise of an earthmover nearly broadsided the stranded vehicle. "Shit. What was I thinking?"

Then he was free and beating a hasty retreat out of the chaotic construction zone populated by a whole fleet of yellow machines intent on scratching out future roads and rearranging the desert floor into enormous pads in anticipation of the buildings that were as yet blue lines on oversized sheets of paper. Some kind of helmeted supervisor honked, and then gestured at Manny menacingly from the cab of his pickup. "Yeah, yeah. I got the idea, Asshole!"

Back on the asphalted portion of the road to nowhere, Manny took stock. He scrutinized the newspaper article lying on the passenger seat that proclaimed "Northern Nevada's Industrial Renaissance" in Fernley.

It was a symptom of his vertiginous fall that he was actually exploring the remote possibility that such raw projects might be ready to hire an ad or PR man. He'd stopped at the completed Stanley Tool Plant, where he was told politely that they had no need for his services. The trumpeted UPS regional distribution center and Quebecor printing plant were still inhabited by jackrabbits and coyotes—at least after dark.

Second largest printer in North America, he read. *Montreal-based.*

"Probably a bunch of Frenchy separatists planning to do their Canuck-bashing from here," he sour-graped, adding one more improbable candidate to the long list of Nevada's sinister desert-based projects. Three months of unemployment had Manny grasping at straws.

He entered the Do-Drop Inn in search of lunch and was immediately put off by its superannuated appearance. Typical of rural Nevada casinos, it was a rectangle with a restaurant at one end and a seedy bar at the other. The lone blackjack table was manned by a gaunt septuagenarian right out of central casting, complete with green visor, garters on the sleeves of his western shirt, and cowboy boots. The hundred or so silent slot machines cast a pallid glow in the otherwise dreary gloom. Two or three middle-aged women played listlessly, chain-smoking and occasionally sipping their highballs. Here, the normal background casino din of a Golden Spur, or even a Starlight, was time-warped into the eerie clink, clink, clink of individual coins dropping into the metal trays of antiquated slot machines. The place reminded Manny of an old floozie on the morning after a hard night on the town, sitting without makeup in her unmade bed, her hair uncombed, her teeth in a cup on the bed stand.

"I'LL HAVE THE BEANIE WEENIE," he nearly shouted at the hard-of-hearing waitress, irritated by her third offer to take his order. *Beanie-weenie, indeed.* He grimaced at some hick wannabe marketer's idea of cute.

"With or without onions, mister?"

"Without."

"Do you want onions, mister?"

"No ... NO."

"Cheese, mister?"

"YES."

Manny contemplated his cheese-less chili dog smothered in onions, sensing his easterner's ire rising within him. Resignation silenced the protest before it had fully formed on his lips. The challenge was too daunting.

"Is everything all right, mister?"

He nodded in assent, as he scraped off the onions.

Sure as hell not kosher, he thought, as he chewed the rubbery, overcooked wiener. Someone had made an offering to the juke-box gods, and Lyle Lovett joined Manny for lunch. He listened intently to the lyrics of *Closing Time*, taking Lyle's suggestion to heart—"turn out the lights and unplug the people."

"What did you say, mister?"

Manny repeated, "I SAID I'M FUCKIN' OUTTA HERE!"

"Where, mister?"

"NEVADA!"

***

"Jer, why did they have to trade Matt Williams?" Sheba's question exploded on Jerry's side of the breakfast table like an incoming mortar round. It was their first communication initiated by her.

"How would Jerry know, darling?" Sue interjected, instinctively shielding him from any potential harm in the revolutionary breakthrough.

However, Jerry beamed as he replied, "I'm not sure. Maybe he's hurt; maybe it's a salary thing. The Giants had an awful season. They were dead last in their division. Remember all those long losing streaks? I guess they had to do something. Williams wasn't their only trade, and they got Jeff Kent."

"I know, Jer, but they won't be the Giants without Matt Williams. Even with Barry still on the team, it won't be the same."

"It'll be all right. Wait and see. Matt's been a Giant for as long as you've been reading the sports page. I know he's special around here, playing for San Francisco and growing up in Carson City. But professional sports are a business, just like the Starlight. You'll get used to it—the trades and all."

"It's not right. It's just not fair," she countered, eclipsing his gray adult rationalization with the black and white of a child's final verdict.

***

"What was I thinking?" Jim mused.

He didn't necessarily regard the living arrangement with Carol to be a mistake, but it had been too precipitous. The temptation to provide his hard-luck lover with her first security in life had been too great. Nor was it working out as he'd expected. She seemed to have made the transition to his support all too easily; Jim was feeling used. He'd been deprived of the privilege and pleasure of rightful patronage! Carol had quit her job at the Starlight, and now spent her days shopping, getting her hair and nails done, and otherwise hanging out. Then there was Tracy. Fortunately, she was testing the limits of an adolescent girl's independence and was often absent. She and Jim had zero rapport. Tracy was long accustomed to the changing male cast in her mother's dramas; she wasn't about to buy into domestic plots.

When Jim returned to the tiny apartment, seeking respite after his increasingly stressful days at the failing casino, Carol monopolized the conversation with vacuous trivia. She'd broken a fingernail that day, the sauna at the gym was too hot, she and Sue were going shopping together on Friday. Blah, blah, blah.

It's all about her, he thought.

There was also the intimidation factor. Dot had always been discreet and soft-spoken. Carol was volatile, given to awesome tantrums when crossed, and prone to victimhood. There was no such thing as shared blame, in which she might have contributed at least something to a misunderstanding. Nor was it necessary to read between her lines. He was jolted regularly by her pronouncements. "Jim, you fart too much!"

***

Jim Fitzsimmons contemplated the white crown pigeons flying from an outer island to Key West, the only immediate source of fresh water and the succulent berries of the holly and poisonwood trees, as Roy Fletcher directed the sleek sixteen-foot-five-inch-long Maverick expertly into the channel that would take them to Renee Richards Flat, so named by the guides for its location halfway between Man and Woman Keys. They passed close by the rusted remains of a shipwreck that resembled the skeleton of a beached whale. When Jim had first fished the area some twenty years earlier, the hapless ship was intact and seemed ready to float off the bank on the next high tide. Now she served as the perch for dozens of cormorants, and two large mangroves were growing from her belly. The derelict was Jim's own Dorian Gray portrait. Watching her deterioration year by year underscored his own mortality like nothing else.

Roy stood erect behind the steering console, flanked by his two anglers. The roar of the ninety-horsepower Yamaha made speech all but impossible, so his angling partner, Bob, flashed Jim a high sign—congratulations for the accomplishment. A few minutes earlier, Jim Fitzsimmons had landed his first permit, that most elusive of quarries for the saltwater flyfishing enthusiast.

For twenty years, like his brethren in the angling fraternity, Jim had targeted the occasional permit, but only half-heartedly and with the certainty of rejection. For it was believed that permit *never* took flies, a verdict that had changed over the past decade to *rarely*. Bob had yet to catch his first, a virginity he shared with most flats fly fishermen. Rather than joy, Jim was suffused with sadness. The successful conclusion to a lifetime quest suddenly seemed another of several abrupt closures adding up to a roaring midlife crisis. Metaphorically, since Jim and Bob were religious catch-and-release fishermen, the lifetime chase had been better than today's kill.

Roy had spotted the impressive twenty-pound fish a hundred yards away as it meandered towards them across the white sand flat behind Boca Grande Key. Jim had plenty of time to discard his twelve-weight tarpon rod in favor of the ten-weight outfit rigged with floating line and a crab-imitation Del's Merkin fly. By the time they were in range, Jim was ready on the bow, poised to cast the coils of line nestled behind him in the bottom of the boat. At fifty feet his quarry passed a patch of floating weed just as the fly landed alongside it. With none of the usual hesitation, the permit tipped its nose downward, its scimitar-shaped black tail momentarily flailing the air. Jim struck, and the line came taut.

Thirty anxious minutes later, Roy slipped his hand under the fish and handed it to the ecstatic angler. Bob took the mandatory photos with Jim's camera while the victor cradled his catch with great reverence. The last shot was of Jim kissing the fish's forehead. He then slipped back below the surface what henceforth would be his totemic animal. After reviving the permit by moving it forward and back to pass water over its gills, Jim released his grip. They watched the fish transform itself into a diminishing speck, sounding for the sanctuary of the greenish deeper water.

"It was the weed patch," Roy opined. "The crabs hide in them, and the permit always check them out. Your fly looked just like a panicked crab heading for the bottom." While Bob took his last thirty-minute turn on the bow as Roy stood perched on the platform high above the stern, poling them quietly along the submerged bank that would funnel tarpon their way, Jim lay across the seat cushion and watched a frigate bird tracing lazy circles in the sky. His mind turned back the clock.

A landlubber from Nevada, he fell in love with the sea at first sight. More accurately, his affair was with its fringe—the flats, where, on the proper tides, hundred-pound tarpon cruise in four or five feet of crystal-clear water, and bonefish seem like gray ghosts with an uncanny ability to appear and then disappear in six inches or less. But it was the total experience, the warmth of moist tropical air on his dehydrated desert skin, the salty taste of unavoidable spray as Roy's craft negotiated a rogue wave, the incidental sightings of sharks from the tiny bonnet to the fifteen-foot hammerhead, the acrobatics of passing porpoises, and the graceful underwater flight of the spotted eagle rays. As he contemplated his first bonefish while nursing the line burn on his thumb and tender knuckles bruised by the screaming reel handle during the fish's powerful first run, he knew that he was hooked. Jim's boyhood passion for pursuing trout in Nevada and northern California paled to insignificance. For the next twenty years, he periodically fished the saltwater flats of the Bahamas, Venezuela, Belize, Mexico, and Christmas Island, but every May he spent a week in the Florida Keys, the one inviolable date on his annual calendar.

At first, Dot came along, but after a while, the hustling street acts of Mallory Square irritated rather than entertained her. She could no longer bear another visit to the Hemingway House or ride on the Conch Train. She became disdainful of the cruise ship crowd that would flow like some fetid tide into every nook and cranny of Duval Street, competing with *her* shopping, and then ebb out to sea a few hours later. The overpriced tourist fare at most of the restaurants invited invidious comparison with San Francisco's far better cuisine. Above all, she hated the flats skiffs with their unpolished captains and all-male universe. Her few attempts at being a sport became day-long ordeals of trying to control her bladder. The logistics of urinating while trapped on a tiny blob of fiberglass bobbing up and down at sea epitomized for Dot that malady otherwise known as hanging out with the guys. Whenever Roy or Jim had the urge, it was 'Look the other way, Dot.' For her, it was over the side to pee through her bathing suit while enduring their predictable shark jokes.

After seven valiant years, she stopped coming to Key West. It was simply too far to go to while away the days in a hotel room reading novels in order to have a string of dinner dates with a husband half-stupefied by a pre-dawn departure and a day on the water under a blazing sun. Jim was not displeased, as she suspected. By then, he'd bonded with several other anglers, including Bob, a retired dentist from Vallejo whose wife hated South Florida's May heat. So, it was natural that Bob and Jim came to room, as well as fish, together. They soon became the odd couple, renting a house and eating in much of the time. Compulsive Bob did the shopping and cooking; Jim washed the dishes and swept the daily patina of fine Florida sand off the floor. Their dinner conversation was the retelling of the fishing stories they never tired of. Dozens of times during the year, Jim would count the weeks, and even days, until his next Key West sojourn.

"Time to go in; reel up," Roy informed Bob.

The Yamaha leapt to life and the exhausted threesome headed into port. As the city loomed ever larger, it assumed its perpetual party air. Three parasailers floated behind tow boats while a squadron of jet skiers frothed the azure waters. Since it was Saturday, a veritable flotilla of weekender sail and motorized craft contributed to genuine marine congestion.

Yet the frivolous fun was overshadowed by the signs of eternal militance and vigilance. Hovering on the far horizon was Fat Albert—a balloon with sophisticated gadgetry emanating invisible feelers far out into the Caribbean to monitor air and sea traffic, particularly drug runs, not to mention TV Martí—the last vestige of the Cold War's mutual suspicions and jammed communications. A flock of AWACs circumscribed an endless circle of trainer pilot touchdowns and take-offs at the naval base on Boca Chica Key. The command towers of an ominous-looking row of Coast Guard vessels seemed to form a defensive picket against any outside force. Jim was bemused at these protections of American bodies from drugs and the American soul from communism—ostensibly in the form of a Cuban invasion.

About as effective as the French one, he opined while thinking of the Maginot Line. The obsession with Fidel Castro struck him as the American version of the movie *The Mouse that Roared*.

Carol Bentley stood on the dock, awaiting their return. The sight of her filled Jim with dismay. He yearned to be alone with Bob to rehash the day's marvelous events. In fact, Carol's daily appearance dockside underscored the awkwardness of the whole week. Bob was staying in a motel by himself. While he'd consented to join them for dinner on two occasions, he'd demurred on three others. Jim wasn't sure whether his partner was being considerate or was inwardly hurt or irritated.

Carol had insisted on coming to Key West. She'd touted its romantic appeal, but in fact, she didn't want Jim out of her sight. She, too, had hooked a fish, but had not yet reeled it in. Nor was Carol Angler into catch and release!

Jim exchanged yet another congratulatory handshake with Roy and reminded his guide that he wouldn't be fishing the next day: "See you day after tomorrow, Bob! Tight lines!"

Carol put her arm around Jim's waist and raised her face for a kiss, as they walked toward their rental car. He feigned a muscle spasm in order to extract himself. He was aware of his sweat-soaked, odiferous attire and skin greased with Banana Boat sunscreen. He was incredulous that another human being might relish close contact before his shower.

"How was your day, Carol?"

"Fascinating, Jim, *fas-cin-a-ting*. They've got six-toed cats all over this one house. Those pusses made some guy named Hemingway famous. It's worth the trip all the way down here just to see the freak show—and I don't just mean cats. The place is full of queers and weirdos."

Jim struggled to smile, or to say something witty and appropriate. All he could manage was an "uh huh" while looking away with narrowed eyes. He'd become a Conch at heart—a true citizen of the Keys. They were his spiritual second home, more sacred to him than the city where he earned his living. He'd watched Key West evolve from a sleepy, if promising, backwater place into a boom town. While he had mixed feelings about the growth, he'd come to respect its unusual architects— the gays who'd discovered, and then gentrified, its aging conch houses and tired small businesses. As a fellow traveler in the tourist business, he could only admire their collective success in converting America's southernmost town into a major destination. While Jim was still made uncomfortable by explicit gay display, his Key West reconciliation had softened his reaction upon first learning of JFK's sexual proclivities.

Carol's remark seemed more a taunt than a comment. The muscles in Jim's neck drew tight. Somewhere deep in the pit of his stomach an alarm was going off. There's one thing worse than lonely solitude— boredom. A little voice in his head said, *Jesus, what have you got yourself into, James?*

At sunset, they dined in the outdoor café area of the Pier House. A nap, cocktail, and the dinner wine had put Jim in a mellower mood.

"So, what did you catch today?"

"Oh, nothing much." He wasn't about to cast his pearl before a swinish listener. At one of their dinners with Bob, she'd complained about the conversation, declaring everything about fishing to be boring.

"Come on, Jim, you guys weren't shaking hands over a business deal. Somethin' happened out there."

For the next five minutes, he tried to explain the significance of the permit encounter, fearful that he might lose his cool if she said the wrong thing. Fortunately, she didn't say anything at all. He wasn't sure how much of his discourse she'd understood.

"So, what's a merkin?" she asked.

Jim laughed long and hard. "Look it up."

"No, tell me. Just because I haven't been to college like you doesn't mean I'm not interested in knowin' things."

"A merkin is a ... is a ... It's a kind of wig that women once used if they lost their pubic hair from pox."

"Oh sure! You expect me to believe that?"

"I'm not kidding, Carol. It's an artificial muff that women wore so their next lover wouldn't know about their illness. It's right out of Shakespeare. I know it's in the dictionary."

"Why would anyone call a fly that?"

"You'll have to ask Del Brown."

After a long pause, Carol stirred. "Like I said, Key West is full of weirdos— particularly the fishermen!"

***

Sue waved at Jerry from across the yard, reminding him of a Roman patrician surveying the ancestral estate. She stooped to run her fingers along the railing of the redwood deck that separated the new gazebo and brick barbecue from the half-completed koi-fish pond. Sue had made all the design decisions, squabbling with a landscape architect whose inspiration for water features was limited to shopping mall fountains. She'd insisted on something far subtler, perhaps conjured up atavistically by her Mediterranean ancestry. At this stage, the brick-and-tile structure looked more like a sarcophagus than the future repository of a self-contained aquatic world.

Jerry wore light gloves, a long-sleeved cotton shirt, Levis, red neck bandanna, and a wide-brimmed straw hat as protection against the searing rays. It was only late spring, but already, the midday sun and dry air of the high desert converted him into a perpetual perspiration machine. As quickly as the beads of sweat could form, they began evaporating, so he interrupted his weeding and tilling to pause frequently for a long drink from the garden hose.

He'd just swallowed a salt tablet when Sheba returned from her neighborhood vegetable-run, beaming with satisfaction. The Joneses across the street had even tried to pay her for the lettuce and sugar snap peas that seemed to flow endlessly from their cornucopia.

The murmuration of honeybees and skirring of songbirds underscored horticultural urgency. It was the day to plant their summer crops. The last patch of snow had just disappeared from Peavine Mountain, a sure sign to Reno's horticultural *cognoscenti* that it was time to put in tomatoes. Three days earlier, Jerry had purchased a dozen pony-packed plants from the Garden Shop Nursery, then left them out for hardening in Reno's brisk springtime night temperatures.

Sheba contemplated a plastic informational tag plucked from the tiny square of soil that was one plant's entire purchase upon the planet. "Early Girl—what a strange name, Jer."

"Not really. The people who develop new plants often give them pretty names. I think they fancy themselves poets—bards of the soil. The 'early' part means that we'll have tomatoes much sooner than we would with other varieties … in about 60 days. The Early Girl was developed right here in Reno—not many people know that—and it's very popular anywhere in the country that they have a harsh climate. What could be better for our garden than a genuine Reno variety?"

Jerry used his small trowel to dig the twelve holes, which Sheba promptly filled with August promises. He then tamped soil around stems and placed a wire frame around each to provide the necessary future support for boughs burdened to the breaking point with rubied fruit.

The squash, carrots, beets, and pole beans were all to be grown from seed. Jerry mounded the soil into little volcanoes, then fashioned calderas into which Sheba planted the flattened oval zucchini and summer squash seeds. He built four tripods of three saplings—their tops laced together so they resembled the skeletal supports of Indian tepees. He showed Sheba where to plant the pole beans that would compete with the others in their race to the sky, culminating in an unruly tangle of green, reminiscent of a starburst in a Fourth of July fireworks display decorated with the hanging green icicles of a midsummer Christmas tree.

They were done and surveying their work with artisans' pride when Jerry suddenly remembered the kohlrabi seeds in his back pocket. "We're about out of space. We can plant one row alongside those bell peppers. I'll make the trench, and you put in the seeds, maybe about three inches apart."

He opened the packet and poured the contents into her palm.

"Oh, Jer, look how small they are. I can hardly see them. How can a big plant grow out of something so little?"

"That's part of the miracle, Sheba. You can barely see the beginnings of most things in this world. You just look up one day, and there they are. In the garden, at least, we have some warning and reasonable expectations. We get to play God … or at least prophets. The really good gardeners are angels, but we have to earn our spot in their heaven."

"Jer, sometimes you talk funny. I'm not always sure what you mean." She paused before continuing, "Mom said I should tell you how I feel about our garden. But I'm not sure how ..."

"Don't, Sheba. I think I know what you want to say. I've seen it in your face. The words would just make things awkward." He put his arm around her slight shoulders and looked intently into her eyes. "Pals?"

"Pals, Jer. What are you laughing about?" He held up his hand to silence her so that he could listen to the rest of the story on the hourly newscast issuing forth from the portable radio that had provided background music and news to their gardening. He chuckled aloud as he said, "It won't mean anything to you, Sheba, but Deep Blue just beat Kasparov!"

***

Jim swore beneath his breath as he contemplated the limp flags atop the Key West Sheraton from the window of his cab. The wind had blown fifteen knots the previous three days, unusual for May, which was why he'd been standing in the bow with his permit rod yesterday. Today, however, was calm and promised great tarpon fishing, and here he was off to Miami for a damn business meeting with Vincent Buong, Thai business magnate and possible buyer of the Starlight.

Jim's mood darkened as he recalled the previous evening's telephone conversation with James Fitzsimmons. His father was practically in old form. "You should have been here, Jimmy. In fact, you *should* have been here. You got us into this mess. Thought you said those Nips or Chinks were going to buy the place. Well, not according to Mr. Big Cheese. I wouldn't give you much for the Starlight, and I'm a cockeyed optimist next to Mr. Big Cheese." His cheeks burned anew at the recollection.

Jim boarded the small commuter plane for Miami and spent the short flight reviewing how it had come to this. Far East Entertainment had seemed genuinely interested in the Starlight. There was the initial feeler from Singleton's McNeal, and the first visit by Trang Luc, FEE's North American point person. Then came the follow-up, which included the head of FEE's hotel division, Wan Fu, an intense, wiry Singaporean. The two visitors had insisted on touring (anonymously) the Pé-Oné facility and had even asked to drive by the Tuolumne site.

Jim had traveled with them to Arizona and listened to their propositions, which were delivered in precise, if heavily accented, English. By the second day, they were kidding one another and exchanging intimacies, like three vacationers who'd met by chance on some cruise ship or tour bus. Instead of posturing for a formal negotiation, Jim's guests stated freely their need to acquire a mid-size hotel-casino as part of a strategy to enter the North American gaming market. By trip's end, he felt thoroughly at ease in his role as member of the new comedy team—the Odd Trio. He was even beginning to believe their oft-repeated assurance that it was merely a matter of time before the Starlight became a part of the "Far East Family."

The only warning signal had been the *telephone call*. While they were discussing Jim's future role with FEE after the acquisition, a call came through from Buong. Jim had noted the instantaneous shift in demeanor—rigid torsos and frozen expressions brushed with what could only be interpreted as fear. The conversation was in Thai, or perhaps Chinese, but Jim didn't need to understand the words to appreciate that Trang Luc had suddenly been transformed from international dealmaker into errand boy and there was little to distinguish FEE's hotel director from any of its porters. In the aftermath of the telling interruption, Wan Fu tried to reclaim the earlier jovial atmosphere by quipping, "Mr. Buong doesn't understand time zones. He might call at 2 a.m. Of course, he likes to do that in Bangkok, too."

Jim stared blankly out the window at the Florida Keys drifting past beneath the plane as he recollected that earlier exchange in a Phoenix hotel room. He shuddered at the thought that he might have glimpsed his future—fearsome late-night telephone calls from an autocrat on the other side of the planet. Now he was flying to a rendezvous with Buong, part of a little test of wills. After the earlier tour of the Starlight, and its external initiatives, Trang Luc had assured Jim that he had a deal—subject, of course, to due diligence, and the working through of a few minor details. Vincent was due to visit the United States momentarily. His itinerary would include stops in Seattle, New York, and Miami, in each of which, FEE had several ongoing, non-gaming business initiatives. Vincent would be coming to Reno to finalize the Starlight deal.

That was two months ago, and Jim had communicated his concern over timing. At one point, he'd confided that he would be unavailable between May 20th and 28th, underscoring the sacrosanct nature of his annual Florida escape with the comment that his daughters knew that if they wanted the father of the bride present, they'd better not schedule a wedding for late May. Then came the one-line message from Bangkok announcing: "Mr. Buong wishes to meet with the Starlight's board on May 24th, 2 p.m." Jim had considered cancelling his trip, but then decided against it. A flurry of faxes established the compromise that Buong would meet with the Starlight's board in Reno, as scheduled, and then with Jim at a hotel near the Miami airport on May 26th.

Jim rang Buong's suite and then settled into a chair in the lobby as instructed. Another wrinkle, he thought, the kind of delaying tactic that one prizefighter might use on another by remaining in his dressing room for an extra few minutes. *For Chrissakes, I fell for good-cop, bad-cop*, Jim thought as he recalled the effusive representations of FEE's emissaries versus what he now knew about Buong's Reno performance. After enduring James's derisiveness, the punctilious Buong had low-balled the Starlight's asking price, justifying his offer with a dissertation about the precarious position of northern Nevada's market while discounting the value of the Starlight's present and possible Indian gaming initiatives.

A nondescript figure exited the elevator, approaching Jim with expressionless face. "Mr. Fitzsimmons?"

"Yes."

"Please follow me."

As they ascended to the top floor, there was little to say. Jim found himself contemplating the bodyguard's medium stature, slight shoulders, and rounded Asian features. There was a certain gentleness about him that belied Jim's knowledge and expectations. Wan Fu had spoken of FEE's armored cars and security entourage in Bangkok, protection against the country's frequent kidnappings, jealousies, and other Byzantine intrigues. When traveling abroad, Buong was reduced to a single bodyguard—one trained in the art of manual killing since he was not authorized in any host country to carry a firearm. Jim struggled with the thought that his underwhelming elevator companion was a skilled, maybe experienced, assassin.

The elevator opened directly into the suite, and Buong approached, smiling and with hand extended. The warmth of the greeting left Jim slightly nonplussed; his reveries had led him to anticipate an icy encounter. "Let's order lunch." Buong proffered a room-service menu to his guest. "Zhan will prepare you a drink." Jim realized that they three were alone. Zhan busied himself in the kitchenette, breaking a tray of ice cubes into a silver receptacle on the well-stocked bar cart. Jim noted that his interlocutor's English was nearly impeccable as he phoned in the luncheon choices of the two CEOs. It was also evident that Zhan was part of the furniture as far as Buong was concerned. He would be present throughout the negotiations.

Jim felt impatient. It was evident that his host was unwilling to engage in serious discussion until the lunch was over. He was also uncomfortable with the formality of two men each sitting alone at opposite ends of a fairly large table. The space between them seemed unbridgeable. They couldn't have touched fingertips had they so wished, the gap would have to be overcome with words and thoughts that suddenly seemed all too feeble. Jim was also conscious of his flamboyant Florida attire, in contrast to his adversary's dark coat and tie. *Shit*, Jim mused to himself. *His turf and terms. This is going nowhere.*

The rest was anticlimactic. Over coffee and the dessert, Buong reiterated his Reno speech. The original asking price had been the five million for eighty-five percent of the stock, and McNeal had exacted a concession that it be half in cash and the rest in FEE stock. Jim had also agreed to stay on as CEO for two years at a yet-to-be determined salary to assist in the transition. (He wasn't prepared to work any longer for Buong.) In Reno, however, Buong had countered with an offer to pay one million in cash and one million in stock now, with a stock-option kicker should the business turn around. Jim and other key personnel would be given five-year contracts, terminable at FEE's discretion should they fail to perform, but otherwise binding.

"Indian gaming is very risky, Mr. Fitzsimmons. There are many tribes; there could be too much product. I'm not optimistic."

"Then why are we meeting, Mr. Buong? You knew our numbers. Your own people have visited and assessed our Indian gaming initiatives. They're the Starlight's hedge, such as it is, against northern Nevada's problems. If you don't believe in our approach, why would you want to own us? I mean, the people … me?"

Zhan held up his hand as a signal for Jim to cease. "I appreciate your willingness to give up a day of your vacation, Mr. Fitzsimmons. For now, I think we should enjoy our lunch. We've discussed enough business for one day."

Jim nodded, knowing full well that the negotiation was over—not only for the day, but forever. After another hour of small talk about Bangkok's smog and American television, the two CEOs shook hands perfunctorily to maintain the fiction that they were destined to meet again. Zhan accompanied Jim back to the lobby, and neither man bothered with a farewell.

Jim called McNeal, who tried to convince him that Buong's offer had merit while Jim expressed his disappointment over being blindsided at the altar after such a romantic courtship. While they agreed to continue the search for a new suitor, after refining and finalizing the agreement between Singleton and the Starlight, Jim knew that he'd just been through his second divorce in less than an hour.

Sitting in the rooftop bar of the MIA hotel in the Miami airport, Jim finished his drink while sorting through the business cards in his wallet. He separated out seven into a small pile, all of them related to the FEE deal. He then tore them neatly in two and rearranged the fourteen remnants into a single stack that he dropped into the empty glass. "At least I accomplished something today," he muttered about his housekeeping.

On the flight back to Key West, he made the mistake of truthfully answering the query of the talkative woman in the adjacent seat.

"Casino owner? Reno? I love Reno. My husband and I have been there two or three times. The Starlight? Can't say as how I ever heard of that one. We stayed at the Golden Spur this year."

Jim tried to shut her up by opening a magazine, but to no avail.

"I just love Reno and Vegas. Every time I go to Nevada I win."

"That's the miracle, ma'am. You know, whenever I talk to somebody like you, they all say the same. I've yet to meet anyone who came to Reno and lost. It makes me wonder how we casino owners manage to stay open!"

***

The Jerry-Sheba vegetable patch was a riot of green, each species claiming its own nuanced variation on the verdure theme. The dark spikes of the onions, knee-high corn stalks, and riotous tendrils and leaves on the pole bean towers all provided vertical visual thrust, balanced by the spreading frilly carrot tops and carpet of juvenile radishes and beets. Jerry and Sheba worked together, plucking out newly sprouted weeds one by one. Jerry was awash in exquisite anticipation of the eventual harvest, as he cultivated the fawn-colored soil with his hand hoe while thinning the thickets of juvenile carrots and beets. He straddled the rows, taking care not to inadvertently squash any plants.

"Jer, can I invite Tracy to sleep over? I'd love to show her our miracle. We even have our own flowers." Sheba pointed to trumpet-shaped zucchini blossoms.

"Anytime."

"Mom asked if I would go to Youngstown later this summer, after I'm done with softball, and maybe Des Moines, too. She promised that Uncle Louie and Aunt Laura would take me to a game in Cleveland to see Matt Williams play. I know she wants me to, but I'd rather stay here. The garden changes every day. I don't want to miss tomorrow."

Jerry laughed and mussed her hair, eliciting a smile. *What a perfect genetic compromise!* he thought, noting the mop twisted lightly around his fingers. Its auburn hue and texture were midway on the color and curling spectrums between Red's tangled flaming locks and Sue's straight ebony mane. On Sheba, her father's flamboyant freckles seemed in perpetual, largely futile, struggle for attention, obscured by the bronze backdrop that she'd inherited from her mother.

Two red-tailed hawks patrolled the firmament.

"See those birds, Sheba? They've been hanging out around here for a couple of weeks. Do you want to give them a name?"

"Sure, Jer. How about She-Bird and He-Bird?"

He laughed. "I wonder if they have Baby-Bird?"

Sue appeared on the deck with two strangers, one carrying a note pad and the other a camera. By the time Jerry reached them, she was leaning on the redwood balustrade contemplating the school of koi fish gathered below her in anticipation of being fed.

"We brought them back from Sacramento … How much? The large ones cost a hundred apiece."

The reporter continued his interview while his companion went about his business of snapping photos of the new deck, fishpond, gravel paths, berms, and screes, all encircled by a latticed ribbon of well-oiled redwood fencing.

"Of course, it will take a few years for the landscaping to mature. It's pretty raw right now, but hopefully you can get a pretty good idea of … Sure, I'd be glad to. Where do you want me?"

Sue followed the photographer's gesture and sat on the raised edge of the upper level. She trailed her hand in the water, prompting two koi to explore her fingertips.

"What does that have to do with anything? I mean … it's so beautiful and we just love it."

But the reporter pressed his line of questioning, and Jerry could tell that Sue was unsure of herself. Before he could distract her inquisitor, she blurted out, "Oh, I don't know. About ninety thousand for everything."

Jerry's eyes narrowed as he watched the reporter scribble his note. *Too late now*, he thought.

They drank their iced tea without any reference to the departed newspapermen. After a few minutes, Sue rose to leave. "See you later, Babe, Sheba and I are going to see *The Lost World* with Carol and Tracy. I know you're not interested."

"What's going on over there?" he asked about life at Carol's apartment. "That's such a small place, and with Jim … It must be really tight. Something's got to give."

"Who knows? Carol says they're getting married, but she's real vague about his divorce. Seems there are complications. But, like I said, who knows?"

Jerry sat alone, contemplating his backyard kingdom. Half-formed thoughts of newspaper interviews, Jim's predicament, Louisiana riverboats, and Tuolumne Indians competed for his attention.

The two red-tailed hawks patrolled the sky over Clinton Gardens. Jim followed their progress, wondering what kind of marvelous pattern they might leave on the sky's canvas were they capable of producing jetliners' misty trails. Suddenly, one of the raptors flared, halted in mid-flight and plummeted towards the ground. Jerry's gaze instinctively completed the trajectory and locked on the fleeting gray blur of a panicked Belding's ground squirrel scrambling for its life. The hawk's perfect calculation created the briefest of ground-level encounters, and then, in an uninterrupted motion, the bird was airborne once again, clutching the squealing rodent in its talons. The successful hunter flew straight to a power pole, where it alighted to subdue, and then eat, its prey.

The explosion was deafening, like the roar of a howitzer round. Jerry felt both shock and heat from the giant flash and immediately detected the acrid smell of singed fur and feathers. Ed Jones bolted across the street and shouted through the fence, "What the hell was that, Jerry? The hill's on fire. Grab your hose."

For a moment, Jerry was a removed spectator, still mesmerized by the incredible event. But then he sprang off the deck and turned on the water with trembling hands. He sprinted toward the back fence, trailing the yellow plastic snake behind him. The brush fire spreading on the hillside was still tiny, and he was able to bring it under control before sirens preceded the arrival of the fire truck.

Half an hour later, he was alone again, staring at the black circle carved out of the browns and yellows of summer-desiccated vegetation. It was then that he noticed the small pile of scorched flesh marking the shared destiny of the predator and its prey. Overhead, another red-tailed hawk searched the firmament futilely for its missing mate, its razor-edged calls penetrating the recesses of Jerry's soul.

E-e-e-e-e-e-e

II

Jerry began his nightly insomniac exercise of reviewing the next day's agenda. He'd take a 6:30 a.m. flight to Denver, where he would transfer to the Little Rock plane. The meeting with the Starlight's silent Arkansas partners was scheduled for the following day at 9 a.m.

Then, it was on to a Memphis hotel for the evening, followed by the next morning's drive to Tunica in his reserved rental car. As a gaming venue, the Mississippi town was clearly overbuilt, and the Starlight hoped to link its fortunes with a local group, which was bottom feeding for a discounted property in a downsizing market, but had no gaming experience and needed an operator. Perhaps the Starlight could strike a deal that would provide a decent management fee, and even some small percentage of the project, but without real financial exposure. Baton Rouge would be his last stop.

Jerry strained to read the illuminated numbers on the clock across the room to verify that he'd set the alarm. *Two and a half hours until up-and-at-'em time*, he thought, rolling over on his side with the hope of drifting back to sleep.

It was then that his connoisseur's eye alighted upon Sue's naked body in the semidarkness. She was certainly no Rubens' model, with mounds of pale flesh gathered together like the billowing white clouds of a late afternoon summer's sky and accented by pink nipples suggesting the first blush of sensual sunset. Instead, Sue's body—swarthy, lean and angular—evoked a Modigliani painting. Her breasts rose abruptly, like twin peaks soaring above some desert valley and culminating in brown summits that defied, rather than blended, with nature. Her pubic hair was coarse, more reminiscent of a wild mountain meadow than Ann's manicured lawn. He imagined himself as the lover-gardener to Sue's Lady Chatterley, braiding crimson strands of Indian paintbrush flowers into her jet-black thicket. He noticed the rounded outlines of the marks that he'd left on her inner left thigh earlier and thought them to be the tracks of some furtive nocturnal creature. All in all, it seemed appropriate that he'd once introduced her to the Sweetwaters.

Such thoughts left Jerry aroused. He lifted her right leg over his and penetrated her while still lying on his side. Since she was still moist from their bedtime tryst, he entered her easily. Her only response was a barely audible "hum-m-m." Jerry couldn't tell whether it was a purr of pleasure or simply the somnolent protest of a disturbed sleeper.

***

When God paints landscapes, He is an Impressionist. Except for the coastlines that separate watery domains from terrestrial ones, and the occasional soaring mountain range, His transitions are subtle and shaded, more processes than events. Not so in the Truckee Meadows, along whose western edge the alpine energies of the Sierra Nevadas dissipate in a last gasp of conifer groves. To the east, juniper- and sagebrush-covered foothills herald the beginning of the vast Great Basin. In short, Reno sits astride the division between verdant California and the arid interior of the American West.

Perhaps following the deity's example, Renoites have long engaged in their own divisiveness. Three ribbons—one of asphalt, another of steel, and the third of concrete—divide the valley and its citizenry, while threatening to convert local politics into a blood sport. Each of the ribbons is its own legacy, rooted in a particular past that largely eludes the collective memory. History thereby becomes myth, especially when the "old-timers" are few and the "newcomers" are legion—as is the case in one of the country's fastest growing cities.

Few Renoites were around for the monumental fight over the location of I-80 in the 1960s, a struggle that postponed completion of the federal interstate highway system for more than a decade. That contest—as well as the contemporary battle over placement of the town's convention facility, which resulted in the anomalous compromise to select a cow pasture situated miles from the closest hotel—is largely forgotten. The mistake, however, lives on.

The two more recent *causes célèbres* regarded the trenching of the iron ribbon—the railroad tracks that cleave Reno's downtown core into two neat halves—and construction of the concrete one: the river-walk walling in the Truckee River as it's suddenly converted into an "urban feature" for a few blocks of its hundred-mile journey from Lake Tahoe to the desert lake called Pyramid. Jerry thought of both as akin to Agnone's boondoggle bridge.

Reno was founded as a river crossing, when Myron Lake exacted a toll to allow traffic to cross *his* bridge over the obstacle between fortune seekers, their suppliers, and the fabled Comstock Lode. Lake's efforts were quickly eclipsed in 1868 with completion of the transcontinental railway, which followed the river's canyons into and out of the valley. As was the custom, the railroad was given land for a town site which it subdivided into city lots.

Reno became a reality—named for an obscure Union general from the Civil War whose French family surname had been changed from Renault.

Jerry lowered his copy of *Tough Little Town on the Truckee: A History of Reno* and rested his eyes. He closed them in anticipation of the nap that should have been his reward for making the 6 a.m. flight, but it was to no avail—his mind kept racing. His patience for the self-imposed homework assignment was about exhausted. He glanced out the tiny oval that passed for a window at the billowy clouds thousands of feet below, on which the slanted rays of the early morning sun created a cotton-candy world of pink peaks and purple valleys that reminded him of Sue's O'Keefe print in the living room.

Jerry replaced the tedious litany of facts and statistics in his briefcase and fingered the fat book that had been Sue's little love offering. She'd read Walter Van Tilburg Clark's *City of Trembling Leaves* in her fall semester Western Literature class and thought that it might help Jerry better understand Reno. He was already a third of the way through the intriguing text, which reminded him of a sequel to *Catcher in the Rye*. The young adult struggles of Tim Hazard seemed to depict Holden Caulfield's probable travails had Salinger explored his next few years.

Most fascinating, however, was the description of a Reno before gambling was king— an undivided community dominated by its university and awash in artistic concerns. The depiction was more like the Berkeley of Jerry's illusions than the Reno of his experience—a kind of Athens on the Truckee where ordinary youngsters aspired to be great poets, musicians, and sculptors. The text's pastel word pictures reminded Jerry of his favorite painter, Renoir. He chuckled to himself as the word play between Renoir and Reno flitted across his mental screen, and then faded into the whiteness of the cumulus cloud that suddenly enveloped the airplane.

***

The cramps began faintly, like the far-off growling of an approaching August thunderstorm in the Sweetwaters. By the time Jerry's second flight landed in Little Rock, he was awash in cold perspiration. The ride to his hotel was excruciating. Once in his room, he thought of calling Sue, but then decided not to worry her unnecessarily. What could she possibly do?

Dinner was out of the question, so he stripped to his underwear and crawled into the bed of his nondescript hotel room to read reports in preparation for the next morning's meeting. In the background, a green Larry King and some blue celebrity looked like two fish floating in a ghostly aquarium, the poorly adjusted tones of the first-generation color set giving an extraterrestrial aura to their interview.

Jerry awoke in discomfort, struggling to remember his whereabouts. The porcelain chill from the toilet bowl pressed against his cheek was his first real sensation. Gradually, it came back to him. The sprint to the bathroom, first the diarrhea, and then sinking to his knees to vomit again and again. He couldn't recall the rest; he'd probably blacked out from retching and wretched exhaustion.

He had no idea how long he'd been lying on the floor but knew the worst was past. Still, he was almost too weak to move. It took several minutes for him to half-crawl back to bed. He'd neither set his alarm nor asked for a wakeup call, so he felt some concern over making the morning's meeting.

Jerry was too weak to turn off the overhead light. That would have entailed an impossible journey to the wall switch by the door. So, he shielded his eyes against the glare with his arm. As he was about to slip into slumber, he became aware that the surface of the water glass on his bed-stand was shimmering with the undulations emanating through the wall from the next room, where its occupants were attempting to replicate themselves. After enduring several minutes of the grunting and groaning, he looked at his watch.

"Jesus, four a.m."

He had five hours to kill before his appointment. Jerry lit a cigarette and began reviewing his notes.

***

The ritual that was the closure for each fishing adventure had begun. Jim arranged the forty or so thirty-five-millimeter slides across the surface of his aged lightbox in order to select the best one for framing and hanging on his trophy wall. In this instance, it was more a search for the permit-kiss one. Fortunately, it was neither under- nor over-overexposed, its sharply outlined features free of photographer-shimmy. Off it would go to the Powers' Frame Shop. Like his casting, Jim's collage of fishing memories improved with time.

Jim opened his desk drawer and extracted a mangled paperback, the fractional tome in his two-and-a-half-volume personal library. He wasn't a book person, excepting on plane flights, his literary indifference another way in which he differed from Dorothy. Throughout their entire marriage, she consumed an average of four novels a week— mainly murder mysteries and gothics. Dorothy belonged to a luncheon circle of women who met periodically, their brown bags bulging more with books than sandwiches—trade material that was as precious as any puka shell necklace to a Trobriander enmeshed in his kula ring.

Jim contemplated the neatly cloven copy of *Hawaii*. The ticket stub from the Dallas-Reno leg of his last Key West trip marked the boundary between his reading progress and the final seventy pages of unexplored territory. Whenever confronted with a lengthy flight, it was Jim's custom to find an appropriately weighty work, usually of the Michener ilk, and slice it in two with a paper cutter. He would read the first half on the outbound leg, abandon it in a trash receptacle at the airport of his destination, and coast home on the remainder. As with the latest example, should the journey prove shorter than the text, he would secrete the manuscript away to be finished someday. That resolution always proved as slippery as a New Year's one. Within a few months, he'd have forgotten the characters and plot, since his reading was more about enforced boredom than curiosity and knowledge.

He now took aim at the wastebasket with the mutilated second half of his airline book and pumped a clenched fist in celebration when the missile careened off the wall and into the receptacle. He regarded it as a good omen for both his next fishing trip and his immediate fate. Five years ago, he'd missed the rim altogether and, on his drive home that afternoon, Jim totaled his new BMW.

"Three points!" he exclaimed.

***

"She says it's important, Mr. Clinton," Priscilla informed him. "She has to talk to you—now!"

Jerry was irritated by the interruption. He was in the midst of preparing his opening remarks to the board concerning his recent trip as he awaited admission to their late-afternoon meeting.

"Sue, I'm right in the middle of—"

"Jerry, she's gone! They've got Sheba!"

He struggled to regain his balance, like some tightrope walker buffeted by an unexpected gust. "I don't understand. Who are …?"

"I have no idea. A man called. Said he'd be back in touch. No police. God, Jerry, what are we gonna do now?"

"I … I … have to think about it. I … better go into my meeting. I'll call you in a little while."

He paused ever so slightly before replacing the receiver, just long enough to notice the stunned silence at the other end.

Having been shown into the boardroom, Jerry took a deep breath, shoved his concern over Sheba to the back of his brain, and dove into his report. "Well, gentlemen, it was more in the nature of avoiding failures rather than landing opportunities. The possibility of gaming in Arkansas remains murky. One thing is clear there, however—certain politicians are expecting a bribe from us, maybe even whether or not they're successful with the initiative. To quote one, 'I'm sure we'll be taken care of at the proper time in the proper way, isn't that right, Mr. Clinton?' I think his definition of 'proper' and mine are worlds apart. We could be looking at a scandal there worse than Whitewater. I recommend that the Starlight drop its Little Rock option. We scarcely have the wherewithal in hand to do much there anyway, even if everything is on the up and up.

"I cancelled Tunica so I could recuperate for a day, as I was really ill in Little Rock. I then went straight to Baton Rouge. As you know, we've been approached by a local group to bid for one of Louisiana's two approved riverboat licenses. Were we to be approved, it should be relatively easy to find a joint-venture partner with deep pockets. We might just be the operator for a non-gaming investor. So, it could be lucrative and carry minimal exposure.

"But that project has to have a shore facility to dock the boat. They showed me a failed amusement park that would be perfect. It's mothballed, but it has several buildings that could probably be rehabbed into shoreside dining and shopping. We could probably lease all of that out. Hell, somebody might even restore some of the rides. There could be a carnival atmosphere that would complement the riverboat.

"I toured the location, and there was just one little problem. A thin strip of private land separates the park from the water. They introduced me to its owner, who's the classic polite and soft-spoken southern gentleman. I tried to get him to state his price, and he just smiled and said I shouldn't worry because the details could be worked out. Afterwards, my hosts tried to assure me that the old guy was a huge local booster and would do anything for the town; he'd practically give away that property if it were critical for Baton Rouge's chances of getting one of those two precious licenses. Besides, they said, that little strip is worthless without activity next to it. Well, maybe. I'm not sure that there's a difference between a southern cracker and a gentleman when he has his hands around your throat. To have real comfort, we need a signed option, not just a handshake over a mint julip.

"The other issue is Governor Edwards. It seems that he recommends we begin negotiating with his list of purveyors of food, beverages, linens, paper goods—almost all of the supplies the riverboat would need. Most of the companies were acronyms, but my hosts acknowledged that Edwards's son owns one of them—wink, wink. At that point, I was up to my ass in Louisiana alligators and Arkansas déjà vu. That night, I had a nightmare in which the Starlight owned part of a forty-million-dollar riverboat and a contract to operate it. The inaugural ceremony and cruise were scheduled for the following Saturday, and we got a call saying that if we expected the state's final approval, we better meet someone the midnight before with a suitcase containing one million dollars in unmarked bills. Our Nevada gaming standards and license were on the line ... in other words, our very existence. We were being called to a come-to-Jesus meeting by the good old boys. We were pregnant, in labor, and with no place to have the kid—not even the back seat of a taxi. I'm not so sure it was a dream as much as a premonition."

Jim Fitzsimmons had listened patiently, nodding more in understanding than assent. A frown darkened his visage, and he ran his fingers through his graying mane nervously. "I hear what you're saying, Jerry, but dammit, I sent you out to look for some hope. We *need* hope. So, Arkansas's a non-starter and Louisiana's another. The bottom line is that the Starlight just underwrote your travel expenses and a week's salary for nothing."

"Sometimes, the best deals are the ones you don't make, Jim."

"I know that, but you just can't always stand pat when you're holding low cards. You have to take risks, maybe even bluff. We've got all our eggs in the Starlight basket, and it's old, tired, too small, and stuck in a bad location in downtown Reno, which isn't exactly America's hottest gaming destination today. We don't have much time, Jerry—I mean hang time—and—"

"I have nothing more to report, Jim. I also have a personal crisis to deal with."

Jerry rose and left the boardroom.

***

"Yes, Jerry." She seemed distant, and he detected an edge to her voice.

"Sue, I apologize. I was up to my butt in alligators. Also, I'm not thinking too well."

"I'm sorry, Babe. I just didn't know what to say. Sheba's gone. What are we gonna do now?"

"I'm on my way home. Everything will be all right, you'll see," he said, fearful that his voice conveyed more confusion than conviction. "Love ya, Sue," he added.

***

"I said no cops, got it?"

"Fine. What do you want? Just tell me what it is, so I can go to work on it," Jerry answered the anonymous voice and then added, "How do I know you've even got her? How do I know she's all right?"

There was a slight pause, and then a tiny voice said, "Jer ... Daddy, help me. I'm scared ..."

"Don't worry, Baby. Don't worry. I'm coming ..."

Jerry realized Sheba was no longer on the line.

"I'll get back to you in a few days. Remember, no cops." Click.

Jerry replaced the receiver while shaking his head slowly at Sue across the dining room table.

"I can't figure it out. He won't show his cards. I keep asking myself who he—or even they—could be. If he wanted money, you'd think he'd get on with it. A deal like this doesn't get better with age. I don't know about the 'no-cops' part. But hell, I'm not sure what they could do. You said Sheba disappeared on her way home from softball practice. Even her bike's gone. I just don't know, Sue."

"We can't call the police. You heard him. Let's at least wait for one more call. My God, Jerry, if anything happens to her …"

"I've been trying to think of who our enemies might be. There are only two concrete possibilities—Frank Wilson and Red. For Frank, I *am* the Starlight, and he sure resents our deal with the tribe. But they're both a stretch. I mean, take Red. If he were an angry father pinching his daughter, like happens with most of those kids on the milk cartons, you wouldn't expect him to contact us, would you?"

"No, I wouldn't. Maybe he just wants money."

"I've thought of that. Anyone who knows me, or the business, should realize that we're not a great target. If you're going after real money, why not kidnap a Ferrarese, for instance? I'm just a minor owner and salaried employee of a smaller property. But it's not impossible. I've been thinking about the newspaper article—the one about our backyard. To most people, ninety thousand spent on landscaping makes you sound like the Shah of Iran."

***

Jerry entered the fortress within a fortress after being buzzed through a second set of bars. Hundreds of rifle and shotgun barrels, arranged into a lower and an upper row, converted the back wall of the gun store into a dress parade without soldiers. A customer, attended by two clerks, was handling a sinister-looking semi-automatic weapon of obscure origin. Jerry hovered about their perimeter, gazing into a display case.

One of the clerks—a neatly-coifed young man with a clipped blond mustache, wearing a name plate proclaiming "Al"—approached. "May I help you, Bud?"

"I need a handgun for home protection."

"What caliber?"

"I'm not sure. What would you recommend?"

"A .38 is sufficient, but you might want to consider a .45. More stopping-power."

"Show me one."

Jerry handled the heavy pistol carefully, yet as nonchalantly as he could manage. He wanted to give the impression that he was experienced with handguns, since he wasn't sure of the requirements. For all he knew, he would be made to pass some sort of test as a condition of purchase. "So, do I need a permit? How long does it take? I mean, do I have to fill out an application and wait …?"

"Are you kidding me? I ask you a couple of questions and call your answers in to the Reno Police Department. We'll have your permit before I finish ringing you up. Unless you've got some sort of serious problem—know what I mean? You don't look like a felon. You pay fifteen bucks for the background check. We add that to your bill."

"I see. What about ammunition? Do you sell ammunition?"

"Of course, Bud. It's $14.95 for a box of fifty."

Jerry scarcely needed that many. He was tempted to ask if he could buy fewer bullets, but decided not to display ignorance over a few dollars.

"That's a used gun you're holding. It sells for $299. It's silver-plated, so it won't rust, and it comes with a lifetime guarantee."

Whose life? Jerry thought to himself. *Mine? The weapon's? Sheba's?*

After answering the clerk's questions for the permit, Jerry waited for five minutes, trying to appear interested in the store's inventory, which reminded him of a museum display.

Finally, the phone rang, and the clerk mumbled a few words into it. "You're cleared, Mr. Clinton. Here's your purchase." The clerk offered Jerry a brown paper bag with metal contents.

"That was easier than a smog check."

The young man smiled at Jerry's crack. "Do you need a cleaning kit?"

"Not yet. When I do, I'll come back for one."

***

Jerry glanced at the Colt .45 lying on the passenger seat. It reminded him of a coiled rattlesnake ready to strike. He thought of putting the pistol in his glove compartment, but decided to leave it exposed while crossing the state line, unsure as he was of California's concealed firearms legislation. He preferred answering some official's questions before, rather than after, a search. A feeble ray of light, exhausted by its space travel, glinted off the gun barrel and into the corner of Jerry's right eye, so he placed his Giants baseball cap over the offending reptile.

Jerry fumbled with the radio knobs in search of distraction from his morbid thoughts. A signal converged on the cruising vehicle and transmogrified into the voice of some interviewee on NPR delivering a monologue on chaos theory. Jerry tried to digest the notion that the flit of a butterfly's wings in Indonesia could cause a hurricane in the Caribbean. This prompted him to speculate about what factors in a remote corner of the universe had set in motion the forces that culminated in Sheba's disappearance. He turned off the radio.

Negotiating the bad road into the Tuolumne Rancheria with a Lexus proved easier at night than in the daylight. In the headlights, the yawning potholes were distinctive shadows and the guardian rocks stood out like miniature mountain peaks. Jerry parked in front of tribal headquarters and used a flashlight to read the rancheria's plot plan lying on the front seat beside him. He could make out only two bright pinpoints in the velvety darkness, and he was in luck—despite the hour, there was a light on in Frank Wilson's dwelling.

Jerry thought about sticking the pistol in his belt, hidden by his jacket, but grimaced at the possibility of an accidental discharge. So, he carried it in his right hand, occasionally using the flashlight in his left to survey the next thirty feet or so before extinguishing it. He wasn't quite sure why he was being so furtive. The irony of a white man sneaking up on an Indian encampment in the dead of night did not escape him. His thoughts turned to dogs. On his previous visit to the rancheria, gaunt curs, cringing around the outskirts, had seemed to outnumber the people. He expected a pack to attack him without warning. At the very least, he anticipated their warning barking to begin at any time. While the whelps were strangely absent, Jerry gagged momentarily on the fecund smell, pointing his beam at the ground to avoid making dogshit a part of his apparel. The only noise to break the silence remained the chirping of crickets.

He paused in front of Frank's door, fingers around the butt of his pistol. It gave him a disturbing rush—a feeling of power. Should he confront the man with the weapon in hand? Jerry decided not to. He slipped his armed hand into his coat pocket.

Frank's grunt at the nocturnal rap was discernible through the closed door.

"Who is it? What do you want?"

"It's Jeremy Clinton, Mr. Wilson. From the Starlight."

A bepuzzled and disheveled Frank Wilson peered through the smirched glass of his screen door. His frame nearly filled the doorway. Jerry hadn't noticed the man's physical size before. "Do you know what time it is? What do you want?" Frank stood aside, the gesture serving as a resigned invitation for the intruder to enter. He motioned Jerry silently to the second chair facing the flickering screen. Frank used the remote control to mute the sound while Jerry struggled to formulate an opening line. *What have you done with Sheba?* seemed far too blunt, and likely even unfathomable.

"Mr. Clinton, don't think you can come here like this, eleven o'clock at night, and try to talk me into the casino project. If you think you can, then you'll still be here trying on the eleventh hour of the eleventh day of the eleventh month of the eleventh year. I'll never negotiate over the spirit of my people. Hey, wait a minute! You're not here to offer me money to sell out ..."

Frank was visibly angry and looked like he was about to spring up out of his chair.

Jerry now knew that his adversary had nothing to do with Sheba. "Easy, Frank, I'm just lost. I mean, I lost track of the time. My wife and I are staying at a bed and breakfast in Jackson, and I thought I'd come over to say hello to Jenny, since I was in the neighborhood—a courtesy call. When I got here, well, it was awful dark; there weren't many lights on. I saw yours and ..."

Frank grunted again, suspended somewhere between his general irritation and skepticism about Jerry's lame story. However, his anger subsided noticeably. "Want a beer?"

Jerry accepted the offer gratefully, pleased that Frank seemed to no longer believe that Jerry's mission was bribery.

"I meant what I said in Reno, Mr. Clinton. I'll never agree to the casino project. It's already divided my people. That's what you've done to us with your white man's greed. There are worse things than being poor."

Jerry hastened to finish his beer, while the two men watched the images of the silent film. He glanced around at the sparse surroundings and wondered if Frank lived alone. Or was he a family man? Jerry saw no evidence of a feminine touch. Yet it seemed presumptuous to ask the question. He swallowed the last of his beer and said, "I'll be going now. Thanks for the hospitality."

Frank grunted for the third time and restored the sound to his program. He didn't so much as acknowledge Jerry's departure into the night.

***

Red Johnson was suspended somewhere between dream and reality, the bam-bam-bam on the door of his mobile home drawing him back into the miserable world of Fresno down-and-outers. At the third series of blows, he swung his torso out of bed and groped through the darkness, flinging perfunctory verbal darts before him.

"What's the matter? All right, all right. Keep your shirt on!"

The answer was no tap-tap-tapping at Red's chamber door, politely requesting entry. There was yet another stentorian bang, prompting Red to fling open the flimsy aluminum flap as he simultaneously flipped on the porch light.

"Jesus! Don't shoot! You … you can have everything. I've got some money, maybe forty dollars. It's yours. Just don't kill me." At first, Red was fixated upon the steely orifice that threatened to flash to life and deliver his almost certain death. Then he looked past the muzzle of the gun to Jerry's face. "Wait a minute. It's you. What the hell are you doing here at this hour? Why are you here at all? I signed the papers. Mom says you and Sue got married. What do you want from me? I haven't caused any trouble …"

"I'm coming in, Red. Put on some lights and back up slowly."

Red did as he was told. He was standing in the middle of the now-illuminated living room, feeling doubly vulnerable in the circle of light that revealed his near-total nakedness. Dressed solely in a pair of briefs, it would have been difficult to engage in a manly exchange with the fully-clad Jerry—even discounting the pistol.

"What's down that hall, Red? The bedroom? A bathroom? Let's see."

"I don't get it. What do you care? Hey, this is embarrassing. I'm not much of a housekeeper," Red babbled as he led Jerry on a tour of the premises. Jerry had had no idea of what to expect. There could have been anyone sharing Red's digs—a live-in girlfriend, a common-law wife (maybe with kids), a short-tempered male roommate. No, Red was clearly a loner. More importantly, there was no sign of Sheba.

Red was getting over his initial shock. While showing his bedroom, he'd put on a bathrobe. "Look, can't you stop pointing that damn gun at me? It might go off. If you were here to kill me, you'd have done it by now. Jesus, three a.m.! You sure keep crazy hours. Why don't you sit down, and I'll make us some coffee? This night is fucked anyway."

Jerry nodded and sat in a living-room chair. He placed the pistol within easy reach on the small end table beside him and watched Red's every move in the kitchenette, wary of some kind of hostile act—possibly with a stashed firearm. As at the Tuolumne Rancheria earlier, Jerry's surprise tactic had allowed him to eliminate (at least to his satisfaction) a suspect. Red's reactions had been far too genuine, indeed ingenuous. Now Jerry faced the unpleasant task of informing her biological father of Sheba's plight.

Red listened to the narration without comment, hoping that there would be some sort of bottom line. "So, you still haven't told the cops? Is that smart? You said yourself that the Indian and me were long shots. What else do you have to go on?"

"I hear you. I needed to be sure first. Actually, I guess we're just buying time, waiting for the call. They must think I'm made of money, but I'm not. I don't think bargain-basement ransom demands are in fashion these days ..."

"Yeah. They're more like athletes' salaries," Red opined.

"You're right. When I get back, I'll try to talk Sue into going to the police. She's afraid that if we do, and it goes wrong ..."

They'd finished their coffee, and Jerry rose with a mumbled "excuse me" and went to the bathroom. When he returned, as he approached his chair, he realized that he'd forgotten his pistol on the end table. Even now, Red had the advantage were they to scramble for it.

Red read Jerry's mind and confirmed that thought with a smile as he nodded Jerry towards his seat without comment. Jerry put the pistol back into the jacket pocket that had served as this evening's improvised holster.

"I can hear her voice now," Red said. "I mean I can just hear her saying to you: 'God, Jerry, what are we gonna do now?' I feel sorry for her … almost more than for Sheba. I can see Sue, hear her, but my daughter is a stranger to me now. That's why, at first, I insisted on seeing her—before signing the papers. More just curiosity than love, or anything like that. Sue sure let me have it. I was really mad when I got home from Reno and wrote that letter. But later I got to thinking about it and realized she was right."

Red's fingers were shaking as he lit his cigarette. "You know, I'm not proud of what I have and haven't done. I shouldn't have walked out on them like that. I should've helped out later. But I was never much of a husband, or father either. I never really missed the kid … until now."

Jerry was beginning to feel a certain empathy for Red. It was the bizarre bond that's possible between two men who've shared the same woman serially and then ascertained that there was no danger of a lingering rivalry. The empathy became sympathy as Jerry contemplated the stark surroundings that, if not abject poverty, bespoke marginality.

"I do casual labor whenever I can get it. Remodels for the most part. Sometimes I carry the lumber, sometimes I nail it. One guy uses me as a carpenter, another as a half-assed electrician. None of it is steady, and none of it is union scale. No benefits, either. The 'no medical' is a real problem. I've got this arthritis called Reiter's Syndrome. Sometimes my knees swell up so bad that I can't walk, let alone work, and they have to drain the fluid. It's better now, since they invented Indocin, but it all costs money. They tell me that Reiter's is genetic. So, Sheba should be tested …"

At the mention of the painful name, they lapsed into awkward silence until Red renewed his monologue. "I'm not going to cause you any trouble. I have enough of my own. I'm two months behind in the rent and a payment on that jalopy out front. It ain't going to last much longer either. So, I sure can't help you with no ransom. If there's anything else I can do …"

Jerry felt an enormous fatigue. The pain deep within his shoulders and neck was impalpable to his probing fingers and they begged for a miraculous poultice. A lugubrious Jerry implored, "Would it be all right for me to sleep here on your couch for a while?"

"Sure."

As Jerry was slipping beneath the surface, he heard Red say, "If … I mean when you get her back, would you try to convince Sue to let me see Sheba? Even if it's just once?"

Jerry awoke at noon and found himself alone. He splashed cold water on his face and then ran Red's comb through his hair. He was tempted to use the razor to remove his day-and-a-half shadow, but decided against it. Before leaving, he placed two one-hundred-dollar bills under the coffee cup containing the cold dregs of their nocturnal libation.

***

For the first time in his life, Jerry wasn't enjoying himself at the wheel. As the Lexus negotiated asphalt slickened by a mid-afternoon summer thunderstorm, he realized that his malaise flowed from both his destination and former company. He was heading back to Reno empty-handed and out of ideas, condemned to join Sue in an unbearable and interminable wait. Something was happening to him lately. It wasn't any one thing—like his illness on the Little Rock trip, or the chest pains during his recent ascent of Mount Rose. It wasn't the tension of the previous evening's confrontations with Frank and Red or the pall that Sheba's disappearance cast over everything. It was none of these things but rather all of them in combination.

Jerry recalled the first time he drove a twenty-year-old Studebaker from California to Reno on a twisting, two-lane U.S. Highway 40. Now his sleek, ultra-modern vehicle exchanged fuel for miles on Interstate 80 so effortlessly that the car was practically driving itself unerringly, reminiscent of a horse sensing its barn. Descending Donner Summit, Jerry contemplated the broken fragments of the abandoned highway he'd negotiated nearly three decades earlier. He found it difficult to relate to his graduate-student self. He really lost the thread, his thread, when he tried to push further back into the past of the awkward teenager, raised by a divorced, single mother—let alone the five-year-old victim of an abusive father. Was this regression into the mists of time or the repression of painful memories?

It was then that he realized he was indeed traversing a critical watershed in this, his mid-century year. Like his Lexus, Jerry's life was now on cruise control. He might be driving through pine forests paralleling the clean, alpine source of the Truckee's waters, but in the distance he could discern the barrenness of brown desert peaks. Jerry wished that he could shut out his travelling companion—himself. He wanted to stop along life's highway and order himself out like some obnoxious, no-longer-welcome hitchhiker. But it was as impossible as shedding one's shadow. More than tired, Jerry felt truly exhausted.

***

"Sue, it's time to go to the police. It's been eight days since she disappeared. We haven't heard from them since the second—"

Jerry's comments were interrupted by the television newscaster: "Today, police found the body of an unidentified teenage girl floating in the Truckee River near Vista. Since no one has been reported missing—"

"Oh my God, Jerry, it's her! I know it's Sheba. Oh my God!"

"You can't be sure. Not yet. Wait for me here. I'll call as soon as I know something … anything."

Jerry drove through the early evening traffic toward the police station accompanied by the image of a hysterical Sue with her arms wrapped tightly around herself, still shouting protests at the screen with the two bantering reporters. His explanations, first to a desk sergeant and then to a detective, were grossly inadequate. Once verbalized, his and Sue's decisions and actions seemed pathetic. Officer Rowley nodded at the description of Sheba and muttered, "Could be, let's go see."

Jerry's nod of assent identifying Sheba's corpse was more paroxysm than gesture. He was in shock as he mechanically signed the form at the county morgue. It's one thing to read in the newspaper about a fatal car accident, quite another to come upon it and contemplate the bloody faces and the broken, rag-doll bodies.

Jerry now knew that he would forever recall the hollow stare and slack mouth on the death mask that once bore Sheba's smile. The silk-stocking gag and her other bonds had been removed, but their ugly marks remained. There were circles around her wrists where the twine had tied her hands behind her back. The suppurating punctures on her ankles from the barbed wire reminded Jerry of the wounds on the more graphic depictions of Christ crucified. The graceful neck bore the markings of the mature hands that had snuffed out her adolescent vitality. So much evidence of pain on such a small body! Jerry blew in the corpse's right ear as his farewell.

"We're not sure yet whether she was molested … sexually, I mean," Officer Rowley explained. "The autopsy should tell us more. I'll keep you informed."

"I don't want to know."

Back at the station, Jerry sat passively across from the two policemen and struggled to follow, let alone respond to, their interrogation. Detective Rowley had been respectful, even gentle, throughout the identification; now Detective Brown was leading the investigation. "Frank Wilson, Red Johnson. We'll check them out."

"I just told you, they didn't do it."

"Right. So, tell me who did."

Jerry shrugged.

"Let's see. You say that the girl disappeared a week ago Tuesday night. You've had two calls. A man's voice. There's been no demand yet, and you decided not to tell us about it. That's all there is, and we're supposed to buy into some kidnapping scenario. One vague call, and all we have is your … whatever. You claim you were in Little Rock or Baton Rouge. That's a great alibi if it holds up. Of course, we're not sure when the girl really disappeared. All we've got to go on is your word, and I presume your wife's."

Jerry was too grief-stricken to even take umbrage at the suggestion that he could be under suspicion. *Just doing his job*, he thought. "Actually, I got back from that trip the night before. When I left for work that morning, Sheba was headed off to school …"

"Let's assume you're in the clear, Mr. Clinton. I presume you do know that you still have some liability here. You didn't report a crime, and now a little girl is dead. It's called obstruction of justice. You should consult—" Officer Brown stopped talking in mid-sentence, silenced by Detective Rowley's gesture.

"We can get into that later, Dave. I think Mr. Clinton has had enough for one day. We may be dealing with loss of nerve here. It's possible that the kidnapper panicked and decided not to make any more contacts. The girl might have been the loose end, his Achilles' heel. She could probably identify him ..."

"It's possible. We'll see," Officer Brown conceded.

As Jerry was about to exit the police station, the desk clerk called out to him. "Mr. Clinton? You have a call, Sir."

How to answer Sue's question? He'd hoped to tell her to her face. Jerry was awash in the miserable realization that evasion of any sort was the same as admission. Her anguished, one-word response flowed out of the receiver and into oblivion.

"No-o-o-o-o-o-o!"

***

The Reverend Thompson waited at the altar as the mourners stood listening to the organist's non-descript sacred music. Jerry glanced over at Sue and sensed the presence of Louie, Laura, and Grandmother Johnson completing the contingent of bereaved kin sharing the first pew. *Nonna* was absent, saddled with the eternal vigil over her incapacitated husband. All eyes, excepting Sue's, were directed toward the central aisle ... where four men solemnly bore an undersized casket toward the altar. Sue's reddened gaze was fixed upon the figure of Christ-crucified that hung on the opposite wall, her countenance tinged with an anger that seemed to blame her God for the senseless injustice of it all. She couldn't bear to look at the impersonal box that contained her child's—her shattered future's—cold remains. Even with Jerry standing at her side, Sue felt utterly alone and hopeless, trapped in an intolerably painful present.

"My friends, we are gathered here today to say goodbye to our little Sheba, who is now with her Maker. I see that some of you are crying. If you must weep, do so for yourself, or for the person next to you in the pew. Sheba is one of the lucky ones, an innocent who was chosen by God to come home without having first to pass the test, the many tests, of this sinful world. She was born an angel and never lost her wings. She is now with the cherubim and seraphim, serving our heavenly Father."

Sue felt more like screaming than crying. She couldn't bear to look at the priest for fear of glimpsing the fateful coffin.

Normally, Jerry shunned religious services, particularly funerals. He felt a pang of guilt at the memory of his avoidance of his own mother's burial. He'd received the "Mom died last night" telegram from his brother, Aloysius, but failed to acknowledge it until it was too late to travel the two thousand miles to Minneapolis for the service.

During his marriage to Joan, he'd attended mass without fail for more than a year. He'd therefore thought that he knew what to expect. However, gone was the familiar Catholic formality—the Latin incantations, the clerical officiousness designed to enhance the distance between the pastor and his flock. As the service wore on, Father Thompson seemed more intent on being one of the boys than preaching sermons to them.

Jerry glanced over his shoulder at the congregation. Tim nodded back solemnly, flanked by Carla, Caroline, and Brett. In the back of the church, separated from everyone else by several empty rows, Red Johnson sat impassively. Jerry felt mild gratitude that the wayward father had at least turned up for the concluding chapter of Sheba's story. Carol Bentley was scarcely recognizable in her basic black dress and understated makeup. With her blond hair pulled back in a bun, she reminded him more of a schoolteacher than a cocktail waitress. She'd avoided eye shadow altogether, so as not to underscore the puffiness around her eyes. Her hand rested lightly upon Tracy's shoulder in silent sympathy for her daughter's pain over the loss of her best friend.

On the other side of the aisle, Jim Fitzsimmons stood stoically, avoiding Carol's occasional furtive glances in his direction. The solemnity of the occasion had forced their breakup off the front page of their lives' newspaper, but it lingered somewhere near the obituaries, like some morning ember from last night's campfire, capable of igniting new blazes if fanned by the breezes of the Starlight's rumor mill.

Jerry was surprised to feel slight disdain for his boss. He was in no position to criticize another man's failed relationships, but somehow it seemed irresponsible of the Starlight's leader to be mired in both a messy divorce and failed affair with the company in such desperate straits. Even Jim's gesture—the arrangements to have the Starlight cater a late-afternoon, post-burial repast at Jerry and Sue's residence—seemed ill-conceived. It was as if Fitzsimmons had sought to fill the void left by Sheba's death with finger food, carbonated drinks, and booze.

However, Jerry's irritation evaporated into the realization that it was his own sense of helplessness over Sheba's death that was really at issue. The "party," with its activity and small talk, would be the first step on the path back to normalcy, the first demand that he exit the inertia of his grief—in short, a very necessary invasion of his privacy. In fact, Jerry couldn't improve on the sentiment and frustration expressed in the Newark telegram in the pocket of his jacket. *Sheba was on our local news. I don't know what to do. Nothing from here, probably nothing if I was there. I don't even know what to say except that she was a great kid. Manny.*

Jerry was genuinely startled from his reverie when one of Sheba's Hispanic classmates was asked to play his guitar and sing *De Colores*. Carlos and Sheba had been fast friends—he'd bordered on becoming her first real boyfriend. Then Reverend Thompson asked Sheba's softball coach to give the eulogy.

"Sheba was a hell of a shortstop, a regular vacuum cleaner. Nothing ever got by her. She wasn't good with a bat, but she was the complete player, the special sparkplug. It was all in her attitude—she never quit and would never let you quit either. Maybe she wasn't the best player on the team, but she'll be the most missed. She was a champion in every sense of the word—our champion." Coach Goodwin directed his eyes toward the ceiling and added: "God, let me be your scout. When she shows up for the tryouts, pick her for Your team. You'll never regret it."

A ripple of laughter passed through the congregation, and Jerry realized that everyone but him seemed more relaxed. The intimate references to the daughter he might have had were simply underscoring his loss. Even Sue's grip on his arm had loosened, and she seemed to be a little more at ease after having stood at attention for far too long.

Reverend Thompson was again center stage. "The Giants are playing the Dodgers today. There'll be 50,000 fans at the park. The pennant's at stake, and I know our little fan will be rooting for her team. Let's join in a last song—not *for* Sheba but *with* her."

Jerry felt the tears course in tiny rivulets down his cheeks to disappear into his shirt collar. Philosophically, he was against the death penalty, but, at that moment, if they were about to fry the bastard who defiled and murdered Sheba, Jerry would have volunteered to pull the lever. He tried to join in the sing-along, but his choked voice seemed half a beat behind the rest of the congregation. He struggled to remember the words to their Epiphany, which, outside the ritual confines of the moment, passed as the plebian melody *Take Me Out to the Ball Game*. Today, it seemed composed by Handel. Jerry felt utterly alone as the only truly morose mourner. He marveled at the miraculous transformation that he had just witnessed, and envied all true believers the power and gift of their belief.

***

Louie and Laura were clearly exhausted. The emotion of the funeral, the graveside service, the alcohol from the late-afternoon get-together back at the house that had served as a belated wake, and the jetlag from the three-hour difference between Youngstown and Reno time, were all translating into nodding heads and slurred words. Jerry knew he should take them to their rooms at the Starlight, yet he tarried out of fear of being alone with his grief-stricken wife. Finally, even the small talk ran out, and it was either deliver the travelers to their hotel or watch them fall asleep in their chairs.

Back from his mission of mercy, Jerry sat in his car for several minutes, contemplating Sue through the living room picture window. She was motionless, her visage barely illuminated by the single lamp. He didn't need to see her face to anticipate the rigidity of its lines.

As he entered the house, he was struck immediately by its emptiness. In life, Sheba had seemed such a tiny presence; now, her absence was enormous. Jerry sat down wordlessly across from Sue, unsure of what to say or do. After a moment, and without even looking at him, she said, in a raspy voice that was more like an echo from a deep well than human communication, "You should have found the money. Things might have turned out differently."

He was too stunned to reply immediately. He struggled to formulate a rational response to a patently illogical observation. "Don't you remember? He never stated an amount. He never gave us a specific order. I thought that I did everything that I could. I would have tried to raise ..."

"But you didn't. We should have had as much money as possible ready, just in case. You never even tried."

Jerry couldn't believe the turn of events. Anger over the injustice of having grief suddenly twisted into blame closed his throat and choked off his ability to speak. He felt a numbing sensation that extended the day's loss to include Sue as well as Sheba.

"So, what's the song going to be?" she asked. "You've always got a song to fit any situation. It's easier to use someone else's lyrics to express emotions that you're afraid of. Maybe you're just not capable of having them. What's the appropriate song, Jerry? Has anyone written *The Ballad of the Murdered Little Girl* yet?"

It wasn't until Jerry was driving once again towards the Starlight— now in search of his own room for the night—that he recovered his voice. He slapped himself hard across the right cheek, in need of a reality check.

"Son of a bitch!" he railed out loud at no one in particular ... and the universe in general.

***

"Sheba! Sheba! Talk to me, Baby. Where are you hiding? In the backyard? No, you must be spending the night at Tracy's. That's it, Tracy's. Call me, Baby. Tell me you're all right. How was the flight? How's *Nonna*? Sheba, Baby, why didn't you go to Youngstown like I asked? If you'd gone to Youngstown, you'd be there with Louie and Laura. Maybe you'd be sitting in some movie theater with Mom Johnson. Oh my God, Baby, what am I gonna do without you? It's my fault. You never had a chance. You really got the booby prize, the short straw. A good-for-nothing dad and a cocktail waitress mom. Too many tears and not enough lullabies. My poor little Sheba, you never had a chance. God, if I'd stayed away from Jerry, none of this would've happened. No one kidnaps a poor kid. We'd be together right now, you and me. Maybe the team has a game tonight. I would've swapped my day off to be there to see my little shortstop. Honest, Baby, I would've. God, I'd give anything to swap the rest of my life just to see you play one more time, to watch you step into the batter's box ..."

Sue's strident voice fell silent as the mention of "box" evoked the fleeting image of Sheba lying beneath the earth. The dumbstruck mother completed filling the suitcases on her daughter's bed. Sue now had no need, or use, for the clothing. Nevertheless, she felt absolutely compelled to take all of it with her.

When he returned home after work the next day, Jerry read the cryptic, block-lettered message left for him on the kitchen counter that bore neither salutation nor signature and said:

This is your house. I'm living with Carol for now. Please forward mail.

The impersonal tone of the note was enhanced by the postscript listing Carol Bentley's address and telephone number. The rupture was further telegraphed by the glint of the diamond ring lying on its side on the Formica. The cat box missing from its corner of the kitchen confirmed the news. Sue was definitely gone, and Jerry was staring once again into the abyss of a shattered marriage.

He struggled to formulate a plan. He'd returned with the intention of picking up a few things with which to resume a bachelor's existence—at least over the short term. He felt caught up in a chess game in which the players had lost track of their moves. Was it her turn or his to call Charles in the morning?

Jerry began walking the house like a security guard making his rounds. Out of habit, he checked the locks on the doors and extinguished a light left burning in the guest bathroom. When he was about to leave Sheba's room, he noticed a faint scratching noise coming from a small cage under the bed. Throughout the kidnapping, it had been his self-appointed task to feed and water Sheba's hamster.

Sue had either overlooked or abandoned the little creature during her flight. Its water bottle was empty. Jerry opened the wire door and groped through the shredded newspaper litter until his hand settled around the tiny, trembling body. "Poor little guy," he said aloud as he stroked the agitated rodent. Since it hadn't been handled for days, it squirmed to be free.

Jerry was startled by the bite that broke the skin on his thumb. Instinctively, he released his grip, and Matt Williams fell to the floor, landing on his back. Jerry was transfixed by the sight of the quivering remains of his last living link to Sheba. He took the tiny corpse out to the backyard and buried it beneath a single spade-full of dirt.

***

A month later, the Starlight's board chairman and director of external relations shared a bachelor lunch in The Westerner restaurant. Jim tried unsuccessfully to stretch his mouth around a first bite of the excessively thick "Wrangler Burger," then dissected it to examine its constituent parts. He made a mental note to discuss its size with François. *It may be the signature item on our luncheon menu, but how many customers is it going to impress if you can't even eat the damn thing*, he thought.

"I learn life's lessons best in the school of hard knocks, Jerry," Jim said. "I've only smoked pot twice. The first time was fantastic, but the second gave me my worst headache ever. I haven't touched the stuff since—or any other drug. Booze? I've always been pretty careful, ever since I stole a bottle of scotch from James's liquor cabinet when I was twelve and got really shit-faced with my buddies. That was the second worst headache of my life. It helps me put on the brakes to this day. I won't bore you with the minor-league whoring at the Mustang Ranch that passed for a sex life before I met Dot. As for gambling, well, the day I turned twenty-one I went to Harold's Club with my only two hundred bucks and a surefire system for roulette that I'd worked out.

In about fifteen minutes, I was broke. It was the best money I've ever spent; I mean, if I was going to live in this town, imagine what might've happened if I'd won that day! I've never placed a single bet since."

"For me, Jim, it's the opposite, my antidote to any of life's excesses is over-exposure. I had to grow pot to give up smoking it. I failed the AA course, but one bad hangover too many did the trick. My first two trips to Reno, I had to bum gas money to make it back to Berkeley. I lost everything at the tables. But after I moved here and started dealing, blackjack just lost its attraction for me. My only impervious weakness is women, and Lord knows, I could use an antidote for them … maybe a vaccine!

"It's really ironic. I've been a swordsman all my life. Four, now five, failed marriages, and I couldn't count all the affairs if Saint Peter was making it a condition of letting me through the Pearly Gates. I always thought of gender relations as warfare. There were the attacks and retreats, threats, truces, casualties, ambushes and set battles, not to mention the eventual winners and losers. If my latest squeeze didn't see through me, well tough—her stupidity was no shield against my cupidity. Maybe cynicism is my vaccine.

"You'd think I'd be used to the wind-down by now—the close escapes and crash landings—but I just can't get over Sue. Two months and I haven't been with anyone else; not interested. I can't even stay at the house—too many memories. So, it's like graduate student days, sleeping in a tiny rented room. Now she's back here at her old job, and it just kills me to see her. I can't go on the floor during her shift."

"I'm kind of in the same place, Jerry, but I got there from a different direction. I was ready—hell, happy—when I broke up with Carol. I felt like the fly that managed to escape from the web just before the black widow injected her venom. Even so, I don't like to run into her here, either. Fortunately, she's usually on the swing shift or graveyard, so I can prowl the place until late afternoon. But I slip out the back way when I leave for the day—just in case."

"What a couple of middle-aged wimps we are!" Jerry exclaimed.

"I guess you're right. In fact, I know you are in my case. I stayed in a loveless and passionless marriage for decades. I lived all that time in Dot's house. I knew that it was just a matter of time before it was over, but there was the daily inertia, year after year. There just never seemed to be the right moment, or the sufficient excuse, to pull the divorce trigger. A piece of me was really glad when she finally did."

"How barren and dreadful that sounds, Jim."

"Maybe it wasn't all that intolerable. I had my squash and my fishing; she had the house and her travels. It kept us out of each other's hair and made it possible to avoid the touchy subject of us. We both found fulfillment outside our little prison cell. I could win a trophy or catch one; she could remodel a room. We were very good at it. We could even feign genuine interest in each other's accomplishments in what passed for dinner conversation. It continued in bed and ate up enough time so we didn't have to make love. It became habit, blessed routine, that allowed us to stay together while raising children. I'm not sure, in fact, whether our divorce was the result of the Starlight's and my financial crisis or the empty nesting. Probably both. Even I know that Carol was a rebound, rather than a genuine relationship.

"After I left them, I thought I was free of Carol, and over Dorothy, too. Life was about to become real fun and exciting. Boy was I wrong. I just can't believe what's out there. I didn't know that there were so many desperate people, particularly single mothers who want to get married the morning after the first night before."

Jerry chuckled at Jim's naivety.

Jim continued, "The worst was my short affair with Sally. I met her at a singles mixer that I ended up at after calling a number in the classified ads of the newspaper. I just wanted to get laid by a stranger, a one-nighter with no strings attached. That first night, Sally and I didn't even exchange real names. We ended up in a pretty sleazy motel with both our cars parked out front. I should have left well enough alone, but I insisted on breakfast together. By the time it was over, I felt like a tree in some jungle with tendrils beginning to grow up its trunk. We exchanged personal histories, fears, and dreams, too. She had two kids, no job, no skills, and was in therapy. She was totally dependent on a cocktail of anti-depressants—mainly Prozac, I think.

"We spent the day together, and that evening, there I was, sitting in her tract house across from two little strangers, and eating her home-cooked dinner. Compared with Sally's slippery slope, Carol was a level playing field. I hung around for a week or so, and then cut the cord. I didn't know what to say to Sally, so I didn't even try. While she was taking her kids to school one morning, I just left. Maybe three weeks later, this strange woman approached me on the floor at the Starlight. I mean, she was unrecognizable until she said, 'What did I do to you, Jim? Was I so awful? I must have done something. You didn't even say goodbye.'

"She'd lost about fifteen pounds, and her eyes were so sunken and hollow that, well, she was just death warmed over. I was pretty much speechless. It was all I could do to mumble, 'I'm sorry, Sally. Don't take it personally; it's me, not you, that's the problem.'

"After Sally, I realized that the best way of evaluating failure in life is by counting how many people you've hurt. I mean really hurt. I suppose we all harm someone, several someones, before it's over, but most of them are superficial wounds—painful for the victims, but survivable. Sally taught me that it's possible to inflict serious and lasting hurt. Most people who go over the edge have somebody giving them a final push. Maybe it's not solely the pusher's fault, in the sense that it probably took a lot of other failures to place the victim on the brink in the first place, but somebody is the catalyst—the final nudge. I'll never forget that look in Sally's eye, the tone of her voice—it was like a visitation from hell. I resolved that day to do my level best to live the rest of my life without ever hurting anyone again—at least not like that. I feel like some honeybee that's likely to die if it ever uses its stinger.

"I can't handle this single scene, Jerry, I'm just no good at it. I don't know how to come on to a woman. I'm out of practice. Hell, Dot and I were so young when we paired up that I'm not sure I was ever *in* practice."

"Don't worry about it, Jim. You don't have to do a thing. You're being sized up all the time. You're a likeable enough guy with a certain amount of polish ... and money. You don't drink, smoke, or even swear much—a paragon of virtue. Believe, me, you're being sized up. When word gets around, you'll be on a lot of radar screens, and in quite a few crosshairs, too. Your problem won't be taking the initiative. You'll have to learn how to play better defense, not to mention recognize the schemes and ploys. Your first challenge is to become a little more cynical about women; otherwise you're just a piece of red meat in shark-filled waters. You'll be taken by the first hammerhead that comes along ... actually, the second, since you've been eaten once already."

"I'm not so sure. I don't believe I'm much of a prize. In fact, I think I'm pretty much a mess. As for Carol, I feel guilty. I'm not positive, but I think I used her. Early on, I began to suspect that it wasn't going anywhere, but I wasn't man enough to tell her so. I guess I needed some sort of haven in the storm, someone to help me get used to being alone ... after Dot, I mean. I couldn't remember life before Dorothy. I needed a little time to get my sea legs."

"You didn't deceive or shortchange Carol. Hell, you took Manny's place in her bed. Do you believe she thought *that* was going anywhere? Wedding bells? House on the hill? Larks singing in a meadow? She used Manny, and she probably used you. I'm not saying that she wasn't likely bummed out. In fact, I'm sure she was, because you were no Manny. She probably did begin to think a little about what might be. I could see the signs. She was beginning to work on you, and that's always a bad sign."

"I don't understand."

"Look, Jim, we're projects. Every woman believes in Mr. Wonderful, the perfect man—as defined by her, of course. He doesn't exist, so they never find him, but every woman believes in her capacity to create him. She's on the lookout for the ninety-five-percent guy—the one with all the basics and a few flaws, ones she can deal with. Not accept, mind you, but correct. So, for women we're all potential works in progress. Problem is that, just like with business deals, the first ninety five percent is easy—it's that last five that's the killer. That's why there are few good business deals consummated, or marriages either. By 'good' I mean win-wins, good for both parties. You're vulnerable as hell right now. That's why I say you need to concentrate on defense."

"Whew! Now I see what you mean about cynicism, Jerry. You're as cynical as it gets."

"Been there, done it all, Jimmy. Learn from my mistakes. I know of what I speak. Hell, lots of women look at even me as a potential work in progress! Someone that they can save from himself."

"Were you Sue's project? You certainly bought into that relationship. Your cynicism didn't make you immune, or even seem to want to be."

"Understanding the game of life doesn't exempt you from it, let alone insulate you from the risks. In fact, failure to ever take a risk is its own form of death. So, for one more time in this trapeze artist's career, I climbed up the ladder and leaped into the void, building up enough momentum to let go of the bar, confident of meeting a partner in midair who would catch my wrists and return me safely to her platform. You even get bolder with age, since you come to realize that your cynicism is your safety net. Should you fall, it helps you rebound.

"Women have their own defensive cynicism. When their man fails to live up to expectations, she gets sympathy—he rarely does. He was her cross to bear. The more oafish, boorish, and beer-swilling the bastard becomes, the more delicious the delight of her plight.

"Maybe the biggest myth of all time is that men are dominant and independent, and that women have to ensnare and domesticate them, if only to preserve the species. Men, independent? No way. Emotionally, most of us are little boys, and most little girls are already matriarchs in training. There's the anatomy, for one thing. Men walk around attached to an erection. Lots of men are only an erection; it defines their whole life. Ask yourself who can go longer without getting laid, men or women, and then tell me about male independence. If all the women locked themselves in one gigantic fortress, we men would be groveling prostrate at its door.

"In one of my Berkeley courses, I was taught that all human thought works through binary oppositions—hot versus cold, up versus down, in versus out, raw versus cooked. For me, the planet's mega-opposition is men versus women. And for men, the female universe subdivides further into lays and no ways. You and I can't order a cup of coffee without subconsciously putting the waitress in one category or the other. She's either your potential lover or stern older sister. It affects how you talk to her, and even the tip. You can't help yourself. It's hormonal."

"So here we are, Jerry, two guys adrift and without any interest in playing the game—at least, not for now. We're both floating. Didn't you say you're in a rented room? Probably a weekly, like me. Tell you what, given the Starlight's crappy occupancy anyway, why don't we share one of the two-bedroom suites on the top floor? We could just hang out together until one of us moves on."

"Fine with me."

**

The next morning, Jerry and Jim shared coffee in their new digs. As was his custom, Jerry probed the yoke of his fried egg with a battering ram of buttered toast.

"The coffee's fine, Jerry. I'll wash the cups when we're finished. You be the cook and I'll be the maid. Do you know how to do laundry? College was the last time I was in a laundromat."

"Don't worry; just follow my lead. I'm used to being on my own— at least periodically. I'm no great chef, but we'll get by."

"Before I left Dot, I had no idea how complicated everyday life can be. We had this magnificent house—I think you were there once for dinner. It was her house, not mine. It was actually more like a museum—each surface had an exhibit and every wall told a story— her stories. But Lord, it was comfortable. It was spotless and with everything in its place. I now realize what a champion homemaker that lady is. I took it all for granted; it was the natural order of things. We had so many rooms that I'm almost sure I was never in a couple. It still has a nursery that no one's used for twenty years. It just sits there, waiting for tomorrow's grandkids.

"Moving in with Carol was a real reality check! It was a claustrophobic one-bedroom apartment for a single working mom and her daughter. We slept in this cramped queen bed—we had to coordinate turning over. There were soiled clothes on the floor, dirty dishes in the sink, and expired crud in the refrigerator. If I wanted a snack, I would actually make a trip to the corner store for it; it beat one to the emergency room. It was different for you, I believe. You have your own house."

Jerry laughed sardonically. "Yeah, I know how to take care of myself. I've lived alone for most of my life ... between marriages and affairs, and sometimes even during them. Sure, I know how to shop, cook, and clean—none of it is rocket science.

"As for the house—I mean the one Ann gave me—that was actually a weird experience. Before then, I'd always rented or moved in with someone, usually a female. Suddenly, I had this building and lot. At first, it was like being given an unwanted puppy. You think to yourself, 'I'm getting rid of it as soon as possible,' but meanwhile you put down newspapers, pour it some milk, buy some biscuits, wipe up the messes. Then it crawls up in your lap and licks your face. So, you postpone trying to find it a new owner, and the next thing you know, you are its owner. It begins sleeping with you in your bed. When you hear it whimper, you wonder if it has a tummy ache. You take it to the vet and pay ridiculous fees. You try to coax pills down a reluctant throat. Then one day, you realize that it's grown into a dog and it *owns* you!

"It was like that with Ann's house. At first, I resisted, but then I remodeled. By the time Sue moved in, for the only time in my life, I was owned by a *thing*. I'd come to really care about that place and wanted her to feel the same way. She was coming around, too, but then our puppy died. So, once again I'm one stray mutt hanging out with another."

Jim and Jerry were quick to discover their deep-seated common interest—San Francisco Bay Area sports, and their pessimistic prognosis of same.

"Fuckin' Frisco's toast for a long time to come—right across the board," Jim opined.

"Yeah, that Tampa Bay bastard trashed Jerry Rice's knee, and Golden State's the crappiest excuse for a team in the NBA. The Giants are up and down. Take Estes out of the mix, and we got a bunch of rubber arms; our pitching staff practically qualifies for social security. It reminds me of George Allen's Redskins. For several seasons, he traded away all his young players and draft picks to get veterans with a year or two left in them. It might work for a short while, but it's sure as hell no way to build the future."

"I like Dusty a lot. But could you believe that game the other day? Our bullpen walked in six runs with twenty-four pitches. Dusty was a hell of a player. I hated him when he was a star outfielder for the Dodgers, and now, I have to love him as manager of the Giants. I can't keep track anymore. Look at that Butler guy. One season a Dodger, then he's a Giant, then a Dodger again. I used to understand loyalty, but no longer. Whatever happened to the days when a guy came up through the farm system, played his whole career with the parent team, and then retired from it—like our Willie Mays?"

"Actually, Jim, we traded Mays. He retired as a Met."

"I forgot."

The previous night, they'd watched the Giants on television while, thanks to the myriad replays, six Rod Becks hung six curve balls that six Dodger batters lined over the heads of eighteen drawn-in outfielders for yet another San Francisco loss. The camera had flashed six times upon Dusty Baker's exasperated visage as he expectorated six times.

"Well, Willie played all of his *real* years with the Giants, Jerry. That's what counts."

"I've got an idea, Jim. Why don't we just digitize old Dusty? We could break him down into his binary components and reconstitute him as our Super Free Agent of All Sports Hero. Tune in Bay Area sports fans. Dusty fades back to pass and hits Baker for a 49er winning touchdown on the last play of the game, then runs into the locker room to change into his Nikes in time to sink the three-pointer at the buzzer for the Warriors, before catching the red-eye to New York to pitch the next day against Willie's Mets! In his spare time, he plays goalie for the San Jose Sharks.

"It could resolve all of this salary inflation crap. If you can't afford a star at every position, create one for all. Why should sports be exempt from the virtual reality that passes for the blurred existence of the rest of us? Digital Baker has a great future in this blood-sucking, money-grubbing, life-denying excuse of a society; Dusty Baker has none. He's just too human. He feels pain and frustration, spits and scratches his balls on television, and grows older by the day—which, of course, is his biggest sin of all. In Virtual World, no one will be permitted to grow old—gracefully or otherwise."

"Are you always this full of bullshit, Jerry, or only when you're sober? Maybe you should give up abstinence," Jim quipped, and then added, "Did you know that Dusty is a bone fisherman? I learned from a mutual friend that he fishes the Bahamas. It makes me feel more than just a fan's pain for him; it makes him like ... like a distant relative. It makes me want to give up on these money sports and root for something like lacrosse, volleyball, or soccer—where they just play the game out of passion for it."

"Ever heard of Maradona, Jim?"

"What's a singer got to do with this?"

Jerry inhaled brusquely to store up oxygen for an appropriately exasperated expostulation, but Jim interrupted with a chuckle.

"I know who Maradona is, I know. I was only kidding."

Notre Dame was scheduled to open its football season against Michigan that morning.

"Should be a great game, Jerry. Should we get some beer and snacks?"

"Not interested, Jim. Maybe I'll just take a walk."

"What!?!"

"I'm more an NFL than a college wonk. I hate Notre Dame. I can't imagine watching them, particularly in their annual big game against USC. I would have divided loyalties watching a game between Papists and Southern Californians! It would be tough to decide who to root against. Joe Montana was my one big compromise—he played quarterback for Notre Dame before discovering true religion by signing with the 49ers. I never once saw him play for the Irish."

***

A new dimension had crept into their relationship, one built more around their respective solitude than friendship. Like two bottles bobbing on the sea of life, Jim and Jerry clinked together and began to float in tandem on the currents and tides. At first, it was a shared dinner, usually of the fast-food variety, to avoid dining alone. Then, it was the attempt to watch rented movies—an exercise that underscored their middle-aged distance from mainstream America. They failed to see any point to *Pulp Fiction*, a film that appalled, more than amused, them. The whir of the VCR had exercised a stronger influence than the plotless special effects of another "blockbuster," putting both into their own *Lost World* with its dormitive powers. Their favorite was the subtitled *Il Postino*, the delightful afterglow of which prompted Jerry to purchase the English translation of Pablo Neruda's *Canto General*. In short, Jim And Jerry now constituted that uniquely American, potentially contentious, household—two grown men, one television set, and a single zapper.

By unstated mutual agreement, the next step was to step out … indeed, seek out evening alternatives to simply vegetating in their suite. They saw the show at Fleischmann Atmospherium Planetarium, twice, and attended a touring company's *West Side Story* at the Pioneer Auditorium. They even took in an occasional lounge act at competitor casino properties. Each was the other's date, a kind of shield against possible fate in that biggest of all minefields otherwise known as the singles scene.

In late September, Jerry convinced Jim that they should attend a reading at the university by Robert Pinsky, America's forthcoming poet laureate. His performance was the crowning event of the Great Basin Book Festival. Jim had protested at the high-brow suggestion, but acquiesced, lacking an appealing alternative.

But his anticipated boredom quickly evaporated into sheer delight, as he listened to one poem after another. Each new creation seemed simpler, yet more complex, than the previous one—glimpses through a myriad of looking glasses into the many recesses of the human spirit. During the curtain call, Jim had clapped so hard that his hands ached.

They queued up with a hundred other admirers to buy the poet's works, then approached the table where Pinsky sat ready to dedicate them. Jim was too reverential, and totally at a loss for words, when asked his preference. "Whatever," was all he could muster in response to the poet's query, so he ended up with the same perfunctory message in each of his treasures: *Best wishes, Robert Pinsky.*

***

"We're here from headquarters to work with you, Mr. Fitzsimmons. Consider us your partners."

"I'm not sure I understand, Mr. Fogelson; the Starlight is only two months behind in its payments." Jim regarded with askance the three dark-suited figures from the bank arrayed before him in a semi-circle.

He appreciated the expansiveness of his executive desktop, which seemed to buffer him, if only a bit, from this new menace.

"That's true, Mr. Fitzsimmons." Fogelson then voiced his captious skepticism. "However, two months is two months. Then there's the winter operating reserve issue. You've got none, and it is already October. We're concerned about more than just the Starlight; our gaming division believes that Reno is in deep trouble. It's certainly not Las Vegas. We have three loans in this town that are in arrears. We're the troubled-borrowers division, if you will. It's our job to work with our distressed customers before their loans are in default rather than after. You don't even want to meet the guys from the dark side of the bank." Fogelson chuckled, as if this last observation was a truly humorous joke that even his miserable interlocuter should appreciate.

Jim tried to take the visitors' measure. Except for Fogelson, the team seemed composed of babies. He wondered if the two silent faces frozen in forced smiles had ever felt the blade of a morning shave.

Fogelson continued. "From now on, I need your monthly statement. I'll call you after I read it and tell … Oh, I mean I'll discuss with you what we'll do next. I'll have to approve any checks before they're issued. By the way, you're not to pay board directors' fees any longer, and I won't authorize your salary. From now on, you're simply an owner here, not an employee. The owner of a distressed business is the last to get a salary."

The bankers rose to leave, and Jim came out from behind his desk. He felt a slight shiver as he exchanged the mandatory handshakes.

"Don't worry, Mr. Fitzsimmons. If we work together, I'm sure we'll get through this. I want to give you back full control as soon as possible. Remember, think of me as your partner."

Jim Fitzsimmons sat in the solitude of his office, staring at the door through which the Fogelson entourage had just departed, taking with them his last source of personal income. He picked up the phone and dialed the Starlight's attorney.

"Jeff, it's worse than I thought. You better file for chapter eleven. I mean immediately!"

***

Swede knew that matters were delicate and tempers short. There was more than one potential fault line capable of dividing the NNCA. Foremost was the Reno-Sparks Convention Authority's recently announced study to ascertain the cost of remodeling its existing, poorly located facility in South Reno, supported by the outlying casinos, mainly in Sparks. Several downtown properties north of the railroad had already announced their intention of building a temporary convention venue in their midst, while lobbying for a public-private partnership to build a permanent one. Several downtowners south of the tracks had their own plans to construct a special-events center capable of hosting trade shows and small conventions. In short, everyone had their eye on the scarce resources, with three agendas in play on how to expend them. So, the meeting table of the NNCA was ringed by both proponents and NIMBYS for any concrete proposal.

"Gentlemen, we all know that Reno needs more conventions. It may be our last competitive advantage. Nevada's monopoly on gaming is history. We thought we were geniuses and impervious to competition. Wrong! A blind monkey can make money with a monopoly on a product that appeals to human weakness. If you owned the only bar in town, you couldn't go broke. Then those Resorts International guys got gaming legalized in New Jersey. No one in Nevada worried much. Resorts was out of Nassau, and their clientele was East Coast. They were just moving closer to their customer base. In fact, some Nevada gamers saw it as an opportunity. Most of the new Atlantic City properties were owned by Nevada interests and certainly operated with Nevada expertise. We even told ourselves that New Jersey might be creating new gamblers who would ultimately want to see Mecca, the big show—Nevada.

"The news for us isn't all bad, even if most Americans now reside within an easy drive of some form of gambling. But tourism along with gaming is another matter. We've got maybe 25,000 quality hotel rooms in northern Nevada and a pretty substantial convention facility already constructed. We can be one of the top ten convention destinations in America if we commit to that goal and work together. Do you think a Des Moines or Omaha can compete with us? Not a chance. Meeting planners all say that they get their best turnouts when they come here or to Vegas. Who in the hell wants to be stuck in Des Moines for a week, or the other hundred Des Moines in the country that are all convention-business wannabes?"

"Okay, okay, Swede, we get the point," George Anderson interrupted. "You're not talking about something that we haven't all chewed on in our board rooms ... regularly. I just don't think that public monies should be used to benefit the downtown properties on whichever side of the tracks."

John Ferrarese rebutted, "No, of course not, George. You want to pour more public money into a convention center that's obsolete and in a terrible location. It must just be a coincidence that it's two blocks from your property. You think we can build our way out of a mistake. I won't pretend that a new facility downtown doesn't benefit me more than you, but I sincerely believe there's a public-trust issue here. If I was no more than a taxpaying citizen, I'd still say that it's crazy to keep expanding a relic in a cow pasture."

Mark Bengoechea interjected, "Guys, we'd better understand one thing. Without a healthy downtown, this whole area can just turn off its neon lights. Lose the downtown, and you're talking about a few stand-alone properties that are too scattered to constitute critical mass. On the gaming side, critical mass is our only competitive advantage over Indian gaming, riverboats, and California card rooms. Sure, there will be more Indian casinos and riverboats, but they're spread out all over the place. You visit one and you are pretty much stuck; you can't walk to another across the street. Only Reno, Vegas, and Atlantic City have that synergism. So here, the customer has a choice. We've all got the same machines and games, so maybe it's not a real choice, but it is the illusion of one. In this business, illusion is much more important than reality.

"Besides, the superstitious gambler thinks he can change his luck by changing casinos. Every time players take the trouble to come here, they're *electing* to do so instead of going to a more convenient Indian casino or riverboat. The outlying casinos in this valley have the same handicap—you can't choose to leave them on foot. So, it's mainly about critical mass. And in northern Nevada, the critical mass is in downtown Reno. That means that if we build a convention facility there, we're not diluting our resources; we're concentrating them where it counts most."

Swede cringed. The pot was definitely bubbling, and it seemed only a matter of time until it boiled over. Who was going to sharpen the edge of his voice next or hurl the first expletive? It all reminded him of his Korean negotiations, in which verbalization of rigid, irreconcilable postures made matters worse. Consequently, there were still two Koreas.

An eerie silence descended over the room. Everyone seemed to recognize that they were at the brink and the next orator risked plunging over the cliff, taking them with him. No one was prepared to run the risk of incurring the blame for that. They were all aware that the community and local press were amused by the factionalism among the city's gaming properties. It was local theater, Reno's palace intrigue, and none of the players around the table relished the prospect of being cast into the role of court jester.

"Let's talk about the commission, Swede," Jerry Clinton suggested, to everyone's relief.

"All I know is what I learn from the media, like you guys. They set it up without consulting the industry. It has gamers, anti-gamers, and presumably neutral 'experts,' mainly social scientists. It seems to be a response to all the media speculation on the negative consequences of the spread of gaming in America and the world. Of course, each new initiative in each prospective venue triggers its own heated debate. Frankly, I think the commission is a typical cop-out by the politicians in DC, designed to get them off the hot seat. Appoint a commission and you've actively *done* something to address the problem. It's being studied and, meanwhile, it fades from the front page.

"It's hard for me to imagine much coming of it. Put casino-industry representatives, anti-gaming activists, social scientists, and preachers around the same table, and it seems very unlikely that they can come up with a consensus that could lead to actual recommendations on some sort of federal policy on gaming. So far, legalization of gaming has been at the initiative of each state. No federal policy; no federal taxation. So, the whole thing opens up the states-rights' can of worms. If the feds try to take a cut of the states' gaming revenues, they're whacking a hornet's nest. We should have lots of bedfellows on our side if it comes to that fight.

"We're not talking about the Kefauver Commission here. That old senator had a rod up his rear about gambling. Nevada had a monopoly, so he was really only taking on one state, and he had a hole card. He supposedly had evidence from the FBI, from Hoover himself, that there was a Mafia connection. When Kefauver revealed the hood influence in Vegas, he had his story—his crusade. He even tried to parley it into his party's presidential nomination—think of where we might be today if he had pulled that off! Thank God for us that Governor Laxalt was able to cut a deal with Hoover to force the Mafia out of Nevada. He also convinced Howard Hughes to invest in casinos, opening the door to corporate America. Bobby Kennedy was also riding the anti-gaming horse, but he got assassinated.

"The present commission is nothing like the Kefauver or Kennedy threats. It seems pretty obvious to me that it'll be a hung jury. I suspect it will produce a report with vague warnings and some lukewarm recommendations that will go nowhere. There may even be a dissenting minority that will enhance the gridlock. The Kefauver investigation was essentially a criminal one. That's a lot different from the present enquiry. These commissioners are examining the social and economic consequences of gaming, and they're looking at anecdotal evidence. There really is little data available on gambling, and a lot of it is questionable. I don't see this coming to a thumbs up or down conclusion. The critics and proponents of gaming will both declare a victory and continue to disagree. I can't see any significant legislation coming out of it, except maybe for Indian gaming. After all, it's a federal commission and the Indian reservations are under a degree of federal jurisdiction. But I think that genie's out of its bottle, and no one is going to shove it back in."

As they were leaving, the Comstock's representative, John Douglass, turned to his brother Bill, half-owner of the Riverboat, and commented, "I think the hood thing is important to our image. Our customers like the feeling that there's a sinister side to casinos. If you lose your money, do you really want to know there's some university professor like you in the back room counting it?"

***

Jerry and Jim gazed out of their suite's window at the stagnating Mapes Hotel two block away.

"That's not a heap of bricks, Jerry; it's a pile of ironies. How many years ago did it close? Maybe eighteen. No one can figure out how to make it work. The city bought it to resell to a casino operator, and suddenly the preservationists came out of the woodwork. Where were they when Karadanis owned it? Suddenly, it's an icon. Reno's icon. Now anyone who touches the Mapes is a crony or a crook.

"The biggest irony of all is that the people most committed to preserving it make a fetish of never coming to the downtown. They *hate* the downtown, and they *hate* gaming. They're embarrassed by the image that it gives to *their* city. Never mind that people come here from far away *because* of the gaming. Now all of a sudden, the Mapes has to be saved in the name of *our* heritage. Where were they when Harrah's knocked down Harold's Club? It was a truer original and at least a decade older than the Mapes … and built before most of the Vegas properties, too.

"So now the Mapes is Nevada's historic casino—as if Hull never built the El Rancho, Moore the Last Frontier, Bugsy Siegel the Flamingo. Suddenly, the Mapes is this art-deco jewel, Nevada's architectural heirloom. Never mind that Charlie Mapes had a stale concept and plans for a copy that he erected twenty years after the Art Deco period was over. Never mind that he wanted to put a cement platform for parking cars over everyone's beloved Truckee River. No, suddenly, it was critical to preserve the place where Marilyn Monroe slept while they were filming *The Misfits* and Sammy Davis Jr. performed. It's as if it were her only bed and his only stage."

"Wow, you're certainly steamed up about this, Jim."

"Dad appointed me the Starlight's government-relations' representative several years ago, and I've sat through dozens of meetings on the Mapes."

"I'm not sure what I think. It is not a bad-looking building. It's got some character. I kind of wish it could be rehabbed."

"There you have it. Like a lot of people, you think that's possible. Well, it isn't. I'll bet a dozen casino operators went through the building when the bank owned it and was practically offering to give it away to any taker. You did your dreaming, but then your due diligence led to some architect or engineer telling you that the building was unsound and unsalvageable. It could never be retrofitted properly to meet the new earthquake provisions in the building code, for example. If you wanted a casino on that site, you were better off demolishing the Mapes and starting over. That may be mission impossible, given the certain opposition of the preservationists, and the dicey prospects of Reno's casino industry. So, there the dinosaur sits, becoming ever seedier with passing time. One day, it'll just fall down by itself—hopefully not on some unfortunate passerby."

"Do you think it'll be imploded, like they do all the time with old structures in Vegas?"

"I suppose so, but there will be hell to pay. I don't envy the council members when they have to take that vote. The room will be full of irate naysayers. It will ostensibly be an exercise in democracy, but not really. The preservationists won't be there to listen or learn. They accept your view as long as it agrees with theirs. If not, your motives are sinister and suspect, and you're unqualified to hold office. Some might not even want to wait until the next election—why not recall you now for the good of the community? But what are the alternatives? If no private party will take it on, are we going to spend millions of public dollars on a municipal hotel-casino run by the City of Reno? Personally, I think the site should be a civic amenity—a little park or plaza that enhances the Riverwalk."

"Kind of makes Arkansas and Louisiana look simple by comparison, Jim."

"You've got that right."

***

Jim entered James's office on a peremptory mission. "You know, Dad, the Starlight's not going to make it. We've had it."

"I've known that for a long time, Jimmy. Even before the flood, we were underwater."

"Then why did you lend that money? Good after bad."

"Because of you, Son. I wasn't investing in this joint; I was investing in you."

"Dad, they say that if you owe the bank a little, it owns you; if you owe it a lot, you own the bank. That's a nice sound bite, but it isn't true. You, personally, are on the line for everything."

"The first thing I ever taught you about business was to never sign a personal guarantee. If the lender believes enough in the asset itself, and its future, then the collateral should be a first deed of trust on it. Period. You didn't sign personally, did you?"

"Yes, I did, Dad. I don't know exactly when you negotiated your last agreement with a bank, but times have changed. No bank will lend money any longer without personal guarantees. No one else will, either. The companies that sold us the new player-tracking system and our neon signage on time both demanded personal guarantees. In this business today, without player tracking, you're flying blind. Without neon signage, you don't exist."

"I'm really disappointed that you did that, Jimmy. How much are you liable for?"

"About two million, maybe more."

"Oh my God!"

"I had no choice. What do you do if you can't make next month's payroll? What do you tell vendors who haven't been paid for six months and are about to cut you off? How do you expect to stay open through the winter without an operating nest egg? What do you say to the State of Nevada about last month's gaming tax? Wait while we catch up? If you don't pay right on time, in a heart-beat they send in auditors to determine if you should even keep your license. For that matter, what do you tell the bank itself when you're asking for your note to be rescheduled after having missed payments? So, of course I signed personally, when Wells made it a condition for more credit. By the way, I was able to win a little victory. The bank agreed not to require your personal guarantee as well. That would have been fun!

"Wells made me list all my assets. I have a few stocks, a little real estate, equity in the house. I put them all down, but I didn't mention the divorce. Dorothy will get the house when it's finalized next month. I guess you could say I have no real assets, except for my stock in this place. Even she didn't want that!

"We haven't made the bank payment here in two, going on three, months. Wells has transferred us to some kind of crisis division in Los Angeles. They're sending up two officers to meet with us next week; meanwhile, they gave us the name of an "advisor" they insist we hire. Fogelson was all about eyes and ears. Theirs. Now it's about complete operational say-so. Some financial wizard with zero understanding of the casino business will make all the real calls around here, because Wells believes we know nothing about finances, or maybe running a casino, either."

James was at a total loss for a reply. He averted his gaze to the muted television on the wall and clicked his remote to restore the sound. A Wall Street guru was giving testimony to a Congressional committee.

"The financial system is about to go under, Jimmy. I mean throughout the United States ... maybe the whole world. I used to watch sports, but now I can't get enough of C-Span. Did you know that they want to deregulate banks? God knows what the financial industry has spent on lobbyists and politicians. They're going to get their way, and then we'd all better watch out. I've been a businessman all my life—a capitalist, if you want to get fancy about it. One thing that I've learned is that business is all about greed. I went to work every morning to earn money. I kidded myself that it was to provide security for your mother and you kids, but it was really all about me. And, you know, the money was just a way of keeping score. It only really matters when you don't have any. After that, it's pretty boring. You know the cliché that money can't buy happiness—whatever that is."

"So, Dad, by your reckoning, isn't it better to be worth ten million dollars than one?"

"I know you'd respect me more if I said no, Jimmy, but you bet your boots it is. Nine million better to be precise. I started with less than nothing, and I made my first hundred thousand one nickel at a time. That's how we counted in those days—if you said millions you meant Rockefeller. I counted those damn nickels and thought that, one day, they'd add up to a hundred thou, and then I'd retire. But when I got there, I decided to keep going. Well, it's all relative. I'm worth maybe twenty million today, and when I look out that window at the Golden Spur, I see three or four hundred million. It would take my entire net worth to remodel some insignificant corner of it. It's humbling, Jimmy. I glance out the window and feel like a failure."

"I don't respect you any less for any of that, Dad. Sometimes, I think that your middle name is 'Networth.' But you're wrong if you believe that the money is only about keeping score. It's really all about power. Your game ruined your marriage, drove Sean to Boston, and made me a hell of a squash player and fly fisherman. Your money couldn't influence that. I learned those life skills on my own, and they were lifesavers. They gave me self-respect. If all I'd been was a useless drone, the pathetic and parasitical son of James Fitzsimmons, self-made man, I would have killed myself long ago, or maybe become a street person in Manhattan. Strangely, I've fantasized about both, particularly recently."

James fiddled with his ballpoint pen and began doodling on his scratch pad, then returned to his former monologue. "Anyway, Jimmy, when the defenders of capitalism talk about altruism or patriotism, it makes me want to puke. I never paid a worker a nickel more than I had to. I never hired anybody for my country. My next employee was always because I needed a job done. Now I sit here, watching C-Span and listening to those self-serving bastards in Washington and on Wall Street drone on about self-correcting markets that only need to be unshackled and we'll have unimaginable prosperity for all through a trickle-down effect. Take off our gloves, deregulate us, and we'll police ourselves—we'll be good. Somehow, self-interest and naked greed will produce Mother Teresa's world. We'll suspend the laws of economics and the New Economy will float every boat.

"Right! Well, Jimmy, I was a kid in the twenties and a young man in the thirties. When you live through the Great Depression, you've seen it all—the best and worst in people. I now see that same train coming down the tracks, and I'm glad I won't be around for the crash. One Great Depression is enough for a lifetime, thank you very much!

"Do you know the changes that I have experienced, Jimmy? When we old farts aren't talking about our health, we carry on about the world. How your generation messed it up. How everything is different now than when people actually worked and appreciated what they got from it. We remember seeing the first television set, our first flight on an airplane, a propeller one to be sure, and the first atomic bomb, not to mention the hydrogen one. Now all your generation seems to care about are material things, mainly of the electronic ilk— geegaws to us."

"Well, we have our own nostalgia, Dad. When I was a kid, we had no plastic. We carried our lives around in paper, canvas, and cotton. You never had to figure out how to open things. My school lunch was in a paper sack and my education in a canvas book bag. My gym clothes were in a cotton bag, and yes, you could smell them through it. When I trapped muskrats, I bought them home in a gunny sack that was wet to the touch. Not like today, when everything is sealed in its damn plastic wrapper so thoroughly that you can hurt yourself extracting it—no feel, no touch, no smell. I remember—" Jim paused in mid-sentence, interrupted by James's gentle snoring.

In the hall, Jim shook his head. He had gone to James for commiseration and maybe advice. His father's soliloquy on the American twentieth century, not to mention his improbable prediction of the world's future, were all beside the immediate point—the Starlight's plight. Jim had never felt lonelier.

***

"Death by a thousand nicks, Jerry. That's what's happening to northern Nevada's gaming industry. Indians, Vegas, Macau, riverboats, legalization everywhere. Even here in Reno, we have more neighborhood casinos and slots in every grocery store."

The two roommates were chatting over their dinner in Vario's Restaurant.

"Steve Wynn says gaming has little future in Nevada. It used to be the cheese in our mousetrap, but now there are mousetraps everywhere, all with the same cheese in them. We have to go into 'tourism' instead. He envisions offering visitors the planet's best food, rooms, shopping."

"That's a tall order for Reno, Jerry. Lake Tahoe is beautiful, but a little too far away. Besides, it has its own gaming. Same with Virginia City. It has some tourist appeal, but there isn't much to do there once you've seen Piper's Opera House, photographed the church, and strolled the wooden boardwalk. We have desert, but no Death Valley.

We have skiing, but the slopes are a little too far away and have their own lodges. Squaw and Heavenly are both over an hour from here. Mountain scenery, yeah, but not the Rockies or Alps.

"Some of the properties have tried to theme themselves. The Reno Hilton went for 'environmental zones' and converted parts of itself into the Pacific Northwest and the Southwest—cactus and all. The Silver Legacy invented the prospector, Sam Fairchild, as the discoverer of the Comstock Lode, part of its mining theme. How far would you drive to experience a contrived desert or phony history?"

"You're right, Jim. Bowling, golf, a handful of weeks of special events, and a movie theater on a two-block riverwalk. Kind of reminds me of Jenny's vision for the Tuolumne. We're screwed!"

"I'd still like to think there's an outside chance that the Starlight might survive. But it's going to take a lot of work, not to mention luck."

"We've got a more immediate problem, Jim. Our new controller is out of control. Simms may be good at numbers, but he also likes to write jeremiads."

"Jere-whats?"

"Bad news. Indeed, the worst possible news. He writes memos to the other department heads, laying out the financial crisis blow by blow, and then rehashes it all at our staff meetings. How can we instill morale if our department heads—the team leaders—think the jig is up?"

"I know, Jerry, I know. What I don't know, or Mary Beth either, is what to do about it. Do we tell Simms to sit on the information? But then aren't the department heads all flying blind? What's worse? Cutting them in on the real details and making them a part of the problem and its solution, or simply telling them 'things are bad, and we have to tighten up around here'? Then imaginations run wild and rumors fly. Pretty soon, everyone believes that the situation is worse than it really is. They may even start dusting off their résumés ..."

"You have a point. There's no easy way around it. We can't just pretend or wish the crisis away. Let's buckle our seat belts, because, if Simms is right, the brick wall is right around the corner. But, Jim, there's something that I can't help wondering—you said that the

Starlight got three million dollars in insurance for the flood damage. Why did you spend it on a remodel? You could have used the money to facilitate the wind-down. You could have saved face by blaming the closure of the Starlight on the flood. It would have been the truth, not just a contrived excuse. Instead, you spent the money on carpeting, new mattresses, and a little paint. Every new casino in Vegas cost a billion, and even the Indians are into joints in the hundreds of millions, and you spent three million on a fleabag."

"I know, Jerry. It was inertia and a lot of false pride. It's hard to admit failure, because then you own it. There was also Dad's legacy. I feared having to tell him that we were closing. He might have been understanding, but who knows? It might have killed him. This place was his life, and he has precious little of that left. In retrospect, sure, it was dumb."

"I knew the game was up a year before the flood, Jim. I remember that September board meeting when I asked for a million dollars for capital improvements—paint, carpeting, and particularly new mattresses. Our guests were complaining that the old ones were literally dumping them on the floor. We needed some new televisions. All of our maintenance crewmen were becoming half-assed TV repairmen. I lectured the board on the need to think about upgrading the slot product. Even with the million, I would have been attempting the miracle of the loaves and fishes.

"We had precious little saved for winter operating, and we were probably going to have to draw down on the two million left in our line of credit with Wells Fargo. Well, I sat there while the board voted to draw down the whole line and give me half a million to work with. You do the math. A mattress cost $400, and a television about the same. We have nine hundred rooms. Then the board voted to distribute the rest to themselves as dividends. I can appreciate that they did so because everyone, maybe excepting James, needed the money. But it was that day that I knew the Starlight was finished. As GM, I was supposed to perform a magic trick without a rabbit, or even a hat to pull it out of."

***

Sue regarded herself intently in the mirror in the employees' powder room—her daily assessment of the progress of the tiny wrinkles in the corners of her eyes. Serving drinks was a soft-sex profession, and her body was aging. She glanced at the voluptuous woman to her right, who was putting the finishing touches on her lipstick. Debbie was ten years younger and seemed to get twice as many gratuities. Sue's days in the profession were as numbered as those of any thirty-five-year-old NFL linebacker. Her scanty costume barely covered her nipples. She was mildly superstitious and had a little ritual before heading to the floor—ostensibly influencing her customers' generosity. With her left hand she lifted her left breast and muttered "bread." She then repeated the exercise on her right side to a plaintive "butter."

Being a cocktail waitress had never been lucrative, but now the former garrulity of the casino floor was absent—there were hardly any customers. She actually missed the Canadians, even if they did think that a tip was a canoe accident. Her discomfort was heightened by the gnawing realization that she'd destroyed her own bright future. It wasn't it that she missed; it was him.

**

On this December morning, Jerry was once again about to check into the *Hotel California*. The Eagles song always captured his state of mind when confronted with a failed relationship. He stripped the cellophane wrapper from the replacement for his cherished former 33 recording, and tentatively ejected the six-CD tray from the player. He substituted his disc for the Hip Hop selection in the top tray and discarded one of Sheba's lingering legacies in the waste basket.

"Why can't they just use buttons and knobs anymore?" Dangling his eyeglasses from the corner of his mouth by a single stem, Jerry squinted at the space-age digital face of the infernal machine. He pushed a protuberance in anticipation that it might transform the oppressive silence.

"Who needs all this anyway? Life definitely used to be simpler—more livable." The strains of the familiar theme song filled his bachelor pad. He poured himself another double Chivas and swigged it down, lost anew in the familiar narcosis of his former threatening, yet comforting, nemesis. His sodden and sottish state helped alleviate the guilt over this latest fall from grace. He strummed his imaginary guitar in time with the lead-in. Jerry began to sway to the music, closing his eyes to better concentrate on the words that he was lip-synching, as if he were the spiritual sixth member of the band.

Jerry meditated on his predicament while listening to the remainder of the disc and sipping his drink. The brown outline of his personality's receding desert peaks stretched out before him like a wasteland. The thought of traversing the rest of his life's landscape alone was barely bearable. There was no question about it, Jerry was feeling very sorry for himself. Rather than deal any longer with the contraption's mechanical mysteries, he turned off the CD player and replaced its music with that of the "easy listening" selections of Reno's FM radio station, KOZZ. His sense of bleak transition was enhanced immediately by the words of Jimmy Buffett's *A Pirate Looks at Forty*.

Jerry went to the closet and extracted the box containing the visual record of his recent family life. It was far too painful to dwell on the photos of Sheba in her team uniform, mugging for the camera with Tracy on their field trip to the Harrah's Auto Museum. Then there were the hundred or so colored snapshots taken by Sue during their Italy trip. Most included him, as if his six-foot frame were the yardstick against which to measure the height of Michelangelo's David or the width of a Venetian canal. He pondered the photo he'd taken of her standing beside her befuddled Uncle Enzo. His mouth was transfixed with the wan smile that bespoke both the pleasures of better times and the bitter prospects of his bleak future.

It was then that Jerry came across the Iowa-postmarked envelope of their wedding shots sent by Tim. Sue was in each, her face alive with the occasion's sheer joy. He studied all the images carefully, delighting in her delight. It was then that he noticed the lyrics of *Un-Break My Heart* that Toni Braxton intoned in the background. The relentless drumbeat of the song's simple message seemed to Jerry like an admonition written for Sue and him alone. He pictured the front door of his house with the realization that both he and Sue had stormed through it. Each had made the grand gesture and walked out on the other; now both were trapped in a cul-de-sac of painful pride.

He slammed his fist on the table and blurted aloud, "No, God dammit! Not again. Not this time."

***

It was halfway through Emmylou Harris's *Bluebird* album that its words moved to the forefront of Sue's awareness. Emmylou continued to abuse their sisterhood by reminding Sue of her own loss of *those blue eyes.*

Sue sobbed, feeling a deep pang of remorse. She'd lashed out at him, converting Jerry to the vessel into which to pour her grief and anger, and not realized until much later the absurdity of her attack. It'd been a hapless mother's desperate maternal reaction. Everyone, the whole world, and even God above, had been to blame. If she'd failed to proclaim their universal guilt, Sheba would have passed unnoticed and unacclaimed into oblivion. Jerry just happened to be a nearby dog to kick.

Sue ejected the disc and carried it with her to be inserted into her car's CD player. The motor purred in time with *If You Were a Bluebird* and Sue sang along, substituting Jerry when Emmylou reached Honey. The last words of the song echoed in her brain as she entered a record store on an urgent shopping mission:

If I was a highway,
Well I'd be stretchin'
I'd be fetchin' you home.

***

Their telephone conversation seemed so inadequate and stilted after the weeks apart. They agreed to meet at the Starlight half an hour before her swing shift the next day. Sue, parcel in hand, walked towards the employee ladies' room where she exchanged her street attire for sequins. Jerry awaited her arrival, clutching a baggie. Without an exchange of pleasantries, they embraced in a lingering kiss. Both had anticipated a more sedate first encounter that would eventuate in another at an agreed time and place after midnight. Jerry took Sue's hand and led her into the mercifully vacant break room.

"I missed you, Sue."

She reciprocated with an equally weak, "I missed you too, Babe."

They exchanged sheepish grins and furtive glances, almost like high school freshmen on a first date.

"You were right," Jerry admitted. "I mean right about my use of song lyrics as an emotional crutch. I have a present for you."

He handed her the baggie. She poured the contents out on the table between them and then spread the remains of the *Hotel California* disc that Jerry had cut up with tin snips an hour earlier. Sue fitted the four shreds together as if they were parts of a jigsaw puzzle, and then contemplated her work, wondering if it had somehow restored the fragments to a viable piece of real estate once again capable of housing the Eagles' fantasies. She began laughing, at first quietly, but then with growing gusto. "I have a gift for you, too, Jerry."

It was his turn to empty a bag onto the tabletop. The plastic case of the portable CD player threatened to crack when it met the marble surface, but held intact. "I don't understand, Sue."

"Push the play button and you'll see."

James Taylor's voice delivered Sue's tailored message in song lyrics, Jerry's favorite idiom (or former one):

When you're down and troubled
And you need a helping hand
And nothing, oh nothing is going right
Just close your eyes and think of me
And soon I will be there
To brighten up even your darkest night …
You just call out my name
And, you know, wherever I am I'll come running (oh yeah, baby)
To see you again.

It was now Jerry's turn to laugh—at the irony, but more out of relief. After such intimate abjuration, it was time to bring Sue home. They agreed to return to his, no *their*, house after her shift.

He fished in his pocket. "Mrs. Mallard," he said with a small formal bow, "please allow me."

Jerry slipped the diamond band back on her finger. Sue *loved* her ring.

***

Jim Fitzsimmons's ears were ringing as he struggled to listen to Jerry's post-announcement rationalizations. The "I'm leaving as of the end of this month" had at first erected an insurmountable aural barrier between the two men, one that was gradually penetrated by tiny disparate fragments of additional information.

"... Assistant General Manager's job ..."

"... Golden Spur ..."

"... $250,000 ..."

"... hard choice ..."

"... great opportunity ..."

"... fifty years old ..."

"... last career move ..."

"... for Sue's sake ..."

The fragments finally added up to a coherent pattern, like some new combination after a fateful twist of Jerry's kaleidoscope. First there'd been Mary Beth's defection to the Ferrareses, and now they were mining the Starlight for Jerry. Jim struggled to control his rage, staring at his former roommate and confidante through narrowed eyes. He was torn between the desire to punch out his ex-director of external relations and simply screaming at him. Despite his near-violent impulses, Jim sat stoically while the waitress refilled their coffee cups and asked if everything was all right.

Jerry dismissed her with a wave and continued: "I know I'm leaving you somewhat in the lurch, Jim. I'll try my best to facilitate the transition. I asked for an extra month to help bring my successor here up to speed. The Ferrareses aren't long on patience, so I'm willing to come down here on my days off for a while if it would help out." Jim had yet to utter his first word, and Jerry was beginning to find the silence to be intolerable. "What I do feel really bad about is the

Tuolumne initiative. I've bonded with them, and I'm not sure how they'll take the news. I mean I assured them they could count on me if they went with the Starlight. They're ready to sign our consulting agreement … at least they were. I'm not sure—"

"Take it with you, Jerry," Jim grunted hoarsely.

"What?!?"

"I said take it with you. Wrap up the Tuolumnes into a pretty package and present it to old man Ferrarese. Tell him it's a present from me. Now put your keys on the table and get the hell out of here. I mean right now."

After Jerry left, Jim deflected the waitress's new offer of more coffee. He fingered Jerry's keys one by one, arranging them into a neat semicircle on their steel ring. His attention fixed upon the frosted glass between the back of his booth and the adjacent one. In the center of the divider, there was a clear, etched starburst—the Starlight's logo. A guttural groan began somewhere within a totally unfamiliar recess of his being, a sinister place. Like some ambitious Caribbean tropical depression, by the time it exited his throat, his conniption-fit had a hurricane force capable of destroying all in its path.

Jim suddenly felt hands upon his shoulders and elbows, restraining his movements. There was a throbbing in his right hand, clenched into a blood-soaked fist and festooned with crystal slivers. The stunned party of four in the next booth stared at him in disbelief while they brushed shards from their clothing. The other diners in The Westerner were agape over the hubble-bubble.

The initial comments of the two security guards—"All right, fella, take it easy now. Someone call the cops"—had dissolved into a confused, "Jesus, it's Mr. Fitzsimmons? What can we do for you, Boss?"

Jim allowed himself to be escorted to the Starlight's employee clinic, where a rotund nurse carefully picked glass from his wounds, closed up two gashes with butterfly bandages, dressed his hand, and pronounced him a lucky man for having sustained such superficial injury. She urged him to go to an emergency room to be sure.

Jim found himself standing in the middle of the casino contemplating his surroundings, only now realizing how much just coming to work every day for years had withered his spirit and bent his will. He felt like some gnarled tree on a windswept coast, all but leafless, bowed, and broken by its relentless surroundings.

At the cashier's cage he wrote a personal check for two thousand, and then approved it himself, unsure whether he had sufficient funds in his bank account. He put the twenty crisp hundred-dollar bills in his pocket and left the Starlight.

At the airport, he worked out a convoluted schedule that, after a red-eye flight from San Francisco to Miami, put him in Key West at ten the next morning. He counted out ten of his bills to purchase the impromptu, nearly thousand-dollar, one-way, first-class ticket.

The wind was brisk, and there was the slightest hint of chill in the air as Jim sashayed across the Florida terminal and entered a waiting cab.

"No luggage? Are you all right, Buddy?" the cabbie asked, looking at Jim's bleary-eyed, stubble-chinned face, wrinkled business suit, and bandaged right hand. Jim looked down at the crimson-streaked dressing. It reminded him vaguely of the red-and-white candy canes and jolly Santa Clauses that Dorothy always used to festoon their tree.

"Garrison Bight," Jim muttered, ignoring the driver's questions.

Most of the charter boats still in harbor were of the deep-sea variety, and Jim knew it would be difficult to find a flats skiff. It made no sense for guides to pay for exorbitant permanent moorage, when the sleek craft could be easily trailered to the water's edge daily and then launched for a modest fee. By this hour, those few captains willing to brave the unsettled weather would have long since departed.

Jim was almost prepared to charter one of the deep-sea boats, when a skiff idled into sight through the narrow channel under the Palm Avenue bridge and made for the launching ramp. He didn't recognize its captain—one of the new guard that had proliferated on the flats after the Billy Pate videotapes popularized fly fishing for tarpon. Jim sat patiently, sipping his beer in the Garrison Bight floating tavern, while the skipper bade farewell to his discouraged client, who'd clearly bagged their trip early because of the lousy conditions. A brief rain squall dimpled the surface of the otherwise calm waters of the protected haven as Jim went to speak to the captain.

"I'd like to charter you for a run to Woman Key, Captain." It was the only one of the outer islands with a structure.

"No way. It's brutal out there. With this sky, you can't possibly see the fish."

"You don't understand, Captain, I'm a houseguest at Woman Key. I missed the boat that took my friends there this morning," Jim's lie was reinforced by his business attire.

"I see. Well, I still won't go back out there. It's gettin' way too rough."

"Look, I'll pay you three hundred. It's worth it to me. It shouldn't take you more than an hour ... round trip."

Captain Simpson wavered for a moment and then waved Jim aboard. "No luggage?"

"My friends took my overnight bag with them."

Captain Simpson grunted, started his motor, and idled back toward the bridge and the open bay beyond. "Want a raincoat?" he asked.

Jim seemed not to hear.

"What happened to your hand?"

"It's all right. My stitches are leaking some. Don't worry about it."

They were into the swells of Northwest Channel, and Captain Simpson stood erect behind the controls' console in order to better time their rhythm. Despite his caution, and the moderation of his speed, the skipper was unable to avoid a wave that soaked them and covered the deck with a couple of inches of water. Once across the channel, the swells flattened out in the intermittent lees of the sprinkled keys. Captain Simpson applied the throttle and removed his drainage plug. The water around their feet quickly dissipated, sucked into the sea as if by magic. Jim contemplated the talons of soaring turkey vultures that provided the living link between sea and sky.

The house at Woman Key came into view.

"Hey, Mister, there's nobody home. There're no boats at the dock."

"I must have made a mistake," Jim muttered. Captain Simpson was about to turn around, when Jim demanded, "Go in for a closer look. I want to be sure."

They entered the narrow boat channel.

"No dogs, Mister. When someone's home, there are always a couple of big dogs on the beach."

Jim ignored the remark. "I want you to circle around Woman Key and take me to Boca Grande."

"This is nuts! Those are high swells on the ocean side. We're talkin' rough sailin' here."

"Do what I said, Captain. It won't take long."

Simpson shrugged; his muttered invectives were snatched away by the steady gale. They pitched their way through the chop, occasionally shipping small amounts of water.

"Turn in here, Captain." Jim pointed the way, and they traversed a long strip of white sand meandering across the seabed between Woman Key and Boca Grande—the precise place that he'd caught his permit. He pursed his lips into a kiss.

As they rounded the western end of Boca Grande, Jim fixed his gaze upon a smear on the horizon—the fifteen-mile-distant, isolated cluster of the last of the Florida Keys. "Take me to the Marquesas, Captain!"

"No way. Look, this has gone far enough. We're headin' in."

Jim extricated the remaining seven Benjamin Franklins from his pocket and extended them towards Simpson.

"It means a lot to me, Captain," he stated in a stiff, imperious tone.

Simpson shrugged, and disappeared the money into his spray-soaked shirt pocket. "It's your nickel, Mister."

The rolling swells of shark-infested Boca Grande Channel caused the skiff to shudder in protest. The skipper was on his feet again, hunched over the controls and staring intently ahead as the bow rose on swells and fell in troughs. It took fully half an hour of skillful navigation before the skiff emerged into the calmer shallows of the flats surrounding the Marquesas and Captain Simpson could relax his vigilance.

"So, what now, Mister? I said what now, Mister?"

It was only then that Simpson realized he was alone.

III

"Mr. Fitzsimmons! Mr. Fitzsimmons! Are you all right?"

Jim lifted his head from the improvised cradle of his right arm. Priscilla's bulbous face was contorted into the only look of genuine concern he could ever recall. It demanded an answer.

"Oh yes ... mmm. I'm fine. Really. Could you get me a glass of water, please?"

It was then that he noticed the throbbing in his bandaged right hand and the red stain it had left on his desktop.

Alone once more, he gathered his thoughts, his gaze fixed on the enlarged image of the snapshot taken last May by his fishing partner. The rapt look on his face as he contemplated his permit was ludicrously out of sync with his present mood, but still possessed an uncanny ability to suffuse him with the first stirrings of a sense of power ... or was it purpose?

The executive secretary returned with a pitcher of ice water and a tall glass better suited to serving frozen concoctions at a midsummer patio brunch. He drank such a long draught that his palate began to ache in protest from the sudden chill, filling his eyes with tears.

Jim was tempted to invite Priscilla to stay, possibly to consolidate, with her human presence, his still-suspect resurrection from the dead.

But contemplating intimacy of any kind with her was a bit like waving a white flag across the minefield at a former enemy. A truce was possible, but you could scarcely expect to throw down your weapons and rush to embrace somewhere in the middle of no man's land! So, he dismissed her with a nod, and a mumbled, "Thank you."

The thought of suicide had receded as surely as the pain in his revitalized mouth. It was then that he noticed the other two poetry volumes perched on the corner of his desk, trophies from the extraordinary expedition with Jerry.

Jim picked up Pinsky's *The Figured Wheel* and tried to open it. With his bandaged hand, his efforts proved maladroit, and he grimaced at the crimson smear now soaked into the pages' edges. With his left hand alone, he managed to open the tome and contemplated the last stanza of "The Saving."

> *In the fresh luxury of breath*
> *And the brusque, flattering comfort*
> *Of the communal laughter. Later,*
> *Falling asleep under the stars,*
> *He watched a gray wreath of smoke*
> *Unfurling into the blackness;*
> *And he thought of it as the shape*
> *Of a newborn ghost, the benign*
> *Ghost of his death, that had nearly*
> *Happened: it coiled, as the wind rustled,*
> *And he thought of it as a power,*
> *His luck or his secret name.*

He read the words over and over, each new reading further staking his claim upon this special message, seemingly written especially for him. When his understanding bordered upon memorization, he began flipping randomly through the pages. Jim's ball settled into another slot of the poet's roulette wheel, and he read the poem "To My Father," Pinsky's ode to a caring and vulnerable person so unlike James Fitzsimmons as to belong to another race of men, if not a different species altogether.

"I guess we each get issued one," he said aloud.

Jim's thoughts about not having been consulted evolved into speculation over the character of the grandfather he'd never known—James's father. His only contact with his hoary ancestor was the portrait on James's wall of the gaunt, stern, bearded immigrant from Carrickmacross, County Monaghan. The sober Comstock miner sat stiff and immobile, flanked by a standing Bridget Murphy, his wild-eyed bride from County Cork, her hand upon her husband's shoulder in the pose typical of the day. Jim's musings turned to Ivy, Heather, and JFK.

"They didn't get much of a bargain, either."

***

Outside, Reno's neon lights began to press their daily advantage over sunlight, prompting Jim to turn on the desk lamp to illumine his work. Over the past hour, he'd used up half a yellow legal pad, the wadded paper missiles strewn across the floor bearing witness that the accuracy of his former three-pointer Michener goal was aberrational. A *plan*—how to write a plan? Maybe in the morning. "How can I write a goddamn plan when I'm not even sure what drives this business?" he muttered aloud.

When Jim entered the elevator, he at first experienced his usual irritation over having to share it with a customer. The middle-aged woman clutched her plastic cup full of quarters and smiled at him politely. He found her blue bonnet, tightly cinched under her chin with ribbon, a bit ludicrous. James's one-note ode to the customer, repeated as often and as predictably over the years as breakers crashing upon some beach, echoed in his memory.

"Having any luck, ma'am?"

"Never do."

"Then why do you play?"

"Because it's fun."

"Losing is fun?"

"No, trying is fun."

"But if you never win here, why don't you play at Harrah's or the Golden Spur?"

"I do sometimes. I might walk to Harrah's, but it's three blocks and we don't have this brutal sun in Canada," she remarked, tugging at her ribbon by way of justifying the bonnet. "Anyway, I always stay here. This place is … well, it's my place. Fred and I used to come here twice a year by bus. On one trip, we met another couple from Vancouver and became close friends. Last year, our daughter married their son. Fred loved the Starlight. I think his ghost lives here now." She laughed. "I wouldn't dream of staying anywhere else. The Starlight sent flowers to his funeral last year."

"We did?"

"Do you work here?"

"Sort of."

They exited the elevator together, and Jim handed her a business card. "Give this to the *maître d'* in The Westerner. Tell him that you're my guest for dinner. Here, let me sign the back." He restored the autographed card to its new owner.

"Thanks."

"My pleasure. Oh, and good *luck*, ma'am."

***

Jim turned off the desk lamp and stood to exit the darkened room as the first step on the journey to his upstairs' bed, negotiating the blackness by habit and opening his office door. It was then that he noticed the light seeping from under James's door. "Wow, Dad's still here." He tapped lightly and then opened the door in response to the muffled, "Come in."

James was sitting behind his desk, its only clutter a lumpy plastic zip-lock bag and a row of ten or twelve pill bottles arranged in a line like a picket fence. Three or four were brown, bespeaking their pharmaceutical origin; the remainder were purchases of wonder drugs from television pitches. The two unopened ones next to their half-filled counterparts underscored James's integral and intact parsimonious nature. He was as big a sucker for twofers as any Starlight customer.

"Good evening, Son, or is it morning? I can't tell any longer."

"It's midnight, Dad."

"Oh, okay, so it's neither."

Jim recognized the voice, but not its source.

"You know, Jimmy, I used to take pills in order to cure something, to feel better, to get on with life. Now, I take them to buy a few more hours before it's time to take my pills again. What's the point?" James waved his hand over the little chemical kingdom and added, "I think about swallowing all of them at once. That would be a sure ticket to … wherever. I think about it a lot, Jimmy."

James covered his catarrhal eruption with a handkerchief, drawing Jim's attention to his father's pallid and wizened face. "Dad, you look so frail. You've lost a lot of weight. Have you been to the doctor?"

James bleated and gave a dismissive wave. "Yeah. I hate those quacks. They never give you good news. They're so full of themselves. They actually believe they're saving lives, when all they're doing is postponing deaths. If you want to die soon, go see a doctor. I went to Cantlon the other day with a little problem, and he thinks he's discovered two new serious ones." James gestured at the brown bottles. "At least your dentist cleans your teeth. When I was younger, I smoked, drank booze, and ate whatever. I wanted to live until I was seventy-five and then die as peacefully and painlessly as possible. Well, I'm now ninety, and I still want to live longer. There are things that I want to follow, even if I can no longer attend them. I want to know who wins the next World Series and Super Bowl, who's going to be the next president of these United States. I also keep score." James opened a black book that looked like a diary.

"What score?"

"Every day, I read the obituaries in the newspaper and see that most of them are about people who were younger than me. If they were famous—athletes, or movie stars, or politicians—I write their name on that day's page in this book. It makes me feel like I'm ahead of them in the game of life. I'm here and they aren't; I'm truckin' on, and they're sleepin' for eternity." James handed Jim the book, and he flipped through it. "There are no entries for this year, Dad."

"I know, Jimmy. I didn't forget; I just lost interest. There's not going to be a ninety-first birthday for me. If someone else out there is playing the game, this year, *he* wins!"

Such finality scarcely invited comment, so Jim changed the subject. "What are you doing here this late?"

"I'm here all the time now, Jimmy. Oh, I still prowl the floor and restaurants to check things out—you know, talk to my people. In good weather, I try to walk to Wingfield Park to listen to the free noon concert. I now have two or three friends there—street people. They live under a bridge, and I live on top of a casino, but we're spiritual soulmates, sharing the oom-pah-pah together. I try to give them a little something, maybe ten bucks. I might then walk along Virginia or Sierra to reminisce. I can still picture Menards' Men's Store, Armanko's Stationery, Herz Jewelry, Sears, Penneys, Monkey Wards—all gone now."

James pointed to the half-masted chaise lounge in the corner. "That's my bed. I can't sleep lying down any longer. In a regular bed, I can't breathe. It gives me a panic attack, like someone is sitting on my chest. Even here, it's hard to sleep. Sleeping sitting up takes getting used to."

"I see you still have Snow White." Jim pointed at the corpulent poodle sleeping at James's feet.

"Right. After your mom died, we both moved here permanently. Someone walks her once a day for me. The kitchen sends up food for both of us." James pointed at the half-eaten sandwich in the zip-lock and then the bowl next to his feet. "She still has a great appetite; I don't. Nothing tastes good any longer. Not even my mother's milk—I stopped drinking my Glenlivet."

Jim hid his dismay over the several landmarks on his father's relentless march to the grave, while dismissing his managerial pique over the flouting of the property's no-pets policy.

***

Jim contemplated the pornographic images flitting across the television screen in near disbelief. He'd punched up the adult channel in search of the stimulation that culminated in the masturbation in his adolescence, not to mention his Jim's World years with Dorothy, and failed to attain tumescence. The raunchy film was more disgusting than stimulating, and his embarrassment over the thought of Priscilla ever learning of such a charge to his room undermined Jim's capacity to concentrate on an erection. He zapped *Floozie Susie Does Everybody*, or whatever, and let his mind wander as he luxuriated on the expansive king bed bathed in the twilight of the full harvest moon. His desire for arousal after months of celibacy directed his thoughts to Carol, but that merely conjured up the emotional barnacles of a failed affair. To think of Sally was out of the question, and there were no erotic-memory diamonds in the Dorothy mine, either.

Jim closed his eyes, mired in the nadir of his lusterless love life. But then his mind wandered to a distant pubescent realm ... and she was there. Janine Beauchamp flitted onto his mental screen, the vivacious twelve-year-old sylph who'd been the fantasy fueling the raging hormones of every eighth-grade boy at Saint Thomas Aquinas parochial school. His pimpled persona retreated before the advances of the high-cheeked, olive-skinned Madonna with perfect lips framing alabaster teeth and arranged in a siren's smile. He experienced, as if it were yesterday, the volatile emotional mix of keen excitation and profound self-doubt that had forced him into the deepest recesses of an omnipresent shyness of a young boy. Of course, Janine sensed her power and delighted in the playful flirtation that stoked his palpable awkwardness. She knew just when to stop—before Jim took flight.

Janine was an anomaly in the ethnic mix of Irish, Italian, and Basque students attending Saint Thomas. Her people were descended from that part of Europe where swarthy Italian and French Catholicism collided with frosty and pallid German Protestantism in the unique cultural and political experiment known as Switzerland. Such geographical complexity was beyond the grasp of the average Saint Thomas grade schooler, but they all appreciated that Janine was different. There was an exotic, almost Gypsy-like, mystique about her. She was Jim's first love, albeit a vicarious one.

Indeed, his certainty that such feelings would remain unrequited, combined with his youthful piety as both altar and choir boy, had prompted his decision to attend Ryan Preparatory in Fresno. His freshman year at the Jesuit-staffed Catholic seminary had brought many epiphanies. He'd embraced Latin with a passion and excelled at

Gregorian chant. He poured his pent-up physical energy into basketball. Most weekends, the entire student body crowded into the back of a truck that would transport them to a nearby mountain campground at Fullerton Lake, or to the Jesuit retreat house in Santa Cruz. It was then that Jim Angler was born. He would slip away from the group to cast bait into mountain waters or a spinner into Pacific surf.

But then there were the self-doubts, which became shame when he had his first wet dream, the object of which, of course, was Janine. At a single stroke, he'd demonstrated his unworthiness for the priesthood and defiled his vestal virgin.

As the fast-forwarded incarnation of his former self, lying naked in the demi-darkness of his Starlight suite while stroking his penis, Jim experienced anew the guilt of *the* fateful night. He'd left the seminary, transferring to Manogue High, once again Janine's classmate. He recalled her deep French kiss during the graduation night party. He then relived his twentieth school reunion, the last time he'd seen her. He'd attended with Dorothy and made the perfunctory introductions between the two women in his life. Then, for the rest of the evening, he maintained his distance from the queen of his former fantasy world. Observing Janine from across the room, he understood the difference between passion and his marriage of convenience. Before tonight's reverie, Jim had perused several Keats poems, and he now muttered aloud, "She was certainly my *belle dame sans merci*." He wondered what had become of Janine.

***

Jim was amused by the perspiration on his forehead and the dryness of his mouth as he dialed the number and waited for … he knew not what. At his age, still the scared little boy?

The female voice that answered was vaguely familiar, and he fumbled to explain his reason for calling. "So, Janine, you still live here in Reno? I almost never see any of the old gang anymore, but the other day I was having lunch in the Prospectors' Club and ran into Ben Pagliari. We started reminiscing about our high school days. I asked him about you and well …"

"I can hardly believe this, Jimby." He flinched at the near-forgotten sound of yet another of his nicknames—the one inflicted upon a timid lad by his classmates. "Ben said that you are a teacher in high school. He wasn't sure of what. He also said that you're single, never married."

"Spanish, Jimby, and guilty as charged." She laughed. "How's life treating you and ... Doris, isn't it?"

"Dorothy. We've been divorced for several months now."

"That's nice ... uh, I'm sorry. I mean, I don't know what to say, Jimby. I hope it's what you want."

"When you put it that way, I'm not quite sure. It was sort of her idea, but it was a really obvious one just lying around waiting for one of us to put into words. It never was much of a marriage ... a very Catholic one. More about kids than us. When they began to move out, the little that we had in common was gone. I don't hate or blame her, or anything. It might even be better if I did. Hating is a form of caring. Just a second ..."

Jim felt the receiver slipping from his moist grip. He laid it on his desk and wiped his hands on his pantlegs and forehead with a handkerchief.

"This is going sideways," he muttered. He slapped himself on the cheek and exclaimed "showtime!"—his confidence-building mantra whenever faced with an anxiety-ridden challenge ... such as public speaking—then picked up the receiver and said, "Janine, I was wondering if maybe you could see your way clear to possibly—"

"I'd love to see you."

"Maybe we could go out to dinner. Are you busy tonight? Oh, you must be. How presumptuous of me. You pick a day and place, and I'll be there. I mean I'll pick you up and we'll go out ..."

She didn't try to conceal her amusement over his floundering. However, her gentle laughter had the tinkle of a tiny bell rather than the rumble of ridicule. She hastened to his rescue. "Tonight's fine, Jimby. 34 Rochester Place. I'll see you at six."

***

Jim listened to the faint footsteps approaching the door with mixed emotions. More than twenty years since he'd last seen Janine; this could be a really long evening! But then, his fondest hope was confirmed—the same electric smile graced the totally familiar face.

Unabashed, Janine tolerated Jim's head-to-toe scrutiny of her svelte body.

"I … I don't remember you being so slender. You look like you'd snap in a good wind!"

"And I don't remember you being such a romantic, Jimby. You say the sweetest things." She laughed.

Rather than feeling consternation over her comment, Jim was suffused with self-confidence. Janine's ironic sense of humor was intact and would likely get them unscathed through any verbal bramble patches. He grinned broadly and touched the shock of hair that tumbled onto her shoulder and disappeared somewhere down her back. "There's some snow on the mountain, but it makes you look lovelier than I remember."

"I've never considered dyeing it. This fits my image as a spinster schoolmarm."

Now they were seated in the living room of her small condo, her tiny hand resting obediently in his capacious grasp. "So, you've never married. I find that hard to believe. Every one of us senior boys would have married you on graduation night. I still remember …"

"What, Jimby?"

"Don't take this wrong, Janine, but there was your trip around the room at Ben's party. You kissed every boy, and they weren't just pecks. It made me feel very special, like I was being seduced, loved, but then betrayed when you moved to the next guy."

She chuckled at the reminder of her coquettish powers, then defused their memory. "We were just celebrating, and like with any celebration, there was a lot of joy and a little bit of sadness. I was saying, 'congratulations for graduating—you're no longer a boy after today.' But I was also saying goodbye. I haven't seen half of those guys again since that night."

"So, where would you like to go for dinner?"

"Chez Janine's. Can't you smell my casserole?"

It was only then that he noticed the pleasant aroma. "If I'd known, I would have brought something. Maybe a bottle of wine."

The spicy chicken and rice, a *faux* paella, accompanied by a 1983 Faustino V Riojan red, provided the perfect props for their dinner conversation, dominated as it was by Janine's Hispanic odyssey. She'd studied for a year at the Complutense in Madrid on New York University's junior year abroad program. After getting her bachelor's degree in Spanish literature at UNR, she was now a veteran Spanish teacher at Reno High School.

They sipped their espresso and then Gran Duque de Alba cognac from a bottle given to her decades ago by a Spanish admirer. "No, Jimby, I didn't marry. There was no time for it. There was too much world to see. Maybe it was Saint Thomas and Manogue. We were given constant Immaculate Conception messages by the nuns. We girls were untouchable *santas*, but whores if we fell off that pedestal. We had to watch out for you guys because you were always ready to give us the push. When you weren't stalking us, you were driving to the Mustang Ranch." Jim stirred in protest at the cathouse aspersion, then acquiesced to the knowing look in her eyes, which seemed to say, *We girls all knew about it—it's okay.*

"If Santa Janine was the flirt you claim, maybe it was my protest against that suffocation—it was pretty innocent. But I never really escaped the consequences of my upbringing. I mean, I spent most of my twenties looking for Mr. Perfect—Mr. Catholic Perfect. I might just as well have been searching for a leprechaun or unicorn. It took most of my thirties before I could relax with a man—really relax and accept him on his own terms as another flawed, lonely, and maybe scared human being ... like me. I'm not alone, Jimby, because now I have me ... and I like the *real* me. I don't want to be beholden to anyone else."

"Other than Spain, what have you seen of the world? I've been to many countries, but it was always in some remote backwater with a fly rod. There were also Dorothy's canned tours or cruises. For me, England is Big Ben and France is the Eiffel Tower. The Mediterranean and Caribbean are a deck chair."

"My story is a little different. After college, I took off for more than a year to South America—no destination in particular. I was in Peru, Chile, Argentina, and Uruguay, mainly staying in youth hostels. I had many affairs … mental ones. With García Marquez, Vargas Llosa, Borges, and some other magic-realist authors."

"What's a magic-realist author?"

"That could take all evening to explain," she said, laughing.

"I haven't even read Steinbeck, let alone Shakespeare. For me, Grisham is a real heavy trip. But recently, I discovered this poet, Robert Pinsky, and he's become very important to me. I have a book that I'd like to share with you the next time we—"

Janine rose, went to her bookshelf, and returned with a tome in one hand and a guitar in the other. "Let me share something with you. These are the love poems of Mario Benedetti, a Uruguayan poet. He's always very uplifting. My favorite poem of his is *Te Quiero*. You read along while I sing it." Janine adjusted one of the guitar strings, and then her crystalline soprano voice intoned, "*Tus manos son mi caricia …*"

Jim struggled to follow her musical flight with the exotic text. "It says, 'Your hands are my caress,' Jimby." The melody was strikingly beautiful, even to someone who couldn't comprehend the words.

"That was gorgeous, Janine. I didn't know you could sing. What does the whole poem say?"

She walked him line by line through Benedetti's magical garden of delights. Jim was particularly struck by the refrain:

Si te quiero es porque sos mi
amor mi cómplice y todo
y en la calle codo a codo
somos mucho más que dos.

He made her write it down along with the translation:

If I love you it's because you are
my love my accomplice my all
and out in the street arm in arm
we are much more than two.

While doing so, she assumed her professorial guise. "The sos for 'you are' is idiomatic in southern South America. It's an anachronism no longer used anywhere else in the Hispanic world. It really underscores Benedetti's Uruguayan nationality."

"Sing it for me again, please."

Jim stretched out on the sofa and closed his eyes to better concentrate on the subtle colors in her lyrical rainbow. His rapture lingered into the afterglow of her performance, all but crowding out her whispered, "I'll be right back."

Presently, Janine was standing in the doorway of the condo's sole bedroom. Her naked body and spindly arms and legs seemed a nearly ornithological apparition. The tiny brown breasts were scarcely the size of walnuts. The only recognizable feature was the radiant smile that had haunted Jim's fantasies since their playground days. He arose and floated towards its promise.

Jim struggled to abandon himself to the moment, suspended somewhere between atavistic Catholic guilt and the excitement of violating a Madonna. There was even a hint of pedophilia, as he penetrated the now gray-haired child. He feared that he might hurt the frail figure moving rhythmically beneath him. However, he became aware of a guttural growl of passion coming from below. Janine's nasal moaning in his left ear was just about the most banal sound that he'd ever heard, culminating in an orgasmic screech accompanied by a painful bite on his ear lobe and the gouging of red trails across the topography of his back.

"That was so wonderful, Janine," he lied, the legacy and fantasies of Saint Thomas and Manogue forever behind him.

***

It was Christmas Eve, nearly a year since Jim had left Dot's house. In all that time, he hadn't passed its architecture or memories. Now, nostalgia and holiday loneliness decided him to do a drive-by for old times' sake. He would be just one of the many gawkers that cruised Reno's holiday decorations. Dot's had always been spectacular, if not prizewinning. They would also likely be familiar; she'd standardized her display over the years.

Jim was correct in that anticipation. However, there was one noticeable change. The impressive holiday lights now showcased the "for sale" sign driven into the front lawn. A startled Jim braked and tried to gather his thoughts. He was paying ten thousand a month in alimony—the main reason that he still lived in the Starlight with both his room and meals comped. Dot's cash flow should have been sufficient to cover her living expenses and service her mortgage.

He noticed the light on in her bedroom, then realized that another was aglow in Jim's World as well. Had he forgotten to turn it off when he left a year earlier! For decades, it had always been his practice to prowl before going to bed, extinguishing his profligate kids' bulbs. Was he now the consummate offender? What did it cost to power a lightbulb 24-7 for a year? Jim dialed the familiar number by rote, as if calling home to discuss some small domestic detail. There were many more rings than he expected.

"H-u-l-l-o?" was the somnolent greeting. Dot had apparently fallen asleep with her television on.

"Dot … er, Dorothy, it's me."

"Jim?"

"Yes, dear."

"Is something the matter? Where are you?"

"Well, I'm here in the driveway. Can I come in?"

"Wait a minute. I'll have to come down. I had the lock changed ages ago."

A few minutes later, Dorothy opened the door, and took a step backward. "I certainly wasn't expecting you, Jimmy. Please come in."

Being seated at the familiar dining room table was its own holiday comfort for him.

"I don't get it, Dorothy. I thought Charles did the math and settled on an alimony amount that would let you keep this place. Dad's in terrible shape and won't last much longer. What I'm saying is that I'll probably have an inheritance soon. I'm not sure how it will all shake out, what with the Starlight's problems, and of course, there's Sean. But I should have something after all the dust settles. Maybe I could give you a little more then."

"No, Jim. You've been very generous. It's not about that. The children are gone, and so are you. This big place makes no sense. I think all the empty space just makes me feel lonelier. I'm tired of the housekeeping and yardwork. I really struggled to put up the decorations this year. I want to downsize. Besides, I want to travel more while I can still enjoy it. I have an offer on this place that isn't too bad. Right after the holidays, I expect to close and buy a cute little condo I've found. I should have some money left over, and no mortgage. Maybe then, we can reduce our alimony settlement."

They'd just exchanged hypothetical Christmas gifts. It was then that Jim blurted out a request. "Dorothy, do you think that I could spend the night in Jim's World? The thought of Christmas Eve alone in my Starlight room is really depressing."

"No, Jim."

"I understand. It was presumptuous of—"

"If you want to stay, you'll have to sleep in our bed."

***

There was a new wrinkle to Jim's daily routine. He no longer knocked on the door before entering. Even with two hearing aids, his father's capacity to respond was now abysmal. Fortunately, the executive office's men's room was adjacent to James's cubicle, as he used his walker to pay hourly visits to it. Gone were the days when he toured the Starlight. Summer was coming, but there were no outdoor noonday concerts on his horizon, let alone strolls down Reno's main thoroughfares. James's universe had contracted to a few square feet.

For an instant, Jim was certain that his father was dead. But then the rasping and gurgling from the head face down on the desktop told him otherwise. Jim placed his hand on the hunched shoulder, and James lifted his upper body. He reached for the thin plastic hose of his oxygenator and inserted the cannula in his nose. Jim noticed the circle of drool where a head had rested and the speckled blood of the hawked loogies in the three well-used handkerchiefs.

"Are you all right?"

"All right? Don't ask me, ask them."

"Who?"

"Maybe my cardiologist or possibly my oncologist. I think they have a bet on what's going to get me first. They've both got good odds."

303

James's attempt to chuckle was more like a death rattle that trailed off into prolonged coughing.

"Dad, I'm calling the para-medics."

"The hell you are. Don't even think about it, Jimmy. I'm right where I want to be; where I belong. I'm not about to go to some emergency room to be poked with needles by strangers, pumped full of crap, and handed a stupid gown with a slit down the back that won't even cover my bare ass."

"But, Dad, you were barely breathing."

"I was meditating, Son. I was communicating with my friends and relatives. They're on the other side of the Great Divide, and they're angry with me. They say, 'Come on, James, hurry up, get the lead out.' Maybe it's pride that prevents me from dying, Jimmy. I've heard that we void our bowels when we die. The shame of shitting all over myself as my last act on earth keeps me going."

James lapsed into another coughing spell that lasted a full minute. He clutched Jim's hand and squeezed it with surprising strength. When his father finally caught his breath, Jim heard the raspy whisper: "I'm proud of you, Jimmy, and I love you. Now leave."

It was farewell.

***

Sean and Jim stood alone by the open coffin. James's expression was considerably less stern in death than at a Starlight board meeting. The funeral director had invited the two sons to spend time alone with their father. Tomorrow there would be the customary funeral mass and graveside service, attended by the forty or so relatives and friends at this evening's rosary. Each of the brothers was absorbed in private thought when the door opened and in walked JFK.

"Hello, Dad. I want to say goodbye to Grandpa."

"I didn't realize you were here, son. You weren't at the rosary."

"I was standing in the back. I felt a little out of place. I'm staying with Mom, and she thought if she were here tonight it might be awkward … you know, after what happened between the two of you."

"Well, I'm glad you came, and I wish she had, too. It would have been okay. Tell her that. Tell her to come tomorrow. It's not about us; it's about him." Jim gestured towards the coffin.

"Hi, Unc. Long time, no see. What's it been, at least ten years? I was just a kid."

Their fragile avuncular tie seemed forged out of their mutual long-term absence from Reno and family. Neither had managed to visit James before his death.

Jim interrupted: "I was about to give Sean this Starlight gaming token. I thought that we might each put one in your grandfather's pocket. The Starlight meant more than anything to your grandfather, so I thought he should take a little piece of it with him. Unfortunately, I only brought two."

"It's okay, Dad. You didn't know I was coming. I think it's a fine idea."

***

Reclusive James Fitzsimmons Kennedy would have been uncomfortable in the crowd that packed his funeral. Jim sat in the front pew, flanked by his brother, Sean, Shirley, and their son, William, to his right, and his three children and Dorothy on his left. Jim locked eyes momentarily with Jerry, Sue by his side, and accepted their telegraphed condolences. He nodded his gratitude to Mary Beth and François, also seated together—an arrangement that made Jim question whether his former colleagues were now a number.

Jim and Dorothy took communion together during the funeral mass; his first time in many years. His mind processed the day's ironies and anomalies during Father Carmody's laundered comments about James's character and life. He detailed the deceased's wanderings as a nomadic slot-route operator in the taverns of central Nevada mining camps during the 1930s while omitting that James had machines in every one of the cathouses. That would have seemed unseemly when praising the bishop's perennial Thanksgiving dinner partner. So many truces and anomalies present in the confines of a single church—Armistice Day or Armageddon?

After the graveside service, Jim lingered behind the other mourners departing for the wake. Standing above the fresh grave, he chuckled at the thought that it was the only time he'd ever towered over James. He uncorked a bottle of Glenlivet and poured the entire contents upon the fresh-disturbed dirt.

***

Jim extracted his notes from the pages of Robert Bly's *Iron John: A Book About Men* and placed the book on the conference table. He didn't intend to quote from it. Rather, it was his talisman and security blanket as he prepared to address his department directors. Bly had taught Jim that it was all right for a man to cry—a possibility for him in this circumstance.

"Gentlemen ... and ladies." Jim nodded at Ruth and Sarah, the Starlight's latest controller and marketing director, seated together with their fingers linked surreptitiously under the conference table. He could barely stand the sad stares from the several sets of hopeless eyes fixed on him.

"I know that this will come as no surprise ..." Jim groped for the magical vocabulary that might accomplish mission impossible—a gentle delivery of harsh news. "We will have to shut down the Starlight at the end of this month."

Ruth's and Sarah's interlocked fingers tightened.

"You all know that we've been in trouble for some time now, and, well, we've come to the end of the road. Yesterday, I met with our bankers, and they plan to file a foreclosure suit. It's early November, and we haven't made a payment since June. We even lost money during the summer. Since September, we've been losing a hundred thou a month."

Heads nodded and their grim faces reflected acceptance of the inevitable.

"God, this really hurts! I just want to tell you how much I appreciate everything that you've done for this place—for me. We all tried our best. I ... I love you guys. I'll never forget you."

"You were a great boss, Boss. We'll never forget you either!" Seth Harris declared.

Jim rubbed his wettened eyes and grappled with the rising emotional tide within his breast. He was determined not to sob. "We have a lot of work ahead of us, a lot of pain. I want each of you to prepare a wind-down plan for your department by tomorrow afternoon. Please keep this to yourself. I don't expect you to make the announcement to your staff. I will. I owe it to you and to them. It's my responsibility. I want to make some calls first to other casinos around here, maybe Las Vegas and Indian Country, too. I'm hoping they can employ some of our people. I'd like to arrange a job fair if there's enough interest among our competitors in participating. We need to make the transition as painless as possible for our employees and their families. Unfortunately, there's no money to give them severance pay or bonuses. We'll meet again tomorrow afternoon at four to go over details. Please come prepared with your plan and any other suggestions. Meeting adjourned."

Alone, Jim laid his head on his crossed arms and struggled with his next move.

The first call would have to be to Gaming Control. The regulators never appreciate being blind-sided. He knew that when a casino closes, the state confiscates the bankroll, and, for a reasonable period, maybe a month, redeems any outstanding gaming chips, which are like money. It then confiscates all the chips and destroys them. Everything would have to be inventoried—cash on hand, value of the used gaming equipment, accounts payable—anything not soaked by the bank.

He had to call Jeff immediately. At their last meeting, two months earlier, much had remained undecided. The Starlight's bankruptcy attorney had mentioned the possibility of a soft landing. He would have to negotiate with all the creditors individually to see if they would settle for cents on the dollar—maybe twenty. It would be better than nothing. Jim had personally signed on the bank debt, which would bite into his recent inheritance considerably. For now, just how much was unknowable, since the bank would surely sell the building and Jim was legally on the hook for any shortfall. In Reno's present gaming climate, a shortfall was inevitable.

Jim shuddered at the thought of making the public announcement. It was a little like being caught in *flagrante delicto*. Business failure seemed a bit pornographic. He knew that it would be months before he again darkened the doors of the Prospectors' Club. The mutual avoidance of the Starlight's demise in conversation with his friends would be unbearable. He considered putting out a canned statement to the media, but found that to be cowardly and intolerable, particularly given his many years as the Starlight's public face and mouthpiece. Indeed, his first call after tomorrow's directors' meeting would be to the *Reno Evening Gazette-Journal*, with successive ones to the three local television stations. He dreaded the inevitable interviews. Ouch! Details, details, details.

Jim remained motionless for the next hour, paralyzed by it all. But then he began to stir, suffused with a creeping sense of relief. For the first time in months, his stress was dissipating. While there was no solution, at least there'd been a resolution. Jim muttered, "And so, Mrs. Lincoln, how did you enjoy the rest of the play?"

The Starlight's flame might be extinguished, but his would flicker on.

***

The month from hell was over. Actually, it'd had its bright moments. Seth Harris and Andrew McDermott had both decided to retire. Shelly Sherman was hired by a Vegas property as its hotel manager. Joshua Threadwell left the casino industry and was director of human resources for a local manufacturer. Priscilla was the new administrative assistant of the dean of the College of Agriculture at the University of Nevada, particularly content to be eligible one day for a pension. Ruth and Sarah were now a team at the Flamingo Hilton, their upward career mobility positively vertiginous. Given their brief two-month stint at the Starlight, they were exempt from any blame for the closure. The Golden Spur's job fair had placed more than half of the rank-and-file employees, and Jim was still receiving daily calls from human resources directors from as far away as Vegas and Atlantic City, not to mention the remotest of outposts throughout Indian Country. In short, everyone would land on their feet rather than face.

Jim picked up the receiver of the nagging telephone and listened to Jeremy Clinton's voice intoning, "Been thinking about you a lot, Jim. Could we get together for coffee?"

"I'd like that. Tomorrow morning? Where? Sure, I've never been there, but I know the Lotus Blossom."

The bank was taking possession of the building later that day, and this might be his last visit to his own office. Jim removed the photograph of the permit kiss from the wall, the very last of his possessions remaining in the now sterile premise. As he walked out the door, he almost collided with JFK.

"Whoa, Son, I wasn't expecting you."

"I know, Dad. I've been worried about you since I saw the news about the Starlight on television a couple of weeks ago. I thought of calling several times, but that seemed too impersonal. Anyway, I decided that I needed to come here. Actually, I was tying up my own loose ends. Jake and I split up about six months ago. I moved into a commune, but that got on my nerves. The other guys were okay, but we all liked different kinds of music. Beethoven and Bowie are not a great mix. I wasn't that happy at work either. Then there's the sadness. I have lost many friends to AIDS, and it's all that my surviving ones seem to talk about. My San Francisco days are over. But enough about me. How are you doing?"

"It's okay. It's pretty much resolved now. There are a few loose ends to tie up, but life goes on. I think you know Mom and I are back together. I moved in with her the day after closing the Starlight."

"Yeah, I do. I'd thought of staying with her. I can't believe that she sold the house."

"*We* sold it, Son. We'll have to get you a hotel; we don't really have room. We're your classic empty nesters, now."

"I'll find a place. I need something more permanent than a hotel. I've got all my belongings in the back seat of my Volkswagen. Imagine that—I can fit my whole life into two suitcases." JFK laughed.

"Been there, Son."

"How did it all go so very wrong? I thought there'd always be a Starlight. Grandpa seemed so good at what he did."

"Grandpa?"

"Oh, sorry Dad, I didn't mean …"

"It's okay, Son; it really was *his* place. Even after the board removed him, I still knew that. He permeated every corner in the Starlight, like the stale tobacco odor in some guest room, even months after it's been designated non-smoking."

"It couldn't have been easy for you."

"No. Easy wouldn't be my first choice of words for it. But it wasn't horrible, either. It was what it was, and I certainly learned from the experience. It was my crash course in life."

"I'm really glad you can take it that way. You don't seem bitter. Please don't think I was ... Well, you know ... sort of suggesting that it was your fault."

"Fault is another poor word to use in talking about the late great Starlight. Was the automobile at *fault* for the bust of the busted buggy-whip manufacturer? Jesus Christ himself couldn't have saved the Starlight. Think of Reno's casinos as a herd of impalas stalked by two lions. In Reno's case, the lions are Vegas and Indian gaming. Each impala is afraid to bolt and become the first to be eaten. So, they herd together, and the strongest make it to the center. The lions bring down the weakest on the periphery, but it doesn't really matter to the fate of the herd, because other hungry lions are about to show up. There are always more hungry lions."

"So, the Starlight was a weak impala?"

"Among the weakest. It was in trouble even before the Indians discovered lions and Vegas found Steve Wynn. The Starlight made money, but it was too small, and no one wanted to nurture it. So, when the lions showed up, it was all spindly and couldn't even keep up with the herd. Hell, Son, even in the best of years we spent the spring paying off our winter suppliers. Maybe, by June, we were even and profitable for the rest of the summer and early fall. But you had to squirrel away money for winter operating. The first year after they opened the Golden Spur, we should have realized that the game was up. That year, it took until July to clean up the previous winter's debt, and there was scarcely time to save for the next snowfall. We couldn't believe the evidence right before our eyes and just kept riding the horse until it bucked us off."

"It makes my gig seem insignificant, Dad."

"What gig?"

"My life. I've never had much to lose—bricks and mortar, I mean. You used to tell me, 'Get some responsibility; hell, get something.'"

"I was just being a concerned parent, a frustrated father who thought he knew best for you. I did care, you know."

"I always knew that, even when I resented the cheap-shot advice."

"I'm sure it wasn't always easy."

"There's that word again. No, it wasn't easy. Even guys without responsibility have to eat every few hours. I've slept in the rain, but that's not your first choice, either. So, you've got to get some bread—money, I mean."

"With your guitar, I suppose."

"Sure, you learn to milk it. The joint only gives you a stage and a plug for your amps. If they're hurtin' and you're real lucky, maybe they throw in some beer and a few bucks. The real money's in the crowd. You have to work it. I always wore a wedding ring, and the first thing I'd say was 'Sorry for being late, folks. Baby problems, you know.' So, in their minds, now I'm married, a family man, and with his priorities at home, not just some doper with a voice.

"Say it's a restaurant and there're kids having dinner. I get them on stage, and a couple of the mothers, too. I give one kid a cymbal, another a maraca, and pretty soon they're performing, and the proud mothers are swaying to the beat. If the vibes are right, I lead a conga dance around the place. Back at the mike, I plant the seed. 'Well, folks, that was a twenty-dollar dance, don't you think?' I then open up my guitar case, put it at the edge of the stage, and throw in a twenty myself. You call out the first party that heads toward the exit without tipping. 'Thanks folks, *you* have a nice evening and come back again sometime.' Everyone else now realizes that they'll have to run my gauntlet if they try to stiff me."

"Boy, Son, you've really got it figured out."

"It's called survival, Dad. I was thinking that maybe we could do something together. Is there any way I could help? What are you planning to do now? I'm prepared to exchange my Paradise for your Pair-of-Dice."

Jim was a little flummoxed. He had no real answer regarding either of their futures ... but didn't want to dismiss JFK's offer out of hand. "Let me think about it. I haven't run that trapline yet. Actually, Son, we might make a good team. We're both survivors."

***

"You were smart to leave, Jerry. We were in freefall, only this pilot failed to fully realize it. No hard feelings."

Jerry stirred sugar into his cappuccino and gestured towards the swimming mallards. "I think they're immortal unless someone shoots them. Shotgun pellets are their only Achilles heel."

"I don't get it."

"A little private joke, Jim. So, what now?"

"Everyone's asking me that question these days—Dorothy, JFK, you ... I've learned a lot about the gaming business, certainly the hard way. But you know, I've come to like it some. I still have a little foothold. Jeff, our attorney, went back and forth with the bank over closing the Starlight. It was the foreclosure that triggered everything. By then, I was personally signed on the note—the only owner. So that kind of made Jeff my personal attorney. He advised me to put the property into chapter seven bankruptcy, and to take chapter eleven myself. I had my inheritance to protect."

"Makes sense to me."

"Maybe, but then you have to live with yourself. I told Jeff that I preferred his soft-landing approach. I offered to put up some of the money if the creditors would settle for twenty-five-cents on the dollar. I agreed to pay five million to the bank, assuming it would waive any further claim against me. Once a Fitzsimmons, always a Fitzsimmons. I think I did it for James. It was his legacy, and mostly his money, too.

"So, here I sit with maybe a million dollars and a gaming initiative in Fernley on Interstate 80. Jeff salvaged that for me out of the settlement. Even though Fernley was making a little bit of money and could have been sold to some slot operator, that was going to take time, certainly more than a year when you consider approval of the new owner by Gaming Control. The bank didn't want to be in the casino business. The Starlight was gaming on steroids; Fernley is gaming on tranquilizers—no food and beverages, no rooms, no marketing—just two employees per shift.

"Dorothy and I are back together. She sold that outlandish house, and we have a little condo. I urged her to accept Shirley's invitation to go to Europe together. The girls met at Dad's wake and have been friends since. They talk on the phone at least once a week and lament their fates as mothers without grandchildren. I guess that's sort of a bond. They're also both into cooking. Anyway, they're in London, as we speak, and heading for Paris to take a short course on how to cook cordon bleu chicken. You would think that a recipe sufficed, but whatever." He laughed.

"And your kids?"

"Those are amazing stories as well. Heather is in Mozambique with her boyfriend. When they graduated from college last May, they joined the Peace Corps. Ivy applied to Denver University's Law School and was accepted. Who would have thought? I'm now delighted to support her studies. JFK just moved back here from San Francisco, and, well, you could say he's a work in progress."

"A whole lot has happened to me, too, Jim. Sue and I are back in the house. I doubt that we'll ever get fully over losing Sheba. Of course, it's still an open case, but the police have no new leads and the trail has definitely cooled. It may have been one or more kidnappers who got cold feet. But given the mutilation of the body, it may have been a wacko. However, if so, why did he call to us to negotiate a ransom? Go figure. I don't think they're going to solve Sheba's case, but to my mind, there's a good chance that he'll kill again. Maybe he'll make a mistake, then get caught and reveal his other crimes as part of a plea bargain to avoid the death sentence. We don't talk about it anymore, and time does heal.

"Sue's pregnant, but even with the morning sickness, she works on her ceramics every day. She has her own wheel in the old family room, and you should see the pottery display on the wall. She is really good. She wants to be a professional potter; that way, she can stay home with the baby. I doubt that she'll ever go back to school.

"I quit the Golden Spur. I was tired of working for someone else. With the spread of casinos, and the entry of the corporate guys with no background in gaming, I thought there might be opportunity for someone with my experience as a consultant. Right on.

"Do you remember when I gave my report on Arkansas and Louisiana? Well, my consulting is a lot like that. I advised the Starlight to stay clear of Baton Rouge, and, guess what, my hero Eddie DeBartolo didn't. Governor Edwards demanded a bribe for a riverboat license, and the FBI taped their telephone conversation. DeBartolo paid Edwards $400,000 in cash, and now has his own serious legal problems. He may lose the 49ers."

"So how goes consultancy?"

"I have more business than I can handle or want. Actually, I owe much of it to you. Jeremy Casino was born at the Starlight and pretty much grew up there. So now I have my own little consulting business and publish a gaming newsletter. I'm even writing a casino novel. Its working title is *The Starburst Hotel-Casino*," Jerry said, laughing.

"Robert Pinsky would probably have called it *Lights Out!*" Jim snorted. "The admiration is mutual, Jerry, because I owe you a lot as well. You introduced me to poetry, and now I read it for at least an hour a day. Pinsky's still my favorite, but I love the Uruguayan, Benedetti, too. Without him and Robert Bly, I don't think I could have maintained my sanity the last six months. Then there's Keats and … so many others.

"One thing I've learned is that the first giant step on the road to wisdom is to be able to say, 'I don't know.' Many years ago, the University of Washington gave me a degree in business. Well, my real education in business began just a few months ago. Then there's the poetry and … and life. In some ways, I feel like a baby who worried his parents because he was two and had never said a word, but then started talking in full sentences. There's so much for me to learn, so much catching up to do, that I'm in a constant state of mental agitation. I'm not sure when, or if, I'll ever enter another squash tournament or visit the Amazon. There's so much to discover, and so little time.

"I'm now beginning to listen to music, Jerry. Mainly classical, if you'd believe that. I donate to the Reno Chamber Orchestra, and they've asked me to be on their board. The thought is intimidating for someone with my background. Talk about a latecomer. I never played an instrument, and I can't read a note. I remember sleeping through my undergraduate music appreciation course at times. But, you know, I think I'll accept the invitation. It's time that I begin to give something back to the community, rather than just to my own family. Don't tell

James if you run into him during one of your nocturnal twilight-zone seances! He wouldn't understand."

"Just one more commonality between us," Jerry said. "I'm now on the advisory board of the Nevada chapter of The Nature Conservancy. I was a fairly substantial donor, and have always loved the outdoors. That doesn't make me a *bona fide* environmentalist, but what the hell. Last year, Sue got a grant from the Sierra Arts Foundation, and I'm on that board, too. I know something about business, so ..."

Jim nodded and commented, "I think it's mainly about fundraising. They need us to help them raise money. It's a never-ending challenge for every charity. But I don't mind. In fact, it's kind of nice to sit across from a potential donor and ask for a good cause; it's clear that you have no vested interest in the outcome. It makes you feel a little like Saint Francis, an altruist beloved and trusted by all of God's creatures."

Jerry laughed. "So, here we sit, two middle-aged farts and *faux* art connoisseurs, trying to bury our feckless pasts while we invent our laudable futures. In search of the furtive copacetic. I think I've learned a few things from all of this, Jim. First, about loyalty. It's the easiest virtue to espouse, and the hardest to practice. We all think we're loyal, and yet, when push comes to shove, we have all been disloyal to someone or something. Second, I now understand how unique each one of us is. If no two sets of fingerprints are alike, how much more unique is a total personality? We stereotype others way too quickly, and then think we've captured their real essence, when we're really fixated on superficial appearances. Finally, the supposed essences in this world are themselves unstable. *Plus c'est la même chose, plus ça change.*"

"What the hell did you say?"

"Think of it as my little private joke with French philosophy. *En garde*, Rousseau! I'm trying to say that change is the only real constant in everyone's life. Nothing ever stays the same—not in our hearts and heads, under our own little roof, or in the universe as a whole.

"Then there is the tricky question of *real essence* itself. Do we even know ourselves? Everyone's present is a mysterious adventure. When we get up in the morning, we might think we have an agenda for the day and, by sundown, our plans have almost certainly gone awry. Life really is indeterminate, even chaotic. No one steps off the curb thinking they'll be run over by a car, yet it happens. We all struggle with the past—our own in particular. It's a never-ending makeover—like your Dorothy's home redecorations—all the little revisions that feed the new versions of us. Each of us is the central character of our own story, and sanity requires that it be sanitized in the retelling. Our villainies, indifferences, and insensitivities need laundering, or at least plausible rationalization. Each of the little stories has to add up to a grand narrative in which we're a little larger than our own life's realities—that is, if life is to mean *anything*. Those who fail to rewrite their own past find it impossible to face the future. So, our active self-justification is also 'survival'."

Jerry nodded for emphasis, and then changed the subject. "Jim, you probably don't know about Carol Bentley."

"No."

"Well, right after you closed the Starlight, she and Tracy moved to New Jersey."

"They did?"

"They sure did. Carol was still in touch with Manny. She told him about the casino closing, and two days later, Federal Express delivered her a little package. It contained a kazoo; no note or anything. She packed up and moved to New Jersey. Seems to me that they might get married."

Jim extracted the single blank check he habitually carried in his wallet, filled it out to Carol, and handed it to Jerry. "Can you get this to her?"

"Sure, Jim. But, wow, five thousand! What should I tell her?"

"Say it's a wedding gift to both of them."

***

Jim Fitzsimmons and JFK drove down Interstate 80, and into their future. After having toured the Fernley casino property, their destination was Battle Mountain and then Wells. Premier Oil was in the planning stages of opening travel centers in each, and had invited Jim to lease both gaming premises. Father and son needed to inspect the two settings before formulating their offer and business strategy.

"What shall we call the company, Dad? Fitzsimmons and Son seems clunky to me."

"I vote for Presidential Gaming. After all, aren't we both JFKs?" Jim asked ruefully.

"Wow, isn't that pretty pretentious?"

"Not at all, Son; this *is* Nevada."

About the Author

Bill Douglass is a social anthropologist and writer. He received his PhD in 1967 from the University of Chicago. He then founded and directed for 33 years the William A. Douglass Center for Basque Studies for the University of Nevada System. He has authored more than two dozen books and 200 articles. He was born in Reno, the eldest son of Jack Douglass—a Nevada gaming pioneer. Bill has extensive personal experience in the gambling industry, having been a part-owner of Reno's Club Cal Neva and the Comstock and Riverboat hotel-casinos. He is currently the president and principal shareholder of Nevada's Leisure Gaming.